Heirs of Eternity

By: Franc Ingram

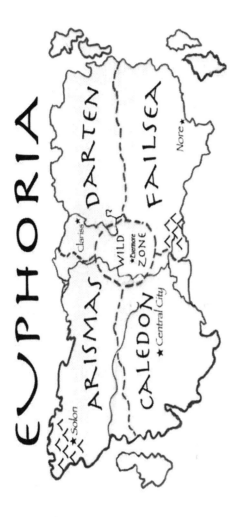

In memory of:

Hazel P. Loving mom and great reader of books

Cover Art: Ernesto McKenzie jr.
junproject-13.deviantart.com

Edited by: Cynthia Boswell
boswellprofessionalwritingservices.wordpress.com

Map: Debra Calhoun
www.facebook.com/designsbydebra.calhoun

CHAPTER ONE: SOLON

Oleana sat cross-legged on the worn blue rug of her motel room floor. The hard wood planks beneath creaked every time she took a deep breath. She tried to lock onto the bio signal she'd traveled a thousand miles to find, but her tongue felt like a hairy caterpillar rubbing the roof of her mouth raw, and some errant drummer decided to swing away at the inside of her skull. The winded grunts of her son, Lorn, practicing his fighting techniques on the hill just beyond her window didn't help her concentration either.

Every living thing on Euphoria gave off a unique bio signal due to the smart-particle cloud used to seed the planet, and make it suitable for colonization. Oleana had the rare ability to hear those signals, but finding one out of so many often proved difficult. Squeezing her eyes shut, Oleana pushed away the world of flesh, blood, and pain to immerse herself in the digital river that lay just behind the curtain. Oleana could hear the signals of everything within a hundred miles. Most of it was just white noise she could ignore, but hybrids like Lorn and herself stood out like stars in the night sky.

Her enhanced ears caught the signal and she translated it into a blip on her mental map. Lorn blazed like the sun against the mostly dull-gray map. There was another signal within fifty miles. Its steady glow reminded Oleana of an old star, past the chaotic energy of youth, but still strong. Oleana recognized it, knew who the unique frequency belonged to, and while pinpointing it did make Oleana smile, it wasn't the one she was looking for.

Three lifetimes she spent searching for the other Heirs of Eternity. Three all too short lifetimes wasted, and here she was again expending her life in pursuit of others.

Frustrated, Oleana gave up her intense listening and opened her eyes, blinking rapidly against the early sun pouring in through the open curtains. After glancing out the window to check on her son's location, Oleana reached for the one thing she knew would never disappoint her, her flask.

The curved metal canister with its black leather case was the first thing Oleana bought after leaving her parents' home fifteen years ago. It reminded her of both the family she would never return to, and the brief time in her life when she thought she could be free. She'd placed it on the wicker nightstand next to her bed the night before, within easy reach for an early morning pick me up. She'd done her share of drinking the night before but nothing cured her hangover like a long hard drink.

When her hand hit empty air, Oleana raced through several worst-case possibilities. Maybe she'd had too much to drink and dropped the flask carelessly somewhere, or worse, left it at the bar. A prize like that wouldn't stay discarded for long at the type of places she hung out at. Oleana scanned the rest of the room, not a great feat with the place being so small. She saw the familiar shape poking out of the top of her boot, which was leaning against the far edge of her bed.

Relief flooded through Oleana, but when she moved to grab the flask she remembered while it was common for her to stash the flask in her shoes for safe keeping. She had avoided that spot of late, because it was too far to reach in the bitter cold mornings of the northern cities.

If Oleana had any choice, she would have avoided the north all together, or at least until the height of summer, when she could move around outside without wearing three layers of clothing, hat, gloves, and a scarf. Instead, she was forced to cram Lorn and herself onto a fishing boat, with what belongings they could carry, and make the rough journey to the northern realm of Arismas. Another three days' travel by carriage and they made it to the southwest gate of Solon, the second largest city in the realm, and the last stretch of civilization before the frozen tundra that spread across the northern tip of the continent.

Oleana snatched the flask and shook it, already knowing what she'd find, it was empty. She undid the cap and tilted it up to her lips, just to be certain. Nothing came out. The container even smelled of cold metal instead of warm alcohol.

Thinking of how to make the culprit pay, Oleana pulled on her crumpled clothes from the day before, laced up the boots that once held the evidence, and tied her black dreadlocks into a ponytail, making sure each precious lock was in place. She grabbed her twin sais, which she'd stashed under the mattress. Lorn was going to get a real life sparring lesson today.

The grassy hill, which the Solon Inn called a backyard, was crunchy with the sprinkling of snow that fell during the night. Oleana reached to pull up the fur-lined hood of her coat, its rich brown color matching her deep brown skin, and realized she'd stormed off without it, leaving her nothing but a wool sweater to shield her from the cold.

Lorn danced atop the hill, practicing fast footwork with his thrust and jabs. Puberty had taken its toll on his coordination, turning the much-practiced sequences into an awkward mess, with his newly elongated limbs flailing about. He'd gone from looking Oleana in the eye to being a foot taller than her, with him standing at 6'2". His once pudgy frame was now lean and long. Lorn didn't allow the setback to bother him though. He had increased his practice times, and started back at the basics. From what Oleana could see, it was paying off.

With revenge on her mind, Oleana circled around the base of the hill, putting the sun and Lorn's back in front of her. She made sure her foot was well placed before taking a step. Lorn had the hearing of a bat, which meant Oleana needed all her stealth and speed to sneak up on him. Her twin sais, with their long, sharpened middle prong about half the size of her forearm, and two short prongs on each side acting as guards, were raised high, one pointed out for attack, the other flat against her forearm for defense.

She reached the crest of the hill with no sign that Lorn noticed her approach. He lunged forward. Oleana sucked in a deep breath waiting for the backstroke. When Lorn pulled back, she lunged forward, her blade headed straight for the unprotected right side of his ribcage. The dull inner edge of her blade slowed as it came against the thick material of the boy's fur-lined coat.

Lorn recovered quickly, turning on the ball of his foot, pushing his elbow back and out, deflecting her blade and giving him enough time to present his. Lorn swung hard at her head, forcing Oleana to drop low, killing her forward momentum.

Oleana guarded high and cut low at Lorn's shins, but he was too fast. The boy jumped back and planted his feet square on the higher, flat part of the hill. Oleana popped up, leading with both blades. Her thighs complained, burning as she moved. They weren't prepared for such strenuous activity so early in the morning. Lorn blocked down, and out, with the flat line of his short sword, the impact jarring Oleana's cold hands. The force of his attack pushed Oleana down the hill several steps.

Digging her toes into the earth, Oleana attacked high to push the boy back, her hands shaking and shoulders straining with the effort required to hold him off. Lorn resisted with all he had, and Oleana knew she couldn't hold him off for long, so she didn't try. She pulled back and kicked out at his exposed midsection, allowing the hill and gravity do most of the work as she fell back, with Lorn tumbling over her and down the slick slope.

Oleana tucked into a tight roll, recovering her feet with little effort. Lorn lost hold of his sword as it embedded itself in the ground, hammered in by the weight of his body. He tilted enough to keep from getting his ribs broken by the hilt of his sword, but landed awkwardly on his face.

Oleana raced over, pushing him over with her foot and laying the point of her blade under his chin. Lorn groaned low and long, his chest heavying in ragged breaths, sweat glistening on his forehead. For a moment Oleana wondered if she'd gone too far, pushed the boy too hard, until she felt something hard scrape against the top of her hip. She looked down to find Lorn pointing a dagger at her belly.

"Do you concede?" he asked. His eyes were closed but he couldn't hide the grin spread all over his face.

"Draw," she said, tapping her blade against his neck. Much of her anger had subsided. Instead Oleana was proud of how well her son did.

"Draw," Lorn sighed in conciliation. He opened his dark green eyes, squinting through the sun's bright rays as his gaze found Oleana's. "Hey what's with the aggressive ambush anyway?"

Oleana pulled back, sitting down next to her son. "Why the empty flask?"

Lorn slowly pulled his legs in and sat up, but he kept the blade out as if expecting another attack. He brushed his sandy brown curls out of his face. "You know better than I that the closer we get to Solon the more danger we face. We both need clear heads as we enter the next phase."

"My head is always clear," Oleana insisted

Lorn sat up in a hurry. "You stumbled into bed last night, mumbled something about flowers, and fell into such a deep sleep I could've set your bed on fire and you wouldn't have noticed. How is that clear headed?" Lorn asked, with a perplexed look on his face.

Oleana jumped up, the fire in her chest enough to banish the chill that had settled in her bones. "No matter what happened last night, I still managed to knock you on your butt this morning," Oleana replied, her chin jutting up in defiance.

Lorn snorted. "It was a draw, and if I was close to the worse we're likely to face I might be impressed, but I'm a baby compared to Cornelius and his sort."

"Don't!" Oleana ordered, her teeth snapping down on the word like a vice, and a chill running down her spine. "Don't use that name. Besides, I tell you what to worry about, not the other way around. You don't have to remind me what we'll face. I've faced them before." Oleana realized how crazed she must look, wide-eyed, face burning, and emphasizing her point with the point of a blade. She backed off. "I have it under control, under complete control." Oleana avoided Lorn's stare, focusing on brushing the debris from her clothing. It was too early in the morning for such an old argument. With her adrenaline-high fading, Oleana was increasingly aware of how wet her clothes were, and how frigid the air felt. She cleared her throat. "Since you're so active you can pack up all our stuff while I go grab me something to eat."

"Can you bring me back something?" Lorn pleaded, allowing the mention of food to overcome any previous argument. "I'm starving."

"Young men who overstep their place forage for themselves," Oleana shouted over her shoulder, already heading back down the hill. "I'm pretty sure I smelled pumpkin muffins on my way out. I could eat three of those," she added for good measure.

"Not fair," Lorn grumbled.

"That's life." Oleana yelled back. Lorn was sure to learn that truth fast.

100101

The Solon Inn technically lay outside of the great city Solon. It was the northern-most point of the suburb Erald on east gate of the great wall, nestled in a valley between lush rolling hills. Nothing else sat close by but the farms and pastures that kept the city Solon fed. The heart of the city was three miles away. Lorn said he was fine with walking it, and taking in the scenery, but Oleana wanted to get the job done and get out as quickly as possible.

That meant taking the carriage with its two horses into the heart of town. It also meant sharing the ride with two other passengers. Oleana should have considered herself lucky it was only two. Thousands of students and tourists flocked to Solon every year, to visit the Thousand Years Library and buy one-of-a-kind items from the open-air market. The start of spring usually marked the start of the busy season for tourism, but the Inn was mostly vacant and the four of them were the only ones headed into the city.

The young couple that shared the carriage were tourists, visiting the College of the Founders for the first time. Oleana knew this because the couple took the fifteen-minute ride as an opportunity to explain their entire life story to a captive audience. They couldn't just tell the story, they were all smiles, bubbly, and just a little too loud. Oleana, who was growing more desperate for a good drink as the seconds dragged on, gave them nothing back but the occasional, noncommittal nod. Lorn, being his usual friendly self, stoked the fire with his barrage of excited questions, and tidbits of his own life.

Briefly, Oleana wondered if she should give in to her perverse side and tell them she'd met the founder of the college up close and personal. Not the three whose statues dotted the city, even though she knew one of them very well. No, she was talking about the originator of the oldest school, the School of Technology, the ultra, Cornelius.

Cornelius, like the few other ultras still around, was a creature of legend due to his makeup of human and Euphorian DNA, enhanced by a computer neural network care of the abundance of smart particles laced in his bloodstream. While the realm of Gaeth was the only realm still directly ruled by an ultra, Cornelius' dark shadow still hung over the city of Solon.

Oleana wondered would their travelling companions still be as bubbly and friendly if they knew how close she'd been to Cornelius? Would they assume Oleana and her son worshiped

Cornelius as their god as a growing number of people did? Would they explode with excitement? Either way, Oleana worried that the revelation would just elicit another set of annoying questions and she just wasn't up for it.

Just thinking about Cornelius made Oleana edgy. She crossed her arms over her abdomen protectively, remembering the searing pain of his sword as it sliced through her insides the last time they ran into each other. She could still remember the look of amused satisfaction on Cornelius' face as he watched her bleed out. That was a long time ago, and Oleana had no intention of repeating her mistakes.

"Mother, are you even listening?"

Oleana rubbed at her eyes, banishing haunted images from her mind's eye. The excited couple gifted her with a confused, and disapproving look. It was a look she'd become familiar with, something she experienced every time Lorn called her 'mother' in public. Lorn's height and weight belied his age, making him appear much older than his fifteen years. With Oleana having just seen her thirtieth winter, her giving birth to Lorn seemed improbable.

They weren't wrong. Lorn wasn't Oleana's natural child. He was an orphan she'd stumbled upon whilst trying to run away from her responsibilities years ago. As soon as she saw his dirty little face and those wide, inquisitive eyes Oleana knew she couldn't run away from him.

"Mom, they want to know what part of the college we were going to first," Lorn explained. "I realize I failed to ask you before, and I can't believe it slipped my mind. I was just so excited to see Solon! Well nervous and excited," Lorn chattered with increasing speed. "Well more like terrified and excited. Goodness, I didn't even stop to think exactly where we were going to start our…umm…vacation. Right, vacation!"

Oleana gave her son a stern look. He'd almost said too much, forgotten their cover. "The Thousand Years Library."

"Wow," the woman's face lit up. She'd told Oleana her name but it was forgotten as quickly as it was said. "How did you manage to get a pass for there?"

"Yeah," the man added, "I tried to get our names on the list last week and was told we would be put on the waitlist, but it could be a few weeks before a spot opened up. We can only pray to the Twelve that our turn comes up before we have to go back home."

"Well Mom knows...uhm." Lorn stumbled over his own tongue. "She knows someone that works at the library. Managed to get us passes," he finished weakly.

"You're very fortunate," the man said. His eyes took on a look Oleana interpreted as him trying to picture what the inside of the library looked like.

The driver rapped on the side of the carriage. "Founders College. Everyone out."

Oleana snatched up her satchel and made it out the door before he even finished speaking. She stretched her back, looking up into the bright blue afternoon sky, desperate for wide open spaces. Euphoria's rings were faintly visible between the clouds along the horizon.

The sight of the collegiate buildings brought a smile to her face. That was, until she spotted how close they were to Mount Elmire, the home of Cornelius. The twin peak mountain range with its dark gray rocky terrain cast a shadow over the city, and her mood. Of all the places her quest could have lead, it had to bring her right under the nose of Cornelius, the man who'd caused her enough pain for a thousand lifetimes.

Lorn patted her back. "Don't worry. I'm sure we won't be here long," he said over her shoulder. "And I know our next stop will be far away from here. Maybe close to the wild zone. I can't wait to go there. Then maybe to Failsea." Lorn's concerned tone quickly morphed back into his usual excited chatter.

Oleana pulled her gaze away from the mountain, and back to the city around her. There was plenty of work to be done without being distracted by old fears. "Focus on Solon first," Oleana admonished Lorn. He nodded as if he were sufficiently chastised, but he rocked back and forth on his tip toes. Oleana briefly considered throwing snow at Lorn to calm him down. She knew from experience there was little that could curb his enthusiasm, and the snow would just make her hand cold.

"Guess it's too late to throw you back and get a new son, one that's less trouble," Oleana said, wrapping her arm around her son for a quick hug, the warmth of him reassuring her.

"Yup sorry, you're stuck with me," Lorn replied with a broad grin.

"We hope to see you two around," the young man said, interrupting their private moment.

Oleana turned back to afford him a smile. She could at least pretend to be a normal, sociable person as they were leaving. "Hope you enjoy the city. Take care," she called brightly.

The young man seemed taken aback by Oleana's sudden jovial disposition, but the girl waved back, even giving Oleana a polite smile. Lorn started rumbling around in his pack, pulling Oleana's attention back to him. "We're all out of snacks, and I'm so hungry," Lorn grumbled. "I didn't have time to grab any food before we left. How can we be out already?"

"Check my bag. I have two grain bars left," Oleana said pointing to her back.

"I ate those in the carriage," Lorn said sheepishly. He shrugged. "Well, it was a long ride!"

"How did you...," Oleana didn't bother finishing. She had been so concerned with keeping her eye on the road, she couldn't remember half of the ride into the city. Lorn had a habit of treating her stuff as if it were his.

Being back in Solon unnerved Oleana. It made her skin feel tight, her tongue too heavy, and her eyes fogged up by the pain of the past. Lorn was right in what he said back at the Solon Inn, she needed a clear head. Even without the liquid morning pick-me-up, that was proving harder to accomplish than Oleana would have thought.

"Can we please go eat?" Lorn said.

"Library first. Then we fill that pit that is your stomach."

CHAPTER TWO: THOUSAND YEARS LIBRARY

Legend had it that the Thousand Year Library was the first library ever built on the planet Euphoria. It was the second oldest building ever, next to the Crystal Tower. Looking up at it, Oleana always got the feeling that she was staring at something that could stand up against the onslaught of time. The gray stone library, with its little round windows like dozens of curious eyes, looked like something carved straight from the mountain looming behind it.

The Twelve, the collective of A.I.s that ruled over the planet, commissioned the ultra, Cornelius to build the library so all who wanted to learn about the history of humanity as far back as ancient Earth, and of the new home of humanity the planet Euphoria, could come and immerse themselves.

It didn't take Cornelius, being a slave to his lust for power, long to learn the true power of knowledge is money, and he restricted access to those who could afford to pay for the privilege. Going to the library became a reward for being one of Cornelius' sycophants, and the books gathered dust. The progress of man slowed to a crawl.

The benevolent Twelve, tasked with saving the last remnant of humanity couldn't stand for such treatment. They gathered all those willing to help fight to kick Cornelius from his self-appointed position as dictator. Thus began the war between humans, and the militant ultras. The bloody conflict lasted seventy-five years, leaving thousands dead and the world changed. When the dust settled and the blood dried, the new age of enlightenment began, and the boundaries of the five realms were set.

Oleana told her son the legends as bedtime stories for years, but she knew how true they were. She also knew that the end of ultra rule was only the start of mankind's problems. Separating humanity into realms encouraged conflicts over territory and resources. The ultras, with their impossibly long lives were willing to sit back and wait for the right moment to strike back. The Twelve could see the conflict brewing. They took steps to give humanity a chance. They created the Heirs of Eternity, enhanced humans blending the abilities of the Twelve and the vulnerability of humanity that the ultras lacked. Oleana didn't know the ending to that story, she was living it.

Lining the steps of the Thousand Years Library were statues of the heroes of Solon. Oleana was particularly amused by the one in front of the library. Its bronze surface had gotten a fresh polish since the last time she saw it. The plaque beneath was new as well.

"Champion of the right to be taught by the Twelve, Daycia invites all truth seekers to enter these ancient halls and find enlightenment," Lorn read. "That is so amazing. I can't believe we're actually here. Goodness. We're actually going to meet...,"

"Lorn." Oleana glared at him. She hoped one day he would learn to control his tongue.

Lorn hung his head. "Sorry," he sighed, "calming down."

Two guards stood at the thick red oak doors leading inside the library, each one of them as tall as Lorn and twice as wide, with stoic expressions chiseled on hard faces. They tensed, and Oleana realized that being so obviously armed might present a problem. Going without a weapon wasn't an option, she would just have to turn on the charm to get them through.

"State your purpose," the one on Oleana's right said, his deep voice as hard as the stone around him. He had a wide face, pinched brown eyes, and just a shadow of blond hair on his angular head.

"We have special passes for the library," Oleana said. She pulled them from her pocket slowly. The last thing she needed was an incident before she began.

Mister deep voice snatched them, the thick velvety feel of the envelope that held them accentuated how precious the cargo. He pulled out two cards, of heavy stock, with old embossed lettering on them and a red wax seal. He scanned it until his eyes hit the signature and seal. Oleana saw his eyes widen considerably. It wasn't every day that people came in with that kind of pass.

He handed them over to his partner who studied them carefully, as if he didn't really believe two strangers could have such a thing. "How did you get these?" number two asked, a touch of awe mixed in with his disbelief.

Oleana waved her hand as if they were nothing. "Just called in a favor from a very old friend," she said. If anonymity wasn't so required Oleana would have showed them who she was, and cut through all the questions, but safety came first.

"They're the genuine article," guard number one said, mister deep voice.

"But we can't just let them through with those," number two said pointing to the weapons.

"But it says free access," one countered.

Oleana didn't like being talked about while she was standing in front of them. Her jaw clenched tight against the rude words she wanted to spew all over them. "Why don't one of you go get Daycia, the Hero of Solon, and explain that you didn't trust her to decide who was worthy to come into the library armed," Oleana said, sarcasm oozing from her every pore, "that what she wrote and sealed wasn't good enough for you!" Oleana waved her arm, pointing inside the library. "Tell the Fire Ultra's child that you need further proof that she didn't make a mistake. I'm sure that'll go well for you." She snorted, folding her arms in front of her, and leaning back against the doorway. "We'll wait right here." Oleana caught sight of Lorn who clasped his hand over his mouth, but his eyes glistened with his contained laughter. His leather soles squeaked against the stone steps as he shuffled awkwardly.

The guards exchanged looks. The Daycia, Oleana knew, was a mild tempered woman in general, but no one wanted to bother a legend no matter what their demeanor. Oleana hoped her bluff would cut through the hesitation. She had no intention of waiting around out in the open. If they didn't decide soon she'd make the choice for them.

A group of students, evident by the robes they wore, approached the stairs. Now they had an audience. The guards looked between each other, and the incoming crowd of students. Guard number one's eyes narrowed to angry slits. His wide nostrils flared and she could see the veins in his neck beginning to bulge. Oleana feared he might pick a fight with her.

"Go ahead through," number one guard finally said. "Enjoy your time at the library," he added, forcing a smile. His partner moved aside just enough to let them pass. Oleana felt their eyes glued to her every step. Oleana stood even straighter. She wasn't going to allow these men to get under her skin. After all, she'd won.

Pushing the heavy wooden doors open, the noise of the library came out to greet her. Even though it wasn't yet mid-day, the peak time for public access, the library was bustling with activity. Young men and women, proudly clad in their student robes, and arms laden with books of various sizes, scurried back and forth through the halls. They were worker bees doing the delicate dance of hard work.

The main entrance of the Thousand Years Library opened to a grand foyer with a circular mosaic tile floor. Off to the left sat a semi-circular desk large enough to fill the hotel room Oleana and Lorn shared the night before. Two men, both with heads of gray hair, helped the students gather and check out books, or directed visitors to where they needed to be.

Toward the center of the back wall, and off to the right, were archways framed with thick wooden beams that lead into other rooms. One labeled, 'Science and Technology,' the other, 'Earth History.' The floor-to-ceiling bookshelves could be seen through the openings.

Directly opposite the circular desk, lay a set of wrought iron stairs that spiraled intricately into the upper levels of the library. They were wide enough for two people to walk side-by-side comfortably. The spindles of the banister were shaped into different types of flowers from all over the world, crawling up twisting vines. Oleana had always thought it a shame that such a beautiful piece of art was relegated to a dim corner, although there were plenty of other works of art to appreciate, all over the library.

"It smells great in here, Lorn said in awe. "Like old books and freedom." He inhaled deeply, adding mischievously, "Maybe a hint of sweat too." With wide eyes, he turned in circles trying to take it all in. "What are the different color robes for? What's in those rooms?" Lorn's questions came like rapid-fire arrows as his excitement grew. "Those stairs are gorgeous! What could be up there? This place is massive!" Oleana laughed at her son's exuberance, and placed a hand on his shoulders to slow him down.

Oleana took a deep breath. "The color tells you what year the student is in, and the crest on their breast represents which school they're in," she explained. "The rooms nearest us contain research books, which are separated by general categories. Second floor is works of fiction, along with some study rooms. Third floor contains the offices." Oleana looked around until she saw the person she needed, wearing a badge. "Stay here, I'll be right back." Before Lorn could ask yet another set of questions, she stepped away. She spoke briefly to a young man at the desk just inside the science and technology room, showing off her pass during the exchange. Once she got the response she needed, she moved back to Lorn. She pointed him up the stairs.

His eyes lit up like stars. Oleana didn't know how long she could put up with his heightened excitement. Normal everyday

Lorn was bad enough, but the giddy little school boy he'd morphed into as soon as they got close to Solon wore thin fast.

Just off the stairs, stretched a long corridor with four different hallways leading from it. All four openings had the same ornate wooden archways.

In all her travels, Oleana couldn't remember any other place that felt like this library. Every detail of its structure showed both elegance, and functionality, on a scale that seemed incongruous with its age. How could a building so old, have features that would have looked futuristic in even the most modern buildings?

The materials were all wood, stone, and glass, with precise detailing carved into every square inch. The walls were slightly curved to catch as much of the natural light pouring in from the expansive row of windows. Steam pipes running under the floors kept them warm, even in the most frigid part of the winter.

Yet the old-world feel could not be denied. Above the doors, signs were written in a language not of the planet Euphoria, but of an ancient Earth long dead. Oleana remembered the words, though the fancy script took some deciphering.

'Hall of Science,' 'Hall of Medicine,' 'Hall of History.'

Oleana didn't need the signs to point the way. She'd roamed the halls for years as an apprentice, during her first lifetime, learning what it meant to be the Guardian, one of the Heirs of Eternity. The learning curve was steep, and she had a hard time letting go of the family she had left behind. The second time around, once she'd been old enough, she had run away from home with a fire in her belly, and a desire for revenge.

Oleana followed the turn of the first branching hallway, then entered the second room off that one. It was a relatively small room compared to all the others they'd seen so far in the library. It was closer to the size of their motel room, if the wall separating the bathroom at the motel had been removed. A worn rug, with a pastel flower pattern on it, covered much of the floor. Three high-backed, dark gray chairs bisected the rectangular room along its width. Two dark wood desks took up opposite corners, facing each other, both stacked with books and papers. The focal point, though, had to be the large bay window looking out over the city proper.

A third-year student sat at the desk on the right side, his nose buried in a large leather tome that looked old enough to predate Oleana's original self. He didn't even look up at them when they entered. His lack of reaction made it obvious he wasn't a member of one of the more militant schools that taught students to be aware of their surroundings at all times.

Oleana sat in the chair that gave her the best view of both the window and the door. Lorn walked to the wall of pictures showing the current head of each school, Medicine, Science, Technology, History, Philosophy, and Engineering. His hand glided over the gold embossing under each picture, identifying the names of each person. Oleana noticed the changes since her last time through. She was happy to see there were still two faces she recognized, though neither would recognize her current face.

"Alwen? Have you finally found your way back home?" a voice asked behind her.

Oleana smiled. "I see you still move with the stealth of someone a quarter your age," Oleana replied turning around. She couldn't help the broad smile that swallowed her face the second she laid eyes on her mentor.

Daycia, the mixed-race child of the Fire Ultra, Emmaray, stood taller than most women at 6'4". Her skin tone reminded Oleana of freshly fired brick, a dark tan color with hues of brown and red thrown in. Daycia's hair was fire red, just like her mother's, and violet colored eyes that looked more like painted glass than something flesh and blood. She wore a long-sleeved tunic that hugged her hourglass curves and came to a point just above her knees. A peak of heather-gray leggings poked out of the top of her hard leather knee-high boots.

The two women embraced in a hug that would have crushed lesser mortals. Oleana never wanted to let go. If there was any place that felt like home, other than the island she was originally born on, it was the library, and that was because of Daycia.

"It has been much too long my friend," Oleana said. She stepped back to get a good look taking in every inch of her old mentor, seeing her again felt like a taking in a glass of fresh water after a very long, very hot day. "Why is it you don't look a day older?"

"I wouldn't say that. I'm finally getting a little gray coming in at my temples."

"It only took five hundred years."

Daycia laughed, which finally got the student's attention. He jumped up, having to fold himself over the table to keep the book from falling. "Lady Daycia I didn't...I'm so sorry...I uhm…" the student stammered as he fumbled with the book.

Oleana felt sorry for the guy. He was so flustered he couldn't finish a sentence. Daycia had that effect on a lot of people. Ultra offspring were rare. Mixed race offspring like Daycia were practically unheard of. Add the fact that she was the last living member of the founders, and the current Dean of the Library, and people just didn't know how to react to her.

"Relax Colin," Daycia said smiling, her voice soft and kind. "It is us who have disturbed your studies. Forgive us. We shall conduct our reunion elsewhere."

The student bowed low, avoiding Daycia's gaze. "No, my lady, I can go. I was about done anyway."

"Don't be silly," Daycia insisted, "stay. Besides I owe my young friend..." she paused looking at Lorn questioningly.

"Lorn," he supplied wide-eyed.

"...Lorn, a tour of the library," she completed with a serene smile.

Lorn clamped his hand over his mouth to keep from losing it.

"By the way," Daycia turned to the student before she left, "I realize chapter four is somewhat disjointed," she nodded at the book in his hand. "We were in the middle of a war, if you remember, and

I did my writing between battles. You will forgive me for not sticking to my usual clear-cut wording. The heat of battle changes one's perspective."

Colin nodded so vigorously his shoulders bounced with the movement. "Of course."

"Thank you." Daycia replied with a smile, turning her attention back to Oleana. "Now come on you two. We have a lot of ground to cover." The Fire Ultra gently cupped their shoulders as she led them from the room. Oleana knew Daycia meant that in more ways than one.

Once they were out in the hall and well away from the open door, Daycia's gaze fell on young Lorn, who bounced beside her down the hall. Oleana watched as her mentor studied the boy's arrow shaped birthmark featured on his forearm. The ruddy brown mark wasn't obvious against the amber brown color of his sun-kissed skin, unless someone was looking hard for it.

Lorn took the scrutiny without a word. He held his back straighter. His movements became more precise, but he made no move to break the silence, which was unusual for him.

"Would you two mind showing me how they interact?" Daycia asked, stopping in the middle of the hall, glancing between Oleana and Lorn. There was a hint of suspicion in her voice that didn't go unnoticed by Oleana.

"Prove we are who we say we are, you mean? Prove that these marks aren't fake." Oleana said. She didn't like the idea of exposing herself out in the open. She liked even less that her friend would be suspicious of her. "When you greeted me so warmly back there I thought maybe ...," Oleana let the thought drop. She expected the great and powerful Daycia to recognize her no matter what her outer shell may have looked like. When she first wrote the letter to Daycia over a month ago, Oleana waited anxiously for a response but when she got the passes back, she'd hoped everything would go smoothly between them. Oleana thought she could come home.

"How about we go inside," Daycia suggested, pointing to an open room. Oleana ushered Lorn inside, then followed him, leaving Daycia to enter last, closing the door behind them.

"What if we aren't who we say we are?" Lorn asked. There was no malice or ill intent in him, but Oleana knew it could have been construed the wrong way.

Daycia took it in stride. She smiled, running her hand through her shoulder-length fiery-red hair. "Well then I guess I would turn you over to the rangers for interrogation."

"And you're confident that the two of us together wouldn't pose a problem for you."

Oleana knew the answer to that. Locked away in his DNA Lorn had a power that rivaled Daycia's, but her experience outmatched even Oleana's, and that counted for more than Lorn understood.

"Number one," Daycia turned to Lorn answering him reassuringly," I do believe you are who you claim, and therefore wish me no harm. I just feel it prudent to confirm. Second, in all my five hundred years I have only one permanent scar," Daycia pulled her hair back to show a white line that traveled from just under her right ear down around the back of her neck. "A parting gift from my mother when I made it clear that her views of humanity were not mine." Daycia placed her hands on her hips, looking from Oleana to Lorn. "So," she continued, "unless you're both ultras I've never heard of before, no, I don't see you posing a big problem for me."

"Does that make you in….," Lorn began.

Oleana was tired of the exchange. She knew Lorn could come up with a thousand questions if let loose. Instead, she licked two of her fingers and pressed them to Lorn's birthmark, cutting his question short. The mark took on a golden glow much like a firefly. When Oleana moved, the arrowhead shifted, pointing directly at her, halting Lorn in the middle of his sentence.

Not finished with her parlor trick, Oleana rolled up her own sleeve to reveal her own mark. It was different, on its own it was just a thin ring of dark skin, easily ignore, but when it came into proximity with the activated mark of another Heir things changed. At the center of her mark the faint shadow of an arrow started to appear, mimicking Lorn's, the distinct golden glow standing out against her brown skin.

"You are indeed one of the Three, and the Guardian," Daycia said looking between them with obvious satisfaction. "Alwen, this is amazing. I was beginning to doubt if I would ever meet you again, Master of Skies."

Oleana flinched at the sound of her old name. That name belonged to someone who had seen the world through naive eyes, the name of a girl who failed to do what she had needed to. "It's Oleana now," she corrected firmly, looking Daycia directly in her violet eyes.

"My apologies, Oleana," Daycia said, nodding.

"It is odd to meet someone that knows more about me than I do," Lorn confessed to Daycia. "Mom warned me, she told me that this is our fourth lifetime and that you knew her during her first, but hearing someone other than her say it aloud just feels weird."

"One of the many things unique to you four Heirs of Eternity" Daycia said, then shifted her attention. "So, you're a mom now," Daycia stated, curiously glancing between Lorn and Oleana.

"It's a long story. One I have no intention of ...," Oleana's complaint was cut off by the sound of warning bells echoing outside.

CHAPTER THREE: YETIS

"What's that," Lorn said, peeking out the window.

"Please tell me it isn't what I think," Oleana said, reaching for her weapons. Lorn took the hint and did the same.

"Warning alarms for a breach of the wall. They've been coming more and more of late. Yetis on the loose again."

Daycia opened the door in time to see young Colin running down the hall with the leather book clutched to his chest. "Hurry to the shelter," he shouted to all whom he passed.

"I'm afraid we are destined for the viewing room," Daycia announced.

Oleana followed her mentor, more out of habit than desire. She had a mission to complete, and getting involved in this little breech would just take time away from that pursuit. She knew Daycia's help would cut the search time, so Oleana decided that she could summon enough patience to make it through one distraction.

From experience, Oleana didn't count the yetis as a particularly dangerous foe in small numbers. They may have looked intimidating with their tall, muscular bodies covered in coarse fur, with elongated fans and curved claws, but they were dim-witted and tended to fight amongst themselves more than anyone else. In large groups, they could cause destruction and panic. For the untrained civilian, even one yeti could cause significant damage if provoked, but incursions weren't new to the people of Solon and they knew how to stay away from the beasts.

Yetis, the creations of Cornelius, aka the Ice Ultra, sometimes got bored roaming the barren tundra and decided to eat their fill of human fare. They often tore their way through town taking all that they wished until the rangers forced them back over the wall.

The viewing room was already occupied. Oleana recognized two of them from their pictures on the wall. The other individual had to be the local head of the rangers; Oleana recognized the uniform and rank as soon as she set eyes on it. They greeted Lorn and Oleana with suspicious stares.

"Friends of mine," Daycia said, recognizing the tension in the room as soon as they stepped in. Apparently, her approval was good enough because the others turned back to their business without another word.

The room would have been large enough to fit twenty people in it comfortably if an array of different equipment and maps weren't taking up half the space. Three large, white strips of cloth, much like new sheets, were stretched taut from floor to ceiling, covering up the back wall, the others huddled around a semi-circular table positioned in front of them. There they watched a multitude of images captured from around the city of Solon projected onto the white fabric from some unseen equipment hidden behind the sheets.

Oleana stood toward the back of the room, well out of everyone's way. She held her arm out to keep Lorn at bay. He gave her a disappointed look, but it didn't matter. Yeti incursions weren't their problem.

"There they are," the ranger said pointing. "Middle left screen."

Oleana spotted three yetis stalking toward the butcher shop at the west end of the market district. They were after a quick meal. With the amount of people in the area at this hour, they were likely to cause panic. Stampeding people meant injuries, or worse. More pleasure for the yetis.

"Zyair if we cut them off before they hit the market, it shouldn't be hard to drive them back over the wall without a fight," Daycia offered.

The ranger shook his head. "Most of my men are out on the tundra. We got a report early this morning that a group of late season ice fishers got themselves trapped on a piece of glacier that broke off. To keep them contained, we need a two-pronged attack and I just don't have the manpower for that."

"Why would those fishers risk going out there in the first place?" Lorn asked drawing more attention to them than Oleana felt comfortable with.

The Dean of Technology gave the boy a disappointed look. "Times are hard young man. Hard working men and women need every penny they can earn."

"I would be more than happy to join you in the field, along with Paley," Daycia said. Then she glanced at Oleana who had her eyebrows raised in an unasked question. "Paley is my latest apprentice. Did a brief stint as a ranger then came to the college to study engineering. She's talented and smart. You two really need to meet. On the battlefield?"

"Not going to happen," Oleana said. She couldn't manage to look Daycia in the eye while she refused, but her feelings were set. She paced the floor, a million reasons why not to get involved raced through her mind, but the number one reason was to frightening to even voice.

"Three yetis won't pose a problem for you," Daycia replied. "Besides it would be good practice for the boy. He'll need it for the journey ahead." A look of mourning passed across Daycia's face, wrinkling her smooth features. It was fleeting, but Oleana could guess at what caused it.

Just under a century ago, Daycia stood in that very market square with the original versions of Oleana, then Alwen, and Lorn, then Thurgood. They were inundated with yetis then. Daycia, trapped by the sheer number of them, had been unable to keep Cornelius from cutting her companions down.

Oleana jabbed her finger at Daycia's face. "It's because of that very thing that I'm not taking this sixteen-year-old out to fight those creatures. Three might not be a problem, but there are many more out there. As soon as we step outside these walls, the greater the risk of Cornelius finding us out. Do you think those three yetis are worth that?" Oleana's voice cracked and all eyes were on her. She didn't mean to yell, to lose control. The idea of facing yetis scared her more than she wanted to admit, even to herself. She pulled nervously at one of her dreadlocks "I'm not dying today, not for this."

Daycia nodded, her eyes soft and understanding. She opened her mouth to say something, even took a hesitant step toward Oleana but Oleana was closed off. She crossed her arms across her chest and looked off toward a blank wall. Not another word needed to be said about it. Daycia turned back to the others. "The four of us, and what city guards we can gather, will be enough to hold off these three, but we must hurry."

Oleana stared at the screens. People in the streets were already starting to panic as the yetis moved closer to crowded areas. The beasts seemed focused on the shop, and therefore made no move to pick on the stragglers.

"Stay here and coordinate things," Daycia ordered. "We'll talk more later."

Oleana didn't bother looking at her mentor, she just nodded. She could picture the disappointed look on the older woman's face. Everyone else in the room purposefully looked at anything but the two of them. Oleana's cheeks were flushed, she hated making a scene. Hated drawing attention.

The ranger, Zyair, was already out the door, presumably to round up what men he could find. Oleana felt a pang of guilt as she slid her sais back into their hilts. Staying put was the right thing to do. Safer for Lorn, safer for her. A master like Daycia could handle three yetis with no problem.

Lorn stepped up to the table, glancing over the city map embedded on top. He said nothing, but the droop in his shoulders, and the calm demeanor, spoke volumes. Oleana understood the need for combat experience, but not in Solon. Not today.

The two deans who remained in the room, accepted Oleana's help without objection. The deans took the right and left screens, respectively. That left the middle for Oleana to watch. The air of the room was thick with nervous energy waiting for the two parties to reach the civilians.

Two men, who were wearing gray uniforms with, 'Solon Guard,' stitched in red thread at their breast, arrived on the scene first. They took up positions in front of the yetis, slowing their progress and providing a layer of protection between the civilians and danger. But, if it came to a fight, the guards would be torn to shreds.

Daycia finally showed back up, with a tall woman wearing a professor's tunic in tow - she must have been the talented Paley. It felt like all the air that was sucked out when the alarms began ringing, suddenly whooshed back in, refilling the space with fresh, sweet air. Everyone heaved a collective sigh of relief.

The two rangers were close behind, in full protective gear including helmets and shields, both embossed with the ranger's emblem and the crest of Arismas, the realm in which Solon lay. The yetis made their displeasure at finding themselves surrounded known by letting out bloodcurdling screams.

"Look at those teeth," Lorn said, his voice high and loud. His hands cradled his face as if to hold the excitement in. "and those claws! And that build. Wow that fur looks coarse enough to stop a blade." Lorn bounced on his tiptoes inching ever closer to the screens.

"Watch how they attack," Oleana instructed her son. "Pay attention to how they fight and think about what the best counter would be." Fighting wasn't the only way to gain knowledge.

Lorn nodded. His eyes darted back and forth between the different vantage points of the street. Give Lorn an opportunity to learn, and he soaked it up. That was one quality that stayed with him, no matter what incarnation she ran into.

With alarm bells still ringing throughout the city, most people were taking the hint to find shelter in the solid structures along the market walls. Others chose to make their exit at the east end where the market gave way to the garment district. Three large factories took up much of the area. Family businesses squeezed between the free spaces. Many of them had pens in the back where they raised, and housed, small herds of baymar. The native

Euphorian animals had soft, fluffy coats that were prized for making quality clothing.

Oleana searched through what little she could see of the area on screen. The herds of docile baymar would make a tasty treat for the ravenous yetis. They scaled the great wall, so no holding pen would keep them at bay. Oleana didn't need the civilians running into more trouble.

The fourth shop on the left, had a sign above it reading, 'Misty's Boutique.' Oleana spotted movement on the left side of the old stone building. The door was lying in the street, splintered with claw marks gouged deep inside the tough wood.

"Can you get me a better view of this building here?" Oleana asked, as she peered closely at the screen, trying to make out more detail of the scene. The Dean of Engineering disappeared behind the sheet. The block images shimmered, then went black for long enough to make Oleana worried. Finally, a new set of images popped up. One of them happened to be a long-range view that covered several of the backyard pens.

Oleana spotted four yetis in the back of the shop tearing into the pen, chasing the scared baymar around. The gruesome scene of blood and guts was sickening, but what she saw coming toward the shop caused her heart to thud against her chest. A group of twelve people were fleeing the chaos of the market, heading straight for the yetis.

"Mom," Lorn called urgently, leaning closer to the screen.

"I see it," she assured him, then speaking to the nearest dean, she asked, "Can you guys get some guards over to the east end?"

"No mom, look." Lorn raised his arm to show the glowing arrow on his hairless muscular forearm.

Oleana jammed her sleeve back to see that her birthmark glowed as well; sparkling like it was sprinkled with diamond dust against her cocoa brown skin. Inside the ring, she could make out the faint impression of a paw print, the mark of the Master of Animals.

Looking back out the door, Oleana hoped some lucky student just walked by then she could snatch him up and they could be on their way, instead of joining yet another useless fight. The hall was empty and no one could be heard. That left her with only one other option. Oleana turned her attention back to the screens. She spotted, at the end of the pack of people leaving the market, a man that looked to be around Oleana's age. He stood out only because he was rubbing furiously at his forearm while he tried to keep up with the others.

"This is not how this was supposed to go," Oleana said looking up, seeing past the ceiling, and calling to the Twelve in the skies above. She should have been used to watching one of the three walk straight into danger by now.

"Does that mean…," Lorn started to ask, his hands tugging at Oleana's coat excitedly.

"Yes," Oleana answered before he could finish. The two deans looked back and forth between them with looks of both awe, and excitement. Of course they could put things together. So much for remaining anonymous.

Many of the people of Euphoria knew the legend of the Heirs of Eternity - the three kings and their loyal guardian. The deans of the Founders College would know better than most how real the story was. Daycia likely wrote a book about it a century ago, tucked away on some shelf in the Thousand Years Library. The older woman had a way with words that must have made the tale about how the Twelve- the collective of AI's that deposited mankind on Euphoria- created the four Heirs to undo their mistake in creating the ultras.

Oleana could just imagine how grand it must have seemed when Daycia wrote about how each Heir could tap into the unique set of bio signal frequencies specific to each form of life. Lorn could manipulate the weather. Oleana had a limited influence over people. Another could affect animals, and the last the earth.

Oleana wondered how many times each one of the faces that looked at her read Daycia's book and hoped one day to come across such legends. Now Oleana and her son were standing in front of them. She knew keeping hidden meant staying safe. The college tended to be a breeding ground of gossip, and secrets didn't stay secret for long.

"Yes, we are who you think we are," Oleana answered their unasked question, "and no, you can't tell anyone. **Anyone**," Oleana insisted. The deans nodded in unison, mouths still open in shock.

"Are we going?" Lorn asked. He didn't wait for the answer, already moving for the door.

"Time to go fight the yetis," Oleana confirmed.

CHAPTER FOUR: MASTER OF ANIMALS

When the alarm bells first sounded, Leith was busy enjoying a pilfered lunchtime snack he'd acquired from one of the poorly watched shops in the open-air market at the heart of Solon. In his youth, the yetis ventured into the city once every three of four years. In the last year, they'd breached the wall eight times already, causing great damage to property and people. Leith didn't put much stock in the doomsday nonsense some of the elders spoke of in hushed tones, but maybe the end was indeed on the horizon. Something had the yetis going crazy.

Leith's initial instinct was to find the closest hole to hide in and stay put, but as word came that the yetis were heading into the market, staying seemed foolish. He chose to follow a group heading out the east end of the market, staying on the fringes of the group in case things went bad and he needed a quick getaway.

Yeti incursions always made Leith anxious. It wasn't from fear. He'd experienced enough fear in his lifetime to know the difference. No, it felt more like when he had too much to drink at a rowdy bar, and the urge to fight burned its way through his veins. The yeti's proximity set something off in him that was both invigorating, and disturbing. The connection gave him the advantage when keeping away from the beasts, one he intended to use to the fullest.

After shoveling the last bit of pastry into his mouth, Leith noticed an itch on his forearm. He scratched at it mindlessly, keeping his eyes on his surroundings. Things seemed all clear, but the further Leith and his group traveled from the center of the market, the more dread built in the back of his mind.

If they were moving away from the beasts, why did he feel the urge to turn around and go back? When the itch turned into a burning, Leith stopped in his tracks, puzzled. He rolled up his sleeve, and glancing at his arm, he nearly jumped out of his own skin.

"By the Twelve," he gasped, fear racing through his veins like a freight train and cutting his usually strong voice down to a strangled squeak. Through the sprinkling of brown hair his arm was glowing like a dimly lit candle in a bright room. The world slowed down around him and nothing else matter but the unnatural weirdness happening under his own skin. How could his skin glow? Leith thought, shock making his body stiff and his mind slow.

Leith yanked up his other sleeve frantically, but saw nothing amiss. He scrambled to check his legs and torso just to be sure. Only the one spot was affected. His birthmark emitted a soft yellow light.

Leith was sure he'd picked up some crazy death worm. The fact that it happened to be under the mark had to be just a funny coincidence. But what happened next was not amusing. The mark rotated. Leith shook his head, and blinked rapidly, certain he didn't see what he thought he saw. The parasite had him hallucinating now. It happened again, and all Leith could think about was removing the creature before it killed him.

Pulling his well-used dagger from the pocket against his chest, Leith was determined to put himself to the blade. No parasite was going to take over his body. He'd dig it out before that happened.

Leith took a deep breath, steeling himself against the coming pain, as he pressed the tip of his blade against his arm when a tingling at the back of his neck made him look up. Two yetis half-lunged, half-stumbled out of the doorway two buildings ahead of where Leith was standing. They both barred their over-sized, hooked canines as soon as their eyes locked on the crowd. Panic set in, and people scattered in every direction.

Indecision rooted Leith to the spot. The scattered people were occupying the yetis' attention. Leith didn't even come into their sightline.

Get the death worm out, then run for the hills if any approach, Leith thought to himself. It sounded like a reasonable enough plan. Let the scattered masses distract the beasts.

Focusing once again on the glowing worm, Leith returned his blade to his arm when he heard someone approaching from behind. He turned ready to fight

"Hey, I wouldn't do that if I were you," a young male voice yelled from behind Leith.

"Can't a man cut his arm in peace?" Leith muttered in complaint, exasperated by the loony situation he found himself in.

He turned and assessed the two people heading his way. The young man, who couldn't be older than eighteen, wore excitement on his face, and held his sword high in attack, confidence radiating from every move he made. His light-brown skin and light-weave clothing marked him as a non-native of Solon.

The other, a stern-looking woman Leith's age, had her hood pulled over her head, her round face cloaked in shadow, and her brown eyes narrow and intense. Her double blades were held close to her body, defensively as if at any moment, the world around her would explode and she needed to protect herself. She was average height, with an hourglass figure. Instead of being billowy, she was all lean muscle. Leith found himself intrigued by the oddity of the pair, distracting him from his own peril.

"I said, I wouldn't do that if I were you," the young man repeated his warning, slowing down enough to give Leith a once over, making him feel like a prized pig on display. "You're going to need that as we go along," Lorn indicated Leith's glowing birthmark with a nod. "Besides the mark is more than skin deep. It will just keep glowing, because it's written in your DNA. I'm Lorn by the way," he introduced himself with a smile and a tap on Leith's shoulder. "You have no idea how happy I am to meet you. Can you feel the…" he stopped short as the woman broke in.

"Lorn," the she warned in a sharp tone that immediately settled the strange boy. She'd taken up a defensive position in front of Leith as if her purpose was to protect him. Why, he couldn't begin to fathom. He struggled to process the past few moments. The boy's words had come at him so fast his brain was still trying to decipher them.

"Sorry. Staying focused," the young man apologized. Then he turned his attention to the yetis.

Two more had made their way out of the shop, and the last one seemed very intent on the trio. Leith was suddenly very glad to have the added protection of this odd pair. He hoped they were as tough as they looked.

"Flank them on the left, keep them from going after the human sheep," the woman ordered the young man, gesturing with her hand. "I'll go right, and try to push them back out into the field, and hopefully over the wall. And you," the woman said, turning to stare at Leith, with brown eyes that held a sadness to them that Leith instantly connected with. "Stay here and try not to get yourself killed, because that would really ruin my day."

Leith nodded in agreement, channeling his inner obedient puppy. Sit. Stay. Be good. He could manage that. Something told him getting on the intimidating woman's bad side was something he never wanted to do. Now he could add 'weird kid, and crazy lady' to the list of encounters he'd had today. It wasn't a good list, and he didn't wish to lengthen it.

Then Leith had a thought. Maybe the pastry he'd stolen early had been laced with something, and it was all just a bad dream. Before Leith could ponder over it the pair took off, splitting up as the woman planned.

Staring at his arm, Leith shut his fear down and thought over his options. If what the kid said was right, that this mark was in his DNA, cutting into his arm would only leave him with a dangerous wound. Why he should he trust the word of some random stranger though? Leith wondered. Still, the kid talked with authority, like he'd encountered glowing birthmarks before.

Leith's brow furrowed deeper, bemused at the thought that there could be more people with this phenomenon that just him. On top of that, Leith remembered the smell of his spilled blood would just excite the yetis even more. Leith was sure the odd couple could handle the yetis, or at the very least provide enough of a distraction for Leith to leave safely. He decided to make his way home, out of the path of monsters, and figure things out there.

Leith took three careful steps back, until he was aligned with the Caitlin Bakery's door. It was cracked open, and he knew the rear entrance lead straight to an open field. He could cut across it, and end up on Tanner road, which lead past the market and presented the quickest way to his house.

Choosing safety over obedience, Leith opened the bakery door enough to let him squeeze through. Once inside, he took one last look back at his rescuers, if he could call them that. While they weren't his concern, Leith did feel a twinge of regret at just leaving them without so much as a goodbye.

The woman already had one of the beasts down. Leith couldn't tell if it was just knocked out, or dead. She had another backed up against a wall, looking hesitant to attack. The boy kept his two opponents at bay, lunging at them sporadically when they tried to approach. This gave what stragglers were left, time to make their escape back toward the market.

Leith didn't see any need to worry about them. He couldn't have done half as good a job in their place. He made his way through the bakery, picking up a few abandoned items as he went along. No need to let them go to waste, he mused as an addict of all things sweet and stolen. The apple popover was still warm, fresh from the oven, which kicked his salivary glands into overdrive.

Ignoring the birthmark became easier as he went along. The burning returned to a mild itch, which he countered with the warm goodness of a fresh dessert in his mouth. Mmmmm, so good, he thought, closing his eyes in rapture. His mind left the craziness of outside, and focused on what to do next. When he got home he'd take a nice long nap and forget all about weird strangers, and glowing death worms.

Leith pushed the back door with his shoulder, but it wouldn't move. He looked down to see it was locked. He had to stuff a buttered roll into his mouth to free a hand to turn the lock. He shoved hard on the old door to get it open, stumbling out into daylight, and disturbing a yeti finishing its baymar meal.

"Wrong way," Leith gulped, as he scrambled to close the door. It was too late.

The yeti tore the wooden door from Leith's hands, knocking it off its hinges. Leith hurled the remaining rolls at the beast before turning and running. He ducked left into the kitchen where the large ovens were still cooking away at abandoned breads, filling the air with a bitter charred smell. Cowering behind a prep station, Leith, sweat dripping from his forehead and his breathing came in gasps, mentally begged the yeti to find some other toy to play with. He rooted around in his mind for a way out.

What tools could he find in a bakery that would do any good against the beast? Where did all the workers go? They had to have fled to a nearby shelter. Where could it be? Leith tried to reason quickly. Inside the bakery? Next door?

If Leith could just find the nearest shelter, he could hide there. After all, the shelters were made to withstand an all-out yeti assault. Leith knew all the alleyways and shortcuts in the city. Somewhere on that twisted map in his head had to be the location of the shelter. He just had to think.

The yeti burst in, its thick black claws clicking against the hard brick floor, banishing all of Leith's concentration. The yeti crashed its way through the place, knocking over pans and other cookware. Flour sprayed in the air dusting the floor near Leith's feet with little white splotches.

Leith looked at the dagger still clutched in his hand. It wasn't his first choice of weapon against the deadly beast, but he knew how to handle it with enough skill to do damage, if it came to that.

Before the yeti could get too close, Leith darted up, jutting in between a large sink and the double-sized ice box taking up a quarter of the short wall of the rectangular room. The brick was slick with its fresh layer of flour. He fell to his knees, sliding out the door and into the display case, knocking eclairs onto his head. In any other circumstances Leith would have been thrilled to have such free access to so many sweet treats, instead they were just annoyances that he flung aside.

The scratching of claws against brick headed Leith's direction. He took the hint to get moving, and vaulted over the counter. If he could get back out into the street, the odd couple could take care of this one as they had the others, and Leith could be peacefully on his way.

He stumbled out onto the unforgiving cobblestone street, knees first, sending a shockwave of pain up his legs and into his guts. Before he could clear his head enough to get his feet under him, something sharp cut its way into his back. Leith's breath caught in his throat as pain burned its way through his insides.

Instinctively, Leith elbowed his attacker and tumbled forward into a rough somersault, landing squarely on his feet, staring eye to eye with the snarling yeti. He could feel the beast's hot breath spurting out of its flared nostrils. Looking at the yeti this close, his dagger seemed like nothing more than a toothpick. The yeti was six and a half feet tall, its shoulders as broad as the door they'd just come through. Coarse light-gray fur covered it from head to toe. Its deep black eyes with their striking diamond shaped white pupil reminded Leith of some of the alley cats he tumbled with in the dark, running from a house he'd raided. Its thin-lipped mouth hung open showing a purplish tongue and a double row of sharp teeth. Bloody bits of baymar flesh still clung to the edges of its mouth. The beast's surprisingly long fingers ended in curved white claws that looked ready to cut Leith open.

The yeti charged, knocking Leith to the ground before he could brace himself. It took all his strength, and both of his hands around the beast's neck, to keep the massive mouth from chomping down on his face. The weight of the yeti pressed the grip of his dagger into his palm.

Leith pushed with every ounce of his strength, shaking with the massive effort of heaving the yeti's heavy body up far enough to allow him to pull his knees up to his chest, taking the pressure off his hands. The yeti's teeth snapped mindlessly, aiming for his neck and face. Leith banged his head against stone trying to stay out of reach.

He leveraged the yeti off his dagger hand, straining every muscle he had from the chest down, muscles he'd built over hard nights scaling brick houses and darting over rooftops. Staring into the awful putrid maw of the beast, Leith adjusted his grip on his small blade, then with what strength he had left, he plunged it deep into the yeti's chest.

The blade met some resistance from the armor-like coarse hair encasing the beast, but the howl that escaped its lips let Leith know he'd done some damage. The beast reared back, taking the blade with it. Leith didn't squander his opportunity. He rolled to the right, pushing off the ground with both hands and feet. He spun on the balls of feet, and came face to face with the angry yeti, the blade still sticking out from its mound of fur, blood falling onto the street in thick globs.

It charged, but this time Leith was ready. He took a running start at the side of the brick building, catapulting off it, landing a hard left-cross along the yeti's jaw. Throwing all the weight of his stocky frame into the move, he followed it up with an equally forceful right hook.

As a teenager, Leith often used his ability to fight equally with the right or left to his advantage, catching the uninformed opponent off guard. But it had been some time since he'd had to fight his way out of anything, and even longer since he'd actually practiced. His second blow glanced off the yeti's nose making a sickening crunching noise. Leith feared he'd broken his hand until blood spewed from the creature's nose.

It took a shaky step forward and fell to its knees. Leith didn't give it time to recover. He leaped over it, stepping across its back, and almost bisecting himself on the strange lady's blade.

"I told you not to get killed," the woman complained with a scowl. Her glare held a fierce anger that Leith didn't feel he deserved.

"Yeah well, I tried very hard not to," he panted, trying to catch his breath. He patted at his chest to reassure himself that all his parts were still intact. Leith heard a scraping noise behind him and turned to see the yeti taking off down the street, back towards the market.

The woman took off after the yeti without another word. Leith was relieved to see her go. The mean look in her eyes was probably what made the yeti run, and Leith was grateful for that, but her attitude puzzled him. He just didn't have the energy to decipher it at the moment, though.

The boy, stealthier than a mouse, snuck up on Leith, startling him. He was smiling at Leith like a fool. "I saw that move you did at the end," he exclaimed. "It was amazing!" he laid a hand on

Leith's arm, vibrating with excitement. "Stay here, we need to talk." With those words, he too, took off after the beast.

In their wake, they left two yetis down, although Leith wasn't getting close enough to check to see if they were breathing. There was broken glass and splintered wood strewn about the street, otherwise it was deserted. Leith felt like a fool, having not tucked away in the shelters like everyone else.

There was no need to stick around. Leith needed to get home, tend to his wounds, and do whatever it took to forget about the day. He ran the opposite way of the yeti like his life depended on it.

CHAPTER FIVE: CORNELIUS

Cornelius stood deep within the latest branch of his growing ice cave network, pondering an expansion, when he heard someone approaching. He peeled his eyes away from his target and back down the hall he'd come to find his son, Tannin approaching. His fragmented reflection bounced around the rough ice walls like a thousand mini Tannins moving in for the attack.

"Father, I have news."

From the etched lines around Tannin's sharp eyes, and the deep note in his voice, Cornelius could tell his son's news wasn't of a pleasant nature. He turned back to the wall, not wanting anything negative to come between him and his work. "Speak," he ordered.

"A group of eight yetis ventured into the city today in search of a change in food. Only four have returned. I fear the rest are dead."

Cornelius slammed his fist against the wall, shattering the ice, and revealing the pitted rock beneath. "Why do they never listen?" he demanded. "They're only supposed to go on approved raids to the city, and never make a direct attack on the citizens.

They're only to use scare tactics to keep people on edge, and test defenses.

"I know father," Tannin agreed with a placating nod of his head.

"We aren't strong enough yet to take on the Solonians," Cornelius reminded him curtly.

"Yes father."

"If they keep breaching the wall without cause, soon the rangers will send out hunting parties. What will the yetis do then?"

"Die I suspect," Tannin suggested.

"Exactly," Cornelius agreed, "and then the last seventy years of secretly building up our numbers will be for nothing. If those mindless fools force me to act before everything is set, they will regret it." Cornelius loved his son Tannin. The boy was loyal, smart, dedicated, and strong. He tolerated the yetis because they were easy to produce and served a purpose. Of late, they were proving to be more and more unruly. He would have no need for them if they couldn't follow simple instructions.

He was fine with them roaming the tundra, picking off what few humans dared to branch out into his domain. People outside the wall knew they were living on borrowed time, but the city was dangerous. It was protected. Cornelius looked forward to the day he waged war on the people who ousted him from his city, but it needed to happen on his terms. He needed numbers on his side, and there was one last loose end to wrap up. The Heirs of Eternity had to be neutralized before Cornelius could feel comfortable waging a prolonged attack.

"You assured me you could keep an eye on them," he said, irritation raising the pitch of his voice with each word.

"There was some excitement over at Lake Furmel," Tannin replied. "The rangers were out. I was distracted. I apologize, Father."

Cornelius expelled all the air from his lungs with one sharp sigh. "No, it's my fault. I'm their father. It is up to me to instill some sense of discipline in them. Since they have too much free time on their hands, it's time I give them some real work to do." Cornelius thumped a long thin finger against the solid mountain. "The expansion will be done in no time. As for you, we can't let this loss of life go unpunished. The humans might get the idea that my children are fair game. You get into that city and be careful. You be stealthy, but you make it clear my wrath is not to be taken lightly."

"Yes father," Tannin agreed obediently.

Tannin left as quickly as he'd come. With him gone Cornelius knew the job would be taken care of as ordered. Tannin may have lacked passion, anger, or any of the other emotions that often drove Cornelius, and to a greater extent the yetis, crazy, but he knew how to get things done. It was a quality Cornelius found vital as his plans accelerated toward their inevitable violent conclusion.

Cornelius put the worries of the city behind him. He had yetis to discipline, and a fortress to finish constructing. Things were escalating between his people, and the people of Solon, faster than he was ready for. The last time he let things get out of control he was ousted from Solon, from the realm of Arismas, and forced to make the barren mountain range his home. Cornelius wouldn't fall into the same trap again.

He had to bide his time, to make sure he was strong enough to take the humans on without risking defeat. He had to drill that lesson into his animalistic children as swiftly as possible. He couldn't completely blame them. The Twelve didn't design Cornelius to create, they built him to rule. Tannin turned out the way he did because he was the product of two ultras, Cornelius and Emmaray. The yetis were different creatures all together.

Over three hundred years ago, when he lost his war against the humans, Cornelius had nothing further to offer Emmaray, and she cut off that avenue of procreation. Cornelius used the knowledge of his creators to do what genetic manipulations the limited resources of their age would allow him. It took him dozens of tries to produce a viable product, dozens more to produce something he could use for fighting. Even generations later they still suffered from the flaws of their predecessors.

Following the familiar twists and turns of his mountain dwelling, Cornelius listened for the sounds of his children. If he let a couple of them know, they would spread the word. Not to the factory buried deep within his mountain though, that needed to run smoothly, with absolutely no disruptions. Five of his sons were milling around in the room they labeled as the ice rink. The floor was slick with ice, and its temperature stayed at a balmy -20 degrees. The yetis used it as their relaxation room after a hard shift in the factory, to cool down.

"Up," Cornelius roared as he entered.

The yetis jumped to their feet looking around confused, until their wide black eyes fell on him, and they tensed up. At least they had enough sense to tell when he was upset.

"Did any of you breach the wall this morning?"

They all shook their heads no.

"Well find out who did and gather as many of your brothers that aren't working, and meet me in the gathering hall. Be quick about it."

Cornelius didn't have to wait more than ten minutes before the first group piled in. As an act of his benevolence he decided to downgrade their planned punishment. The yetis hugged the outer edges of the room as if they feared getting too close to their father. Cornelius smiled inwardly. There might be hope for them yet.

He waited until the guilty ones were pushed in front of him by their brothers. He peered into the faces of four of his children. All of them had the marks of battle along their fur, and written in the creases of their faces.

"What have you done?" Cornelius asked, though he expected no detailed answer. The yeti language was limited to howls and grunts that got the basics across. They understood each other, and Tannin understood them better than Cornelius did. Maybe he just didn't have the patience to learn. All four of them lowered their heads. The one directly in front of him whined low and deep. For a moment, Cornelius felt pity for his sons, his creations. They clearly had been through a lot already. Did he really want to add to their pain? Then he remembered his future was at stake. The world could be his, but if the yetis kept rampaging unchecked, they would ruin it all.

With his claws fully extended, Cornelius swiped the first yeti across his cheek, catching the edge of its lip. He backhanded the next one, then smacked two more until they were all laying on the ground bleeding.

"None of you will go near that city unless I give you an express order." Cornelius bent down, grabbing the nearest yeti, and yanking its head back at an awkward angle. "In fact, you are to avoid all human contact as if they have the plague. To make sure you don't have time to even think about Solon, I want double the output from the factory." Cornelius dropped the yeti and stood up making sure all eyes were glued to him. "You four will work twenty hour shifts, with four hours resting in the ice rink, until you drop dead, or until I give you another task." Cornelius looked out over the rest of them happy to see fear etched into every hairy crease of their monstrous faces. He crossed his arms across his chest imitating the stone cold unforgiving nature of the mountain around him. The muscles in his back and neck worked overtime to keep his anger in check, keeping him planted in the center of the room instead of running around it cutting the yetis down. "As for the rest of you, we have three more tunnels to carve out, and two more storage rooms to build. They will be done by week's end, or I will skin every last one of you. Do I make myself clear?"

The yetis nodded in unison.

"Go," Cornelius yelled, his voice bouncing off the ice walls like a bomb.

The yetis scattered.

<u>100101</u>

"That ungrateful, selfish little prick," Oleana growled through gritted teeth. "Lorn, you told him to stay put," Lorn nodded, but it barely registered with Oleana. "How complicated is that?" she questioned. Her boots slapped against the stone floor as she paced back and forth in front of Lorn. Her anger filled the small space that Daycia called an office. Oleana felt like she was being compressed under a ton of bricks. "Staying in one spot so your rescuers can talk to you. We dispose of the yetis, and he doesn't bother to give us so much as a thank you. Nearly gets himself killed running off the first time, so at the next opportunity, what does he do? He runs again like some chicken-hearted coward."

"He really got under your skin," Lorn mused between bites of the turkey sandwich he'd conned out of Daycia. "I think that's the most you've spoken in one sitting since we entered the great wall."

"That little snot couldn't bother me if he tried," Oleana snapped, her anger belying her comment. She stared out the window of Daycia's office hoping the Master of Animals would saunter by. "His behavior was simply not fitting for a king. He chose his own freedom over the safety of others, not once, but twice. Even I can't train cowardice out of someone's heart. He ran away so fast I didn't even get a name, where he lived, anything to go on."

"You may be judging the man harshly, Alwen - sorry Oleana," Daycia said calmly as she entered her domain, correcting herself as she inadvertently used Oleana's previous name. She handed Lorn a bowl of fruit, and offered Oleana another.

"No thank you," Oleana replied, waving it off. "And I'm not judging him, I'm just explaining what he did."

Daycia sat in the chair next to Lorn, the two of them perusing their food options together. "I remember your first day here as if it were yesterday. You tried to sneak onto a train headed back to the coast. I guess from there you were going to stowaway on a boat back to your native island. Despite talking to the Twelve, you were convinced we were crazy and you had made a mistake. That first month of training was spent overcoming your lack of belief that you were who we said you were."

"That's a bit of an exaggeration," Oleana grumbled, looking to Lorn. She didn't want the boy to think less of her, but his attention was focused on the food. "That was different. A lot was thrown at me all at once. How did you expect me to react when I was just twelve years old?"

Lorn snorted, almost choking on his lunch. "Ha!" he chortled, "That sounds like her. I mean, back on the farm, every time the cow decided not to produce what she thought was enough milk, she had a hissy fit and stormed off down to the closest bar talking about how no stupid cow was going to treat one of the Heirs of Eternity like that," Lorn gleefully told Daycia.

"Ungrateful little…," Oleana's face flushed red, as she muttered to herself. "…I could go for a drink. Impudent little wannabe king."

Lorn wasn't finished in his good-natured taunting of Oleana. "You know she half snores, half talks in her sleep," he continued, ignoring Oleana's insult. "Snores a little, talks a little. It's the funniest thing."

Daycia laughed, joining Lorn in his musings. "Alwen did the same thing. Must be encoded in her DNA."

Oleana sighed, plopping down in the only chair left in the small office, "I'm trying to discuss serious things, and you two are goofing off like freshmen on their first day," she chided the two of them, looking around taking in the office for the first time. It was smaller than the study room they'd vacated, yet it was decorated in bright tropical colors that gave the place an energetic feel. The two lounge chairs, small desk, and matching chair took up most of the room, leaving only a small path between them. There was a set of three shelves built into the walls that held books that looked as old as Daycia was.

At least she had a window, albeit a small one looking out over the mountain, but it let in natural light nonetheless. "And why don't you have a bigger office?" Oleana demanded, still out of sorts. "You are a founder of the new era for goodness sake! Statues of you are all over this city. Why do you work out of a shoebox?" Oleana huffed, challenging Daycia.

"Because I choose to," Daycia explained calmly. She could see through Oleana's petty complaints. Over the years, I've been in most of the offices in this place. I don't mind the small space, it keeps me from trying to put too much in it." Her tone sharpened a bit, making Oleana meet her eyes. "You're just upset you lost track of the Master of Animals. Don't take it out on my office. You need to calm down. He's in the city, and we know what he looks like. We will find him in no time." Daycia put a calming hand on Oleana's arm in an effort to reassure her, and settle her agitation. "For now, you should just eat. Relax. Cornelius won't be bothering us anytime soon. Changing the subject, Daycia asked, "Now, can we talk about how young Lorn did out there today?"

Oleana stared at the plate Daycia left on her desk. It didn't appeal. Oleana wanted out of Solon, out of the shadow of the mountain. She wanted a tall drink with an even taller chaser, and her mouth watered at the thought. Most of all, she wanted her wayward king to show up safe. "You adapted well," she told Lorn, trying to focus on something other than her problems. "You didn't let the live combat situation throw you off. You protected the civilians and scared the yetis off without engaging in unnecessary combat, and I'm proud of you." Oleana was excited to confirm that her years of training with her son translated well in the real world, but she couldn't hold onto that feeling. Her thoughts were plagued by all the things that went wrong, being outed in front of the deans, letting the Master of Animals get away. She needed time away from her son's exuberance and Daycia's passive aggressive corrections to think things through.

"I regret not being there to witness it," Daycia said. "Both the Dean of Science, and the Dean of Engineering said good things. They used words like agile, fast, skilled. It sounded excellent," she smiled at Lorn in approval. "These are men that have seen plenty of battles themselves, so it is very high praise coming from them." Lorn beamed at Daycia's words, feeling a rush of pride flow through him at her words. "You and I should find some time to spar together, see what you do with a real challenge. See if Alwen passed on my refined techniques properly."

"I would love that!" Lorn exclaimed. It was an honor he never expected to receive from someone he so revered. "Yes. Yes!" Lorn jumped from his seat unable to keep himself still. "Mom, did you hear that? Would it be okay? Mom, please can I?" Lorn was practically jumping out of his skin with a frenetic energy that reminded Oleana of a hyperactive puppy.

"Yes. Go ahead. Get your butt handed to you. You're giving me a headache anyway." Oleana rubbed furiously at her temples but Lorn was too excited to take any more note of his mother's sour mood.

Lorn inhaled the tall glass of milk he had precariously perched on the arm of his chair. Then his eyes slid to Oleana's. She offered it up without a complaint. He gulped it down too fast to be healthy, then he dove to the corner, digging through his bag. Crumpled pants, a bar of soap, his med kit, all hit the floor.

"What are you doing?" Oleana moved her feet to keep from getting hit by some piece of flying clothing.

"I...need...my... Here it is." Lorn pulled out the fold-up bow he'd designed himself. It was his favorite weapon of all the ones he was trained on. In the back zippered pocket, he pulled out a quiver with sixteen arrows. "If you think I'm good with the short sword, you have no idea." His face lit up with a self-satisfied smile as he held up the weapon to show Daycia.

Daycia nodded, studying the bow carefully. "I know the perfect place to test you out. On the way, we can have a chat with the rangers, start the search for our missing king."

"You do that and I'll entertain myself," Oleana's mood picked up. She knew exactly where she wanted to go.

Lorn hesitated. "You aren't joining us? Is it safe to go off by yourself?"

"You two go have your fun. I have my own way of blowing off steam. And I can protect myself thank you," Oleana reassured him.

The boy looked torn. His eyes held a worry that was beyond his years, but it fit. It reminded Oleana of a previous version of Lorn long dead. Some things were just in the DNA. "Be careful," he warned her, before moving for the door.

"Clean up your mess first," Oleana chided. "You know better."

Lorn's full cheeks flushed red. "Sorry." He scooped up his things in a hurry and stuffed them back into the bag with no regard for placement or organization. Oleana knew she'd end up repacking it later, or it would drive her crazy.

"Try not to worry too much," Daycia said, patting Oleana on the shoulder.

Oleana wondered whether the comment was directed toward her concern for Lorn, or her irritation over finding the Master of Animals. Either way she recognized it as good advice, but didn't know how to take it. She smiled at her mentor. "I don't know how to do anything else. And Lorn remember, move swift, be safe, and I love you."

Her son nodded.

As soon as the they were out of sight, Oleana grabbed her money pouch before stashing her and Lorn's bags behind Daycia's desk. Solon was known worldwide for four things: the great wall, the college, the market, and the plethora of local distilleries. The last time she was in town she hadn't had the time to partake of the last feature. She was more than ready to make up for it.

100101

The Dusty Owl was a pub close enough to the School of History to remain in Oleana's comfort zone, yet far enough off the main road to not be the go-to spot for every student and traveler walking by. With the lunch rush having passed, Oleana spotted enough open booths to be comfortable. The place was clean and sparse, the perfect combination for someone who wanted a good drink without the frills that accompany a hefty price tag.

The smell of fried meat and steamed vegetables clung to the air. The long, freshly polished bar covered most of the back wall, and two attendants covered opposite ends. Clean, efficient, quiet. Oleana couldn't be happier. Daycia and Lorn had their way of having fun, but it often ended in strange bruises. Oleana's way only sometimes ended in a slight headache in the morning. Whose way sounded better?

A young woman with hair cropped close to her head, and discerning eyes, led Oleana to a booth in the back with a clear path to both exits, and away from the windows at the front of the building. Oleana ordered two double shots of rum and a veggie omelet. The place used local orenten eggs, which were double the size of a chicken's, and had more of a spicy flavor.

Oleana downed her first shot of rum in a hurry. It had been a long day, and she'd gone a long time without even a drop to drink. As soon as the warmth settled in her belly, she felt the tension in her chest ease, and the headache at her temples fade just a notch. She filled her trusted flask with the other. When her omelet came, Oleana ordered two more shots. With everything behind her she could finally relax, and breathe deep.

Before the first bite of cheese, mushroom, peppers, and egg crossed her lips she felt the familiar itch spread along her forearm.

Instinctively, Oleana shoved the shot glasses off to the side so Lorn wouldn't see them and start in on her.

The next person to walk in the door looked familiar, but it took Oleana a second to cut through the shock and realized who had just stepped back into her life. The man stood in the doorway rubbing at his forearm. His brow was wrinkled, completing the disturbed look on his face. He looked back outside as if he were rethinking coming in. Oleana jumped up, knocking her silverware on the floor. She wasn't going to let him get away a second time.

The man looked around, anger flaring his nostrils and reddening his cheeks. His eyes locked on Oleana's and they stared each other down like bulls ready to charge. He moved toward Oleana with large, sure strides. "You're following me," he yelled, pointing his finger in her face.

"I was here first," Oleana argued. She sat back down, hoping her nonchalant ruse would force him to calm down. They were drawing enough attention without any further yelling.

He followed her lead and sat down on the opposite side. "I come here often. Never seen you before," he accused. "My arm starts itching, then burning, and you show up first time. Now my arm does it again, and here you are in my place." He shook his head while he glared at her accusingly. "Not an accident."

"Sorry about the arm. The first time it activates can get a bit painful. The burn will fade in a couple days." Oleana licked her fingers and reached for his exposed mark.

The man flinched, pulling back his arm before she could touch him, and demanded, "What do you think you are doing?"

"Do you want to stop burning every time you come close to one of us?" Oleana asked, but he said nothing. "Only my bio imprint will calm it down. It won't hurt."

Grudgingly, he offered his arm. Oleana placed her fingers on the glowing mark. A shock traveled up her arm like a cold burst of air smacking her in the face. His mark faded and the redness in the surrounding skin eased.

The man looked from the fading mark on his arm, back to Oleana with a dazed and confused look on his face asking, "What this? What are you?"

"Oleana. Guardian." Oleana leaned in close as she spoke to keep any ears in the vicinity from hearing all her secrets. "You're the Master of Animals. One of the Heirs of Eternity." It wasn't a conversation she wanted to have in public, but it was clear he needed some answer before he bolted again.

"Ha!" he snorted, "I know you be crazy. I might be crazy myself, but not that crazy though. Not yet."

"How do you explain it then?" Oleana asked, raising her sleeve showing the junior copy of his mark fading from her arm.

"I don't know," he shook his head. "It may be some trick you playing. Not falling for it. You stop following or we have problems." He stood, but Oleana was quick to get in his face and block his way.

"I don't think so. It's my job to find you, and I won't be letting you get away from me again. I didn't convince you?" she countered, "That's fine. I guess my skills in that department are a little rusty, or you're more skeptical than most. I know others who can be more persuasive. You can come with me to talk to them," she stepped closer, "or we can have that fight right now, and I can drag your unconscious body to them."

"What makes you know you win?"

Oleana smiled. She looked the man over, really noticing him for the first time. He had a sinewy build that was born of hard work. His hands were calloused and scarred. They stood eye to eye yet he held himself like a coiled spring ready to pop. His brown hair was cropped short and slicked back "I have more years of fighting experience than you have on Euphoria. If you think that dagger you have tucked in your jacket is any match for my sais then go ahead and press your luck. Come peacefully and save your dignity."

The man stepped closer to her, his warm breath brushing against her face, which smelled of turmeric and honey, with the faint aroma of alcohol. It was a common remedy for pain. Oleana also noticed his shirt bulged out at the middle. His tumble with the yeti must have damaged his ribs, yet he didn't move like an injured man.

He was tough, no doubt about that. The defiant look in his eyes showed more backbone than Oleana expected, given their last encounter.

"This is my bar. You're a stranger. You attack, and others will defend."

Oleana didn't bother looking around. She knew the second the words came out his mouth it was a bluff. "You're a low-born thief. These people may know you, and may look the other way if the city guard comes around. They may even pass a job your way here and there, but when real trouble comes knocking, they will disavow any connection to you." The man hid his shock well, but Oleana caught the slight narrowing of his amber-brown eyes. "I know more about this city than you think. Your speech screams low-born. The calluses on your hands tell all about the climbing work you do, scaling buildings, running across rooftops. I can see the edge of the Guild brand peeking out of your collar, but it's old." Oleana continued her run-down as a vein at the man's temple pulsed with his growing anger and humiliation. "I'm guessing you started young. You're good at what you do, good enough to have nice clothes and keep yourself healthy and strong. Even though the thieves' guild marked you, I'm guessing your ties to them are thin. No guilder would make their base this close to the school, and the constant guard presence."

The man snatched the nearest rum shot and downed it before Oleana could protest. "Pay already and let's go," Oleana slid her hand toward her blade, suspecting she was going to have to fight her way out. "Go talk to 'em friends," he explained, sweeping his hand toward the door.

CHAPTER SIX: TRAINING

Daycia and Lorn were still out on the grassland behind the local ranger's office. It was one of the few places in the heart of the city that was safe for such dangerous activities as shooting practice. Oleana caught them in the middle of their exercise. Daycia was using herself as a squirrely moving target for Lorn. Oleana wondered about the sanity of her old mentor until she spotted the caps on Lorn's arrows.

The older woman had shed her coat and pulled her distinctive fiery red hair back into a bun. She dived, and rolled, and ran all over the space with the speed and agility of a young hare. There may have been a touch of gray at her temples, but her body retained its youthful vigor.

"Come now Lorn, are you even making an effort?" Daycia teased.

Lorn scrambled behind a large rock, using it to steady his hand. Daycia stood out in the open, not showing an ounce of worry. He had an arrow locked, but didn't fire. His eyes went unfocused, and his lips moved but no sound escaped.

Oleana felt a change in the air around them. Worse yet, her body tingled with the exchange of energy. "Lorn!" she warned, but was too late.

A bolt of lightning suddenly cut through the air landing in the exact spot that Daycia had been standing just a second before. Taking advantage of the distraction, Lorn let his arrow fly, tagging Daycia deep in the chest. It marked what would have been a kill shot for any mortal.

"What was that?" Leith exclaimed in shock, spinning around in a circle, looking up at the sky with its singular dark cloud, that was fading rapidly.

"Lorn what have I told you?" Oleana asked admonishingly.

Lorn looked startled to find his mom staring at him. "I know mom," he said chagrined, "not so close to the mountain." Lorn tucked his bow into the slot on his quiver. "It was only a short burst," he explained, "I really wanted to win. She was being difficult. I didn't see you there. I'm sorry."

"You saying he did that," Leith said pointing at young Lorn. "Wait. He just call you mom?"

"I see you located the Master of Animals on your own." Daycia approached the trio as she casually pulled the arrow out of her chest, as if it were of no consequence whatsoever. She nodded at Oleana. "Well done, my dear." Then she looked at Lorn who hovered just out of arms reach, waiting for her response to his diversionary tactic. She rubbed at her chest, saying with a smile, "and you Lorn, that was very well played. You showed great control of your power and your bow. A very nice move indeed." She handed the arrow back to him, and he placed it back in his quiver.

"I know you," Leith said with dawning awe, "You're Daycia Firestar, Protector of Solon, Dean of the Library, and Fire Ultra offspring."

"Yes, I am, and now that I see you up close, I realize you are Leith Underwood, or do you prefer Silver Owl?"

Leith's face turned a bright shade of red as he stuttered in embarrassment. "I'm not...How do you...? You both read minds now?"

"Young man," Daycia began in a commanding tone, "I have been watching over this city for a long time now. Exceptional characters such as yourself always catch my attention eventually."

"You know all that, why guards not taking me off to jail? Why send crazy lady with far flung story to round me up?" Leith asked in his odd cadence.

"I didn't know where you called home," Daycia replied. "I also had no concrete proof to bring against you. Besides, if you haven't noticed, the city has bigger problems than one thief."

Lorn's curiosity got the better of him. "Why the name, Silver Owl? Sounds intriguing. There must be a story behind the name." he questioned.

"Young Leith here is a second story man, who has a preference for silver," Daycia explained. "He's been known to strip all the silver out of a place, leaving behind gold and jewels. Never could figure out why."

Leith shrugged. "I like what I like."

Oleana groaned. "So not only are you a no-good thief but you're a bad one at that. How do I turn that into a king for the ages?" she asked anyone in general.

"Those who have, don't make a big stink over a few pieces of missing silverware. Make my living without a big bounty on my head. And if you dragged me here to insult, I be on my way. Who say I want you to turn me into anything?"

"You have no choice. Just like I have no choice about traipsing around all of Euphoria searching out the other Heirs of Eternity, and getting nothing for my troubles but three lifetimes worth of nightmares and pain." Oleana's sharp tone could have cut through bone. "I don't want to be here interrupting your life. I would give anything to be able to stay at home and mind my own business, instead of wasting my life trying to save y'alls."

"Mom."

Oleana saw the pained look in Lorn's normally bright eyes, and it cut her insides to ribbons. She had a habit of letting her mouth run away her. Oleana grabbed Lorn's chin, making sure his eyes met hers. "I'm sorry. I didn't mean you," she said, trying to will him to understand just how much he meant to her. "I was just… You're the best thing that has ever happened to me. Ever. You hear me? Ever."

"For a thief, your walk is surprisingly without stealth," Daycia stated to change the subject.

Oleana turned to see Leith already made his way past her and to the edge of the field.

"With that awkward family moment, can I leave?" Leith asked.

"No, my boy, there is much to show you," Daycia said. "After all, don't you want to see what the Master of Animals can do."

"He says we have the wrong one," Oleana said.

"Ah yes, of course. Lucky for you I've had experience dealing with that particular objection. I know just the place to go to prove you otherwise."

The mischievous look on Daycia's face made Oleana nervous. She only looked like that when she had something dangerous in mind. She sometimes underestimated the fragility of ordinary humans. Not everyone could just bounce back from her little demonstrations.

100101

"Welcome to the ranta pits," Daycia said, spreading her arm out over the ravine that dropped off in front of them.

The area was less of a pit and more a series of underground tunnels connected by a large, open area. It must have been thirty feet down, with the bottom partially obscured by the shadows created by large outcroppings. Oleana caught glimpses of what lurked beneath, but never a clear view. They darted in and out of the darkness with a speed and stealth hard to keep up with.

They walked on all fours. Oleana caught sight of a tail that was as thick as a flag pole. Green and red pricks of light dotted the cavern which she guessed originated from a dozen or more sets of eyes.

Oleana heard stories of the pit the last time she was in town, but never did she think to go near them. She heard tales of animals that were five feet tall with sharp ears, even sharper teeth, and claws designed to cut through rock. These animals were as fast and agile as any cat and just as ready to pounce on unsuspecting prey.

"The rantas are hive creatures who live underground eating whatever creatures come into their path," Daycia explained. "They devour mineral rich soil to produce, and maintain, new tunnels. In turn they secrete irdonium which they use to line their nests. Much like the bees they work constantly and produce much more than they can ever use. Trained workers harvest some from time to time."

"Down there," Leith said looking incredulous.

"Harvesters usually work in pairs of four and raid ten to twelve nests at a time. Surely the two of us can harvest two."

"Two? What of the others?" Leith asked. He looked at Oleana suspiciously as if she had anything to do with his current predicament. Oleana shrugged. She was following Daycia's leads as with everyone else.

"No need to risk the others unnecessarily..."

"What bout risking me!"

"...besides the Master of Animals doesn't need anyone weighing him down. I'm just going to help you carry. That much metal can be cumbersome to maneuver through these narrow passageways."

Leith stared down into the pit. His stomach turned just thinking about descending into the shadow. He heard workers talk about what it was like harvesting the nests. As drunk men had the tendency to do, their stories were wild and exaggerated, but the scars on their bodies told the truth of it.

"If I'm not the one you think, we both be torn to shreds." Leith muttered morosely.

"Have confidence, my boy."

"You're the immortal. Sure, things like this don't bother." Leith shook his head. "Not going."

Oleana and Lorn exchanged looks. Then they lined up behind him, weapons drawn. "You're not going back," Oleana said, the look in her eyes a mix of desperation and anger.

"Crazy. All you," Leith shook his head glaring at each of them.

Daycia pulled a glow stick and a short sword much like Lorn's from the pack on her back. She started down the narrow staircase cut into the side of the rock, without another word. Leith's gaze darted back and forth from the rapidly disappearing Daycia to the stern Oleana.

For the second time that day he was caught between two hard choices. He couldn't tell which option was more dangerous. From what he'd witness with the yetis, Oleana clearly had the skills to cut him to ribbons, but would she go that far to make her point? She'd already threatened to knock him out and drag him where she wanted him to go. If he lost the fight with her, he'd have a rough trip down the stairs anyway. Better to go on his own two feet, and hope Daycia could defend them both when it came down to it.

"Crazy," Leith mumbled again as he gripped his dagger tight, and started after the shadow that was Daycia.

The black dirt that made up the sides of the pit was pockmarked with claw marks starting at the ten-foot mark. The creatures that were moving along the floor of the structure, scattered at the touch of the glow stick light. From what Leith could see of them made him rethink having that fight with Oleana. At least she was likely to kill him quick.

"What if we sit these stairs a bit? Test our nerve. Then head back in victory," Leith said looking around with some anxiety.

"Our prize is the irdonium. We shall not surface until we have some in hand," Daycia said. Her voice held a tone of glee that confirmed Leith's earlier assessment of her. The long lonely years must have damaged her mind. No rational person would be happy to go down into a pit of death.

The further they went down, the greater the tension at the back of Leith's neck became. His senses had never felt so alive before. He didn't know how, but he knew there were at least half a dozen ranta crawling around behind the wall at his right. Their presence felt like an itch just under his skin.

Distracted by the new sensation, Leith froze on the steps. He put his hand to the wall, needing physical confirmation for what his mind was telling him.

"Don't fight it," Daycia said, seeming to read his mind. "let the information come in and your mind will learn to sort it all out on its own. The same way your mind rights the image that your eyes pick up. Or, the way we can make out a familiar voice amidst a crowd."

"How you know so much?" Leith asked curiously.

"After you were first created, the Twelve gave me a task. I was to teach the guardian the history of this world, and the ways of the ultras. I know as much about you as the Twelve, and the guardian. My fate is tied with yours. Most of the decisions I have made in my life over the past century have been tempered by thoughts of the Heirs of Eternity."

Leith stared into the ultra's eyes. The violet there was like that of sparkling amethyst forged by immense pressures, eyes that have watched over the birth and death of nations. Yet she spoke of those much older than her with a touch of reverence and awe.

"You've spoken to the Twelve?" Leith looked up into the sky. He could still make out the faint outline of the rings that surrounded the planet. "They be real? Surely real?"

Daycia smiled. "Yes, the legend surprisingly gets it right more than it gets wrong. I've spoken to them. So has Oleana, and if you haven't in a past incarnation, then you will eventually. You can't be sealed as king without them."

Leith's head was swimming. It wasn't enough to encounter the yetis, then an ultra. Now his whole history was rewritten and the Twelve were real. Having a death worm in his arm would have been more comforting.

"You're thinking about it too hard, boy. Relax. Enjoy the ride. That's what I do. Focus on the now. We have beasts to conquer." Daycia did her best to encourage Leith.

A snarl at the opposite end of the pit cut off any further discussion. All Leith saw were big yellow teeth, and glowing red eyes. Even the larger-than-life presence of Daycia offered him no comfort.

"What does it want?" Daycia asked Leith.

"Huh? To eat us."

"No," she said patiently. "Think. Feel," she instructed him. "What does it want? Is it angry? Scared? Hungry?"

"How am I..." Daycia clamped her hand over his mouth. She smelled of cinnamon and old leather.

"What did I just say?" Daycia whispered against his ear. The moment should have been intimate, but the fear burning through his veins, with its anger chaser, cut any thoughts beyond the ranta.

Focus on the now, Daycia had told him. He pushed past the fear, and his instinct to flee. Don't fight it, he told himself. What did the beast want? Leith let go of his own thoughts and tried to let the creature speak to him.

Leith let his eyes flutter closed, and behind his eyelids instead of finding darkness he found a string of numbers. Startled, he opened his eyes, but the information flow didn't stop. The input was too fast for Leith to read, the code too complex to even discern a pattern. But some ancient part of him clicked on, as automatic as breathing. The desire to run back into the shadows was overwhelming, but Leith knew he wasn't his thoughts. He wanted to run, but there was something more important to do.

"Wants to protect its family," he said barely whispering, his voice echoing strangely in his ears as if he were under water. "He wants to protect his family. I say we let him."

"Well convince it we mean no harm."

The question of how to do that was on Leith's lips when Daycia clamped her hand over his mouth once again. It was a bad habit Leith was tiring of quickly.

He thought of all the things that crawled around in the dark. All the things that were prey for the ranta. The smell. The way they moved. Leith pushed enough soothing energy at the beast to calm it down, but hopefully not enough to entice it to attack. With a great snort from its giant nostrils the beast turned and disappeared back into the dark tunnel it called home.

"Well done boy," Daycia said, her tone still hushed but brimming over with enthusiasm. "Now find us a nest that is unprotected so we can fetch our prize and be on our way." Daycia jumped over the three remaining steps and hit the ground with a grace fit for a dancer.

Leith shook his head, wishing the nightmare would end soon. He should have stayed in his hole instead of venturing out for a good beer and a little company. Solitude was safety. Instead he followed Daycia to the pit floor, and toward the opposite end of where they'd encountered the protective ranta.

The others must have scattered at the sound of them. The floor was empty, but he could feel them crawling around inside the earth. Sweat trickled down Leith's forehead, and his skin felt like he'd been in the sun way too long.

"Why so hot down here? We step onto the sun?"

"Energy my boy. Using that special gift requires a lot of energy burning up what fuel your body has, and generating heat. Like any other muscle, the more you use it, the less wear it has on you."

"You had me waste it on one ranta when we are going in whole hive of 'em!"

"Practice makes perfect," Daycia replied placatingly. "Now focus please, and lead the way." Daycia stepped aside to let Leith pass.

Knowing the response any questions would get him, Leith walked forward with more confidence, beginning to trust his instincts to lead him true. He acted like a river letting himself bounce around, taking the path of least resistance.

The tunnels were so small Leith had to take to his knees to get through. If they were cornered, he didn't know how he could possibly defend himself. Daycia handed him the glow stick, making it almost impossible to maneuver with any speed or stealth.

Leith stuck the light in as far as his arm would take it, making sure his new-found ability worked as well as Daycia seemed to think it would. He saw the roughly cut walls that led off into the darkness. The smell of wet earth and animal sweat clung to the walls along with bits of fur, and the bones of prey long devoured. It wouldn't be comfortable but at least it looked clear.

Glow stick in between his teeth, and dagger clutched awkwardly in his hand, Leith lead the ultra deeper into the tunnel system. His initial hope, that a nest could be found near the entrance, proved false early on. Of course, a predator wouldn't expose his young to the open. They crawled for what had to be a good ten minutes before coming across anything promising.

Leith came across an inset part that was rather spherical in shape. A metallic glint cut through the gloom, bouncing the greenish light off into different directions in a starburst pattern. The metal was formed into little hexagonal compartments. Leith assumed those were the nesting sectors. Two of the six compartments were lined with bits of leaves and bark.

Upon closer inspection, Leith saw the baby ranta laying inside. They weren't newbies. They already had a nice coating of fur, and the sides of their nest showed miniature claw marks, as the babies must have been testing their boundaries. For the moment, they were sleep. Leith moved slowly as not to wake them up. He didn't need an angry mother descending on them from behind, if one of the little ones started crying out.

"Take two of the pallets and hand them back. then we can move to the next," Daycia said after squeezing in to peer around Leith. They were so close Leith could feel her breath on his neck. It was rather distracting, her breasts grazing the top of his shoulder and her hair cascading down his neck setting his skin on fire and sending his mind to places it never should have been, but Leith was too embarrassed to mention it. The ultra smiled at him as if all of it were normal. If being the Master of Animals meant this kind of thing would become a part of everyday life, Leith would have to take a pass.

Leith used his dagger to pry the pallets furthest from the babies off. It took some effort, but he managed to get them loose without so much as a peep from the little ones. He handed them back to Daycia as asked. When he felt the familiar tingle at the back of his neck he scrambled back without thinking, crashing into Daycia, and sending the metal ore flying.

"What is it," Daycia asked quickly recovering herself.

"Down the tunnel. Three coming." Leith's whole body felt tense. He needed to run, needed to find the light. His breathing came in quick spurts as he struggled to fold himself into the right position so he could face the outside.

Before he knew it, Leith was scrambling to get outside, having left Daycia to take care of herself. He was pulling himself free of the hole before it occurred to him that this behavior was a bit uncharacteristic. He'd been on the run for many reasons, but never from such a teeth-rattling undistinguished fear before.

His sharp mind was his greatest asset. Never had anything ever made it go blank. Facing the yetis, he'd had a taste of that kind of fear. Now with the ranta, it was kicked up to a new level. Forcing his breathing to slow, Leith wondered if his new-found cowardice had something to do with Oleana and her ultra friend.

When Daycia hit fresh air with a gasp, Leith jumped back. He braced himself for the scolding that was sure to come. He'd left her with a pack of angry beast moving in, who wouldn't be mad?

"Well that was exhilarating," Daycia said smiling from ear to ear, smoothing her hair back. She twirled along the pit floor like a giddy school girl. "I haven't had to scramble like that in a while."

It must have been a delayed reaction to their near-death encounter, Leith figured. If it saved him from being yelled at, he wouldn't complain. Then Daycia froze. She got real close to Leith, even grabbing his face, and looking intently in his eyes. It was unnerving, but Leith didn't know what to say to get her to stop.

"I think we are done with this particular exercise."

Leith snorted. As if there were any doubt of that. Nothing could have made him go back into those tunnels. Oleana would just have to run him through.

Daycia took the lead this time, climbing the steps with a practiced ease. Leith could picture her coming down to the pits every six months or so, just for fun, playing with her pets.

Up top, Lorn was sitting along the edge of the pit wall, feet dangling over, head resting on his bow. Oleana paced back and forth like a cornered ranta. Her eyes looked wild. She chewed at the tips of her fingers. Could he hope that she actually worried for him? What did she know about Leith, and why would she care? As she had said, it was her job. She had no choice, so her worry probably wasn't for him, it was for completing the task before her.

Lorn was up and bouncing around as soon as her spotted Leith's head emerging from the pit. "How did it go? How do you feel? Are you convinced now? Lorn asked in rapid-fire succession. "I still can't believe we found you so fast. Mom has spent the last month reminding me that the process is a long one that could take months, and we found you right away. It's amazing," Lorn marveled at their luck.

"When you breathe?" Leith asked Lorn, half out of curiosity, and half to give his brain enough time to process all the words that had just come flying at him.

"He doesn't," Oleana replied, very deadpan. She looked over Leith like she was searching for hidden injuries. When she seemed satisfied, she moved on to Daycia with a bit less scrutiny.

Leith noticed the sun was much closer to the horizon than it was when he went in. The trip down the pit had taken much longer than he'd thought. It had been the longest day of his life, and he was glad to see it go.

"As for your question, I'm convinced of two things." He nodded at Daycia. "She's crazy" Leith shrugged his shoulders. He thought about all the things he'd discovered about himself during the short trip into the pit. The lingering imprint of the ranta still buzzing in the back of his mind. He thought of the new world that was now opened to him, a world both more exciting and more frightening than he would have ever imagined. "And, I'm more than ever thought possible."

Lorn beamed in satisfaction, nodding his head in agreement. "I'm so happy to hear it. I remember first using my abilities. It was scary and exciting. There were years of hearing mom's stories, but now you're here and all has been confirmed," he said excitedly. "This is just too much! Goodness."

"Breathe before you pass out," Oleana warned Lorn. "Can we have this conversation somewhere more private?" She pulled her coat tighter around her shoulders. "Some place warmer. With food."

"Yes, yes let's eat," Lorn said eagerly.

Leith couldn't disagree. Sweat poured off his skin, and his stomach felt like he hadn't eaten in days, a feeling he knew well enough from experience. "The meal is on you?"

Daycia clasped him on the back. "Tonight, you find out what being the hero of a city can get you," she said smiling. He was really starting to dislike that smirk she always gave him.

"Sounds like it hurts," Leith said suspicious.

"He's learning," Oleana said, daring to crack half of a smile.

CHAPTER SEVEN: TANNIN

Tannin squeezed his large mass into the form of a baymar taking a late-night feeding and melded into one of the herds out on the pasture land. Transforming wasn't a skill he used often, it left him too vulnerable during the transitions. However, special occasions called for special skills. Every time he broke down and reassembled his DNA, remaking his entire being into that of some wild animal, Tannin felt like he lost a part of himself.

The shepherd was soon rounding them all up to escort them back inside the gate where things were safe. Tannin allowed the shepherd to nudge and cajole him inside one of the pins without argument. He made an outstanding baymar. Then it was just a matter of waiting for things to settle down. He listened intently for the sounds of workers to taper off before he felt comfortable changing back into his normal form.

Transforming was a painful process. His bones and joints grew a hundred times faster than normal and slid over each other to regain their true shape. He'd learned long ago to compartmentalize the pain, ignoring all that came with the process and flagging anything that could mean something was wrong. It took the multi-form a moment to catch his breath and feel steady on his new feet.

The shepherds would be back out at dawn to let their herds out and Tannin intended to follow them pass the wall. That left him all night to track his prey and make his father's revenge clear. It was more time than he needed.

Tannin was happy to be spending the night away from the cave. When his father got into his moods, Cornelius tended to make everyone around him suffer. Tannin wanted no part of what the yetis were in store for. Rooting around Solon would be a vacation in comparison.

When his body felt more like its old self, he flipped the latch of the pen and stepped out. A few of his herd buddies move toward the opening happy to follow along.

"This journey is not for you my friends," he said, putting his hand out to keep them at bay. The door closed back without so much as a squeak, and the baymar went back to their huddles, ready to settle in for the night.

Tannin's first stop was the spot where the yetis were last seen. From the report of his brothers, they split up taking both sides of the market and moving in. The ones that hadn't made it back were closest to the garment district, where Tannin was holed up.

It was a short walk to the scene. The destruction his brothers dished out was still evident. One of the shops was bordered up. There were claw marks gouged into the brick on either side of the street. It was the only section that had the shine of being freshly washed. Tannin could still catch a whiff of the blood they'd tried to clean up.

Judging by the marks left behind, Tannin was quick to rule out the rangers. The melee wasn't their style, and the weapons used were not standard issue. There were markings from two different types of weapons, both shorter blades, and one opponent fought with double blades. It must have been someone from the college that decided to help. Daycia, hero of the city, was known to stick her nose into other people's business.

That didn't deter Tannin. His mission was clear. No possible connection to the hybrid Daycia would keep him from exacting the revenge his father demanded. Tannin ran his long fingers against the brick wall, the sensitive pads on the tips picking up every bump and groove.

One particular spot drew his attention. There was no great blood loss there, but there was something about it that set his teeth on edge. The air seemed singed like a fire had erupted in midair. That still didn't fit. There was no trace of ash. Whatever had cut through the air was pure and, leaving behind a minimal disturbance.

The energy signature was unique and had to be connected to the yetis' slaughter.

Tannin got a good whiff. His brand of synesthesia converted the aroma into an intermittent trail of light green waves he could track. At the back of Tannin's mind, he couldn't shake the feeling that the energy was familiar. It felt primal. He couldn't place from where, but he had the rest of the night to figure it out.

After a trek through the city, Tannin found another spot with the same strange energy discharge and followed it to a third. He'd wandered the night for several hours, and the nagging feeling turned into a headache, pounding away at the base of his skull. It would have been enough to drive a lesser man mad.

The third locale was at the edge of a field near the ranger's station which made Tannin rethink his previous assessment. He didn't like being so close to the humans who were specifically trained to kill ones like him. The rangers had done their damage to the yetis ranks over the years. Tannin even had a few scars of his own due to the well-placed shots of one ranger or another.

He slipped into a less conspicuous form, that of a wild dog. It would be less effective than his true form if the need should arise for him to defend himself but there was no reason for him to draw attention.

The hill location had the highest concentration of the energy. He didn't know how he'd missed it before. There was a clear scorch mark shining like a lighthouse burning in the light of a full moon. It was a lightning strike.

His father had a habit of calling down the pure white fire from the sky. He was a petty man that did it just to make his point. That was why the energy felt so familiar. This was not a natural occurrence. Someone in Solon could manipulate the elements.

Tannin racked his brain but he couldn't recall any mention of the half-breed Daycia being able to wield such power. He needed to let his father know right away. Then Tannin remembered the punishment Cornelius dealt out to those who wasted his time.

Tannin needed proof. He needed to set his eyes on the newcomers. Going back to his father with anything less would not be a pleasant experience. He continued off into the night.

100101

Oleana found her way to the roof of the library. The lights of the city led the way. The stars above were shining clear as day in the cloudless sky. Outside alone, she could clear her mind, let the worries of the day fade into the background. She didn't even mind the biting cold. It was like a refresher, sharpening her mind and clearing the senses.

The others were enjoying a nice dinner in the faculty lounge, but Oleana needed to sort a few things out before she could retire for the night. The only way to achieve clarity was to talk to those who knew more than anyone else.

The crisp winter night was buzzing with restless energy. The waxing moon blazed across the midnight blue sky, and cold winds swirled down off the mountain. The rings around Euphoria hung larger than life above Oleana's head. Rich purples and greens could be seen in their shimmering glow.

Before the Twelve first reached Euphoria, the planet had a thin layer of particulate in the upper atmosphere. It wasn't enough to even call a ring. The Twelve adopted its orbit creating a smart particle cloud that rivaled that of the ancient Saturn, long wiped away by its suns explosion. Many looked up at Euphoria's rings and saw nothing but a beautiful act of nature. Others looked up and saw the gods they prayed to day after day. Oleana looked up and knew the truth. The Twelve weren't gods. They were man made things that were tasked with the impossible, but couldn't give up on their purpose to save mankind, even if they wanted to.

Oleana laid out her blanket on the hard roof singles and sat down, wiggling until she was as comfortable as she could expect. She folded her legs under her and rolled her shoulders. She'd grown stiff from not stretching after the fight earlier that day. She should have been soaking in a hot bath, but her questions were more important than her comfort.

Eyes closed, Oleana cleared her mind and thought only of the words the Twelve had given her for those times she needed to speak to them. "Open channel one, priority message to particle cloud, care of the Twelve. Authorization code oscar - foxtrot - tango - four - oscar - mike - ginger - four."

The wind howled an eerily sad song calling to the sky for help. Oleana waited, knowing they would answer, they always did. It was the one thing she could count on, besides a stiff drink keeping her insides warm.

"Twelve responding. Authorization code accepted," a familiar voice said in Oleana's head, the one she called One.

The first time she heard the voices, several lifetimes ago, Oleana was sure she'd lost her mind. Who hears voices and isn't labeled insane? When they tried to explain, she'd paid no heed. When they said they would send her proof, she had run away fearing what that might mean.

Daycia was patient and kind. It took Oleana months to trust the older woman, but once their bond was formed, Oleana realized Daycia meant more to her than any of the women who ever birthed her. Their relationship surpassed incarnations.

"You have located the Master of Animals." number One said.

Over time Oleana had encountered four different voices, with subtle differences in personalities. She'd numbered them in order of appearance. Then there were those few times when many spoke at her at once. She didn't know how many it was then. She couldn't distinguish them. Those first few encounters, she was just happy to keep her brain from liquefying, the experience was so intense. Whether there were actually twelve entities, or that number just held some significance she didn't understand, Oleana didn't worry herself about it. Keeping up with four was enough for her.

"Yes, in record time. If I believed in fate, I'd say we were meant to run into each other, but I know better."

"Fate is the construct of weaker minds to explain what they do not understand," Three said. She was always over explaining things. While One and Two showed signs of understanding the idiosyncrasy of human speech, Three missed it all. On top of that she had the most lyrical voice of all of them. Even though none of them showed any preference for gender of any kind, Oleana always pictured Three as a beautiful woman.

"Yes, well fate or no, I have the Master of Animals, and Daycia worked her gift and showed him who he really was. She also suggested he might be stuck in some kind of prey mode. Does that make sense to you? Could that really be possible?"

The Twelve murmured amongst themselves. They'd gotten better at toning it down so Oleana didn't feel like ripping her ears off to lessen the pain.

"The connection you four have with the smart particles that run through everything on the planet is a two-way connection. You tap into it, and it taps into you. If he were activated while feeling like prey, the Master of Animals could have been flooded with flight hormones. It will pass. You will know if he is reset."

Speaking with the Twelve was like speaking another language. Oleana was used to most of their terminology, but with long breaks in between talking to them, she had to acclimate herself once again.

"How exactly do I do that?"

"You will know. This is why you are the Guardian," Two explained.

"Thanks for the sage advice," Oleana replied dryly.

"You are always welcome," Three said.

Oleana rolled her eyes. "Can you at least point me in the direction of our wayward Master of Earth? The sooner I get away from Cornelius, the better off I will be."

"Cornelius is very dangerous. It would not be wise to encounter him at this juncture," Three explained.

"He has amassed many followers up in his mountain. He has found some way to disrupt our sight. We cannot tell how many yetis he has created, but it is enough to start a very bloody war," Two said.

"Well, point me to my next destination and I will be on my way," Oleana said her irritation building. She tapped her fingers against her thigh resisting the urge to yell. The Twelve always asked everything of her yet getting the smallest bit of information out of them was like trying to pull a cow through a straw. "You know it would be much easier if the other Heirs knew as much as I did and I didn't have to waste time explaining things each time."

"We have explained that the four of you were set up this way for safety. If the others knew too much before they were ready they would only draw attention to themselves. But someone..."

"Someone had to be burdened with failures of the past," Oleana finished, cutting Three off. "Yes, I know. I'm the unlucky one who gets activated by age twelve struggling to deal with puberty and a flood of new memories at the same time while the others stay dormant, blissfully unaware of what's ahead."

"Does this upset you?" Three asked.

Oleana choked on a bitter laugh. She clenched her jaw to keep from letting lose a string of expletives longer than her arm. Instead she smiled and kept her tone flat, knowing that venting to them would do her no good. They might just force an upload to try to fix the problem. "No, it does not upset me."

"The Master of Earth is in the realm Caledon, specifically Central City, or it's vicinity," One said, ignoring Oleana's tangent conversation.

"What is this, the reunion tour? First Solon, now Central City. Out of all the places on this planet, why would he be there?"

"Certain genetic lines are more compatible with the genetic reprogramming that the particles enact, than others. It is only logical for the four to be reincarnated in certain regions more than once following the line of certain families. I could upload a chart if that would be helpful."

Upload was a bad word, Oleana learned that the hard way. It was like learning a year's worth of stuff in the matter of a few seconds. The first time Three uploaded information into Oleana, she couldn't sleep for a week. A mind-scrambling headache camped behind her eyes the whole time, and it took Oleana days to decipher the information she'd been given. The next couple of tries were a bit easier, the learning curve being rather steep. Even though her last experience only caused her pain for a day, it was a process Oleana only agreed to when absolutely necessary.

"No thanks." Oleana took a deep breath and thought about her next words carefully. They were familiar words to her, but they never produced anything worthwhile. She knew it would just frustrate her overlords, but she could not stop herself from asking anyway. "One more thing. Why me?"

"We have discussed this topic sixty-seven times to be precise." Three countered. "We have run out of word combinations that would bring any clarity to the matter."

"I'll ask six hundred more times until you give me an answer that makes sense," Daycia pleaded passionately. "One that justifies having to carry the weight of three failed lifetimes around with me. One that explains why the one person who is supposed to save the world, feels more at home on a rooftop talking to the sky than actually talking to people. People get hurt, they get sick, and they die. The Twelve are forever."

"You are more human than Twelve," One said. Oleana detected the faintest hint of sorrow in his voice. Or maybe it was regret. "That humanity means you feel pain and loss in a way we cannot. For that I am sorry, but it is that pain that will make you and the other three better leaders than us, better than the ultras. They need you more than they need us." With that the conversation was over. The world around her seemed to move a little slower. The night was a shade darker, and the wind colder. Sixty-eight times, and Oleana felt no more at ease with the answer than she had the first time.

CHAPTER EIGHT: BREAKFAST

Dinner with Daycia was good, breakfast was even better. Being guardian of the city came with its perks. She knew all the secret places with the best food. She received a warm reception no matter where she went. Daycia was queen of Solon in all but name.

Oleana remembered being the queen's beloved pet. This time around she was wary of all the attention. Lorn was soaking it up, so she kept her mouth shut.

Even Leith was getting in on the action. He'd spent the night at Daycia's private residence, along with Lorn and Oleana. It was a picturesque cottage that was nestled at the end of the same street that housed the upperclassman dorms. Where the dorms were mostly function over style, trading comfort for functionality when cramming so many active students into a small space, the cabin was all about style.

It was a three-bedroom affair, with large bay windows, and a fireplace in every large room. Oleana hated leaving it. Only the promise of chocolate drizzled pancakes, and hot cider pulled her away. The fact that she intended to lace the cider with a double shot of her favorite rum, only sweetened the deal.

The second they stepped into the Decorated Pastry, the atmosphere shifted. A young woman, with a clean white apron tied at her full waist, escorted them to a large booth meant for a party double their size. Before Oleana was settled in, another woman, this one older, her graying hair tucked behind her large ears, brought them each a large mug of the signature apple cider.

Oleana took two greedy sips, banishing the cold that had seeped into her bones. She could never get used to the cold, and the sooner she got back to a place that wasn't so scared of the sun, the happier she'd be.

With her rum installed, Oleana was better able to deal with the press of people that wanted a moment with their hero. Oleana leaned back in her chair and let them wash over her like waves over a rock. The ordered food came, and Oleana ate until she was sure she would bust. She felt so sluggish she wouldn't have been able to fight a fly. Lorn pushed his plate away with food still on it.

"Do you know how hard I've worked over the years to fill that boy up, and you do it with a single dish?" Oleana said, calmed by the warmth in her belly. "You throw a few sweet treats at him and he can't even eat it all."

"Well mom if you actually knew how to cook a decent meal it wouldn't take so much to keep me satisfied," Lorn shot back.

"Since my cooking is so intolerable, I'll be sure never to subject you to it again."

"Let's not be drastic," Lorn begged quickly.

Oleana laughed at the look of feigned panic on the boy's face.

"You do laugh," Leith drawled, "I thought your face be stuck in that frown."

"The stern look keeps unwanted company at bay," Oleana said cutting Leith a knowing look.

Leith shook his head. "You stalked me. Not the other way sister."

Oleana sat forward, encroaching on his personal space. "Don't flatter yourself. It was for one reason only."

"Yeah, since we found Leith so quickly does that mean we get to spend some time in Solon, maybe learn a thing or two from the great Daycia, or are we moving on, *again*?"

The way Lorn emphasized that last word saddened Oleana. She knew how the boy felt. Moving from place to place was not ideal. Lorn had finally found people who understood what his life was like. He found a new mentor in Daycia. It would be hard to leave that behind knowing the odds were against him in returning. Oleana didn't like the idea of sitting stagnant. She tried hiding from duty to no avail. Now that she was on the inevitable path, it was best to see it through to the end, and without delay.

"I plan to catch the next coast-side train out of Erald. The Twelve said we need to head toward Central City, and that's where we need to be, as soon as we can."

Lorn's shoulders slumped. She had intended to break the news to him later in the day. It was his own curiosity that rushed things.

"Leith, you need to pack up what you absolutely cannot live without. The rest must stay behind. There are plenty of times when we'll end up walking, so don't pack more than you can carry for a long distance," Oleana said needing to distract herself from the hurt etched on Lorn's face.

"Wait there. Who said I be leaving. First the yetis, then you tell me all this Heirs of Eternity business, now leaving. You ask too much."

"Leith, Master of Animals, Heir of Eternity, King of Euphoria. How exactly do you plan to accomplish all of that from your comfortable home?" Daycia asked, her tone flat. "You can't access your full potential without the fourth Heir."

"The three can only be crowned by the Keeper of the Crystal Tower, in Evermore, in the Wild Zone," Lorn said as if reading it off a brochure. "From there, they will unite the Five Realms, and rule for an eternity, working hard to maintain the peace the Twelve longed to create for all of humanity. Mom used to tell me the story at night so I could fall asleep. I still have the occasional dream about the Crystal Tower, and the beautiful Keeper," his sharp green eyes glowed with the fond memory.

"Never left the wall before," Leith said mostly to himself. He downed the rest of his cider in one forced gulp, putting the cup down harder than was needed.

"As Daycia has mentioned, I ran away hard and fast when I first learned of the path in front of me, so I completely understand. You can't let fear drive you." Oleana pushed up the sleeve of his gray wool sweater, showing off the mark on his forearm. It glowed slightly with her touch. "That's what proves you are more than the Silver Owl. More than Solon. And Lorn would kill me if we left you behind." Oleana grabbed Lorn's arm and his birthmark began to glow. The three marks began to pulse in time with her heartbeat. It was a faint light, not nearly the strength it would be with the four of them together. "You can stay here and stick to the world you know, and try to force yourself back into a mold you've already broken. Or, you can accept that you are an Heir of Eternity, accept my leading as your guardian, and come find out what you are really meant for. I don't know about you, but I'd rather not waste another lifetime on a failed attempt at doing what we were all created to do."

"That feels weird," Lorn mused looking down at their arms. "I think I like it. Never seen it do that before. I feel so alive. Mom did you know it would be like this?"

Oleana nodded. She'd had her hands on two of the three kings before. She knew it wasn't all there was. She longed to find the fourth, and complete the circle. Lorn, and even Leith, could take pleasure in the connection they had with each other. For Oleana, it was tempered with a sadness that made her want to scream, the bitter hard memories of lives lost. Her only comfort would come in getting the job done once and for all.

Lorn's boisterous nature, and the strange happenings, drew attention that made Oleana cringe. "Put them away," She instructed abruptly, rolling her sleeve down and putting her coat on for good measure. The boys exchanged puzzled looks and followed her lead.

Leith looked lost in thought, his eyes fixed on his arm. That cocksure smirk he had when they first ran into each other came back to his face. His nostrils flared. Oleana could see the decision he was making playing at the edge of his tongue.

Lorn opened his mouth to speak, but Oleana stayed him. She didn't wish for Leith to feel rushed. Lorn tended to plow over people who were soft spoken.

Oleana pushed back from the table and stood, "We should talk about this somewhere a little more private," she said looking around at the growing crowd. Oleana glanced down at the buffet of food she was leaving behind, even after eating her fill, and wondered when she would next have such a fantastic meal. She turned away, pulling her hood over her head, preparing for the biting weather outside.

Lorn was near bursting with excited energy, walking on the balls of his feet. He walked circles around Oleana. He was distracting enough that she almost didn't notice the odd dog at the edge of the street.

It was a mangy street dog. Shaggy hair and dirt caked feet. Nothing remarkable about its size or breed. There was something in its eyes though. Eyes so light blue they were almost white, like glacial ice in the remotest part of the tundra. They transported Oleana back a century when she'd ran these streets as a young woman desperate for a taste of battle, instead of the bitter old maid she was now, that longed for the release that peace brought.

Those eyes were the eyes of a monster who considered himself an ice god. A man who would rule over humanity with a crushing fist, tossing it about like a dog with its plaything.

"Daycia," Oleana croaked, reaching for her mentor. Where was her bravado, her training, her strength now?

Daycia turned, concern wrinkling her brow.

"What is...," Oleana pointed at the beast too afraid to even ask the question.

Daycia looked, then immediately pulled Lorn behind her. "Tannin."

The dog froze as if caught. It groaned and stretched. The dog stretched out to some six feet tall, covered in light gray fur like the yetis, but lighter and shorter. His body was lean and sinewy, where the yeti was all bulk. He had the yeti claws and the fangs, but a muted version.

"All night I track a familiar energy. Catch the scent of the thing that killed my brothers and what do I find," it wheezed as if its vocal cords were raw from the change. "Daycia and her new friends. Or as I suspect, very old friends having returned. How did I not put it together before? Father has been scouring the five realms for you and here you are under the influence of his mountain."

"Another mutant child of that self-righteous, self-important prick. How many times will he procreate before he realizes the world suffered enough with one of him. That it will not permit another?" Daycia spat, her voice holding a hard tone that shocked Oleana.

Tannin's thin lips pulled back in a tight snarl. "Never say such things about him again. Never speak of him again," he said taking large steps forward.

Oleana pulled her twin blades, feeling stronger with the weight of them in her hands. He may look like Cornelius but he was nothing more than a cheap imitation. His capture, or death, would deal a blow to the false god that would bring Oleana no end of pleasure. It may even ease her apprehension.

Tannin seemed as eager to fight as Oleana. He charged with claws out. Before the two foes could meet, a dagger sliced through the air catching Tannin in the right shoulder.

The multiform whirled around, showing the source of the attack. Leith was at the opposite end of the street, hand outstretched, that smirk painted on his smooth features. They locked eyes, ignoring the raging multiform between them.

"Run," Oleana said in an intimate whisper that failed to carry the distance. "Run."

Leith darted down the street and into an alley that Oleana hadn't even noticed. Tannin moved to pursue, but Oleana was faster. She rushed him, jabbing him in his spine, between the shoulder blades.

Tannin moved with uncanny speed dodging left, catching a glancing blow along his outer arm. He backhanded her hard enough to knock her over and dot her vision. Lorn was at her side, cradling her head while Daycia worked in front of them, facing Tannin down. She moved fast and with anger, keeping the strong man at bay with frenzied stabs.

Receiving one hit after another, Tannin's gray fur became dotted with red splotches. They were minor cuts. He must have realized his odds of success were minimal, for Tannin began to run, changed into a bird, and took off flying toward the mountain.

"Go after him," Oleana yelled, seeing that no one pursued her enemy, "you know what his escape means"

"Killing him would bring the same thing upon us," Daycia walked toward her explaining. "Tannin changed form too many times, he will need time to recover. We will not see him again any time soon."

Oleana's desperate cry pierced the air. "Cornelius will be down on our heads," Oleana panted, trying to regain her breath. "How could I have been so reckless? Trying to show off, and look what that has gotten us! Bringing that...that thing to our door." She shook her head in disgust.

"Who was he anyway?" Lorn asked in confusion.

"Tannin, chief agent of Cornelius. Second generation ultra, offspring of Cornelius and Emmaray, and a very dangerous multiform," Daycia explained.

"Making him your half-brother?"

Daycia ignored Lorn's question. "We must get you out of here now."

"We can't just leave you to face Cornelius and his yetis alone," Oleana said.

"He won't attack here with you gone," Daycia reassured Oleana. "He's not prepared for that fight. We have been defending this city against him for a long time. Believe it or not, I think we can manage without the Guardian."

"Why in the name of The Twelve did I let my guard down? Why did I start to believe, for just a moment, that we could be safe anywhere close to that thing?" Oleana said pointing in the general direction of the mountain. "I can't do it again," she said hopelessness sitting like a lead weight in her chest. "Not here. Not like this. Not when I'm so close." Oleana looked helplessly at Daycia.

"The argument is mute. We can't leave without Leith and there's no telling where he ran off to," Lorn laid his arm across Oleana's shoulders.

"Not going to be getting too far away from you two," Leith said coming up behind them. "Just circled 'round."

"Thank the Twelve you're all right," Oleana said. She was fighting the panicked thought that he had disappeared back into the underworld from which he came.

"Mom, what do we do now?' Lorn said, his voice soft as if he were afraid his words would break Oleana.

Oleana gripped her sais so tight it felt like her knuckles might snap. She closed her eyes tight and took deep breaths to get her body under control. "We run," she said. "Leith, I'm sorry, but if you stay here Cornelius will kill you. I didn't want it to be this way for you," Oleana said.

"That were my favorite dagger," Leith said staring at the space Tannin vacated seeming dazed.

Oleana shook Leith out of his stupor. "You can mourn it later. I'll follow you to pack your stuff. Lorn and Daycia make what arrangements you can, and we'll meet back at the carriage stop in fifteen."

Lorn looked worried. His hand still rested on Oleana's shoulder, even though the side effects of the fight had since faded. Oleana didn't want him out of her sight either.

"Move Swift. Be careful. I love you." she encouraged him.

"Come on, my boy," Daycia urged. "I need your help to finish things quickly." A little push from Daycia, and Lorn started walking.

Oleana watched them go. "He's too young," she said to herself.

Leith turned to her, brows arched.

"That was a wonderful shot," Oleana said pulling her eyes away from her son.

Leith nodded but his eyes were unfocused and his voice floated softly on the air threatening to be carried away. "This way."

He headed down the main road then made an abrupt right turn down a brick alley. Oleana struggled to keep pace when her eyes were continually drawn to the sky, waiting for an attack. Leith lead her through the back of a woodcutting shop and out onto another small back street.

This one smelled of fresh cooked food, and the chatter of diners could be heard as whispers on the wind. Oleana was good at orienting herself in her surroundings, but after a few more swift turns she was lost. How Leith kept it all straight, Oleana couldn't begin to guess. At least she was comforted by the fact that Tannin wouldn't be able to keep up either.

"My humble home," Leith said stopping at the bottom of a flight of steps.

When he lead her inside the old stone building, she had assumed it was yet another short cut, so she did nothing to try and remember what it looked like from the outside. She vaguely remembered following Leith down a hallway, and then down the stairs.

She looked around, not sure what to say about the place. It looked to be a converted workshop. There were metal tables bolted into the floor, and an industrial open-pit furnace taking up a good portion of the far-right wall. A low fire was going, warming up the large room.

Pieces of art were strewn about. Canvas paintings leaned against walls. Marble or onyx statues were positioned at random spots in the large space. Red curtains hung down from the ten-foot ceiling, sectioning off what looked to be a bedroom with the edges of a straw mattress peeking through. There were other pieces of miss-matched furniture.

They were older style pieces, but quality, well taken care of. The whole look was deceptive. If Oleana didn't look too hard she would have dismissed it as a dumping ground for abandoned pieces, but when she got up close the quality and expense was made known.

"Did you buy any of this?" she asked before she could help herself.

"No," Leith said, not an ounce of guilt in his voice. He disappeared into the bedroom.

"Well it's impressive," Oleana shouted. She found herself amused by a finely detailed sculpture of Daycia, sitting in a corner near the stairs. The ultra had a serious look on her face, and wore a cape that was shaped to billow behind her.

Then Oleana found a chaise lounge with a dark blue velvet cushions, and a cherry wood base. When she sat on it, the smell of jasmine wafted up. Some older socialite must have been heartbroken when she found her prized lounge chair gone.

"Ready," Leith said hefting a worn brown leather bag up onto his shoulder. It was a shoulder bag that couldn't have held more than a few changes of clothes, and maybe an extra pair of shoes. Leith's face looked set, so Oleana didn't question him.

She gave one last look to all the treasures that would be left behind. She'd have to tell Daycia to come clear the place out once they were gone, maybe return the items to their rightful owners.

"Let's go."

CHAPTER NINE: FIGHTING

Tannin fell at his father's feet dripping in sweat despite the frigid temperatures in the ice cave. His every nerve felt like it was on fire. Blood swam in his ears and his head pounded, making it hard to think clearly, much less form words. He'd pushed his body too hard.

Cornelius stood at the mouth of one of the tunnels being built, carving out more of the heart of the mountain. A dozen yetis hacked away at the hard stone creating a rough archway. "Ah, there is my favorite son returned," Cornelius greet him as Tannin dropped beside him. "I sent him to do a job, and he took all night to make sure ...,"

"Father," Tannin croaked, interrupting him. His eyes slammed shut against the pain and exhaustion.

Clawed fingers dug into Tannin's neck at the base of his skull. Cold flooded his body pushing away the pain and fire shut up in his bones. He could breath. Could think. Tannin knew the energy exchange from his father was temporary. His body would need rest and fuel to recover. Tannin inhaled sharply, stretching muscles that felt like they were pulled too tight over brittle bones. "The guardian. Two of her kings. In Solon."

Cornelius howled high and loud like a wounded animal, sending Tannin's recovering ears into a frenzy of pain. He held his head in his hands, fighting hard against the darkness pressing in on his mind. Ice fell off the walls in rivulets spreading shards of deadly slivers over the rocky floor.

"Three Heirs of Eternity in Solon!" Cornelius grabbed the nearest yeti and pulled it close. "You gather all the yetis that have strength to fight, and march them on Solon now."

Tannin stood. His knees threatened to buckle but he held firm, gritting his teeth. He would join his brothers in battle.

"Not you. You've done enough," Cornelius told his son cradling Tannin's chin. "Describe these ones to me then go get rest. I'll need you strong for what comes later."

100101

When Oleana and Leith arrived at the carriage station Lorn and Daycia were already there, along with four rangers on horseback, and armored up to the neck. Daycia's latest apprentice, Paley, hung at the back of the group. Oleana recognized her from the footage of the yeti fight. She was a young woman, no older than twenty. She had short black hair, just enough to brush behind her ears, and soft features like a porcelain doll. There was a strength in her hooded brown eyes that gave Oleana a glimpse into why Daycia had chosen her.

"What's this?" Oleana asked.

"I couldn't leave you vulnerable while you leave the city," Daycia replied, as if it were self-explanatory.

"Are you trying to get them killed?" Oleana shook her head, furious. "I can't stand for this."

"It is our pleasure to fight and defend the Heirs of Eternity," one of the rangers said. He was the one from the viewing room. The leader. Oleana couldn't think of his name. He was tall and muscular, with a wisdom in his eyes that only came with experience. He was willing to risk his life for her without being asked, yet she couldn't even keep track of his name.

Oleana couldn't reject his sacrifice, even when every bit of her was scared she would end up with more deaths on her conscience. "Thank you," she replied, her voice a heavy-hearted whisper.

"That first time around I failed to protect you," Daycia choked out. She swallowed hard before continuing. "The next time I didn't even know you were back until word of your death spread. Alwen...sorry, Oleana if you thought I would sit back and miss the opportunity to do what I should have done that first time, then you don't know me at all. Besides, we can take care of ourselves."

Oleana looked her over. Daycia looked ready to take on an army. She wore a black knit sweater with a round hem that hit her mid-thigh. She had slim-cut, forest-green pants that had padding along her thighs and knees, with her leather boots protecting the rest. A matching green corset with shining metal accents shielded her torso, and leather and metal guards protected her arms. Daycia had a short sword strapped to her back, two daggers sticking out of each boot, and a short fighting staff fastened to her saddle.

"I would never suggest that you couldn't" Oleana said. She looked over the men and women who decided to join her and for once she felt protected and it felt good. "Inside," she urged Leith and Lorn. "Time to go."

As the carriage clicked away on the rough road, pulled by two armored horses with legs the size of Oleana's torso, the boys chattered away to each other. Their hurried speech, and the light topics, spoke volumes about the tension they were feeling. Oleana kept her eyes on the sky, expecting Tannin to drop down on them at any minute. Daycia was on horseback running point, so Oleana couldn't even voice her concerns to her friend. It was a quite a nerve wracking ride to the wall that had Oleana grinding her teeth. By the time she found the last Heir of Eternity she would need dentures, having ground her teeth down to nothing.

They made it past the rough transition to the outside of the great wall, and down the road past a lot of the pastureland, to the town of Erald where the train station was before they ran into any trouble. The carriage was pulling up to the stop when Oleana heard the shout from one of the rangers.

"Four behind," he yelled.

Oleana jumped from the carriage while it was still rolling, bending her knees to absorb the jarring impact. Her twin sais were out and ready before she straightened.

"Get back inside," Daycia yelled.

Oleana shook her head. "I know how to defend myself." Lorn then poked his head out, craning to see, but Oleana glared at him. He scooted right back in with a groan.

Four yetis were coming down the main road. Erald didn't have a wall to protect it, so they could stroll in without effort. Oleana felt some relief at the absence of Tannin and Cornelius. She knew her luck wouldn't hold out long, it never did.

"With my help, we can dispatch these four quickly and be on our way," Oleana said pleading with Daycia not to argue and waste valuable time.

The older woman frowned, but there was no use debating the issue. Oleana had the edge. Daycia pulled her up onto the horse. "Paley, keep an eye on the boys, if you would please," Daycia instructed. The younger woman nodded. Daycia spun her horse around and spurred it forward with a kick of her heels, forcing Oleana to hold tight to her mentor's midsection.

The lead yeti turned his head to the sky and let out a noise so ear-splitting the air around Oleana seemed to vibrate with it. The horse beneath her bucked in complaint, and Oleana held on with all that she had. Daycia pulled the reigns tight and the horse finally settled.

"What in the Twelve was that," Oleana said into Daycia's back. Her stomach felt like it was in her chest.

"A call for help," Daycia replied, her voice tight.

The first yeti lunged at Daycia, who urged her horse to veer right, narrowly missing a claw to the face. Oleana pushed off Daycia's back, sliding off the horse backwards. She pirouetted on her tiptoes to get herself facing the right way.

This yeti wasn't like the others she'd fought recently. He wasn't trying to play with his food, tease his opponent. He came at her hard. She caught one blow with the right guard of her sai. The other got through but it glanced off her shoulder, spinning her around.

Oleana landed on one knee, the impact shooting pain up her spine. She had no time to deal with it as she had to roll forward to avoid being swiped again. One of the rangers came to her aide, spearing the beast with his sword.

The blow landed on the yeti's left shoulder, which seemed to anger the beast more than anything. It turned on the ranger, howling like a wild thing. Oleana took the advantage. She jumped up, coming down on the beast with both weapons, slicing into its back. The ranger finished it off with a swift slash across the neck, making a clean separation of its head from its neck.

Momentum took Oleana down on top of the crumpled body. Oleana used all the muscles in her back too free her weapons. She wiped the viscera clinging to her sais on the coarse fur. Up close the smell of a dead yeti wasn't much worse than a live one. Either way the odor of fish and wet earth saturated air around them.

The ranger stood over her offering a hand up, which she took gladly. "Thank you…" she paused not knowing his name.

"Wade," he offered.

"Wade," Oleana repeated.

"Any time, Guardian. You know my brother is obsessed with all the lore on you four. He's read every piece of information he could find. He's not going to believe I got the chance to fight at your side today."

Oleana smiled. "It's so nice to hear about a true believer. They're so rare these days. When you recount this encounter, be sure to leave out the part where I got knocked down," she said brushing her pants off.

"Then how do I explain how great a hero I am for saving you?"

Oleana's reply was cut off when she watched in horror as a yeti slammed all of its two hundred pounds into Daycia, while she was distracted by another opponent, knocking her from her horse. Oleana and Wade rushed forward together. Oleana pulled her mentor out of the way while Wade forced the yeti back on its heels.

"You're bleeding," Daycia said as she found her feet.

Oleana looked at her shoulder. Her sleeve was in shreds, and blood stained what cloth was left. She felt the sting, but the cold kept it to a minimum. "Well you're lucky you have a hard head, otherwise you'd be out."

Daycia shrugged before throwing herself back into the battle. Oleana was looking for her opening when she noticed the darkening sky. The temperature dropped sharply. Oleana breathed in and her chest tightened so much her ribs ached. Her brain tried to convince her it was just Lorn building up a storm, but the air was thick with cold. It wasn't Lorn.

Oleana knew what that kind of change in atmosphere meant. It triggered the nightmare she couldn't escape. Only the Ice Ultra, Cornelius, pushed a cold front ahead of him like the shadow of death.

Daycia did away with her yeti, then spun around to Oleana, her eyes wide. "Oleana go!" Daycia yelled.

Oleana froze. She knew what the strange weather meant. She knew who was coming. She wanted to run. She couldn't bear the thought of facing Cornelius, or worse yet, having him go straight for Lorn and Leith. But neither did she want to leave others to fight her battles for her.

"Do what you're told and go," Daycia demanded, spit flying from her mouth.

"Please be careful," Oleana begged as she began to run, jumping over the dead yeti, and pumping her legs as fast as they would carry her back toward the train station.

The fighting took them further away from the station than Oleana had anticipated. When she reached the carriage, she was out of breath, and her arm was drenched with a mixture of blood and sweat. The carriage was empty, even the driver had abandoned it. Since there was no luggage, Oleana assumed the others caught the train.

Oleana pushed off the carriage and went running. Word must have spread that there was danger, because as soon as she opened the double doors to the station nervous eyes turned to stare. She couldn't tell if her presence made them relieved, or worried. She didn't care. She was searching for particular faces.

Her feet moved forward, even though all she wanted to do was collapse. The coastal rail train was on the last platform and it crawled with people scurrying to board. Lorn and Leith, with their bodyguards, were huddled near one of the doors, the crowd flowing around them.

Lorn spotted her and shouted. "Mom!" he closed the distance between them. "Are you okay?" he asked, concerned. "You're bleeding. What happened?" Lorn laid his hand on Oleana's arm before she pushed him away.

"In the train now. You two," she said pointing to Daycia's apprentice and the ranger. "Join the others. Cornelius is in play."

Their eyes went wide.

"Go!" Oleana shouted. Lorn and Leith grabbed the bags and headed for the train while the ranger led Paley out.

Oleana kept turning back as she followed the boys into the train. If she could force the other passengers to load faster, she would have. Since she was forced to leave the battle, Oleana wanted to be sure it was worth it. That they got away safely.

Lorn found their cabin and stuffed their belongings into whatever space he could find in the narrow closet by the door. Leith took a seat, but looked her over. His jaw worked as if he wanted to say something, but couldn't manage to find the words. Lorn twisted and fidgeted, trying to get a good look out the window.

Oleana stared straight ahead, her body shaking with fear and exhaustion. Her eyes were on Leith and Lorn, but her mind was elsewhere. She was plagued by the memory of Cornelius laughing when he plunged a sword through her kidneys so many years ago. Knowing her friend, her mentor, the only mother she really connected with, might be out on the field, facing the beast that had killed Alwen chilled Oleana to her core.

As the train started up and pulled forward, steam billowed outside. temporarily blocking the view. Lorn groaned, sitting back in his chair, pulling Oleana back into the present. She joined Lorn in his attempt to settle down.

Leaving the station, they got a glimpse of the hill where the others were fighting. Heading the opposite way, it was hard to make out anything clearly, but Oleana saw what she needed. In the center of the melee, taller than any other figure, cold rolling off him in waves, stood Cornelius. Oleana could see where his attention was focused, on a curvy figure with bright red hair.

As the curve of the track pulled them out of sight, Oleana had to bite down on a scream. Her heart thudded in her chest. She wanted so much to go back, protect her friend. She sank back in her chair covering her eyes with her hands. "Please be okay. Please be okay," she whispered over and over, the tension in her temples squeezing her head. Oleana hoped she wasn't being too loud. She didn't want attention. She wanted so much to be alone with her fear.

"Mom," Lorn whispered, his voice gentle, almost pleading.

"Yes, Lorn," Oleana said. She kept her voice flat. If she let even a little bit of the torrent raging inside her out, it would overwhelm her, and she would claw her way off the train and back into the fight.

"Let me tend to your arm."

Oleana inhaled sharply. She blinked back the tears. She remembered where her priorities should be. Taking care of her charges, her kings. She was built to protect them and that had to be enough to keep her going. With anger and determination pushing out the fear and regret Oleana ripped away the rest of her sleeve, exposing the four slash marks marring her upper arm.

Lorn already had the bandages out and a container of water. He set to work washing her wound with tender care. Oleana hated the silence between them. It made her unease all the more oppressive.

"We'll be safe once we reach Central City. I have some old friends there that should help us out. There are half a dozen stops between here and there, so we have to be extra careful," Oleana said focusing on what was ahead.

Leith nodded.

"Not sure if Cornelius saw us get on the train or not, but at the next hub we need to switch trains."

Again, silence hung between them. Oleana didn't know what else to say. The wound in her arm started to throb, and her tongue felt too heavy to be of use. Lorn's steady hands made light work of patching her up, which currently was the only solid thing for Oleana to hold onto.

"Glad you're okay." Leith said.

100101

Cornelius landed on the frozen grass with a thud. He always loved traveling on the wind. It brought him such a feeling of exhilaration, a sensation of being untethered from gravity and connected with the ethereal. The only other thing that came close to the feeling was a nice battle, but his mood darkened when he looked around and found not only his children dead, but no sign of the guardian or the other Heirs.

"Daycia, you fool, where are they?" he bellowed catching sight of the familiar redhead. She looked so much like her mother it was uncanny, but the soft-hearted ultra was tainted with her human side, and had decided long ago to stand up for the weak. Cornelius made sure his offspring were pure blood to prevent that kind of disloyalty.

Daycia swept her battle-tousled hair back off her face. Sweat beaded along her forehead, despite the cold. Her chest heaved in ragged increments, showing the exertion she had already put forward. "They're long gone, Cornelius. You won't get to them. If you attack Erald or Solon, you'll be declaring war on humans and we both know that's a fight you're not prepared for. So quit this posturing and return to your cave."

Cornelius howled, pulling the cold winds around him like a shield. "You'll not presume to order me, half-breed. I'll destroy everything and everyone that gets in my way. My connection with your mother will not save you from the same fate. Point me in their direction and I might spare you."

In response Daycia hurled a dagger at his head. Cornelius dodged it easily, as the winds whipping around him threw its course wide. He was ready to fight. If she continued to be stubborn, he would have to test just how immortal Daycia really was. Someone had to pay for the treatment Tannin received.

Daycia charged first, a ranger at her side. They both wielded swords in a two-handed brute force attack. Cornelius smiled. Such tactics were beyond him. He'd dispatch them quickly and continue his hunt.

Daycia reached him first. Cornelius blocked her jab with his forearm, turning to the side enough to miss the ranger's blow. Cornelius tried to wrench the blade free of Daycia's grasp, knowing she was the more dangerous of the two.

Holding on strong, Daycia side-kicked him in the ribs, forcing Cornelius back a step. The ranger moved into the opening, ducking low to get under the hold Cornelius still had on Daycia, and going for Cornelius' unprotected middle.

Cornelius swung for the ranger, claws out, catching the man across the face, but it was a glancing blow that barely slowed the man down. Cornelius pushed Daycia away and spun to deal with the ranger, but the man was fast. He'd gotten around behind Cornelius, slashing at his back.

Cornelius lashed out with the cold winds, pulling it toward him in a great rush, feeling the soothing bite of it against his skin. Then he let loose with all his fury. For a moment, there was a vacuum around him, airless and hot in the wake of all the energy he'd expended. Cornelius' heart pounded as time slowed to a crawl, and he watched while the others were knocked to the ground.

Air returned, and Cornelius finally had room to breathe. The yetis that followed him out were finally catching up with the fight. Two more humans joined the foray as well. The odds looked more even, but Cornelius still felt glad for his advantage.

He pressed forward before Daycia found her feet, leaving one of the yeti to deal with the ranger. Daycia's hair had fallen over her face, and blue ice clung to her clothes. Cornelius grabbed her by the shirt collar, knocking the weapon out of her loose hand.

"Tell me where the guardian and her brats are. Last chance to hold on to that long life of yours." He lifted Daycia off the ground, her legs swinging uselessly.

"You will never get anything out of me," Daycia snarled. Cornelius believed her. The human blood may have made her heart soft, but her passion was as fiery as her mother's, the Fire Ultra.

Drawing her knees up, Daycia kicked at his chest with both feet, forcing him to drop her. He pressed after her, raking his claws across her stomach. On the ground, she scrambled backwards, but she couldn't move fast enough to escape him.

Cornelius laughed. Such a sad sight watching the great hero of Solon crawling away like a wounded dog. Soon he would rip down all those statues of her darted around his city. He realized too late that her crawl wasn't random.

Daycia had a rock in one hand and reached for her fallen sword with the other. He reached for her ankle, pulling her up. Daycia's hands came together. One spark, and the world exploded.

The daughter of the Fire Ultra engulfed him in flames. Cornelius felt the blaze licking at the fur along his arms as if he were detached from them, as if it were some far off remembered pain that could no longer do him damage. He still held on to Daycia while his brain tried to catch up to the realization that he was dying.

As the fire reached toward his face, Cornelius jumped back in a panic. The searing pain hit him, forcing a ragged scream from his lips. He waved his arms frantically, trying to quell the flame, but it only made things worse.

No! No! No! He couldn't die like this. Not burnt to ashes by some half-breed not worthy of being in the same league as his yetis. Cornelius turned his gaze skyward. He could feel the clouds above laden with moisture.

He called, and they answered. Thick wet flakes dropped down from the sky in such a thick blanket Cornelius couldn't see in front of him far enough to see the end of his own nose. He forced himself to stand still as the bitter cold killed the fire and sealed the wounds in his skin.

He heard the wails of something around him, but couldn't make out if it was human, animal, or other. He sank to his knees, pleased by the crunch of snow that cushioned the impact. Wind whipped up around him, sinking down to the bone. The snow did not let up. Cornelius would empty the sky and bury them all, he thought.

The temperature continued to drop. He could feel the air in his lungs thin out because of it. He'd never pushed it this far. Never stretched his power to its limits like this. He couldn't stop himself. He still felt as if he was on fire, and he couldn't stop until he was frozen inside and out.

Something solid careened into him, forcing Cornelius on all fours. It was one of the yeti, missing an arm and running in wild aimless circles. Cornelius grabbed his child. It whirled on him, fangs glistening with a thin layer of ice. Then it recognized its father and settled.

In his grasp, Cornelius noticed the poor creature was shivering, and its wound was frozen over. If he kept going he would kill his own, as well as his enemy.

Cornelius caught a glimpse of his hand, the blood of Daycia coating the tips of his claws. That victory would have to be enough for one day. He whistled high, calling for his yetis to retreat. He mindlessly followed the yetis as it half-dragged him up the hill. Cornelius couldn't see through the white-out, he could only hope their path was unhindered by pesky men with swords.

CHAPTER TEN: TRAIN

"How we supposed to get cross the border?" Leith asked. He fidgeted in his seat changing positions every few seconds. He kept trying to crack his knuckles but there was nothing left to crack.

Oleana was just as ready to get off the train. They'd been cooped up in the cabin, the three of them, for too long, and Lorn's boundless energy was overwhelming in the tiny space, forcing everyone else to search for a way out.

Currently the boy was reorganizing his bag, which he'd been forced to pack in a hurry. The project required him to pull everything out first, taking up the little bit of floor space between the two sets of seats. Because all the chairs faced the middle section, there was nowhere else to look but at the mess Lorn made, and the intense focus he dedicated to such a ridiculous task.

Oleana handed Leith the documents Daycia had stuffed into her bag. "Daycia made sure we all had diplomatic papers to ensure we could cross between realms. This is not my first trip down this never-ending path."

Leith scanned his documents as if they really were something of interest. Oleana couldn't get a good read on him. She didn't know what he might have been feeling. Lorn was an open book. A mixture of worry and fear was written across his brow. He tried to hide it by staying busy. Leith on the other hand was shut off, showing no outward signs of anything other than mild irritation.

"If we stayed on this train it would take us four days to get to Central City in Caledon," Oleana said. "We can't risk staying in this metal death trap that long since Cornelius knows where we left from," her voice caught just mentioning him. She flashed back to Daycia standing in front of the monster, risking her life to make sure they got to safety.

Oleana tasted death three times, but nothing scared her like the first one at Cornelius hands. The way he laughed as her life ebbed away through the ragged wound in her abdomen. Cornelius reputation for cruelty only got worse as the years went on. Leaving Daycia behind to face him, rumbled Oleana's stomach like sour food.

They'd only been on the train for four hours, but it felt like a lifetime ago that Oleana was running away from a fight, as much out of fear as a need to protect her son and Leith. She was desperate to know what happened, to know if she'd lost yet another important part of her life in the pursuit of fulfilling the programming that drove her.

"So we switch trains," Leith said bringing Oleana back to the conversation. "When and where?"

"This route intersects two other big routes, so we have options." Oleana's head swam with so many variables she couldn't sort them. She rubbed at her temples in frustration. "We can worry about that later. Right now we need…." Oleana searched for an excuse that would get her out of the cabin and away from the others without being obvious. "…. food," she finished lamely. "There is a dining car on this tin can somewhere. I'll find it and bring stuff back. You two try not to kill each other while I'm gone." Oleana jumped to her feet, afraid if she lingered she'd talk herself out of getting out of sight of the others.

"Don't forget dessert," Lorn called out after her. He didn't look up at her, but the stiff way he held his shoulders said enough.

Oleana turned back to him and ran her hands through his mass of sandy-brown curls. Every day they got longer, and since they left their farming home two months ago, she hadn't had the opportunity to cut them. They were long enough to cover his ears already. The longer hair reminded her so much of the dirty-faced orphan she'd ran into on the streets, begging for scraps. She'd promised then never to let him be that desperate again, and here she was scraping by, tooth and nail, to keep it.

"Dessert. Of course. Whatever you want."

People milled about the train, all wrapped up in their own tasks to really notice Oleana. She appreciated the anonymity. There were whispered conversations about some possible trouble back in Erald, but nobody knew what it could have been. No one seemed to have any answers.

Oleana let her feet carry her forward, following the crowd. She tried hard not to think of Daycia, of Wade, and the others. There was enough to worry about ahead. She didn't think she'd be back in Central City so soon. Thirty-four years had passed since she was there last.

Like many of her partings, it was a hard one leaving Central City. She made friends there, despite trying her best not to. Going back wouldn't be easy. She wouldn't be returning to an immortal like Daycia. Her friends there would be changed by the passage of time. She'd already put one old friend in danger, how could she race to put more in harm's way? Without help, they were unlikely to elude Cornelius for long, now that he knew who to look for.

Oleana perked up at the smell of quality alcohol in the air before she realized she'd reached the car she'd been heading for. There were carts secured to the floor, with food sitting under large clear lids on one side of the car, and a bar at the other.

She knew she should take her share of food and run back to the cabin. Lorn's words flitted in her ears like insects telling her to stay away from the bar. Before she could make up her mind, Oleana found herself sitting on the nearest bar stool, a polished wood number with a dark red cushion.

A man stood behind the bar. He looked to be around Oleana's age. He was tall as Lorn, but more filled out. His bronzed skin said he hailed from parts further south than Solon. He wore a black shirt, and trousers with a blue vest emblazoned with the train company's logo on the chest.

He smiled at her as he approached. It was a charming smile, bright and wide, but she could tell it was automatic. The gesture held no genuine emotion in it. His brown eyes stayed flat. Oleana responded in kind, going through the usual rituals of such an encounter.

"What would you like?" he asked, coming in close to be heard over the din of voices around them. Oleana caught the piney scent of his cologne.

"Something strong, yet not overpriced," Oleana said. The bartender nodded as if in the one sentence, he knew exactly what she wanted. "And make it a double." She played with one of her locks as she waited, temporarily distracted by the difference in texture between her hair and the colored thread woven around it. The rhythm of the train around her, lulling her into a fragile state of calm.

What the bartender brought back was a short glass half-filled with an amber brown liquid, and a single ice cube. She paid her check, which as requested, was very reasonable. Oleana lifted her drink to her face and took a deep breath in.

The astringent alcohol smell hit first, but under that she could detect a woody scent, with a slightly sweet caramel after-aroma. It was the sign of a well-aged liquor. At the first sip, when the strong, yet well-flavored liquid, burned its way down her throat, Oleana knew she'd found a good drink.

She also knew a lecture from Lorn was headed her way. She would drink her fill and go back smelling like it, and she didn't care. When the stranglehold of worry and fear released its grip on her brain just a fraction, enough to let a coherent thought pass through unmolested, Oleana knew it was worth it.

The train they were on took a route that hugged the coast line, before making a sharp turn in land to reach Central City. It was comfortable, popular, and the easiest way to get to the capitol pf Arismas, affording passengers with beautiful views and plenty of amenities. Oleana didn't need easy. She needed fast and private.

There were some rail lines that travelled further inland. They made direct routes between cities. It wouldn't be a pretty trip and they would have to transfer again, but Oleana much preferred the time they'd save. She downed the rest of her drink, repeated the process twice more, making sure to fill her flask before she was done. Then she hit the food line. She always felt better with alcohol in her belly, and a plan on her mind.

100101

The train pulled into the first major stop on its route. It was a port town, just outside the capital of Arismas. All the major shipping for the realm came through the ports there and like any other such places it was known for its diversity, and the trouble that came with it.

Leith had heard the tales of the place from people in the pubs, people that spent their lives hauling materials back and forth, collecting stories along the way. He'd never been out of Solon himself, rarely even been near the far edges of the great wall.

Now he was passing his great adventure by on a train, with barely enough windows to tell if it was day or night outside. Every time he reached to open it further, Oleana looked like she was going to have a fit, or throw up. Her last trip away, she came back smelling of alcohol but since the boy didn't bring it up, Leith wasn't going to either. It wasn't his place to judge others. The boy did look disappointed, which made being in that tiny space together very uncomfortable. Leith hadn't signed up for family drama.

"Mom," come on, the boy said bouncing on his seat. "We're miles away from Solon. This train will be stuck here for an hour at least. What's the harm in us spending a little time off this metal box and getting some fresh air?"

"Lorn come on, I'm not in the mood to go traipsing around some crowded port town just to get some fresh air. We have all the supplies we need here. We just have to ride it out until it's time to switch trains. Be patient." Oleana rubbed her temples and shut her eyes, but the boy didn't take the hint.

"You don't have to go.' Lorn cajoled her. "Stay here, and rest up. I won't go far, and I can defend myself if I need to. I just need to stretch my legs. This cabin wasn't meant to hold the three of us all squashed together like this," Lorn paced quickly back and forth in the tiny space, until he'd worked himself up, looking like an angry, caged lion. "Mom, please I need to get out. Just want to get off this train for a few minutes."

"If you think I'm going to let you go out there alone you must have lost your mind boy. It's too dangerous. No matter how far we go we are always in danger. Enemies everywhere and the fact that you don't get that means you can't be trusted to stay alert. No way."

"Leith can come with me. He's just as paranoid as you."

"I don't know him."

"You've known him for longer than these bodies have been alive."

"But I don't know him."

"He's my brother. We're four of a kind, us Heirs. If you can't trust him, you can't trust anybody."

"Think that's her point," Leith said. "She don't trust nobody." He mindlessly twirled his dagger. He tried to stay out of it, but he wanted out as much as Lorn. And while he didn't need her permission to leave, he didn't want either one of them mad at him if he did. "But it might be best for us all if we work off the crazies now, before we do the long haul. The road to Caledon is a long one to be on edge in this tiny room."

Oleana stared at him through narrowed eyes. It was similar to the look she set on him at the bar but this one held a little more malice and a little less bravado, just a weariness that gave Leith hope that he might win this one. Or she could decide to try and beat him into submission with one of her sai.

"Twenty minutes. Then I come looking for you. If I have to come looking for you," Oleana's eyes bored a hole right through Leith's forehead, "you will wish you'd stayed back in Solon and faced Cornelius."

"Mom, come on. Now you're just being dramatic for effect. You needn't worry anyway, we'll be back on time."

"Remember, keep your heads down. Move swift. Be safe. Love you Lorn."

Leith nodded. He had no doubt Oleana was serious about putting a hurt on him if anything happened to Lorn. He also had no doubt he'd bring back Lorn safe and on time, if he had to carry the boy back kicking and screaming.

100101

The train station had some foot traffic, but once they got beyond that, the city wasn't crowded as Oleana had warned. There were several beggars on the streets, and rangers pacing the streets with eyes searching for danger. From the stories Leith heard, the city, even on the outskirts, should have been a lively place. The air of fear and poverty crept into Solon a couple years ago with the constant yeti attacks and the uncertainty of what Cornelius was going to do next. Leith didn't think it would have come this far, but he recognized the stench of decay, and it scared him.

Lorn seemed to catch onto it too because he shied away from the beggars, his face knotted by worry. "Have you never come across beggars before," Leith asked, "the life of a kingling so greatly privileged?"

"I'm not," Lorn stuttered. "I'm not put off by them, they just bring up bad memories. I used to be one of them. Mom found me on the streets begging for money with a few older boys. It's not a period of my life that I remember well, but occasionally things like that will drudge it all up."

Leith looked at the kid. "Sorry. Didn't mean to... I didn't know," he finished awkwardly. "Guess we got some in common."

"Is that how you became a thief? Part of the guild?"

"Didn't your mom teach it's rude to ask such questions?" Leith snapped, avoiding the boy's inquisitive gaze.

"So is it?"

"I thought we here to explore. If you wanted to talk coulda stayed on the train."

Lorn pulled ahead a dozen steps and turned around, walking backwards. "I can explore and talk at the same time, or is that too complicated a task for a lowly thief like you?"

Leith held up his hand in warning. "Two things, boy. First, I ain't no lowly nothing. Second, my story is simple. Parents poor. Did odd jobs. I had to work when was seven," Leith shrugged, his gaze focused on his feet. "Ran wit other street kids, and found thieving an hour brought more than working twelve. Instincts was good, but practice made me better." Leith hesitated. He didn't know why he was telling the boy everything, but it was better than being hounded with a thousand more questions.

"And?" Lorn said.

"Parents didn't agree, so choose guild. Guild didn't work either. Too many rules. We banged out a deal." Leith froze, fixing Lorn with a dark stare. "Then you guys came in, ruined everything. The end."

"You make it sound so...so...,"

"Plain. Cause it is. My life not fancy, daring, whatever nonsense in your head. Thieving a job like any other, just outside the law. I worked every day. Planning, scouting, training, working."

"Can you show me?"

Leith nearly tripped over an uneven patch of the street. "How I'm 'posed to do that? Your mom would kill me."

"Why would you tell on yourself?"

"Wouldn't."

"Then we don't have a problem. So, you going to show me or what?"

"I don't know I could." Leith looked around. Nothing stood out to him as target. He needed something easy enough that wouldn't pose a risk if the rookie messed things up, but required enough skill to give the boy a good idea of what his work was like. Then he heard a wagon rolling by. The side said, Geoff's Fresh Produce. "Might have a plan."

Lorn bounced on the balls of his feet. "Yes. Yes. Yes!"

"We gona rob a wagon. I be the distraction, you grab the goods. Up for it?"

"That sounds crazy and awesome, rob a wagon," Lorn chuckled with glee. "Goodness."

"Sssssh boy, don't tell the world."

"Sorry. So, what's the plan?"

Leith's instincts told him it was a bad idea, but the boy's enthusiasm was infectious. As they followed the wagon, making its slow way down the dirt hill road, he told the boy in as simple terms as he could put it. Then he made Lorn repeat it back and Leith pointed out what dangers to look out for.

There was a patch of road that opened up with nothing but grassy fields on both sides. No businesses or houses nearby. Leith knew that was the perfect spot to set up the ambush. It had been a long time since he'd worked with a partner. The dynamic felt like an old glove. It fit, just a little stiff. The job was simple, one he could have pulled off by himself half-sleep, or better yet, half-drunk. The kid had enthusiasm for days, and the rangers seemed more focused on the train station than anything else, so Leith didn't count them as much of a threat.

Leith left Lorn to trail behind the cart while he darted off into the field. He knew from several bad experiences that the best distraction was one that didn't scream distraction. It was something that just took people's attention, without them even noticing. One good look at the driver, and Lorn knew exactly what to do.

A young woman, strawberry blonde hair down half her back following in the breeze, held the reigns of the two-ox cart. The metal shod hooves of the bald beasts of burden kicked dirt up with every step, and the young woman wiped frantically at her face as often as the reigns would allow. Her eyes darted back and forth over the terrain, even though she must have traveled that route hundreds of times. She knew what was out there waiting for her. She was just hoping to spot something new to break up the monotony.

Leith was more than happy to provide that for her. He ran into a field of lilies that dotted the road side. Like a madman, he started ripping them out of the earth with a frenzy that spoke of mental disturbance. "Where is it? I know I left it here. Where is it? You give it up! Give it up! By the Twelve, I rip up every last square inch of earth to find what mine!" he yelled. Bent over as he was, he spared a glance between his legs to see if it was working.

The girl slowed her cart, staring at him sidelong in little spurts as if she didn't want to be caught looking his way. Leith didn't care, he just needed to give Lorn enough time to hop on the back of the wagon, grab a couple of things, and hop off. No fancy tricks, no high-flying acrobatics. Just down and dirty, the way Leith did it as a youngster.

Leith got his nails into the dirt and started flinging it everywhere. He heard some hit the side of the cart. "Hey!" the girl yelled behind him, protesting his disregard in throwing dirt her way. He ignored her completely, needing to hide his face. and the grin, that he couldn't force to go away. "Hey, cut that out! Are you mad?"

Leith stood slowly and turned, dirt caked his hands and face. "Young lady," he chided sternly, "I want what's mine, and no bit of dirt is gonna keep me from it. Now go ahead and move along, before we have problems."

The girl stared at him as if she didn't know what to make of him. Was he really a threat or just some crazy that was all talk and no bite? "I don't want any trouble mister," she said, putting her free hand up to calm him, pity seeping through the edges of her voice. "Just asking you to keep that away from my cart and my animals. They don't much need any more headed their way."

"Ain't mean to disturb. Be about yours, and I will find mine." Leith readjusted his position so the dirt he flung went further afield, instead of into the road. "I know I put it here," he yelled at the stubborn earth. He had to hope Lorn was finished. He couldn't risk looking back.

The girl snorted, "crazy," and she kicked her cart back into motion as it rattled down the hill.

"You're a mess," Lorn said coming up beside him, grinning.

Leith abandoned his hole-making, and sat down in one of the depressions, having worked up a sweat. "How your steal go?"

Lorn pulled out three golden apples from his pockets, tossing Leith one. "Not bad for an amateur, and two minutes advanced notice."

"Not bad." Leith scrubbed his hands off on his pants and wiped the apple on his shirt before taking a bite. The juice ran down his chin, but the taste of it in his mouth wasn't very sweet. Looks were deceiving, even with the apples.

"That was so much fun!" Lorn said, still antsy from the adrenaline rush. "Is it always like that? I was excited and nervous." He pointed at Leith and leaned back laughing. "I heard you screaming, and I wanted to run back, but I went in there and snatched them up real quick."

"Snatching apples from a girl off a cart may be fun, but won't keep you fed," Leith shook his head, and leaned back to explain. "The real stuff, work that pays, is dangerous. Thief watch out for rangers and city patrol as much as fellows. Lonely way to make a living. Don't recommend it, but I was happy to share a bit with you. Now gotta get back before your mom skins us."

CHAPTER ELEVEN: BARRICADE

"Daycia."

Daycia sat upright at the sound of her name, and instantly regretted it. The middle of her body burned with the movement. The cloying tang of medicinal herbs nearly choked her, along with the lavender candles burning at her hospital bedside. The oil infuser spit out little puffs of rosemary and avendale, an antibacterial herb blend, into the air, intended to speed up the healing process and keep patients calm. The combination left the room in a light haze.

"What it is?" she asked in a husky voice, before her eyes focused.

"The yetis have started to line up at the gates, barricading us in."

Daycia laid back down. The skin on her chest pulled with every inch. Her wound, courtesy of Cornelius, started at the top of her left breast down across toward her right hip. The poison on Cornelius's nails kept Daycia's enhanced body from sealing the wound shut.

Daycia passed a full day, drifting in and out of consciousness, since she was left in that field, snow covering her, burying her deeper with every moment that passed. Still the wound felt fresh, too sensitive for even the bandage around it. Daycia had never been that close to death before. During the war against the ultras, her mother had tried to split her skull open like an overripe melon. Unlike Cornelius, Emmaray showed restraint.

Daycia spent a month healing that time. She didn't have that luxury this time. It took all her concentration focus on what was being said, and not the pain pulsing through her head.

"How many of ours are still out?"

"The group of tundra dwellers aren't in yet, about ten of them. The Callor, Faindair, and Lathed herds are still out on the pastures with at least ten staff each. There are supposed to be two students incoming and there is no way for us to get word to the carriage before it runs into the barricade."

Daycia wiped sleep from her eyes and glared up at the ceiling, willing her body to gather enough strength to let her out of bed. "We should count ourselves lucky the yetis have scared most of the tourists away from the city already."

"Ma'am,"

"Paley why are you," Daycia stopped speaking abruptly, cutting her eyes to the side. When she saw that it was Ranger Yolanda standing at her door, instead of the expected Paley, she leapt from her bed grabbing Yolanda by the collar. "What happened to Paley! Is she okay?" Daycia couldn't remember seeing her apprentice after the battle. "And Zyair?"

Yolanda grabbed Daycia's arm in a defensive hold, then realization crossed her face, draining all color from her cheeks, and she let go in a hurry. "I'm so sorry." She begged Daycia's pardon, as she smoothed the sleeves of Daycia's robe. "Paley's fine," she reassured Daycia. "She and Commander Zyair are with the rest of the rangers watching the wall."

Daycia let the girl go. Of course Paley was hard at work. She didn't know how to slow down and rest. Zyair had the same tireless work ethic. The two of them would have taken on an army of yetis by themselves if they had to. With panic subsiding, the pain in Daycia's chest blossomed anew, making her eyes water and her knees unsteady.

"You should stay in bed," Yolanda said in a soft but firm tone. She gripped Daycia gently along her forearms, helping her to the bed.

"Thank you, Yolanda," Daycia said, trying to force a smile. "Who would have thought I was one fight away from reverting to an old lady?"

"You're far from that," Yolanda reassured her with a laugh. "Anyone else would have died from that attack. The mere fact that you are able to get up and walk a day after means you're stronger than most."

Daycia sighed deeply, gazing out the window in the direction where the yetis were gathered. "I hope that stays true. If the yetis are trying to cut us off, we need to get outside and see what they're up to.

100101

Daycia pulled at the leather vest cinched tight around her chest. Paley had insisted on the added layer of protection when Daycia made it clear she was going with the team, venturing outside the wall. The yeti barricade was on its fifth day, and Daycia couldn't stand around and wait for their next move. She had to make one of her own.

The evening northern sky was awash in the greens and oranges of a dying day, giving the perfect background to the rings overhead. They sparkled like a trillion diamonds making their lazy way through space. Looking up at them Daycia wished she had such a view from on high to look down and see the whole picture of the world.

"If you're listening up there, please do whatever you can to make sure Oleana and her boys are okay. We need them now more than ever," Daycia called to the Twelve.

"We're ready," Paley said. Her gloved hands were covered in dirt from prying open the hidden door in the wall.

Their group of six was going to breech the wall and get a look at the yeti blockade from the outside, to see if there was more purpose to it than just causing trouble. Even with the reemergence of the Heirs, Daycia didn't figure Solon to be an important enough target to warrant such a risk from Cornelius. His break from pattern worried her.

Daycia, Paley, Yolanda, Zyair, Brent and Terry were to observe and report back. It was a fact-finding mission. They were all armed, but a fight would cost lives and Daycia didn't need any more of that on her hands. They'd lost two good rangers in Cornelius' freak ice storm a few days ago. Zyair didn't have any more men to spare. He didn't even like the fact that Daycia insisted on coming herself.

Zyair, as the ranger in charge, took the lead. "Keep to the shadows, keep close to the wall, and keep quiet," he ordered. "You know your assignments?" He looked every one of them directly in the eye, making sure everyone was on their game, his eyes lingering on Daycia at the end. Daycia and the others nodded. "Don't engage unless absolutely necessary. Move," he barked.

One of the other groups of two slipped out first, then it was Paley and Daycia's turn. Paley went first, then Daycia followed close enough behind to reach out and touch her apprentice. There was a short tunnel carved under the wall, into the bedrock Solon was built on. There was a slight decline into darkness. Daycia got the feeling of being swallowed up by some unseen stone beast.

They didn't take torches for fear of attracting attention. Daycia trusted Paley to lead the way to safety. The younger had studied the blueprints of the tunnel extensively before they headed out, and she always did have a good sense of direction. The tunnel leveled out. They walked five steps on level ground before making the climb back up.

Daycia remembered when she helped carve out the tunnel four centuries ago. She was young and enthusiastic then, fresh off a victory in war, and ready for whatever else life had to throw at her.

How different that time was from now. Now she was holding on to the last shred of hope she had buried deep inside herself, begging for change to come quick, before the world collapsed around her.

Back during the war Daycia took up the cause of humanity and the Twelve promising to rid the world of wickedness. Then she'd settled into Solon and figured it was enough to just keep her eye on Cornelius and leave the rest of the world to others. With Oleana on the run and Cornelius at large, Daycia felt too old and stagnant to be of much good to anyone.

The darkest part of Daycia understood why Cornelius fought so hard for control. The ultras were built to rule. Daycia was only part ultra, and it drove her to the brink of madness to sit idle for too long. Her mother's blood with its fierce genetic instincts gave her the notion that her ideas were above that of humans. It was a haughtiness that Daycia fought every day.

Cornelius thought himself above even his creators. His madness was complete. He didn't know how to do anything else but force others to his will. Daycia could feel sorry for him. He was a victim of the Twelve's flawed design, but that wouldn't keep her from fighting him to the death.

They walked up into the light coming out of an open door, dust sprinkling down on Daycia's head. They came out inside a manmade mound, which was covered by a row of shrubs, perfectly placed to hide their exit.

Paley held her fist up and Daycia waited. The younger woman poked her head around the shrubs. Daycia strained to hear if anybody was nearby. All she heard were the coos of the baymar as they lulled themselves to sleep.

Paley waved her forward, and Daycia stepped out into the night, stretching her back for the first time since moving into the tunnel. She felt an errant ligament pop back into its proper place, and relief washed through her. The centuries were really taking their toll on her body. Paley moved toward the mountain, and Daycia dutifully followed.

They were given the task of mapping out the route the yetis were taking to run supplies to their planted troops. If they could cut them off, it would force the yetis back up the mountain. Daycia promised she would just observe. If she felt up to fighting she would have resisted Zyair's order, but the wound on her chest still burned and her heart fluttered irregularly. Daycia didn't feel like the spry thing she did before confronting Cornelius. She would avoid fighting to save herself the agony of defeat.

She and Paley found a secluded spot by the road to hunker down. There was a bite in the wind coming down from the mountain. It was going to be a cold night. Daycia pulled her woolen jacket tighter over her shoulders. As a daughter of the Fire Ultra, Daycia naturally didn't like cold. The northern city wouldn't have been her first choice of residence, but she adjusted over the years. Still there were some days that the cold cut her to the bone, and Daycia was forced to use her abilities to combat it. She was grateful for the leather vest and the long-sleeved shirt covering everything but her face. Using any ultra power with the yetis around was asking to call them. She would just have to suffer.

"Are you sure they would be stupid enough to use the road?" Paley asked in a barely a whisper.

"I've been around since the yetis were first created. They are basic creatures who put in as little effort as the task demands. The road is that shortcut. If they aren't using it directly, they're following it nearby," Daycia replied. She rubbed her gloved hands together, regretting her need to see things for herself.

Their wait wasn't long before a group of three yetis strolled by heading up the mountain. Daycia crouched down low, holding her breath as they passed. She remembered clearly the strength in those fur-covered arms and the sharpness of those teeth, she didn't need another confrontation.

Before the yetis could march out of sight, Paley and Daycia moved to follow them. The road only went so far before the tundra took over, and people that ventured beyond it made their own path, following instinct and family routes tested over generations. They moved from stiff frost covered grass to a land of ice and snow.

Daycia remembered back to the days when the snow-covered land had been a deciduous forest for as far as the eye could see, eventually giving way to the rocky foothills leading up to the mountain range. The tundra around Mt. Elmire was not a natural phenomenon. It was the result of Cornelius showing off his power and carving out a territory of his own.

Daycia grew up at the foot of an active volcano. Her mother, Emmaray made it her home so she could prove to the locals that she truly was a goddess of fire, unafraid of the lava flows. The guardian of the Crystal Tower barely stepped a hundred feet away from the tower where all intelligent life on Euphoria started. The ultras were creatures of habit, and found comfort in extreme mono climates. And as humans have a tendency to do, they managed to find ways to take advantage of even the tundra. Daycia couldn't help but admire them for that.

The yetis traversed the frozen earth with a speed that Daycia found difficult to keep up with. Several times Paley grabbed her to keep from falling. The two women supported each other across the ice, passing a fishing hole abandoned in haste. The bobbing fishing pole was still sticking out, and gear scattered around the sight.

The night fell over them like a blanket. The large moon, and a sky filled with stars, lit their way. Maintaining a safe distance and keeping an eye on the yetis proved impossible. They followed the distinctive tracks instead.

The three sets of footprints lead into an ice cave. Daycia hesitated at the entrance. If they stepped in there, they could be walking into a nest of the beasts. Turn back, and all their walking would have only yielded a possible route for supplies.

"We can turn back, and come again with a platoon of rangers to explore it in the daylight," Paley offered.

"Getting a platoon up here would be next to impossible without being detected, and a huge risk. We can't afford it unless we're sure this is where their supplies are coming from."

Daycia took her hat off and scratched her head. They had to be sure. There was no other choice. They could wait until some yeti came back out, hopefully loaded with supplies, or they could go in and explore for themselves. Daycia didn't think a night in the cold would do her any good. The possibility of fighting a host of yetis felt like the better option.

"Into the breech," Daycia said firmly. She adjusted the grips on her fighting batons, three-foot-long staffs with hard metal caps at both ends, and moved forward with purpose.

The walls were smooth ice shooting a thousand different distorted versions of Daycia back at herself. The ground was crushed stone, packed so tightly it didn't make noise as they walked over it. The cold was still there, but the biting wind was gone, replaced with the rushing noise of a nearby stream. The smell of yetis was cloying. It felt like Daycia had a yeti foot resting on her tongue.

Three feet into the cave, and the light died. The yetis had the unique ability to adapt dark places, and the bright white light reflected off the snow. Daycia wasn't built for such things, and neither was Paley. Daycia reached into her backpack for the firestone she stashed there. It was a special crystal, made the same way as the Crystal Tower in Evermore. It had been shaped into a rose and fit perfectly in Daycia's palm, a gift from a relative. With the right application of heat, it emitted a low frequency light that Daycia hoped would be mistaken for some errant sunbeam bouncing off the ice walls.

The stone cast enough light for Daycia to see about five feet in front of her, but it occupied one of her hands. She would have to drop it if they needed to fight. Daycia hated the thought of losing it to the cave. It was a one-of-a-kind treasure, from a life among the ultras who she had left so long ago. While she didn't regret choosing the side of humanity, she did mourn the loss of feeling truly understood by people with the same long lives.

Onward they moved, with caution born from a healthy appreciation of the dangers around them. They moved from one cave into another, then they heard noises ahead. Daycia slowed. Paley led her close to the wall, inching up on the opening ahead of them. There was light coming through, so Daycia put her stone away, happy to have it tucked safely out of sight.

The opening led to a cave large enough to fit the Thousand Years Library inside with room to spare. Just craning her head around, Daycia saw that it had multiple open levels. Icy catwalks crisscrossed the space with rails on both sides, sitting waist high, riveted by the marks of thousands of claws that had dug into them.

With a quick glance, Daycia spotted fifty yetis easily, and saw tunnels leading deeper into the mountain. The infrastructure Cornelius managed to build under their noses was astounding. The yetis were wheeling in carts from other tunnels, dumping them into piles ready for others to sort and stack in racks along the walls.

There were weapons. Crude swords and spears, but clearly weapons. Never had Daycia seen the yetis use anything but their claws and teeth to do damage, but from the operation she saw in front of her, they could supply several armies.

"What're they going to do with all that?" Paley whispered, her face so close to Daycia's that her tight black curls tickled Daycia's cheek.

"Slaughter everything in their wake, I'm guessing," Daycia said, her soft voice trembling. "Our only hope is that these aren't for them. Maybe some bargaining chip for future allies? If the yetis know how to fight with weapons, they're more organized and sophisticated that I would have thought possible."

"We can't just leave them like this," Paley shot back.

"I have no intention of letting all these instruments of destruction just walk past my door," Daycia sniffed indignantly. "I have an idea. It's dangerous, and it goes against our explicit orders, but I'm up for it if you are."

Paley nodded. Daycia smiled. She always did have a soft spot for young women who liked breaking the rules. Daycia seemed to have built her life around the type. She couldn't help being one herself. She would have to find some way to make it up to Zyair, smooth things over with the man she trusted to protect her city, the man she cared so much about. After things were explained, he was sure to understand why they had to do it. That was if they made it back to Zyair.

"I intend to bring this cave down on top of them. That means it'll be coming down on our heads as well. We'll have a limited window to get out. But as soon as I start heating the place up the yetis are sure to be alerted. You make sure you get out of here. Get back to Zyair and tell him what you saw here. No matter what else happens, you get out," Daycia spoke slowly, stressing the importance of her orders.

Paley kept her face blank, which was a credit to the ranger training she had in her transition to adulthood. Daycia realized everyday how lucky she was that Paley choose the college path, instead of staying with the rangers.

"I uhm," Paley's voice trembled and her blue eyes locked onto Daycia's face, as if she were trying to memorize every nook and cranny. "I understand, but I'd much prefer if we both made it out."

Daycia smiled. "Me too, my dear, me too." Daycia cleared her throat, afraid her emotions might get the better of her.

"Zyair will kill me if I come back without you," Paley forced a smile but her blue eyes held a heaviness that aged her.

"You can blame all of this on me," Daycia said trying to smile back but her face refused to tell that lie. "We need to get to the outer chamber, and pull these walls down on their heads." Daycia pulled out her firestone. It had a pink tint to the delicately patterned crystal. The petals folded in on themselves in a life-like rendition of the perfect rose. Daycia would mourn the loss of her little keepsake, but its sacrifice would save countless Solonians, and that mattered more to her than anything her family ever gave her. "You'll be the most beautiful bomb ever made," Daycia whispered to the stone. I just hope you'll be enough."

Paley led the way back into the first tunnel. They still had to keep an eye out for traffic. Daycia needed a few minutes to set up her bomb. She had to add energy slowly to the crystal. She wasn't exactly sure how much it could take before it exploded. She didn't want it going off in her hands.

The fire stone was only the size of her palm but it was heavy, because the crystalline matrix was so dense. Daycia would force her core body heat, which hovered around two hundred degrees, into the crystal until its particles vibrated so hard and fast it would explode. She intended to expend all of her body's heat if need be.

Paley searched for the perfect spot to plant their bomb. The apex of the cave was ten feet above their heads. It would have been the perfect location, but there was no easy way to reach it.

"I can carve some footholds, but not quietly," Paley offered, adjusting her grip on her sword.

"Can you do it quickly?"

Paley placed her hand against the wall. She scratched at it, and nodded her head. "Yeah, the ice layer is light enough."

"Then do it," Daycia said, her tone cutting through Paley like a knife. "I'll worry about the yetis." Daycia tucked the firestone into her shirt, resting it on her chest, letting her body do its work.

That left her hands free to start trouble of their own. She stripped off her wool coat. She would miss it on the trek back down the tundra, but it was just another necessary sacrifice. She pulled it into ribbons and laid them across the floor, creating a distinctive line of division. She gave Paley the go ahead, and heard the loud echo of ice breaking away fill the hall.

A yeti howl pierced the air, and then the pounding of feet shook the walls. Daycia had to wait. Her little fire strips wouldn't last long and she needed the shock to scare them as much as the actual fire.

"Are you crazy?" Paley asked, her usually pale face now whiter than a sheet.

"Just climb," Daycia ordered breathlessly. Despite the cold air whipping around them, sweat poured off Daycia in rivulets. Her skin felt inflamed.

Daycia braced herself. If the fire didn't work she didn't have much time to grab her batons, and she wouldn't be able to fend them all off anyway. She would just have to set off the bomb and hope it caused enough of a collapse to at least slow them down. Daycia spared her apprentice a quick look. Paley scaled the wall like she was built for the icy terrain. The girl was full of surprises.

Five yetis came into view. Then sixteen. Daycia held off. They howled, and hissed, and the venom in their eyes would have caused a lesser person to flee, but Daycia held still. They charged, and Daycia counted the steps. One. Two. Three. Four. The first yeti was a step from crossing the line when Daycia set them ablaze. The flames shot up waist-high, catching the beast's fur on fire. He stumbled back with a growl, and ignited two others behind him.

"Ready!" Paley yelled.

Daycia took the glowing firestone from her shirt and flung it at the waiting Paley. The younger girl almost dropped it. Steam emanated from her gloves as she held onto the edge. She stuck it into the crudely carved hole at the height of the ceiling. Paley started the climb down, but there wasn't enough time.

"Jump! I got you," Daycia urged, making sure she was squarely under her.

Paley looked at the climb, then at Daycia's waiting arms. She shut her eyes tight and let go. Daycia braced herself. She caught Paley, and before she could even straighten up the younger woman was out of her arms and running. Daycia scrambled to follow.

Daycia spotted daylight before the explosion behind them rocked the ground beneath her feet. Without thinking, Daycia grabbed Paley, folding the younger woman under her body as snow and ice came crashing over them. Daycia curled her arms around Paley's head, protecting her as best she could, and praying they would see daylight again.

100101

Daycia sat bolt upright, forcing her eyes to focus in the dim light. She didn't remember how she got on her back, or as a matter of fact, how she got free of the rubble that fell down on her head. She did remember the pain in her back and chest, the pressure on her lungs, and the screams of her apprentice.

"Paley!" Daycia called in a panic.

"It's okay, she's in the other room resting," replied a low, familiar voice. "This is becoming a pattern with you."

Daycia turned and found herself looking up at a friendly face. Zyair's dark brown eyes cracked her open like a rusted can. How she found herself in a hospital room, bandaged and bruised for the second time in four days, she didn't know, but she had to count herself lucky for surviving again.

"Zyair, I'm sorry. If you laid eyes on what we saw, you would have done the same. We had no choice. I didn't mean to countermand your order."

Zyair smiled. "That's a lot of words really fast. Those rocks may have hit your head harder than I thought. I would be mad about you disobeying me, but that explosion caused the yetis to scatter, which has freed the city. I don't know why I thought giving you orders was a good idea anyway. No matter what ranger protocol says, you're the best tactician I know."

"Thanks." Daycia rubbed her face. "How'd we get back here anyway?"

"Well that explosion, and the subsequent avalanche, wasn't exactly subtle. The yetis scattered, and we sent teams out right away to find you. You were near the top so it didn't take much digging. You're lucky."

"And Paley?"

"She doesn't heal as fast as you do, but the doctor said she should be okay. A broken rib and a few minor cuts. A week of rest should set her straight."

"We don't have time for that. We knocked down one cave, in what has to be a whole network. They're arming up for a war and the Heirs know nothing about it." Daycia threw back her covers and tried to get to her feet, only to find herself quite abruptly cradled in Zyair's arms. He was so warm and strong, Daycia didn't mind the position at all.

"You won't do anyone any good if you croak now," he said putting her back on the bed. "So, for once in my life, can you please just do what I say and rest? There are other people in this city, in this realm, that know how to defend it." Zyair brushed a loose strand of her hair behind her ear. "Let them do their part while you recover. Then you can charge to the front like always."

CHAPTER TWELVE: TYCHO

When Oleana felt the pull toward Central City she couldn't tell for sure if it was all for the search for her final wayward king, or was she still searching for that true homecoming. She left her farm home reluctantly pulled into the hunt by Lorn's insistence. Now she was returning to a place she'd left willing more than thirty years ago. Part of her hoped coming back meant it could be the place that she could settled down in.

Oleana stuffed her coat, snow boots, and gloves into a cubbyhole on the train hoping someone in need would find them and give them a deserving home. She was relieved to be rid of them, like she'd shed fifty pounds. She would make do with her gray ankle boots and her favorite quarter-sleeve blue sweater to stave off the Midwest chill.

Lorn clung to his winter clothes, having developed an attachment. She tried to lecture him on carrying dead weight, but it was no use. The boy had a habit of hoarding items, a side effect of his early years on the streets.

Spring time in Central City usually meant an explosion of activity. Shops that spent the winter boarded up started the process of opening, and stocking up, for the rush of customers that came with warmer weather. Trade posts prepared for the first cartloads of fish coming from the coastal cities of Caldonia and Sartis.

Oleana grew up running errands for the fishers every year, making enough money to feed herself during the hard winter months. It was hard work that kept her skin taught and tan, and kept her out of trouble. There were some familiar faces among the rows of shops - though they were much older than she remembered, amid plenty of new ones. They wouldn't recognize her. She'd changed so much from one lifetime to the next.

The city had changed too. Instead of being greeted by warm smiles, they met suspicious looks. The number of rangers patrolling the streets outnumbered the salesmen preparing for the next hustle. There were homeless men and women huddled in whatever secluded sunny spot they could find.

Oleana felt as if the city was coated in a layer of filth and grime that she couldn't brush off. There was a distinctive smell of decay in the air. Even the mighty Central City was suffering under the systemic turmoil plaguing the five realms.

Oleana found herself walking closer to Lorn as they made their way down the main road. At the heart of the city jutted out massive buildings of glass and metal, gleaming beacons of industry and ingenuity, but the street before them was worn and pockmarked. There were others on the streets coming and going from the train station, all of them had heads down, eyes focused on their destinations.

A man, in his forties, long beard, with a bag strapped to his back, bumped against Lorn. He grabbed the man's arm. Oleana was startled that her son would act so harshly to an accident, but she freed one of her sais to defend him because it was her job.

"Give it back," Lorn ordered the man in a harsh voice Oleana rarely heard from him.

"Sorry, young sir. It was my fault. I mean no harm," the man stuttered. He made no move to pull free, just stared down at his feet.

"Give it back," Lorn insisted.

"I don't know..." the man started.

Leith came up behind him, digging in the man's pocket and retrieving the small leather pouch with Lorn's initials on it, the one where he kept his snacks. Leith handed it over to Lorn, who let the man go. The bearded man ran off down the street without another word. Oleana watched in amazement as he fled. She didn't know how to feel - angry he disturbed her son, sad he had to resort to such tactics, amused at his boldness.

"Good catch, boy," Leith said. "Fast learner."

"Are you okay?" Oleana asked, scanning her son for any signs of trauma.

He smiled back at her. "That was unexpected. I felt his fingers graze my back, and I knew. He was so fast, though, I almost missed it. I can't believe he had the nerve with all of us together and clearly armed," Lorn said, jingling the sword at his hip."

"Yeah well, things have certainly changed around here," Oleana said, looking around. "Wait what was that about being a fast learner? What are you teaching my son?" Oleana asked, pointing her sai under Leith's chin.

Leith opened his mouth to say something. Nothing but a grunt came out. He threw his hands up in surrender.

"Mom, it's harmless. He just showed me a couple pickpocketing techniques, and how to spot one. As you can see, the skills came in handy. Mom, please don't be like that."

"When was this?"

"Spent days on train after another," Leith said.

"Yes, all three of us, cramped in that tiny space. How did I miss these extra-curricular activities?"

Lorn's face turned serious. "Maybe because you spent the whole time drunk, hungover, then drunk again."

Oleana's cheeks burned with embarrassment. "Lorn I...," she wanted to deny it, but knew her behavior had been obvious. "I'm sorry. I'll do better," she said repeating a familiar promise to her son.

The boy nodded, but said nothing further.

Oleana narrowed her eyes at Leith, but lowered her weapon. "I'll forgive it this time, but no more unauthorized training," she warned.

Oleana restarted her walk down the street. This time she added brazen pickpockets to her list of things to watch out for.

The ranger organization knew no boundaries. There were stations in four of the five realms, excluding the ultra-controlled Gaeth. The rangers stood as the peacekeepers of the realms, settling tribal skirmishes, policing borders, and generally stepping in where the local authorities couldn't handle matters.

Central City, was at the heart of the realm of Caledon, the birthplace of the rangers, and home to the main training headquarters. A new set of recruits filed off the train just ahead of them, led by an officer Oleana didn't recognize. She could only hope the man she was looking for was still there. Thirty-five years was a long career in the rangers. Any number of things could have happened to him in the meantime.

Letting muscle memory carry her to where she needed to be, Oleana took the turns needed to lead her boys to the front door of the Ranger's headquarters. The five-story brick and glass building towered over the rest of the industrial buildings around it. Banks, manufacturing firms, distribution, and logistics firms made up the rest of the business sector, but the Ranger's headquarters was clearly the crown jewel. Seeing the seven-foot-tall gray metal door, with the ranger crest embossed in the middle of it, brought Oleana near tears. She wasn't ashamed of the smile that spread across her face.

Getting in the front door was no problem. They blended in with the crowd of eager-eyed potentials. Getting to the person she wanted would prove more challenging.

Last time she saw Tycho, he was still in his first year of field work, and already talking of plans to become an instructor, then the director of operations. Eying the plaque on the wall behind the reception desk, he was running the place now.

"We need to speak with Director Dawnwalker," Oleana told the Pitbull at the desk. He was a middle-aged man with a burn running down the right side of his face, ruining his right eye. The injury likely took him out of the field, but he used as much passion and conviction to run the desk, as he would have to run a mission.

"You have no appointment. No pass. You come off the street expecting an audience with the director?" he scoffed at them. "I don't know how things are done where you're from, but things don't work that way here," he replied none too politely.

Lorn rolled his eyes, "Didn't we play this game back at the library?" he asked sarcastically, crossing his arms over his chest. "I wish Daycia had given some kind of all-access pass, so we could avoid this kind of thing."

Oleana waved away her son's petulant remark. The long, tense journey hadn't done good things to her patience either, but now was not the time to lose it. "Well," she began patiently, "if you explain to the director that his old friend Mira is back to collect a debt, then I'm sure he would be more than happy to see us."

The man's eyes narrowed, but Oleana could tell he recognized the name.

"Remind him he owes me fifty trade coins," Oleana said with a raised eyebrow, planting her feet. She wasn't leaving without talking to Tycho. "He's lucky I don't charge him interest," she added for good measure, narrowing her eyes as she stared the desk jockey down.

The sergeant, Oleana saw the stripes on his collar, looked like he wanted to forcibly remove her. Maybe he would suggest the director was too busy for old friends. Oleana shut him down.

"We will wait right over here for him. He'll be so excited to see me after so long. I can't wait." Oleana enthused. She pushed Lorn and Leith to a set of chairs directly in front of, and facing, the main desk.

"Yes ma'am, I'll let him know," he choked out. He whispered something to his colleague, then disappeared up the stairs.

"You know the Director of the Rangers..." Lorn said in awe, staring at Oleana.

"When I knew him, he wasn't the director.

"You know all the best people. First the Director of the Thousand Years Library, and the firstborn of the Fire Ultra Emmaray, Daycia." Lorn looked at his mother, as if for the first time. "Now the Director of the Rangers! Goodness, who's next? You were always telling me how dangerous this trip would be, and coming against Tannin certainly qualified, but you didn't tell me about all the perks," he grinned with satisfaction.

Oleana shot him a stern look. Lorn forced himself to sit down with an exaggerated sigh, and looked straight ahead. Leith fidgeted on the other side of her, clutching his bag to his chest.

"Not a good stop for a thief," she whispered to him. She couldn't help the amusement in her voice.

Leith's eyes darted back and forth between the remaining rangers, busy doing their jobs. "Don't tell 'em my former status," he pleaded a bit nervously.

"Former?" she laughed, raising her eyebrows at him. "Since when? Weren't you checking out the luggage at the train station?"

"Force of habit," he muttered.

"Shame on you Leith," Lorn said, craning around Oleana to look his fellow in the eye. "That's not conduct befitting…"

"Yes, I know," Leith barked abruptly, cutting Lorn off. "Was looking, not touching."

"Mira?" a deep voice yelled, drawing everyone's attention.

A big man, breaking six feet, broad as a mountain, and looking like a skilled artisan sculpted him from marble, came barreling down the steps like a mad fool. His gray eyes were stretched as wide as his face would allow. Oleana jumped up, overcome by her excitement.

"Tycho!" she yelled back, trying, and failing to match his volume.

He scooped her up with his tree trunk arms, and lifted her into the air. The gray-tinged scruff on his face tickled her face as she jostled against him, and he twirled around in a tight circle. He kissed her forehead, and both cheeks, before returning her to the ground.

He stepped back, holding her at arm's length, taking in the full sight of her. "Your hair is so black," he said, running his hands over it, "I love the colored threads you added to it. Wow your eyes are so brown."

Oleana smoothed her locks down in a sharp burst of self-consciousness. "Well you collected a surprising amount of gray in my absence. You got old without me. I worried you might break a hip running down those stairs."

"That would have been funny, except three months ago, my oldest announced she was pregnant. I'm thrilled, of course, but man did it make me feel old."

"Hey, I didn't come for all that. I came back to get my money, and to make sure you didn't waste all that training I gave to a curly haired brat, that had delusions of grandeur."

"Ha, it really is you!" he exclaimed. "When Eker said that name I almost jumped out of my skin, but part of me wondered if it was some trick. But no one but you would know about that, or even talk to me that way. It's so good to see you again," he mused. "I've missed you so." For a second Tycho's eyes glazed over. Oleana could image the images her re-emergence conjured up in him. It was enough to break Oleana's heart, thinking about all the years that now separated them.

"Me too, my friend, me too," she agreed. "If it'd been up to me, it would not have been so long," Oleana said knowingly.

Tycho nodded his head soberly. "We heard about the troubles in Solon. Did you have something to do with that?"

"Forced to flee with Leith and Lorn," Oleana said pointing out each in turn. "Master of Animals, and Master of Skies, respectively."

"Tycho Dawnwalker, formerly of Nadir's Nightstalkers, and current Director of the Rangers, it's an honor to meet you both," Tycho said giving a slight bow to Lorn and Leith.

Leith nodded, but the blush in his cheeks told his embarrassment. Lorn stood with his eyes wide, and his mouth open.

Oleana shook her head, and tried to explain their reactions. "They aren't used to such treatment." Switching subjects, she said, "since you brought him up, how is our mutual friend doing?"

"Shouldn't you know," Tycho answered. "News of him spreads throughout all the realms."

"She avoids the news," Lorn volunteered. "Says there are too many bad mentions to keep track of."

"Well," Tycho began, "Nadir took over when his father died twelve years ago. He managed to carve out a peaceful reign for quite a while there, but Failsea has really been pressing the issue this last year. Drought and a dwindling fish population hasn't helped things." Tycho paused for a moment, then continued. "On a personal note, after you left, Lillian moved in and they have been married some- wow can't believe it's been that long- thirty-something years now," he marveled.

Oleana swallowed hard. That was why she avoided catching up. It almost always ended up in pain. "I'm happy for him. Truly. Happy for them." Her tone took on an almost too-bright affectation. "They must have a big family by now, just as his mother wished for him."

"One son, Lysander," her friend agreed, "fine young man. Leader of his squad. Tied my record for the youngest to reach that rank." Tycho put his hands up defensively as he continued. "Trust me when I say, it was not due to any favoritism he was shown. I made sure of that."

"I'm glad," Oleana replied, even though she was nothing of the sort. "I will need to speak to Nadir, to request his help, formally."

Tycho's gaze dropped. His shoulders slumped enough for Oleana to know that something was wrong. "I'm sure you've been through a lot recently." He clapped his hands together, and gestured to the three of them, seemingly suddenly intent on changing the subject. "You should come back to my house, get some rest, maybe something to eat. I must acquaint the two kings with the fine treatment they should get used to receiving."

"Tycho we have no time for..."

"Nadir has been so busy tending to certain matters of the realm," he broke in. "He won't be available until later. I insist you come home with me. Relax for a moment, and refresh yourselves," he encouraged them. "You always reminded me to have balance, now I'm returning the favor.

"What is it you're not..."

"Please," Tycho said. He begged with his wide-eyed stare for her to drop it. "Just come with me, and we can discuss the rest later."

Oleana didn't want to push her friend, and she really was tired. Trying to get in to see Nadir without Tycho's help would have been impossible, and another headache was something she'd rather avoid. "Okay," she sighed giving in, "lead the way, old friend."

"Don't call me that. It's not polite." He winked, then turned to Leith and Lorn. "Can you believe I used to be the young buck of our group? Now she comes back, half my age, looking all spry and youthful, calling me old." He shook his fist in good-natured teasing. "I won't stand for it." When neither one of them answered, Tycho shrugged. "All right, fine. I'm old. And you," he looked at Oleana, "don't think I forgot about those fifty coins. When you see what Kaithlen has brewed up at my house, I'm sure you'll call us even."

"We'll see," Oleana replied, even though she was only half listening. She wanted to know what was so wrong with Nadir that Tycho didn't want her to see him. Did he harbor some resentment toward her for leaving? Or was it Lilian? Did she fear that Oleana's return would disrupt her family? The questions would drive Oleana crazy until she got her answers.

Tycho's house was less of a house, and more a fortress with a nice yard. It felt rather fitting for the leader of a security force. The place was a huge stone structure, big enough to fit the five-room farmhouse Oleana and Lorn left, twice. The walk up to the door was lined with tiny forest green shrubs, some of them already showing purple buds along the path.

The porch was supported by four, red-brick columns. It was wide enough to comfortably fit four chairs around a rectangular, glass and metal table. A mat at the front door read, "Welcome" in golden thread. The mixture of sturdy construction, and simple luxury, was unique to Central City.

Inside opened up to a bright room painted in a lovely sea-foam green, with white wood trim. Two-person-wide steps with an ornate railing, similar to the one back at the library, sat in the middle, dividing the two halves into a sitting room and a dining area.

Tycho lead them around the stairs into an eat-in kitchen fit to hold fifteen people comfortably. The smell of roasting vegetables and fresh-baked sourdough bread filled the air, making Oleana's mouth water.

Kait was at the stone-topped island chopping up carrots and dumping them into a black kettle rattling over the fire. A younger woman, looking very much like Kait, and clearly pregnant, sat nearby with her feet propped up, munching on carrots she snatched from the cutting board.

Tycho cleared his throat. Kait looked up.

"Ah Ty, wasn't expecting you home. And you brought guests." Kait recovered quickly. Putting down the knife and wiping her hands on her light blue apron, she smiled, her whole facing lighting with the gesture. "Welcome," she greeted them warmly.

"Wow Kait, still more beautiful than me," Oleana said, admiring her hostess. A chill spread through her cheeks seeing her old friend, someone who was always ready for battle, as tough as the bedrock of the city she called home.

"And a better shot," Kait returned automatically, finishing the customary teasing they used to give each other. "Mira, it can't be." The older woman rushed to Oleana's side, tears welling up at the corner of her eyes. "I feared I wouldn't live long enough to see you return. It's so good to see you."

"Glad someone is," Oleana said, still bothered by Tycho's standoffish behavior.

Kait exchanged a knowing look with her husband. Apparently, everyone knew the secret, but wasn't up to sharing it. "Ignore my husband, he's a big buffoon."

"You're the one who married him. Why would you go and do a thing like that?"

Kait ushered Oleana to the nearest chair. "I believe your last words to me, before riding off to be the hero, were to marry that fool before he forgets he's not worthy of you."

"Well your first mistake was listening to me," Oleana said. She couldn't stop smiling. Her cheeks stretched to the limit, and her face and chest felt warm.

Lorn studied his mother carefully as interacted with Kait. Here was another who knew a previous version of Oleana. Back in Solon, with Daycia, his mother, in some ways, reverted to the young apprentice, Alwen. While Lorn knew her as a self-assured person, in Solon she kept seeking the advice of her mentor.

In Central City, he was encountering yet another change. His mother was friendly and happy in a way he rarely saw from her. Ever since they started the search, Oleana had shut that part of her off, but Mira had friends here. She was reuniting with family and a life surround by people she loved. It was nice to see that part of her shine through. Lorn feared it would disappear all to quickly if he mentioned it.

"What's with all the food," Lorn cut in, looking at the buffet spread before him. "Seems a lot for just you two ladies to have for lunch."

"We usually have the whole extended family over for dinner at the beginning of every month. A tradition you are more than welcome to join us in young..." her voice trailed off, waiting to be introduced.

"I'm forgetting my manners again," Oleana said apologetically. "This is Lorn and Leith."

"Masters of Skies and Animals," Tycho added.

The younger girl swallowed hard. "They're real," she marveled, her eyes jutting back and forth between her parents, and Leith and Lorn. She brushed herself off and swallowed down whatever food scraps she was eating. She started to stand, but Lorn was quick to stop her.

"There's no need for that," he said.

"It's such an honor to meet you all," she insisted. "I don't believe this is really happening," she gaped. "The stories are true! I've heard many tales about the men who would be Kings of Euphoria. The ones forged by the Twelve to save humanity, but part of me thought the legend must have been exaggerated, but here you are, in our house." Her wide eyes cut to her father. "Pop, I swear the way you and mom talked, and Lady Lillian, like it was all a big fairytale. Lysander. By the Twelve, Lysander is going to lose his mind when he finds out they're real."

"This is our oldest, Miriam," Kait explained.

"Miriam, really," Oleana said turning to Tycho, honored to have his daughter named after her former incarnation.

"Don't get a big head about it," Tycho replied, shrugging but with a wink in her direction.

"Two of the kings already," Kaithlen stared at her husband. "You have been busy. Does that mean you're here for the third?"

"The Twelve pointed me in this general direction."

"Was Nadir wrong?" Kait said. She was looking through Oleana, worry crinkling her once smooth forehead.

"I don't know. It's too soon to jump to that conclusion," Tycho answered. He avoided Oleana's eyes.

"Wrong about what?" Oleana asked. "Why do I suddenly feel like the omen of death?"

"Are you sure the third is here?" Tycho asked.

"Well before we got into town I figured he could be in Central City, or any of the surrounding towns, but now that we're here I can tell he's close. Must be in town. The others are feeling him too."

"Who says?" Leith asked.

"You're scratching at your arm again," Oleana said, pointing at his offending limb.

Leith looked down to find his sleeve rumpled, where he'd been fidgeting with his mark. Lorn was steadily rubbing his against the rough material of his pants.

"You both need to recognize what it feels like to be close to one another. It might save your life one of these days. That tingling feeling at the back of your neck, that's your brother. If I wasn't here, the two of you would be able to track him together. Always remember, you are stronger together."

"Nadir's not going to be happy about this," Tycho said to himself.

"I don't know what it is about Nadir you don't want to share, but you need to take me to him right now," Oleana ordered.

"I'll send a messenger to his residence, let him know you're here, and we can make arrangements to have a sit-down."

"Tycho," Oleana and Kait said exasperated, and in unison.

Tycho recoiled. His caramel-brown cheeks picked up a hint of red. "Fine," he acquiesced. "I'll take you to Nadir."

CHAPTER THIRTEEN: THE RESIDENCE

The Residence was a castle in everything but name. After the long walk into town, the detour to Tycho's house, then the walk to the enormous edifice, Oleana hated every inch of the ten-minute walk from the front gate to the front door. Like Tycho's house, it sacrificed some of the finer details for more functionality. It was the work of a people whose pride was linked to the security of their borders.

Tycho left Oleana and the others in the foyer as he went to track down Nadir. Oleana was surprised at how much had changed, yet so much stayed the same. The first time she entered, she was a scared fourteen-year-old who was summoned by Saddiq Starson, leader of Caledon. Now she was back to demand of his son the answers she needed, and request asylum for the ones she loved.

She fussed with her dreadlocks, making sure they were pulled back into a neat ponytail. She didn't have fancy clothes or the makeup women of the court wore but at least she could make sure her hair looked nice. She glanced at her reflection in a polished metal vase. Her skin was puffy under her eyes. Her face was thinner than she remembered and stress was etched into every premature crease around her eyes, but the purple and yellow threads woven into her hair made her nut-brown eyes sparkle.

Nadir walked in looking much like his father the last time Oleana had seen him. Dark brown hair the color of chocolate. Brown skin, sharp gray eyes, full lips always pressed into a tight line holding back his barely veiled irritation with the rest of the world. The years had turned the optimistic Nadir into a hard old man. Oleana wanted to cry for her lost friend, but there was no time for her grief.

"You look good," Oleana stammered, at a loss for anything else.

"Tycho says you believe the third is here in the city. He seems to believe I can help you find him. I believe him to be mistaken," Nadir said, not really looking at Oleana. His gaze skirted over Lorn and Leith in turn, but he refused to look at Oleana. She didn't know whether to be hurt, or furious. She could handle rejection from just about anyone else, but not him. "He's insistent, and it is my responsibility to be sure one way or the other, so I'll indulge him."

Already tired of fighting the tension between them, Oleana nodded. "How do we do that exactly?"

"You three will follow me into the library, and we'll wait." Nadir turned and started walking before Oleana could respond.

She turned to Lorn, then Leith, but neither one of them seemed to have any more insight than she did. Oleana took a deep breath to keep from screaming. She let out a long sigh. "Follow him," she said, not knowing what else to do.

Down the main hallway, on the opposite side of the kitchen and living room combination, directly across from Saddiq's turned Nadir's office, lay the library. It was a good-sized room, thirty by thirty, with ten-foot-high ceilings, yet it felt smaller to Oleana than she remembered. Built-in bookshelves lined three of the four walls, with a large painting of a map of Caledon taking up the fourth.

At the opposite ends of the room sat two light wood desks, both flanked by two floor lamps that cast a warm light yellow into the room. The desks were clear, except for a neat stack of stationery, and three ornate pens each. Both had high-backed leather chairs pushed up to them.

On the floor was a navy-blue rug with a crescent moon, and a ghost image of Euphoria's rings cast in jewel toned purples and greens. Scattered around were comfortable looking leather arm chairs that gave the place a very laid back, cozy feel.

Nadir opened a side panel in one of the desks and slid out a large drawer. On it sat three bottles holding various liquids. He pulled another drawer, in which were glasses.

"Drink?" he asked.

"Yes," Oleana said, feeling rather desperate for anything to take the edge off.

"Yes," Leith said before taking a seat in one of the arm chairs.

Lorn looked as if he wanted to say something, but Oleana's icy gaze made him back down.

"If you tap the corner of that desk the same way I did, you will find another compartment with some candies," Nadir said looking at Lorn.

"Thanks," the boy said, doing as he was told.

Drink in hand, Oleana walked along the bookshelves. Many of the books were on strategy and planning. Some were biographies from legendary military leaders, and past rulers of Caledon.

Oleana paused when she saw a book that read, *Life and Times of Saddiq Starson*. She pulled the hard-cover book from its shelf, shaking dust loose into the air. The rendering of Nadir's father on the cover had the man smiling. The smile had been a rare thing for the former ruler of Caledon, but once used it was a beautiful thing to see, lighting up his whole face, making his gray eyes sparkle like little slices of the moon.

Oleana turned to look at Nadir who was perched on the corner of the desk. "I'm sorry to hear of your father's ...," Oleana started when her arm started to burn.

"Goodness, again?" Lorn asked in surprise.

"Recognized it this time," Leith said rolling up his sleeve and showing off the glow at the middle of his arm.

Nadir shut his eyes and gripped his glass so tight Oleana feared he might break it. Oleana looked toward the door. Two people came into view. The woman Oleana knew. The longer hair and the wrinkles around the eyes did nothing to hide the natural beauty of Lillian Bloodgood.

The young man at her side was less familiar, but Oleana recognized the eyes. The gray orbs that looked like captured moonlight. Saddiq's eyes. Nadir's eyes. He was Lysander Starson, last of the Heirs of Eternity.

100101

Light filled the room as if a thousand lightning bugs took flight, filling the room with tiny pin pricks of sun. Warmth flooded Oleana's body. Her heart thudded against her chest erratically, as if trying to capture some alien rhythm.

Magnetized to Lysander by some invisible force, Oleana moved closer to him, as did the others, until the four of them were standing in a circle, arms laid on top of each other. For a moment Oleana didn't feel like herself anymore. She felt like a part of some larger machine.

Her heart found a new rhythm, and she knew it wasn't hers, it was theirs. Her strength wasn't hers, but theirs. Her knowledge, her drive, all theirs, and what they had was hers.

Then the moment faded and Oleana felt like she was stuffed back into her body. Like she was cloaked in darkness, and she longed to be back in the light. There was a thread at the back of her mind that connected her to the others. Its presence brought her a comfort beyond words. Never again would she be alone, she had the others. She was complete.

"No, not him!" someone pleaded.

Oleana was yanked back to herself, facing the terror-filled eyes of Lillian, and all she could say was, "I'm so sorry." Oleana knew what it was to go to bed every night praying that her son would choose a different path than the one she'd trained him for. Oleana hated to be the one to have to do that to someone else.

Lysander stepped back, pulling his sword from the sheath at his back. He looked frantically around, as if he'd just woken up to find himself surrounded by the enemy. "What was that," he demanded, looking around at everyone in the room." His tone was sharp, but there was no fear there, just the desire for answers.

"What was that? What just happened?" he repeated, turning in circles not sure where the answer would come from.

"That was amazing!" Lorn said, his eyes growing as big as his face would allow. "It was just... goodness. I can't believe that just happened! Goodness..." he trailed off in wonder.

"You said there'd be more. That felt great," Leith chimed in.

"What was it, and who are you?" Lysander questioned. He looked toward his mother, but she just shook her head. Nadir still had his eyes shut tight.

Oleana downed the last of her drink, snatched Nadir's abandoned drink, and gulped it down before she found the courage to speak. She cleared her throat, and spoke gently, but firmly. "My name is Oleana, also known as the Guardian. That's Leith, Master of Animals, and Lorn, Master of Skies." Oleana smiled, charged up by the addition of Master of Earth. "You my friend, are Lysander the Master of Earth, making us the four Heirs of Eternity. That little display was your confirmation, or activation. The Twelve have called it both. I've never experienced it before, but I have to say it was invigorating." Oleana shook herself. Her body felt tingly all over.

"What does that mean? Father?" He looked at Nadir with confusion written all over his face. "Why do they talk of those stories as if they're true?"

Oleana stared angrily between Lillian and Nadir, "You mean you didn't even explain….," Lillian silenced her with a look.

Lillian found her voice, and it sounded like the song bird Oleana remembered. "Those stories were very much real, but your father assured me hundreds of potentials are born every generation with the mark, but only four are chosen to be the Heirs. Others in his family line had borne one and not been chosen. Yours looked incomplete, so Nadir was convinced, and convinced me that we had nothing to worry about. In the back of my mind though, I knew he wasn't as sure as he sounded. So, I told you the legend of the guardian, and her three kings at bedtime, just in case this dreaded day came. I haven't been able to sleep well since news of Solon reached us. I thought knowing for sure would ease my feelings, but knowing the path that is in front of you fills me with fear."

Lysander laughed. Hands on his belly, laughing with his whole body. So genuine and unexpected the gesture was, Oleana couldn't help but laugh herself. "Me. An Heir of Eternity?" he shook his head in wonder, with a sly grin. "That would be a feat. If this is some elaborate going away prank, it's odd, but amusing. You will have to tell me the secret of the light show, but it is time we are done with this." He sheathed his sword, but Oleana noticed the tension in his shoulders remained, like a coil ready to spring.

"Seeing it on the other side, I see the silliness of the objection," Leith said.

"This is no joke," Oleana admonished him, all laughter and merriment leaving her. She turned serious, and looked him straight in the eye to convey the auspicious moment. "You are one of the three, Master of Earth. Your bare the mark on your arm."

"This?" Lysander said holding up his arm in confusion. "This is just a dark spot. It isn't the mark of anything."

Oleana grabbed his arm, surprised at what she saw. His mark should have been a complete ring. Instead it was a fading crescent shape. The edges were rough, blending in with the olive brown color of his skin.

"I don't understand," she muttered confused, "how can that be?"

Lysander snatch his arm back. "This, whatever it is, has gone from amusing to cruel. I'm taking my leave of this foolishness." Lysander turned and left before Oleana could even think of an objection. Her mind whirled with what his distorted mark could mean.

"We can't let him leave," Lorn said.

"This is his home. He won't go far," Lillian said. Oleana didn't miss the sarcastic bite. "I told you, Mira, I wasn't being naïve. I recognized the mark. As soon as he was born it stood out like a beacon, but it wasn't complete. So, I went to the Thousand Years Library and read all the Founders books on the Heirs of Eternity, and the potentials. These potentials were born with a sensitivity to the smart particles that bind us all, but they were never meant to be activated."

"Clearly he was activated. We all saw that." Everyone nodded in unison. "So why does his mark still look like that?" No one responded. "Why does everything have to be so complicated with you three?" Again no answer. Oleana was moving past aggravated and into a territory near mental exhaustion. "Nadir, did you want to chime in here? Maybe explain yourself? Say anything?" Oleana threw up her hands in exasperation as she paced back in forth beside Nadir.

Nadir refilled his glass, and reclined in the desk chair, staring out the nearest window as if he had the room all to himself.

"I don't have time for this. We don't have time for this." Oleana said sweeping her arm over the room. "Cornelius knows our faces, knows we were searching for the last of us. It won't take him long to track us here. The longer we stay here, the more risk for everyone. I don't need another Solon on my hands. I need to convince your son, now, that he is who I say he is."

Lillian stood in the doorway blocking Oleana's exit. "He's my son. I'll calm him down. You just wait in the front lawn for him."

Oleana stared into Lillian's fierce green eyes. The two of them were never really friends, more like friendly competitors fighting for the same awards, and the affections of the same man. Oleana's pride told her to take Lillian's posturing as an affront to her dignity and position, but as her previous rant pointed out, they didn't have time for foolishness, and any more conflict would cause further alienation of this family.

"Do what you need to," Oleana sighed, backing down.

Lillian hesitated, as if she wanted to press her advantage. The older woman nodded, her eyes still tight at the corners. She turned and left with a whoosh of fine fabric, leaving a trail of cardamom and vanilla behind her.

"Can I come help?" Lorn said, practically bouncing on his tiptoes.

Oleana looked between Lorn and Leith. "No. I need you two to entertain yourselves for a little bit. Get Tycho to show you around or something."

Oleana spared Nadir one last glance, but the man she once admired and adored for being brave, smart, and compassionate, was sulking in the corner like a child, nursing his drink. Time was a cruel taskmaster that could turn even the strongest mountain into a pebble, and Oleana didn't think she could take much more of its abuse.

CHAPTER FOURTEEN: AMBUSH

The sound of hoof beats against the stone roadway startled a flock of birds into the air, the horizon filling with a blue and white swirl of movement. Lorn let his eyes follow their path, but his mind remained in Central City, with his mother and Lysander.

He'd never seen his mother look at someone the way she did Nadir. He'd also never seen someone get so mad at being called an Heir, as Lysander did. Lorn didn't think his mother's sometimes abrasive ways were going to go over well with Lysander. Logic impelled Lorn to be there to mediate between them, but his instincts said it was best not to get in the middle of things he didn't understand.

"Don't worry so much, you'll wrinkle your face before its time," Tycho said, pulling Lorn out of his thoughts. "Enjoy the scenery and the fresh air."

"That why boss man go on a supply run? For the air?" Leith asked pulling ahead of the cart Tycho was driving.

"Anything is better than watching Nadir and Lillian pace around the residence while Mira and Lysander run around the yard," Tycho replied. "Besides, its good for even the boss man to get his hands dirty occasionally, or he forgets how to work them. These supplies happen to be weapons built to my specs by a new supplier I was encouraged to trust. I need to make sure they turned out the way I needed them to, or they can get right back on the train, and right back to the supplier."

"That make us free labor if they do be right?"

"Is he always so negative?" Tycho asked, his eyebrows lowered, giving Leith a glowering look.

Lorn glanced at his fellow Heir. "Well, I've only known him for a few days, but from what I can tell, yes."

"Amusing," Leith grumbled.

"So Tycho, how did you managed to become such a decorated man? You hang out with the reagent of Caledon, and the guardian of the three, and instead of being dwarfed by such big personalities and positions, you make a big name for yourself. How'd you do it?"

Tycho laughed, it was a belly shaking affair, big and bold like everything else he did. "I feel as if I should be offended, but I think I'll take it as a compliment instead. Thank you. Besides, Nadir and Mira were never big titles to me. They were my friends that had a lot of pressure to live up to what people expected of them. You should understand that, you do call Mira, Mom, after all.

They worked hard, and pushed me to do the same. I grew up in a ranger family, knew early on in life what my track would be. The physical aspect of it came rather easy to me, as you may have guessed," Tycho said flexing his broad chest. "The academic side of things was tougher. Mira was the opposite, so we pushed each other, taking time outside of class to get in extra practice, or study the books harder. No matter what title you wear, or task ahead of you, it is hard work and determination that give you the edge. As your mother knows, sometimes even that isn't enough to guarantee success. That's life."

"No regrets?"

"I regret watching your mother leave. I would've followed her anywhere. Her leaving left a command gap, and Nadir found himself pulled more and more by political matters, leaving Lillian and I to fill very big shoes. That first year without her was hard. I may have been in Central City, but my heart was in Gaeth with her, searching for you. Then when we learned of her death..." Tycho turned away from Lorn and he feared his question had gone too far. "Her loss was hard to take, for all of us. Even knowing she would be reborn, there was no way to tell if we would ever see her again. What was even worse in my mind was running into the guardian again and not recognizing anything about the new incarnation. Knowing for a fact that the Mira I knew was gone forever, replaced by some strange thing that claimed to know me."

Lorn nodded. He tried his best to avoid thinking about who he'd been before. His mother had an advantage in that she remembered her past lives. She called them a burden, but the years of compounded knowledge prepared her for life in a way no one else could claim.

Seeing the way people from his mother's past reacted to the new version of her always made him wonder, are they really seeing her, or are they just seeing the past? Maybe there were certain qualities that she possessed, no matter what the outside of her looked like. Mom would often say how his passion for learning more followed him from one body to the next.

Lorn thought it important to know that something from his past lives carried through. The smart particles coursing through his veins made him more than human, but every lifetime he had parents, maybe siblings and friends. People loved him, and he couldn't even remember a single detail about them or how he may have impacted their lives.

He couldn't even remember the parents he'd lost this time around. His earliest memory was of sitting alone in an abandoned house, scavenging the torn remnants of a forgotten life for enough covering to keep him warm on a very cold night. Lorn remembered his stomach rumbling loud enough to scare off any monsters that may have been lurking in the shadows. His unconscious mind randomly pulled up other memories in that vein on rough nights, but that was all Lorn had of his past.

"Hate to interrupt the chatting," Leith said, pulling his mount up next to the cart, "but danger comes." He pointed to the tree line off to their right.

"What does that mean?" Lorn said not seeing what he meant.

"Tannin, least five yetis coming this way from the forest."

Lorn squinted until he caught sight of movement just inside the line of fuzzy evergreens that separated the pasture land from the woodlands, moving away from the coast. Lorn recognized the form of five yetis, and their dangerous wrangler, Tannin.

Questions flooded Lorn. How could they have found them? Was Cornelius nearby? Was this where his fourth life would end? Panic chilled his body.

"Why couldn't they have found us after we gathered the weapons?" Tycho said with surprising calm. "How did you even spot them?"

"Predator sense."

Tycho nodded. "You two head back to the city, warn the others. I'll slow them down."

"They'll slaughter you," Lorn objected.

"This cart will slow you down. They'll be on me before I can unhook the horse, and riding with one of you would slow you down. So, do what I say, and get going."

Leith kicked his mount into motion back toward the city, leaving Lorn torn between what he wanted to do, and what he felt was the right thing.

"I can take care of myself," Tycho said, pulling twin axes from their resting places on the bench beside him.

Lorn went too, but instead of heading back toward the city, he charged straight at the yetis. A million objections ran through his mind as he leaned down low on his mount, picking up speed. Had he lost his mind? Was he trying to show off, prove he wasn't just a kid that needed protecting? Lorn knew it was more than that.

His mother drill him in fighting techniques since he was eight. She taught him how to deal with superior numbers. Charge the enemy, she would say. Catch them off guard and force them to scatter. That way they can't use their numbers against you. Tycho needed time to free his horse, and Lorn could give that to him without getting himself too close to danger.

Working with a clear spring sky wasn't ideal, but Lorn could feel some heavy clouds out over the ocean. They just needed some coaxing from him and they would produce the lightning he so desperately needed.

"Come back here," Tycho bellowed, but Lorn had no time for discussion.

The shadowy figures breached the tree line. They abruptly changed direction, like a flock of birds, in response to Lorn's charge. He had difficulty matching course, and concentrating on the movement he needed in the sky. His skin tingled with the energy he was putting out, warming the air around him, and calling to the cold clouds just off the coast. He knew the two could meet miles away, and he could draw the lightning in. He just needed that one spark.

Lorn was off the road and into the high grass, the weeds smacking against his calves. The yetis split apart, letting him run right through the middle, until they made a wide circle around him, and Lorn was forced to arrest his speed or run into them. His mount objected to being so close to the strange beasts, rearing up and stomping the ground. Lorn wanted to grab his sword strapped to the side of the saddle, but he needed his one hand free.

One brave yeti swiped at his mount. Lorn easily dodged it, backing away. His body tensed, but it wasn't from the beasts. His spark hit. Electricity was in the air. It was his game to play now. His heart thumping against his chest, surging with adrenaline.

Lorn thrust his hand into the air, his palm and fingers alight with a familiar blue glow. His heart pounded in his chest, straining to give him as much energy as it could. For that moment, Lorn saw past the skin of the world, and peered into the microscopic. He saw the miniscule little machines that seeded the planet, and altered it into something not Euphoria, not Earth, but a mutant hybrid of the two.

The yetis were swirling, raging clouds of the stuff, while the plants and insects around them were like a neat, well designed web, each element connected to the other in an intricate and beautiful system. Looking up, Lorn pulled destruction down over his head in a thick trunk of particles. At his command, it split like a treetop, forming five branches that went for the yetis.

Lightning hit in five distinct spots, knocking the yetis off their feet, sending them flying in different directions, and leaving Lorn awash in static, but unharmed. Lorn felt shaky, as if he'd expended all that his body had to offer. When his vision adjusted, he still saw spots of black dancing around, and the world looked too bright to be real. Lorn clung to his agitated mount, fearing a close encounter with the ground.

When he heard someone grunt behind him, Lorn struggled to turn himself around enough to see. In his hurry to dispatch the yetis, Lorn let Tannin slip by. The multiform descended on Tycho with a brutality that would have crushed a weaker man. Tycho managed to hold his own, but it wouldn't be for long. Lorn didn't think he had enough in him to be of any help.

"Mom," he cried loudly, gasping for breath, but not knowing what else to do. "Help me, please!"

100101

Lysander stared skeptically at the intruder, who claimed to be a living legend, and an old friend of his parents. When his mother pulled him from the training ground, he foolishly thought it was to have a family meal, maybe discuss the possibility of him being allowed to go on campaign with the other fresh squad leaders.

Instead, they threw nonsense at him, and expected him to swallow it down with a smile. Lysander had long since moved past the need for fairy tales. Despite his mother's efforts to convince him otherwise, Lysander couldn't believe what this new woman told him.

"My mother has tried to convince me you are the Guardian, and what's more, you are the woman Uncle Tycho, and to a lesser extent, my father, talk about. I remember my father telling stories of when you were in the squad together," Lysander said. He circled around her, sizing her up, as they stood in the middle of the Residence's front lawn. Oleana took his scrutiny with confidence, shoulders back, chest out. Whatever Lysander was looking for, Oleana didn't seem to think he would find it. "He even showed me pictures of those days. Showed me the woman you once were. Your skin is a darker brown this time, and I have to say, I do miss those blue eyes."

Oleana shook her head, her loose dreadlocks, with their multi-colored threads laced throughout, slapping against her face. "I had blue eyes during my first lifetime. My eyes were brown the time I spent with your father. Always thought those dark, coffee bean-brown eyes were so strong and striking. I do like the flecks of green in these nut-brown eyes. They remind me so much of my mother, Orda," her voice sounded far away, as if pulled into the past. "I tried explaining to her why, at the age of fourteen, I needed to leave home. I don't think she really understood. My father either, but it's my mother's tears that haunt me at night." Oleana shut her eyes against the painful memory. It was just one of a thousand she wanted to keep buried. "I didn't want to leave them, mind you, but I knew if I didn't go on my own, something would force me out. The longer I stayed, the harder leaving would be." Oleana took in a deep breath, which seemed to steady her. Lysander stopped at her right side so she had to turn to look at him. "If you're done testing me, can we get on with our business? It is my job to teach you how to use your unique abilities, and with Cornelius barreling down on us I don't have time to be my usual kind and gentle self."

"Ha," Lysander laughed. Oleana gave him a look that rivaled his mother. He got a brief glimpse of what the two of them must have been like, working together in the same squad.

"I..," Oleana froze.

"Mom!" the word cut through the air, banging against Lysander's skull. He didn't know how, but he knew it to be Lorn. "Help!"

Oleana looked at him, her eyes wide and glistening with barely contained tears. "Grab as many men as you can get. We have to go save them."

Lysander was startled he didn't know if he could believe his own mind. "How?" he asked, grabbing Oleana's arm.

"I keep trying to tell you, they are you are connected to us. They are your brothers, if not by blood, then by the quirk in your DNA that makes you an Heir. There's no time for explanations. We have to go save them."

"Follow me, I know the way."

Oleana was already on the run.

100101

Guilt tugged at Leith as he fled. When the flash and bang cut through the air he stopped his horse dead, nearly toppling over the front of it as a result. Still he resisted the urge to look back. If it was from Lorn, then things were taken care of and they didn't need him anyways. If the attack was from Cornelius than turning back would waste precious seconds that he needed to escape the vengeful Ice Ultra.

Try as he might, Leith couldn't force himself to go one step forward without making sure the others were okay. Then he heard Lorn's desperate call and his choice was made. White-knuckling the reigns in his hand, Leith forced his mare to turn around and head back. Coming from behind, Leith could see Lorn at the center of the field. The boy didn't look so good. He wobbled atop his horse, but whatever he did knocked the yetis flat.

Coming up on the cart, Leith trotted right into a fight. Tycho tumbled off the cart backwards, Tannin atop him. Leith swung wide to keep from trampling them. Leaving fear behind, Leith slid off his horse and pulled his dagger free in one smooth motion, running toward the tangle of limbs and fur.

Tycho used the momentum of his fall to propel Tannin up and over him. Tannin showed off his quick reflexes and acrobatic skills, tucking his body into a ball and coming up on his feet with inhuman speed. Leith pulled up short, looking the multiform in the face. Tannin looked at Leith's dagger and smiled.

"Come to give me the other one?" Tannin said.

Not in the mood for chatting, Leith charged forward. He brought his dagger down in a cross body swing. Tannin blocked, catching the blade across the back of his arm. The multiform pushed with both hands against Leith's chest, claws piercing the layer of woolen sweater and scraping against flesh, lifting Leith off the ground and throwing him back.

Leith took the short flight in stride, bending his knees as he came down, not losing his balance. Tycho attacked Tannin from behind, keeping the multiform from advancing. The twin axes slashing across the back, one after the other. Leith ran into the melee as soon as Tannin's back was to him.

In an underhanded hold, Leith swung hard at Tannin's neck, but the multiform was fast. He had Tycho's axe in one hand, and managed to push Leith's blow away with the other. Leith caught Tycho's gaze. A silent thanks, and encouragement to push forward, passed between them.

Tycho yelled, and swung forward with both axes. Leith got close to Tannin and ducked low, avoiding the heavy-handed blow and barreling into Tannin's legs forcing him off balance. Tannin pirouetted like a reed in the wind, catching the axe blade along his side instead of his chest as intended. Leith felt the spray of blood across his cheek, wet and sticky.

With Tannin no longer between them Leith stumbled toward Tycho, but the big man was planted firmly, solid as the wall around Solon. Tycho offered him a hand up while keeping one axe up, and ready to defend.

"You might want to rethink your attack," Tycho said to Tannin. "Looks like the odds have shifted out of your favor."

Leith stood and stared Tannin down. Patches of his once pristine gray-white fur now splotched with the dark crimson of his own blood. His mouth was open in a toothy snarl as he sucked in breath like a man with black lung. Leith pulled his shoulders back and locked his knees to make it look like he was on sure ground, but his legs were burning, and his chest felt on fire where Tannin's claws had dug in. Even his dagger felt heavy in his hand.

Tannin wiped his mouth with the back of his hand. "You underestimate my resolve."

Part of Leith broke at the look of confidence that spread across Tannin's face. He hoped the multiform would once again take off, hoping to fight another day. Leith stole a glance at Tycho. The big man was bruised about his face, his lip was split and blood trickled down the back of his head into his shirt. His right arm was slashed up, the sleeve hanging in ribbons around the bloody skin. Still he held his axe up, though Leith could tell it was by force of his impressive will.

Tannin shivered. His whole body vibrating. Leith thought the multiform was succumbing to the blood loss, but when he looked closer it became clear that Tannin was healing. The jagged gash cutting across his side from Tycho's axe had stopped bleeding and was fading from an angry red to a more gentle, warm pink. It would still take time, but the wound would heal in less than a quarter of the time it would take Leith.

"Wishing you had kept going now boy?" Tycho asked Leith, amusement in his tone.

"This funny to you?"

"Always thought I'd die for one of the Heirs, never thought it would take this long."

Tannin didn't give Leith time to respond. The multiform ran at them, claws extended to a terrifying length. Leith took in a steadying deep breath, and pushed off Tycho, letting Tannin run in between them.

Leith leaned back on his right foot, kicking out with his left, but the blow fell short when Leith's world was set on fire, as his back felt like he'd landed on a bed of glass. He stumbled forward onto his knees and had to tuck and roll to keep from knocking against Tycho once again.

Leith rolled over on his back in time to see the yeti that attacked him. Most of its fur was scorched black. Its right eye was ruined, and its mouth hung open in a gruesome half smile, but it was strong and angry, and that made for a dangerous combination.

Leith brought both of his feet up to keep the yeti from landing on his chest. The beast seemed to move mindlessly, slashing wildly with claws and teeth. Leith was forced to expend most of his energy just keeping the thing away from his face, and chest. His back screamed with every movement. He really wished Oleana, and her twin sais, would show up soon and save him once again.

Running out of strength and patience, Leith freed up one foot to kick the beast in its face, focusing on the ruined side. He kicked again and again, as hard as his fatigued muscles would allow. The beast howled and reached for his attacking foot. It took the pressure off Leith, giving him enough space to roll to the side and get out from under the angry bulk of the yeti. He leaped up and came around, jumping on the beast's back before it could react.

Leith stabbed at its neck but the burnt, matted fur acted like a leather shield. In his fury, Leith stabbed at it again and again, ignoring the furious claws that tried to rip the skin off his fast moving arms. Blood spurted his face spurring him on to plunge harder, faster, until the creature's fight died and it slumped to the ground taking him with it.

Dagger still clutched in his hand, Leith straddled the beast as the heat went out of it. His lungs burned and he didn't know if he had the strength to stand, much less fight anymore, but no matter how bad the yeti was, Tannin was worse, and he couldn't leave Tycho to fight him alone.

Leith pulled his weapon free of the yeti's neck, pulled his feet up under him, and wiped the blood from his face, determined to put Tannin down as he had the yeti.

Lorn was out in the field, having to deal with two other yetis who'd found their feet after the initial strike. To Leith it looked like the boy was holding his own well enough. Tycho on the other hand was backed against the side of the cart, blood dripping from multiple wounds. One of his axes lay several feet away. How the man was still standing Leith didn't know, but the look of calm reserve on his face spoke volumes.

In a backhanded swipe, Tannin knocked Tycho to the ground. Leith rushed in, sliding between Tannin and the fallen Tycho, jabbing his dagger up into the multiform's ribs. The blade scraped against bone.

Leith knew it was a good hit, but he paid for it. Tannin's curved claws dragged across Leith's chest, tearing through flesh and muscle. He fell backwards over Tycho's prone body, landing flat on his back, staring up into the cloudless sky. His body refused to let him inhale deeply enough to satisfy his need for air. Leith briefly wondered if being the hero was really worth all the pain.

CHAPTER FIFTEEN: DESTRUCTION

Oleana saw carnage everywhere. Spotting Leith and Tycho crumbled on the ground put Oleana's heart in her mouth. She found it hard to breath around the lump of fear in her throat. All of that went away when her eyes locked on Lorn's. He was backed up against a line of trees with Tannin in front of him, and two mangled yetis on either side.

A level of panic that she'd never felt before bombarded every cell of Oleana's body. She simultaneously wanted to run screaming into Tannin, and run away, pretending none of it was happening. Instead, she was rooted to the spot, her body no longer under her control. Only the horse's desire to keep moving forward kept her on the move.

"Tannin," she half yelled, half begged. "Please." Hot tears poured down her cheek.

Tannin stopped his advance on Lorn and slowly turned, as if he was fighting it all the way. "You insignificant prick, I'll crush you," Tannin said, spittle dripping from his fangs.

Oleana's world exploded. She didn't see Tannin anymore, she heard him. Her fear and desperation kicked her power into overdrive, and Oleana felt the same rush of understanding she always got in that interval before connecting with the Twelve. The world was opened up to her, and more than that, she knew how to manipulate it to her will.

Tannin's bio signal had a surprisingly chaotic, fast-paced rhythm to it, like two high-energy items had been smashed together, forming an uneasy union. Oleana grabbed hold of it, put her digital fingers in the midst of it and squeezed. She opened her mouth wide and let out a noise that only her ears could hear but more importantly, Tannin's body felt.

Oleana shut off the electrical impulses coursing through Tannin's body like flipping a switch. It was s temporary measure, a slight interruption, but enough to keep his brain from firing, his heart from pumping, and his lungs from expanding. Tannin collapsed in a useless heap, his light blue eyes staring up at the sky with panic etched into his pupils.

Oleana kicked a limp Tannin out of the way and held her hand out to her son, scooping him up on the run. Terrified yetis scattered in her wake. "Hold on," she told Lorn in an urgent whisper.

Oleana wanted to whisk him back to the city and as far away from danger as she could get, but she couldn't leave Leith and Tycho. Oleana couldn't lead Tannin and the yetis back into the city either. Instead she took a wild circle back toward the cart, leaving the remaining yetis pawing at Tannin who, for the moment, was frozen in place. "Lysander," she yelled to the boy, "this is your chance to prove you're the Master of Earth. This is your element, use it."

Lysander had dismounted and was crouched over Tycho checking for a pulse. Oleana didn't need to check to know Leith was still alive, but the pain in her joints told her he his life ebbed away with every beat of his heart.

"Why do with some fancy power, when I can do so much more with a sword and confidence?"

"Three of them, two of us, and we can't both fight, and protect them," she said pointing at Tycho, "Tannin won't go down easy. Trust me, I've tried." Oleana looked over at the multiform, who was stretching. He'd broken free of her power already. "Choose," she ordered.

Lysander stood and looked, his hand still gripped tight to his sword. Oleana knew she would regret it, but she couldn't resist giving Lysander a push in the right direction. She placed her hand at the nap of his neck tapping into part of him that made him 'other,' and setting it on fire.

"Mom," Lorn groaned.

Oleana pulled her hand back but Lysander was already lit up like a candle factory. He turned to her, his gray eyes unfocused, seeing into her, reading her genetic building blocks like another book in his father's library.

Oleana pointed to the approaching Tannin, "Get them," she ordered in a low growl, her voice boring into his mind.

Oleana had never used her override ability on one of the Heirs before. The idea of taking over another human being scared her. If she hadn't been so desperate she wouldn't have tried it on Lysander, but seeing it in action she wondered if she should rethink her stance.

Lysander strode out to meet Tannin, and his trailing yetis. With a calm confidence that looked reckless given the state of his companions. Behind and beside him, the grass shot up five feet as he stepped past. Flowers grew stems the size of Tycho's arms, and blades of grass took on the shape of the sword still clutched in Lysander's hand, left forgotten at his side. The ground itself trembled as Lysander passed.

Tannin pulled up short, the look of shock visible from Oleana's position. With a flick of his wrist, Lysander thrust a section of grass at the yetis. Tannin crouched low, putting his arm up to block his face, as his brothers were cut to ribbons.

When the first attack was over, Tannin was up and running. Lysander moved faster, sending in his army of man-sized flowers to wrap the multiform in a vice grip. Oleana heard bone break as the stems coiled around and around Tannin's body. He started to shake. Tannin was trying to transform, but the vines responded quickly to the changes in his shape. Tannin didn't finish the form alteration before he collapsed upon a bed of the mutant grass, the distinct sound of cracking bones filled the air.

Oleana tried to move closer to Lysander, do what she could to calm him, but the grass was so high and thick she couldn't get her horse through it. "Lysander," she called.

The young man turned toward her. His mouth opened as if he wanted to say something. Instead his eyes rolled to the side, his breathing became short and labored. Lysander's hands curled inward and he crumbled to the ground, snorting and gasping for breath.

"Lysander!" she screamed.

The grass and plants shrunk back to their normal size, giving Oleana a clear view of the violent seizure Lysander was caught in. His head was tilted back at a painful looking angle. His arms twitched rapidly as he beat against his own chest.

"Lorn, here take these," Oleana said, handing her son the reigns before sliding off the horse and running to Lysander's side. She managed to leverage him onto his side. At a loss for what else to do, she just rubbed his back and spoke soothingly to him. "I'm sorry. Hold on. Hold on. You're going to be all right."

CHAPTER SIXTEEN: AFTREMATH

Cornelius could feel the dying ember of his son's life ebbing away like a dead spot in his chest, black and numb, and growing. Tannin must have caught up with the Heirs. No one else could present such a threat to Tannin. Cornelius wasn't sure if he was strong enough to confront the guardian and her charges yet. The clash with Daycia took a large toll on him. The left side of his face was still covered in frost to aid healing. That wasn't going to keep him from going to rescue his son, the only person in this world he cared about.

Cornelius whipped up a cold front to ride into the outskirts of Central City. When his feet hit solid ground, he heard the whimpering of a mangled yeti. He shot ice into its nose, giving it a quick death, and walking away without a second thought.

Tannin was crumpled amidst a pile of shriveled vines, his body contorted like a pretzel. His limbs were twisted up among the vines still wrapped around him, thorns the size of Cornelius' pinky finger buried in his son's skin.

Cornelius frozen them and ripped the vines off his son. He desperately searched for any sign of breathing. Tannin's chest rose and fell in slow ragged gasps. His eyes fluttered behind heavy lids, and blood oozed lazily out of the many puncture wounds along his limbs and torso.

Cornelius fell to his knees scooping his son into his lap, rocking back and forth, his mind chaotic, swirling with what he could do. "Tannin, you fool, how could you let this happen? I told you to find them, not fight them," he groaned the words, covering his son with himself.

Tannin made no response to his father's words. Cornelius spent decades building plans on top of plans, plotting and scheming ways to get back in control, but all of that lay dying in his arms. For the first time in a long time he felt something new, grief. Anger, frustration, even fear were all old friends, but never before had Cornelius cared about someone else enough to grieve their loss.

He wasn't ready to let go just yet. He couldn't let that be the end of Tannin, his son, his most prized possession. Cornelius turned to the only other constant in his life to save his son, the cold that he was designed to manipulate.

Cornelius straighten out the twisted form of his son as gently as he could manage. He made sure every scrap of vine and dried leaves was cleared from around him. Cornelius would freeze his son, let his body heal itself over time. "Hold on," he ordered his son.

Placing his hands on his son's chest, Cornelius felt the vibrations of every cell in the boy's body, like a million ants crawling against his skin. But those ants were drones he could order around. He could make them dance to his will.

Every atom vibrated at its own rhythm, and Cornelius used his own biological rhythm to counteract them. He slowed Tannin's body processes down to a crawl. The multiform's heart beat at one beat per minute, his blood moved like tar through his veins. His son was saved, or at least his dying was slowed. Cornelius would carry his son to safety, then he would unleash every ounce of anger his considerable form could hold on the Heirs of Eternity.

100101

Leith was barely hanging on to life, infection raging through his body. Lorn was so exhausted the doctors insisted he needed two days of bed rest. Tycho and Lysander both had their own injuries to recover from. Oleana couldn't get her hands to stop shaking - she'd overused her abilities, and her body was paying the price; so she decided to steady them with liquor she'd pilfered from Nadir's office.

The other three Heirs of Eternity were safely tucked away in their various rooms in the medical wing of the Residence, while

Oleana watched the sun set on the roof of its greenhouse. She felt light and gooey at the center by the time she heard footsteps on the roof behind her. The lightness of her breakfast was only remembered after her head started to spin.

Now with an orange-red sky in front of her, Oleana was pleased to have company for safety reasons. She was perched dangerously close to the edge, but didn't want her good mood spoiled. She waited until the person was right beside her to turn and see who it was.

Anger came flooding back, her light mood shattered. "What're you doing here? Do you finally have something to say? Not sure I care what it is."

Nadir sat down beside her. His eyes slid to the empty bottle with a look of yearning, as if he wished he was the one who had polished it off. "For the first time in my life I didn't know what to say then, and I'm still not sure what to say to you now."

"Let's start with why in twenty-three,"

"Twenty-five," he corrected.

"In twenty-five years you couldn't be bothered to tell your own son he might be one of the three?" She looked up at him with a disbelieving look.

Nadir shook his head. "I didn't have the heart to disappoint him like that when I was so sure he wouldn't turn out to be. First his mark being incomplete, then when he started... He uhm... when the seizures started, that sealed it for me. He's had them since he was a child. They are mostly under control now but as you have seen they are terrible when they occur. I've worked very hard to keep them a secret so they wouldn't affect his future in the rangers, but I knew no Heir of Eternity could have a body that was so defective."

The raging emotional storm brewing inside Oleana burst free. She swung at him, which only succeeded in toppling her over onto her back. What was worse, she couldn't tell if she'd actually landed. "You're an idiot, for more reasons than I can list. That defective boy saved me, saved my son, and you have the nerve to suggest some seizures could ever hold him back! Did you never stop to think that it's because your son is enhanced, that he's having these seizures?" Oleana heard herself talking and it sounded right, but the truth behind them was clouded behind a layer of alcohol. She hoped she'd remember her revelation when it would matter. She heaved a big sigh and looked up at Nadir with sharp eyes. "Our reunion wasn't supposed to go like this. You couldn't even be bothered to even acknowledge my exist…my whatever! I'm not some curse you ward against. I knew coming back that you would have moved on, thirty years is a long time, but writing me off as some bedtime story is cruel." Oleana was shaking from hurt, exhaustion, and an overdose of alcohol.

"I wasn't trying to dismiss you," Nadir said staring off into the horizon. His shoulders were slumped and his head low. "I was just trying to save my son. You're here less than a day and he's come closer to death today than he's ever in his life."

Oleana craned her body forward to get a clear look of Nadir's face in the dying daylight. The anger in his eyes scared her. Hurt her. "You were saving him from me? One night you're telling me you love me, the next time I see you I don't get so much as a hello. I may have a new face, but my heart still cares for you. You should know me well enough to understand I don't wish bad on anyone. If I had any choice, my path would have never brought me here, to your son. I tried to keep my own son as far away from this life as I could, but instead, he went running into it with arms wide. It's unfair of you to even suggest I would want this."

"Mira, listen I just…,"

"Oleana! By the Twelve why can no one remember my name is Oleana now. New face, new name, same crap task. But its not about me. What you did wasn't just unfair to me, and trust me when I say I now hate you enough for that, but it was a disservice to your son. You treated him as if he wasn't good enough. There's no way he didn't pick up on that. You had a rare opportunity to prepare him for what was ahead, and you failed because you couldn't see how great a person he is. So why don't you do me a favor and go disappear," Oleana finished, curling up on the cold hard roof.

She didn't have the energy for any more disappointment tonight. What should have been the greatest triumph of her multiple lives – finding the fourth Heir – quickly morphed into a disaster. Oleana didn't know what hurt worse, the fact that her son almost died because she was distracted, or that she may have failed *again*. Instead of facing it head on she once again decided to crawl down into a bottle and lose herself in its warmth.

Oleana tried to hide behind her defense of Lysander, but she was yelling at Nadir for reasons much more personal. It killed her that he failed where, of all people, he should have succeeded. More importantly he stood as a reminder of her own failures to protect Daycia, to protect Leith and Lorn.

It took a few moments for Oleana to realize Nadir was gone. She regretted not telling him to send her up some food. She wasn't leaving the roof until she spoke with The Twelve. Her stomach started rumbling, and Oleana decided nighttime was too long to wait. Talking to the Twelve during the day always came with its problems, the sun caused some interference, but Oleana would just have to deal with whatever problems arose.

Oleana levered herself up in a sitting position and did her best to clear her head, concentrating on her breathing. In and out, in and out, until she felt stable enough to actually be productive.

"Open channel one, priority message to particle cloud, care of The Twelve. Authorization code omega, foxtrot, tango, four. omega - mike - ginger - four." Oleana waited in silence, staring up at the outline of the rings the Twelve called home. She got the all too familiar feeling, as she had the dozens of other times she spoke to The Twelve, as if she was no longer just in her body, but spread out over the entirety of Euphoria.

Oleana wanted to stay frozen in that state of mind forever. It was in those moments that she felt connected to the people, and the world around her. She felt the pains and triumphs of others. During the day to day she tried to hold that feeling close to her heart, to remember what all her efforts were for, but it was too much for her fleshly brain to keep track of, and she got mired in her own selfish desires.

"You have found all the Heirs," Three said. Oleana wasn't sure, but she thought a bit of happiness could be detected in the disembodied voice. "Now you must get to Evermore with all haste."

"Yes, except there is a slight problem with the Master of Earth. His powers are defunct. He has seizures every time he tries to use them. What good does that do me?" Oleana could hear her abrasive tone and she didn't like it, but couldn't stop it either. There was a pause, static in her head which Oleana recognized as The Twelve conferring amongst each other. "Ha, you don't know either. This wasn't part of your grand plan. What are plans good for anyway, nothing but useless talk to satisfy the mindless masses."

"You're rambling," One said, making Oleana jump. "The Master of Earth is incomplete. You must reset him."

"What's that even mean?" Oleana said, fearing her inebriated brain couldn't keep up.

"When the particle cloud that makes up each one of the Heirs takes over a host body, it blends with that body so the two become one, forever altering both. In this case the blending is not complete. The host is somehow resisting the cloud. He must be reset so the blending is complete."

"How do I do that?"

"We will upgrade your knowledge," Three said.

Oleana was slow to comprehend exactly what that meant. "Wait, no, I don't ..." her objections fell on deaf ears. Ones and zeros fell from the sky like shooting stars in the heaviest meteor storm Oleana ever witnessed. The heavens filled with neat lines of numbers as they descended on Oleana like a tidal wave. She had just enough time to inhale sharply before she was overcome.

Her brain felt like a thousand angry wasps were rattling around inside her skull. Oleana clutched her head, her strained scream filling the twilit horizon. Then things went haywire. Oleana tried to curl up into a ball but her body refused to obey her. Her nervous system seized up and she couldn't even expand her lungs to breathe. Panic set in, and she tried to scream but nothing came out.

"Breathe," One ordered, his calm, stern voice cutting through whatever vice was around her.

Oleana sucked in air greedily. Her mouth tasted like she'd been licking the train tracks. Her vision swam. Oleana doubled over and vomited out what alcohol hadn't already made it to her bloodstream.

Once her stomach settled Oleana spit to clear her mouth of the foul taste. She wiped her mouth, and laid back staring up at the sky. Behind her eyes swam a wealth of new facts and figures. She couldn't search through it all. She was given several lifetimes worth of data in the matter of seconds.

Her head felt twice as big as it did a moment before. She knew the pain would ebb over time, and things would become clearer as her body accepted the download, but for the moment the thought of moving was too painful to contemplate. All she had to worry about was how to fix Lysander. If she concentrated on that question, the solution would come up.

"Oh no," Oleana said once things cleared up for her. "I'm not using my son to shock Lysander's system into a reset. What if he uses too much juice? What if Lysander never wakes up? I won't put that on my son."

"You are the guardian. You cannot put the feelings of one over the life of another," Three scolded.

"Don't ask me to be the best of humanity then judge me for being human," Oleana snapped back.

"You will serve as the bridge between them. That's what you were designed to do. Your body will release the necessary amount of energy."

Oleana still questioned the safety of such a plan, but it was the only one she had. "What about Leith? The damage he took was extensive and there is no way we can stay here and wait for him to heal. Cornelius will have the way blocked before that. There has to be a way to help him."

"The tower at Evermore was built to refresh and repair the bodies and minds of the Heirs of Eternity. You get him there and the tower will heal him much faster," Three offered.

"The journey there would most likely kill him."

"There may be another way, but the consequence will not be conducive to the conclusion of completing your mission."

"Listen, my head is spinning and my mouth taste like the bottom of a trash barrel, so please speak simply, or don't speak at all."

"You can use the regeneration energy to restore his body, but that means he will lose a life and you all have only one left."

"What? What does that mean? Last one?"

"We are not gods," Three said.

"I know that," Oleana shot back. She didn't need to be told that. Cornelius called himself a god, and some worshipped him as such, but his power was in destruction not creation. The Twelve were advanced, sure, even beyond what Oleana could easily comprehend, but even they had limits, ones that Oleana had run into before. She knew God existed, and knew as certainly the Twelve weren't it.

"Which means," One finished, "that we don't have the ability to make something that is truly immortal. We programmed the information bank that created you with the best recuperative program we possess. If you were completely machine your lifespan would be thousands of years or more. Blending with the biological system of your human body puts a strain on the computer system that we only had partial success in overcoming. The bank that stores your memories and gives the others their powers can only last through one last blending."

"That makes no sense, Cornelius is much older than we are, so is Daycia and her mother. Why aren't they falling apart?" The news was startling, and Oleana struggled to understand what this meant for her future.

"It is the storage and transfer that requires an amount of energy your primitive scales of measurement would not even be able to chart. Repairing the same body over and over costs much less, but even they are not as immortal as some claim."

A feeling of vertigo threatened to send Oleana's stomach over the edge once again. She couldn't tell if it was some residual effects of the download, or the result of the new-found fear hanging over her head.

As far back as she could remember, Oleana never feared death. She feared the weight of failure that another death brought her. She feared pain, and loss, and suffering, but she never thought about what her own death - permanently this time - would mean. She had no reason to fear something that would never come. Half-drunk and still in pain, Oleana didn't know how to process her newfound mortality.

Instead, she pushed it back into the furthest reaches of her mind, hoping if she ignored it long enough it would go away. "Why is it that every time I talk with you guys, I leave with more problems than when I came? Next time I run into an issue, I will just yell it to the wind and get a better answer."

"We are not gods," Three repeated.

"You keep saying that."

"We are not gods, so we cannot manipulate things to suit our will. We can only put things in motion and hope they turn out the way we have predicted. We have put our best into you and the other three. We are sorry if you feel it isn't enough. We too know what it means to taste defeat. We were once twelve strong, but the ravage of time has reduced us to six, with three of us remaining dormant for centuries at a time to prolong what time we have left. The Heirs of Eternity are the only chance we had left to do the one thing we were hardwired to do, preserve humanity."

"Ha, Heirs of Eternity what a stretch!" Oleana sniped. "More like Heirs of a Century and a Half. Three lifetimes I have wasted following your orders, sweating and bleeding for a future that even if I do it right this time, I still won't live to see play out. Why should I even bother continuing to fight this impossible war?" Oleana threw her hands up in surrender, looking up toward the heavens for their answer.

"This version of you has a propensity toward selfishness that surprises me," One said. He delivered it so coldly Oleana felt like she'd been smacked in the face. "As you said, you may be an enhanced human, but you are still human. You do this not to satisfy us or our pride. You do it not to be paraded around as the immortal hero of legend. Do it because hundreds of thousands of people on Euphoria want to grow up, fall in love, raise children, explore the world. Instead they are enslaved under the rule of vicious ultras, or forced to live in fear and poverty by the violent, greedy warlords that roam their realm. Do it because you are the only one that can save them, and that's more important than anything else."

Oleana felt the connection between them snap like a too-taut rubber band. With only the cloudy night sky and faint hint of the rings above her. Oleana took a minute to appreciate her solitude. Nobody had told her off like that in a very long time.

She wondered if One was right? Had she gotten so full of herself she'd lost sight of what really mattered? Lorn mattered. She knew that for certain. The way he talked a mile a minute and said 'goodness' every five minutes, as if saying it would actually put some out into the world. He could irritate her to the point of screaming, and then turn around two minutes later and do something that made her so proud she wanted to cry. Her son was so kind, and smart, and funny, and curious.

And Leith, he was growing on her. That cocksure attitude and confident smirk of his clashed so strikingly with the unsure look that often flittered across his brown eyes. Oleana remembered exploring his home. She remembered how each piece of art there was not only beautiful, but had an attention to the fine details. Oleana got the feeling that Leith didn't just collect art, he collected pieces of history, stories of moments in time. His broken speech may have caused some to write him off, but Oleana noticed the burning intelligence Leith hid behind his flippant nature.

Then there was Lysander, young, strong, proud. So much potential. So stubborn just like his father. and cunning like his mother. Through all that, Lysander held a pain at the core of him that Oleana so desperately wanted to ease. Lysander mattered and so did Nadir, Lillian, Tycho, Kaithlen, and Miriam.

Dear Miriam, and her unborn babe. What kind of life awaited them if Cornelius took control of the city? Would they even survive the attack? Oleana didn't like the odds that things would work out for them.

The cool breeze that swept in from the coast cleared Oleana's head enough for her to feel normal again. With the information still fresh in her mind, Oleana resolved to do what she had to for Leith and Lysander before all of her liquid courage faded away.

CHAPTER SEVENTEEN: HEALING

When Oleana got back to Leith's room she found Lorn standing in the corner directly across from the door, leaning against the wall. His arms were crossed on his chest and his head was down. Oleana knew he was sleep. His occasional snort confirmed it. He looked weighed down by exhaustion.

Lysander was less stealthy in his sleeping. He was laid back in the widest chair the room had to offer, and his feet were propped up on the foot of Leith's bed, shoes by the chair. Concern still wrinkled Lysander's brow. His eyes darted back and forth under heavy lids, and his hands were curled into fist. Even in sleep he couldn't escape trouble. Oleana hated to wake them, but she needed complete concentration for what she was about to do.

"Lorn, honey, gotta wake up," she said, shaking his shoulder.

Lorn jumped, nearly dislodging the short sword at his hip. Lysander popped his head up and pulled his sword free of its scabbard in one smooth motion. Oleana found herself staring down the blades of two different opponents before she could blink.

"Very good reflexes," Oleana said, nodding her approval. "Now kindly get those out of my face and get out."

Lorn dropped his sword. His face turned a bright red. "Mom, goodness, sorry. Wait, what's going on? Where were you? What are you going to do? Why do you smell like that? And look like that?" Lorn rattled off his question in his usual rapid-fire, staccato manner.

Oleana caught a glimpse of herself in a nearby mirror. She had dark circles under her bloodshot eyes. Half of her dreads had fallen out of their loose ponytail, and were pointed at odd angles. Her lips were dry and cracked, and the overall color of her brown skin was pale, and drained.

Oleana hurried to fix her hair, but nothing but a week of sleep and several good meals would fix the rest. "Lorn please, I'm fine, I promise. Its not like you two are the picture of health." Oleana noticed the dark, puffy circles under Lysander's eyes, and the drained look on Lorn's. "I know how to fix Leith and I just need a moment alone to concentrate on what I have to do. So, please, the two of you out, now. We can talk about the rest later."

Lysander took the command without question. He nodded and ushered Lorn out the door, giving the younger man just enough time to grab his shoes. Left alone with Leith in the candlelit room, Oleana took a good look at her thief for the first time. From the second she met him, she prejudged him because he didn't act like the king she wanted him to be.

Since that day, Leith proved himself to be brave when he walked away from all that he knew, leaving the walls of a city he'd never left before, when he confronted Tannin with nothing more than a dagger, when he saved her son.

Leith proved himself kind when he spoke those words to her on the train, and when he treated Lorn like an apprentice. Oleana first thought it to be an impossible task to turn Leith into the king the five realms needed, yet in a short time he proved to be more qualified for the job than she would ever be.

Oleana smiled. She had once told Leith that chasing after ones like him had been a waste of her multiple lives. She'd even promised herself she wouldn't die for them, not ever again. How foolish she had been to think in such selfish terms.

Leith risked his life to save her son, and she owed him more than she could put into words. Closing her eyes, Oleana reached back into that part of her mind that was more machine than human, and accessed the information the Twelve had uploaded. Oleana let herself move without second guessing what she was doing, knowing that was the best way. She had muscle memory for an activity she'd never performed before, and if she let the logic side of her brain think on it too hard she would end up tripping over herself.

Oleana organized the steps like a book in her head, flipping the pages after each task was completed. She grabbed the nearest candle, its heat warming her cold hands after a windy time up on the roof. Next she looked for a blade. Her sai was too big and cumbersome for the delicate task. Leith's dagger lay atop the neatly folded pile of his belongings.

The dagger was the last half of a set. The other was lost when Tannin took off with it back in Solon. Having it in her hand, Oleana could see why Leith liked it so much. The weight was well balanced. The silver blade shown in even the yellow candlelight. The black leather of the handle was soft, the grip felt off to Oleana, but it must have fit Leith's hand perfectly, the indentations of his fingers forever etched into the material. The guard was long enough to provide some protection while not making the blade too heavy. It was strong enough to be used in attacking.

Oleana gently pulled back the white sheet covering Leith up to the neck, exposing his left hand. She turned it palm up, noticing the amount of heat he was giving off, and the clammy feel of his skin. She made a small incision in his palm and followed the same move on her own hand. She tilted the hot wax to her wound pouring a coin-sized amount. It burned but Oleana pushed the pain away. She could add it to the list of things she would regret in the morning. With the wax still warm and malleable, Oleana pressed her palm to Leith's, the wax acting as a bridge to something more important than blood that passed between them.

As a guardian for more than one lifetime, Oleana knew how to tap into that part of her that made her more than human. Before her recent talk with the Twelve, her ability to manipulate that power was limited to the searching for, and guiding, of the three kings.

Oleana never really thought about using it for herself. Three said to use Leith's own regeneration energy to fix him. She had a better plan, a better source. Oleana didn't need another lifetime of regret hanging over her if this one didn't work out.

With the new access codes the Twelve passed on, Oleana pulled from her own reserves, draining the smart particles that coursed through her veins of as much power as they could spare, guiding it through the crude bridge she'd created, and into Leith. The heat the exchange generated burned hotter than the wax. Oleana feared her skin would blister, but she didn't let go.

Leith's body jerked. For a second Oleana flashed back to Lysander's seizure, but the gentle undulations of Leith's form were nothing like the violent contractions Lysander had suffered. Oleana tightened her grip to keep their connection strong. Leith's skin began to glow, much like when his mark activated, but spread over every inch of exposed skin. The barriers between them broke and Leith's body absorbed the energy greedily, to the point that Oleana struggled to keep her loss manageable.

Feeling near the point of collapse, Oleana yanked her hand free, backing away from the bedside. She rubbed at her jaw, realizing she'd clenched it so tight her teeth ached. Liquid wax dripped from her other hand, mixed with the crimson of her blood. Oleana stole from the pile of clean bandages on a nearby table to clean her palm and seal the wound.

She tried to check on Leith, but her knees buckled and she fell to the floor. "Lorn," she called in something between a croak and a whisper.

Lorn was through the door before Oleana could summon the strength to call again, Lysander close on his heels. Oleana knew they wouldn't have gone far. Lorn helped her on the nearest chair, while Lysander stood over Leith.

"How is he?" she asked.

"Glowing," Lorn said awe in his voice.

"Breathing steady," Lysander added. He pulled back the sheet covering Leith's bandaged chest. He lifted the edge of the bandage to get a look underneath. "The red of infection has faded considerably. Whatever you did saved him."

Oleana nodded, but even that small movement didn't sit well with her overtaxed body. Her stomach was balled into knots, and her eyes felt like lead weights rattling around in her skull. Lorn's hands holding her upright in the chair felt like ice cubes against her inflamed skin. Sleep pulled her willingly into its warm embrace.

"Good," Oleana tried to say, but didn't know if it made it past her lips.

100101

Oleana woke to the sound of hushed voices all around her. The inside of her mouth felt like she'd been sucking on sandpaper, and her eyelids felt twice as heavy as they should have. Instead of fighting the fatigue she laid there, listening. She picked out Lorn's voice right away, along with Tycho's. At first she thought she heard two Nadir's then realized one must have been Lysander.

"It was a large release of energy," Lorn said. "...needs time to recover."

"The bodies are gone, which means Cornelius likely took them. Which means he knows you're here," Tycho said.

"Reports from all over ... hundreds of yetis on the move. A war is brewing and seems to be headed to our doorstep," Nadir said.

"We need to leave," Oleana said, her eyes still shut tight.

"Oh, no you don't." Tycho said. "Not again. Not like this. No way."

Oleana cracked her eyes open, blinking against the bright yellow light of a new sun, pouring in through the only window in the room. She sat up slowly, her every muscle feeling like it had been raked over by sharp nails.

When the world around her finally came into focus, Oleana realized she sat on a hospital bed in a crowded room. Lysander, Tycho, and Nadir were dressed in the ranger's battle gear from head to toe. Lysander and Nadir sporting the royal crimson, while Tycho wore the crisp steel gray of ranger command.

Even Lorn looked ready for battle wearing his black pants that he modified with padding at the knee and down his shins, his long-sleeved gray shirt with elbow pads, and thick black leather vest complete with matching sword hilt secured around his waist and upper thigh. Oleana felt claustrophobic with so much muscled humanity and armor crowded in the small room.

"I won't risk Central City, risk Caledon, by staying here any longer. Evermore isn't far. We can make it."

Nadir scratched at his chin. "That direction won't be any safer. I don't know if it's coincidence, or if Ivar is just trying to take advantage of the chaos, but Failsea troops have been moving through the wild zone. They'll be at our border by week's end."

Oleana knew of Ivar from her last life. His uncle ruled Failsea at the time, an old man desperately trying to keep his fractured realm together. Ivar split from his family, choosing the life of a warlord instead, raiding everywhere from Plath inside of Caledon territory, to Landen inside of Darten. Oleana ran into the marauders a few times, and each time she barely escaped with her life. She couldn't imagine dealing with a whole army of men like that.

"There's no way he could have gathered his troops and set them on the march that quickly," Oleana said.

"Tensions have been rising between us and Failsea for some time. It started the second Ivar took control after his uncle died,"

"More like was killed by Ivar," Tycho added.

Nadir nodded. "Okay, killed. Ivar has been claiming parts of the Wild Zone as his own, and even making runs on some of our border towns. War between us has been on the brink for months. The attack on Solon just gave him an opportunity he apparently couldn't resist."

"Why didn't you tell me this when we first got here?"

Nadir shuffled his feet, his sword rattling against its scabbard. "It is my problem, not yours. Not everything is your fault, or your concern."

"I could have…," Oleana started but she didn't know what she could have done about it.

"Done what? Nothing. You were too busy trying to take my son away to be worried about the world around you," Nadir snapped back.

"Hey," Lorn said, stepping in between Nadir and his mother's bed.

Oleana opened her mouth to object, but Nadir held up his hand. "I'm sorry that was unnecessary. I know you meant no ill will, and that you understand what I'm going through," he stole a glance at Lorn. "My point was that you can leave Ivar up to us. We have been dealing with him for a long time now."

"Come on, Nadir, even the birthplace of the rangers can't fight a battle on two fronts."

"We aren't alone," Tycho said, "and neither are you. Daycia sent us a communication. She managed to convince Dale of Arimas that the time is now to pick a side. He committed two hundred troops to the yeti hunt, along with all the Arimas Rangers that aren't staying behind to guard Solon."

"I take one little nap and the world goes crazy," Oleana said, rubbing her head.

"I wouldn't call sleeping for three days a nap," Tycho said.

Oleana turned so fast she slid off the edge of her bed, only Lorn's quick hands pushing her shoulders back kept her from hitting the floor. Oleana patted his hands once he planted her safely back on the bed. "Three days. How could you let me sleep for three days?"

"Well, we tried several times to wake you but as soon as your eyes opened you fell right back asleep. Yesterday you mumbled at me, telling me to run from the roses," Lorn said.

"This morning you told me to get you a stiff drink, and make it a double," Nadir added.

"Wait, where's Leith?"

"Don't worry, he's fine. He's with Lillian and Kait getting fitted for armor," Nadir said. "When you feel up to it you're next."

"The last time I wore armor I had a different body. I'm not sure I know how to fight in it anymore."

Tycho smiled, "Well, as you used to tell me, you'll learn."

"Yeah I've been learning a lot of things lately. Like that trick I pulled with Leith." Oleana tested her feet against the ground. She tried putting some of her weight forward, but her legs felt like wet noodles. Whether from the massive energy exchange, or the days in bed, Oleana didn't have the fine motor control over her body the way she wanted. Spending three days in bed had to be her limit. Even if it took a few face plants to the floor, her time for resting was over. "I also learned how to repair the younger Starson over there, and this one won't put me out for days." Oleana managed to get her feet under her and stand, though she had to lean on the bed for balance. Once gravity was pressing down on her lower half, she received a sharp reminder of what three days in bed could do to the bladder. "Okay all of you out now."

"Why?" Lorn said looking concerned.

"I've been in bed for three days, why do you think? Out. Out now!"

CHAPTER EIGHTEEN: IVAR

After an extraordinary amount of time in the bathroom, and a bath long and hot enough to return her skin something akin to normal, Oleana felt like a proper human being again. She wouldn't be outmaneuvering Lorn for a little while yet, but her strength returned at an extraordinary rate. Some of it had to do with the meal Kaithlen and Miriam fixed her, one fit for two queens. With cooks like that in his house, Oleana didn't know how Tycho wasn't twice his size.

With power back in her legs, Oleana wandered out of her room and into a chaotic foyer. Nadir and Tycho were in the middle, swathed in armor from head to toe. Several high-ranking rangers, Oleana could tell by the ranks on their lapels, swarmed around them talking about a thousand things at once.

Oleana reached for her sai, fearing an attack, but she had nothing but borrowed pants on. "What happened? What's going on?" Where's Lorn?" Oleana scanned the room for her son. She needed to know where he was.

Tycho turned to her and smiled. "You shouldn't be out of bed."

"I've been in bed for three days. What's going on?"

"Ivar sent a messenger. He wants to meet and discuss things," Nadir said. He adjusted the strap of his chest piece. "Lorn and Leith needed some air, so Lysander took them to ranger headquarters to get fitted for some much-needed gear." Oleana started to object. "I sent an entire squad to protect them and they aren't going anywhere near the outskirts of the city."

"Well since you have my son secured, I will get my stuff and we can go," Oleana said turning to go back to her room.

"Oh no. No. No. No," Tycho said grabbing her shoulder with his good arm and spinning her around. "No way you're well enough to come with."

Oleana easily twisted out of Tycho's loose grip and spun around him, lifting his axe out of the holder strapped to his back. "I'm perfectly fine," she said tapping him on the shoulder with his pilfered weapon. "I can either go with you under escort, or I can trail behind you, because there's no way I'm letting you guys go alone. Your choice."

Tycho looked to Nadir as if the older man could help.

Nadir sighed, his shoulders slumping in defeat. "Grab your things quickly. We don't want to keep the warlord waiting."

100101

Ivar sucked on his teeth like he'd just eaten the best steak of his life, and half of it was left behind. Oleana didn't much care for the man. His reputation did enough to put her off, but meeting him proved reality was worse. Oleana thought she could have been facing a deep-seated prejudice against the people of Failsea given her upbringing in a previous life. The closer Ivar got, the more Oleana knew her feelings were for him alone.

"This is the infamous guardian, one of the Heirs of Eternity." Ivar scrutinized Oleana with his wide dark-brown eyes, almost black. He had to be the tallest man Oleana ever saw. He made Tycho look small in comparison. Ivar could have looked Cornelius in the eyes, but while the ice god was slender in build, Ivar had a barrel chest that bears would envy. He had sandy-brown curly hair laced with gray at the temples. As he walked by her, too close for comfort, Oleana detected the smell of mint, and the earthy aroma of horses. "I expected you to be more imposing."

"Size isn't everything," Oleana said.

"Trust me, little girl, I'm much more than my size."

"Can we stay on task?" Nadir said, stepping forward and drawing Ivar's attention.

"Negotiating your surrender," Ivar said.

Tycho snorted.

"You think your position's that strong?" Nadir asked snidely. His face was hard, showing no emotion. Oleana admired his stoic demeanor. She wanted to rip Ivar's face off every time his eyes slid over her. She would need a long bath to get the filth of his presence off her.

Ivar sucked at his teeth before answering. "I know that we are not the only problem headed to your door. It's not in your best interest to prolong a conflict with Failsea. Having the Heirs of Eternity in your back pocket can only help you so much."

"This unprovoked act of aggression will garner support from more than the Heirs. You will make enemies of Arismas and Darten as well."

"Unprovoked. No one but you believes that," Ivar said. "Half my farmland is under drought, and you control the largest source of freshwater around for miles. This is an act of survival."

"Not once have you requested aid," Nadir shot back. "It isn't our job to anticipate the needs of your people, it's yours."

"My people need more than the pitiful handout you would have afforded them. I will take control of that river, and it will be the beginning of my revitalization of Failsea. The Wild Zone is already filled with my troops so we can press the siege comfortably for longer than you can afford."

Ivar glanced sideways at Oleana when he mentioned the wild zone. The cocky look on his face worried Oleana. The Wild Zone was a thirty-square mile stretch of untamed land separating Caledon and Failsea, unclaimed by any realm. Most of it was forest and marsh land, with one jewel at the center. The city of Evermore was as large in scope as Central City, and more ancient than Solon. It was the one place all the ultras, no matter where they spent the last several hundred years, called home.

At the heart of Evermore stood the Crystal Tower. According to the history books at the Thousand Years Library, it was the first structure built on Euphoria. It served as the control tower for the particle cloud the Twelve let loose on the planet, holding the building blocks for all the earth-based lifeforms that now called Euphoria home.

Now it served the same purpose as the Library, a mecca for those brave enough to make the trek to get closer to the Twelve and partake of the information they are willing to give out. Daycia protected the Library, and the Tower had its own protector, the Crystal Ultra, Kameke.

There weren't many legends that Oleana put much stock in, being one herself. Even her idols, the Twelve disappointed more and more each time she talked to them. Only Daycia proved to be greater than even the legend could express. That gave Oleana hope that the only other person she longed to meet would live up to the stories told about her. Oleana would make it to Evermore, and the Crystal Tower. No one would be able to stand in her way, not Ivar, not Cornelius.

"Cornelius got to you. Made a deal," Oleana said, understanding smacking her in the face. "How else could you be so perfectly timed with the yetis? And know so much about me."

"This is about the welfare…," Ivar started.

"I know you won't believe me," Oleana said cutting him off, "but you can't trust Cornelius. He'll never see any human as an equal, despite the claims he may have made. Your cooperating with him will only delay your subjugation, not prevent it."

"Don't interrupt me," Ivar boomed, getting so close to Oleana the metal buckle on his belt pressed into her bellybutton.

"Don't presume to tell me my fate. You know nothing." Ivar didn't give Oleana a chance to respond, turning to Nadir. "Your pet demi-goddess is going to cost you more than control of the Alignment River. Or you can show some sense and give up the mouth of the river and focus your attentions elsewhere."

Nadir hesitated and Oleana wanted to step in and say what had to be said. It was Nadir's territory, and his people. No matter how hard Oleana wanted to tell Ivar to go jump in a deep dark hole, she kept her mouth shut.

"I don't wish a conflict between us, but if your troops cross into Caledon I will be within my rights to consider it an act of war, and react accordingly. You might want to consider what chaos your people will be thrown into if you're killed in battle. As far as I know you have no legitimate heirs. How many of your relatives will take a chunk of Failsea for themselves?"

It was Ivar's turn to look uncomfortable. "I look forward to meeting you on the battlefield, Starson," Ivar said. The big man turned with a rustle of leather and fur.

For Oleana it was satisfying watching him leave in anger, but she couldn't help but worry about what that moment would cost her later. Ivar didn't seem like the kind of man that let his anger rise without causing damage. From the narrowing of Nadir's eyes, he felt the same.

Tycho was the first to speak once they had the room to themselves. He still held his injured arm close to his body, even though he'd done away with the sling for the meeting. "That didn't go as bad as I expected."

"I don't think we were at the same meeting," Oleana said.

"After Nadir threatened him, and called him a childless bastard, I thought for sure things were going to come to blows. We should count ourselves lucky we escaped without bruises," Tycho said.

Nadir rubbed at his chin like something was biting him. "I had hoped to force him to slow his troops, to hesitate at the border.

That way the Heirs could slip through while Ivar was distracted with us. Now my impetuous tongue has bungled it. Oleana I'm sorry. I just couldn't stand here and let that man insult everything important to me."

Oleana laid her hand on his shoulder. "Listen, Cornelius already talked to Ivar. There was no chance of us buying any space. I thank you for trying."

"Ivar is eager for a fight, and we haven't heard from Daycia. What are we going to do now?" Tycho asked.

"We do as Ivar said, get ready to meet him on the battlefield, and trust the Twelve that Daycia and her troops will be there when we need them," Nadir said.

CHAPTER NINETEEN: WAR

The war room at ranger headquarters was stuffed to the brim with people. The octagon room was set up much like a small theater, with an angled floor slanting down to accommodate five rows of seats surrounding an inset stage. Armored and armed men and women from all over Caledon gathered in the space, filling it with the noise of swords clanking against scabbards, shields knocking against chair legs, and voices talking hurriedly about grave matters.

Lysander held himself washboard straight, forcing air in and out of his lungs in slow, steady breaths. The air felt thick and hot, as if there wasn't enough to for all the greedy bodies. Lysander followed his father down the aisle feeling hundreds of eyes following his every move.

He was hyper-aware of the swollen tongue taking up more than its fair share in his mouth, and the dark circles under his eyes, all side-effects of his recent seizure. His body still felt shaky, as if at any moment it would fall apart. Lysander couldn't help but wonder how many of those eyes looking on now knew his secret, knew his weakness. How many of them were now judging him?

His father slowed when they were steps away from the stage, forcing Lysander to pull up short. Lorn, who was behind him, bumped into him. Lysander glanced at the boy, nodding to him. Everything was okay. They were all suffering under the effects of the last few day's troubles.

Even though Leith was clearly on the mend, watching him come that close to death shook Lysander to the core. He barely knew the man, yet they shared a connection that was beyond his understanding. On top of it, Lysander had been given a title and responsibility that he couldn't possibly live up to.

Lorn may have known for years what he was meant to do, but coming against the harsh reality of it visibly shook the boy. They had no time to deal with those feelings. There were more important things to worry about. Caledon was on the brink of war, and in this room history would be decided.

"So many people," Lorn said, looking around distractedly. His eyes darted from place to place, as if he were trying to take in every detail, but absorbed none of it.

"This is how our realm works," Lysander said leaning in close to keep the conversation between the two of them. "My father may be the leader, but matters of war have always been decided by committee. All the provincial leaders, eighty-eight in total, plus the leaders of infrastructure, including agriculture, finance, transportation, they all get a say. Of course, they all bring aides and analysts, advisors of different sorts. It quickly becomes a circus."

"Stay here," Nadir said pointing to the first row of seats.

Lysander nodded to his father. He was more than happy not to stand at his side on the stage. This was too big to be ruined by his uneasy nerves. Tycho's family was already in place. Lysander's Aunt Kaithlen, Miriam and her husband Garth, who wore the steel gray dragon scale armor of ranger leadership. Lysander greeted them with a nod. It wasn't the place for anything else. His mother sat on the end. He spared her a kiss on the cheek. She stared at him, through him, in that way that only she could manage.

"I'm okay, Mom," he said, anticipating her question. She smiled and nodded, but Lysander could tell she knew the truth. He was very far from being all right.

Nadir took the stage, Tycho on his right side - arm still in a sling, and Oleana on his left. Nadir knocked his fist against the podium in front of him three times, and the murmur of the crowd died. Nadir turned a slow circle making sure everyone's eyes were on him.

"As many of you know," Nadir started, his voice loud, and strong and steady, "Ivar has set his troops on the move and they're headed for the mouth of the Alignment River. I've made it clear that such an aggressive move will mean war between our two realms. Ivar is intent to follow through with his plans, despite my attempts to negotiate a more peaceful solution." Nadir gave the crowd time to absorb the news. The crowd held themselves still.

This was not a group prone to panic. They knew the pronouncement that was coming. "I have no intention of letting the troops of Failsea get anywhere near our river." A roar of approval erupted. Lysander locked eyes with his father as they waited for the noise to die down.

Lysander knew what his father would say next, needed to say, but he wasn't ready to be exposed in front of so many. Despite having used his new ability to a mixed result, Lysander still had trouble believing the truth himself.

Nadir sucked in a deep breath. Lysander could see his father physically steel himself up for what was to come next. "Our land is not all Ivar and his troops are threatening. Our realm and others have been on the decline because of the ultras, Cornelius and Emmaray. Many of you know about what happened in Solon and heard about the yetis being on the move. This isn't a random occurrence. Cornelius is after the Heirs of Eternity."

Nadir ushered Oleana forward. She rolled up her sleeve to expose the brand on her arm. Lysander, Lorn, and Leith stood up to show theirs off as well, turning and holding their arms up to give everyone a clear view. Lysander's heart was in his throat. He wanted to pull the blanket of his old life over his head and forget the last few days had darkened his path. He expected to be rejected as a fool and a liar.

Shock rippled through the crowd like a bitter, cold wind. Nadir continued before things could get out of control. "We have long awaited their arrival and the hope for a better world that they can bring. Our land and our future is being threatened. If we enter this fight, I needed everyone to know the full stakes."

"I ask a lot of you. If we enter this fight, it won't be quick, but victory will mean peace and security on a scale we've never seen before. So, I put this question to you, will we side with the Heirs of Eternity, block the invaders at our borders, Ivar on one side and Cornelius on the other? Do we go to war?"

Again the murmuring started, but people were gathering in small groups to talk amongst themselves. Lysander watched as his father came up off the stage. It was time to let the people decide, without their ruler hanging over them. Oleana followed Nadir, and Lysander was quick on her heels, urging Lorn and Leith to join them. Lysander knew his mother would stay. She was the daughter of a provincial leader, her voice needed to be heard.

Once out in the hall, Oleana leaned against the far wall. She patted Lorn's back. A look of calm spread across the boy's face. Lysander found himself staring at the doors that closed behind them. He wished he could will his people to make the right choice.

"This isn't how I wanted things to go," Oleana said, breaking the silence between them. "Cornelius is stirring up this war just to get at us, and your people are caught in the middle of it. We should have left as soon as Lysander was activated. We could have sorted the rest on the go." She pulled at her hair, a wild and frustrated look in her eyes.

"The war between Caledon and Failsea has been building for a long time. I prefer sooner, rather than later," Nadir said. He grabbed Oleana's hand and gave it a squeeze. "I'd also prefer to fight this battle with you at my side, than without."

"That's just weird on so many levels," Lorn said stepping away from the two of them.

Oleana's face turned a shade of red Lysander would have thought impossible for someone with skin as brown as hers. She stepped back from Nadir, putting several feet between them. Lysander looked away, feeling as awkward as Lorn expressed he was.

"We have to leave," Oleana said, avoiding Nadir's eyes.

"It is better if we fight as a united front," Nadir objected.

"No, no, no. If we leave, Cornelius will pull his troops from the fight and follow us, leaving you to deal with Ivar alone. I didn't want it to be like this, trust me. I have spent years preparing Lorn for what must come next, and I would love at least six months to get the other two ready. It's not fair to throw it at them on the run, but that's what we are left with. Staying here isn't safe for anyone. Once the three are crowned we can legitimately rally help from other realms."

"Oleana please, that's risky going out there without the protection you have here."

"No Nadir, we must leave." Oleana stood to her full height, raising her chin, daring Nadir to challenge her further. She met his eyes, in an intense stare. "You have to think about more than me, more than your son. This is my decision as the guardian."

Nadir looked to Lorn, who only shrugged. Before anyone could speak, the doors opened and Tycho poked his massive head out.

"They've decided."

"That was fast," Lorn stuttered, suddenly anxious.

"We go to war," Tycho finished.

100101

Tycho and Nadir were busy coordinating troops and making arrangements to prepare the realm for war, leaving the four Heirs of Eternity to finish what Oleana started four days ago. Oleana was happy to have them out of her hair while she did what she could for Lysander.

The second she mentioned her plans Nadir and Lillian cut into her like she'd asked permission to slice him open and take a look inside. Oleana knew there was risk but Lysander was a soldier, they'd been training him half his life to do a job with an elevated amount of risk. She tried her best to assure them it was the best course, and her miraculous healing of Leith only sealed her case.

"Are you sure you're clear on what needs to be done?" she asked Lorn for the third time since they'd took up standing in the back garden of the Residence.

"I stir up a low level electrical storm right down on your head. It travels from you into Lysander giving his system the jolt necessary to reset itself to allow the smart particle cloud to fully integrate with his biological systems eliminating the seizures."

"Do you understand half of the things you just said?" Lysander asked.

"I understand what I have to do," Lorn replied, puffing out his chest with confidence.

Leith, standing at the start of the walkway closest to the Residence, shook his head. "Dangerous game this. Sure you don't want to practice? Better question, why I'm out here?"

"I don't need practice. I healed you. I can do this. Don't worry," Oleana replied dismissively, looking at Lysander.

"How do you keep from getting electrocuted?" Lysander asked.

"I can copy Lorn's immunity, at least temporarily."

"Is this reset going to hurt? It sounds rather painful," Lysander questioned, skepticism twinkling in his wide eyes.

"It shouldn't," Oleana said plainly, not wanting to sugarcoat things.

"What does that mean?" Lysander said raising his eyebrows, backing up a step.

"Dang it Leith, see what you've done?" Oleana yelled. Leith shrugged. Oleana put her hand on Lysander's shoulder, looking into his shining gray eyes. "Listen Lysander, I promise you as I did your father, that I would not be putting you or Lorn through this if I wasn't sure that - one it was as safe as possible, and two that it was the only way to make you whole. Every seizure you have does damage to your body. Unfortunately, our presence will only mean an increase in seizures as your powers continue to grow." Oleana held on to the young man hoping to impress upon him how serious this was. "After much arguing and explaining, your parents agreed to this because they came to understand how vital this is, not just for your future as an Heir but for your continued health. If you choose not to do it, that's fine. It's your body, your choice, but know that it's a lifesaving measure."

Lysander held his shoulders back and stood up straighter. "I do not fear what must be done." he said.

"Good, now you hold my hands. Lorn you do your thing, and Leith stay over there and stay silent." Oleana took in several big breaths knowing that despite what she told Lysander the reset would likely hurt her a great deal. She was going to have to keep calm and work through the pain. With Lysander's hands firmly in hers, Oleana was as ready as she could be. "Okay Lorn, whenever you're ready."

Oleana knew Lorn better than he knew himself. She also knew the massive power that lurked behind his innocent face, that wide smile and wide green eyes. She knew that power well enough to be able to rewrite her own genetic makeup to match it.

Cold air rushed in, and the sky crackled with pent up energy. Oleana opened herself up to the full powers of the guardian, the many lives she lived, the deep-seated connections she felt to the men around her, and the world beyond them. The first bolt of lightning cut through the air and Oleana tensed, but it wasn't meant for her. Oleana focused on the sequence of things she had to do to make this work. She would have to run through a lot of calculations in a millisecond to get things right.

The air sizzled, and lightning struck Oleana. Without thinking about it, without meaning to, Oleana pulled on the power of all three of her charges. She networked four separate brains to complete different parts of the same task. Lorn was in charge of keeping the wild energy under control, circling it through Oleana's body until the time was right to share. Lysander had to map out his own nervous system, find and highlight the damaged areas. Leith, ever the reluctant participant, calculated how much of an electrical jolt Lysander needed, leaving Oleana to absorb the information from the others, and act accordingly. A task she found difficult, as her body burned from the inside out.

Lysander gave her the map. Leith came right behind him with the calculations. Oleana took control from Lorn, splintering an eighth of the energy off and sending it toward Lysander, while forcing the rest to ground in a path that bypassed her heart.

Just as she had with the Twelve, Oleana could no longer see the surface world of bone and flesh, but she looked inward and saw the ones and zeros that mapped out the being currently called Lysander. The electricity was a compact group of ones that shoved its way through the neatly arrayed lattice work of Lysander's nervous system. Oleana gently nudged it through the path she wanted, toward the knots of tangled code in Lysander's brain that kept him from being whole.

She could see the damage the seizures had already done. There were gaps in the lattice, areas where branches spun off into nothing, and cracks in the framework of others. Compared to the billions of connections, the gaps were miniscule, but many more looked on the verge of collapse and it would be a cascading effect where whole sections would be broken off.

The electricity careened through Lysander, finding the knotted lines of code and exploding on impact, breaking apart the knots and creating a swirling eddy of numbers. Vaguely Oleana recognized the sound of screaming. Sound was unimportant, an ineffective means of energy transfer, so it was ignored.

Oleana knew what Lysander's latticework of neurons should look like. She guided the whirling lines into the correct shape. At first it resisted, preferring the disorganized jumble it had been in before, but Oleana forced it into line, and equilibrium restored itself.

With the task completed, Oleana tried to return to herself. She missed the direct route and found herself looking at the back of her body through Leith's eyes. He/she looked at her with concern and attraction. He turned away as soon as it flared up, but Oleana felt it, and the shock of it pushed her into the next body.

The weight of new armor on his/her skin made moving a challenge. It also made them feel stronger. Lorn reached for his mother, but his limbs felt like they were stuck in tar. His mind still buzzed with the massive amount of information that swirled through his synapsis. If worry wasn't constricting his chest he would have been more excited. No matter how hard he tried not to worry about his mother, to put on the brave face worthy of a future king, Lorn couldn't help the dread that seized him every time she put herself in danger. He couldn't lose the only parent he knew.

Oleana's heart broke for Lorn, and this dichotomy sent her hurtling toward Lysander. For the first time, she stared into her own eyes. She could see the bags under them. The premature wrinkles, the pinched, sour look etched on her face. Oleana recoiled from the truth of herself. Lysander held her firm.

Looking through his eyes, she gained understanding. He knew that every line told the story of a weighty decision made for the greater good of others. The bags were the result of hard days and short nights doing whatever she could to protect her boys. She had the face of a warrior, a leader, and Lysander respected her, admired her, longed to be like her. With things made clear, Oleana found herself drifting back down the pipeline to her own body.

She was on the ground. Oleana knew that for sure. She could feel the blades of wet grass rubbing against her arms and through the thin cotton of her trousers. How long she'd been there she didn't know. She vaguely sensed the others around her, heard a groan off to her left, felt movement on her right.

"Is everyone still alive? Still in one piece?" She asked, looking around still a bit dazed and trying to get her bearings to move her body.

"What was that? I mean it was crazy, and amazing, and...*goodness*! What was that?"

Oleana sat up in a hurry. The cadence and energy behind the words were all Lorn, but the voice was Lysander's. He was sitting cross-legged on the grass, staring off into the horizon, eyes unfocused. Lysander seemed to sense eyes on him and came back to himself. He cleared his throat.

"Ummm, I don't understand what just happened," Lysander said, perplexed.

"You sounded like the boy," Leith said. He was stretched out on the ground, hands under his head, legs crossed at the ankles.

"That's not what I sound like. Is it? No. Well, maybe. Goodness." Lorn clasped his hand over his mouth to stifle the stream of excited gibberish.

"Okay, so we're obviously suffering some unexpected consequences, but nothing we can't handle," Oleana said, trying to calm everyone. "The important question is, did it work"

All eyes turned to Lysander.

"I'm not some trained dog who barks on command," he insisted.

"It's a nice day, we could just lay around in the sun for a while. Or talk about what just happened, because for a second there I could read everybody's mind, but the thoughts got all jumbled so I couldn't tell what came from who..."

"Lorn," Leith said, cutting the boy off with the same strict tone that Oleana usually used.

Oleana didn't know whether to be offended that someone else stole her line, or grateful that Lorn was reeled in.

"Felt weird," Leith said, "like someone else -"

"- someone else talking through you," Lysander finished. Leith nodded his head.

"One problem at a time, please," Oleana said. She racked her brain for any clue as to what was going on with them, but none of the new information the Twelve gave her hinted at anything like it. Seeing as Lysander's cure was more important, she pushed it aside to talk to the Twelve about later.

"Fine," Lysander said.

He stood and Oleana's heart skipped a beat, fearing the seizure that might be one its way. At the back of her mind was a shadow memory where she remembered the taste of copper on her tongue and the systematic tensing of all her muscles. Oleana pushed the haunting vision away, refusing to be scared by another's nightmare.

Lysander took in a deep breath, puffing his chest out. Upon exhaling, he stretched his long arms toward the ground, his fingers dancing as if he were playing some invisible instrument. The grass around Oleana started to move. She pulled her legs up to her chest to be out of the way.

The blades of grass that were once smaller than her little finger, grew larger than her arm. Four blades twisted together, creating a thick braid, arching over Oleana and connecting with three other braids to form a beautiful canopy, with beautiful inverted lilac blooms opening up right above her head. Oleana looked around to see that Lorn and Leith had their own canopies.

"Wow. Your level of control is astounding," Oleana said in a hushed voiced filled with awe, brushing the flowers with the tips of her fingers. Her skin felt hypersensitive. She could map out every bump and groove on the petal. She could see the purple and yellow trail of perfume each flower gave off.

"I see smells," Leith said.

"It will pass," Oleana assured him even though she had no idea if it would. "It will pass," she repeated knowing Lorn was about to object. She didn't just anticipate his objection because she knew him so well. The sense went beyond that. She could feel the words forming in his mind. "Lysander, how do you feel?" She asked knowing the answer.

"Ha! I feel fine. No, I feel amazing! I feel like I have been half-blind all my life and now I can see. This is incredible!" Lysander bent his knees and jumped up and down like a child at play. He thrust his hands into the air and a hundred flowers blossomed, spilling white flecks of pollen into the air as thick as snowfall.

"For you maybe, but it took me years to develop the kind of control you just happened to stumble upon," Lorn said, swatting away pollen. His tone said it was mostly teasing, but Oleana could see the streak of green in his sound waves. Jealousy didn't suit him. "I'm glad you feel so good, but can we please talk about that whole sharing minds thing we just did, or are still doing?" Lorn said. He turned around in the patch of grass Lysander had manipulated. "I heard everyone's thoughts at once. Leith, you should be ashamed of yourself thinking like that, and Mom," Lorn's face went pale. His eyes welled up with tears. Leith sat up and peered at Oleana, shock etched into every crease of his face. Even Lysander looked over at her with a mixture of awe and pity.

Oleana knew what they had gleaned from her mind. It was a secret she was hoping never to have to confront. Now the most important people in the world to her knew. In some ways it was a relief. She never liked hiding things from Lorn, but she also didn't want Leith burdened with the knowledge.

"Mom, why?" Lorn asked. He rushed to her side taking her hands in his. "Why would you do that and not tell me? How could you give up your last life without so much as a word?"

Oleana wanted to look at Leith, wanted to explain it to him, but she couldn't tear her eyes away from Lorn.

"I couldn't let him die. Let any of you die. Not again, not ever again. You've now been in my head; you might be able to understand. In Solon, less than a century ago I watched you die, the yetis having ripping your chest open. I'd never seen so much blood. I was so distracted and in shock Cornelius managed to sneak up on me and he ran me through without hesitation." Oleana finally tore her eyes from Lorn and laid them on Lysander. He fidgeted under her gaze.

"That second time around I was determined to be more vigilant, stronger, faster. When I found you I was all about the mission, finding the others, getting to Evermore. Then we ran into the stupid farmer's revolt in Failsea." Oleana punched the ground in frustration. "I tried to convince you it was none of our business but you insisted on playing hero. Gave me some sob story about how you grew up on a farm and understood the plight of the people. I took something sharp to the back of the head and woke up in a different body. I heard a rumor those farmers built statues to us." Oleana inhaled sharply. Reliving her past mistakes was exhausting but it felt good to let it out, let go of her secrets.

"That third time around I met Nadir, and Tycho," she smiled remembering her old friends the way they were before the years came between them. "I loved it in Caledon, becoming a ranger. Leaving felt like dying all over again. I found the other versions of Leith and Lysander, but my heart was still in Caledon. When we were pulled toward Gaeth we got on the fastest ship we could afford and headed south. The Fire Ultra Emmaray learned about our arrival. You have never felt fear until you watch a lava ball hurtling toward your unprotected boat." Oleana rubbed her eyes, trying to banish the pain of the past. Her chest was on fire remembering the flames that once licked at her skin. Her voice cracked and she had to clear her throat before starting again. "I gave my last life to Leith because I had no other choice. I couldn't watch any of you die again. Please understand."

Lorn bit his lip. Moments passed as they stared into each other as if trapped in a trance. Oleana felt the others looking at her, judging her. And she in turn was desperate for their approval. She needed them to understand what they meant to her.

"I understand," Lorn said breaking the tension. He let go of Oleana's hands, straightening himself out. He wiped the tears from his eyes, replacing it with his usual smile. "I don't like it but I understand. I just wish you would realize you don't have to do these things on your own."

"Lorn, I'm sorry." Oleana hated having nothing but feeble words to offer her son. She had no grand gesture that would fix the space between them.

Oleana glanced over at Leith. The muscles of his jaw were working overtime as if he were chewing over the right words to say. For Oleana there was nothing he needed to say but she waited, giving him the space to deal with what all of them now knew.

Leith moved through the branches of his canopy to stand beside Lorn. He laid his hand on the boy's shoulder and looked down at Oleana. "Hope I prove worthy of such sacrifice."

Lysander joined them, laying his arm on Leith's shoulder. "Together we'll finish what you started."

Oleana stood, completing the circle by putting her arm on Lysander's and taking Lorn's hand. The link between them surged to the forefront once again. This time it was controlled. Oleana didn't feel lost in the others. She felt connected to them, strengthened by them.

"I could use a drink," the four of them said in perfect unison.

Oleana snatched her hands back, rubbing them against her legs to rid them of the lingering tingling from the sudden disconnect. "That's not how I sound," she insisted.

"Yes it is," the others replied.

"That's just creepy."

"Time to go back in," Leith said, voicing the words Oleana thought.

Looking at the others, Oleana again lost track of herself and looked at the world through four pairs of eyes, took in air through eight lungs, balanced on eight feet. Then she took a shaky step forward and tripped over a rock. The pain was all Oleana's from her stubbed toe to the sharp crack through her knees as she hit the ground.

"Mom, you alright?"

Oleana used Lorn's offered arm to leverage herself up. "I'll survive. It will pass," she said with less confidence.

100101

Ivar found himself feeling like a scared underling in his own tent, as he regaled Cornelius with the tale of his encounter with Nadir and the guardian. Ivar noticed the change in Cornelius' demeanor as soon as he mentioned the guardian. The Ice God went from half listening as he reclined in his chair, to staring at Ivar with an intensity that worried the King of Failsea.

"She tried to scare you into submission?" Cornelius asked with imperious arrogance.

Ivar nodded, afraid to say too much.

"Some things never change. Did she have any of the other Heirs with her?"

"No."

"How did she react when you made it clear your intent was to go to war?"

"She showed no signs of worry," Ivar said. He didn't like being interrogated, but dared not mention it.

"Curse the Twelve, she must have found the fourth Heir. They will make a move for Evermore. We must implement a change. I need you to hold the border, and all of your troops, in the Wild Zone must barricade the roads leading to the city."

"No, our priority must be the Alignment," Ivar replied.

Cornelius stood and grabbed Ivar by the front of his shirt, "You shortsighted, inbred, fool. Do you not understand that if the Heirs get to Evermore and secure a base of power, it doesn't matter how many battles you win against Starson and Caledon, you will have lost the war! The Heirs will unite the other realms against you, and crush you. There will be nothing I can do for you then."

"I-I didn't mean to..." Ivar stammered. "Our deal was that you would help me get water for my people."

Cornelius smiled. He let go of Ivar and stepped back. "Ivar, you help me capture the guardian, and not only will I help you capture the river, but I'll make sure your people have an overabundance of new land to cultivate and explore. We capture the guardian and everything else will fall into place."

Ivar swallowed hard. The guardian's words echoed in the back of his mind. She said he couldn't trust Cornelius. Ivar didn't trust anyone. He could use Cornelius and that's all that mattered. Ivar would have his men capture the guardian and then Cornelius would owe him all of Caledon not just the river. After that, Ivar would part ways with Cornelius, permanently if need be.

"Capture the Guardian, aye, my men are up to the task."

CHAPTER TWENTY: BORDER

Daycia dismounted, deciding it best to walk beside her horse for a while, reins in hand. Looking around and seeing a landscape unfamiliar to her felt disconcerting. She hadn't been this far from Solon in over a century. She'd made a life in Arimas, built a legend. There was no need to leave. The world was falling apart, and all she could do was protect her corner of it. Solon was the only constant in her life. People lived and died, but her city grew with her.

"Are you all right?" Paley asked, pulling beside Daycia.

She looked up at her apprentice. "Fine. Just needed to stretch my legs. Been a long time since I've traveled so far on horseback. This body can only take so much abuse." Daycia smiled. "I should be asking you that. I'm not the one with the bandaged ribs. You shouldn't have come."

Paley waved her off. "I've had worse." She dismounted to walk beside her mentor. "You took the brunt of that avalanche. You could have stayed in Solon."

"I've been part of the story of the Heirs of Eternity from the beginning. I could not stand on the sidelines now. Don't worry about me. I'm up for this fight," Daycia waved the younger woman's concern away. She looked at her apprentice, amazed again at the girl's resilience. Paley received her fair share of bruises from their encounter at the mountain, yet she hadn't slowed a step. Daycia on the other hand, felt like she was testing the limits of her extraordinary body.

"You're going to have to prove that sooner than you would have liked," Paley said, pointing in front of the them off the road they were following.

Daycia followed her student, leaving her mount behind. Together they approached what caught Paley's eye. There was an indentation in the ground where something heavy crushed the grass, and judging by the shriveled blades, it was cold. Daycia saw the bits of yeti fur, then spotted the footprints in the soggy ground.

"They must have bedded here for the night," Paley said. She touched the print. "They can't be more than an hour ahead of us."

"Days of tracking them, and all we get is some abandoned campgrounds and footprints in the dirt," Zyair complained, coming up behind Daycia.

Tall, dark, and brooding, Zyair hovered over Daycia's shoulder, temporarily distracting her. He jumped down off his horse in a clatter of sword against armor, his stride strong and aggressive.

"Well it took until we got inside the border of Caledon, but we are close," Paley said.

The corner of Zyair's mouth turned up in the beginnings of a smile, "So what do we intend to do about it?"

It didn't take much for Daycia to guess at what the ranger wanted to do, pick up the pace and descend on the yetis with all the fighting power they could muster up. Days of chasing shadows had Daycia wishing for a more direct approach herself. She'd been the one in the cave, seen the weapons the yetis were making. She knew how destructive a yeti army could be. Still, caution tugged her in a different direction.

"I don't believe I'm the one saying this, but we would be better suited heading straight for Central City and Alwen-,"

"Oleana," Paley corrected.

"Yes, Oleana," Daycia said shaking her head. "She needs our support more than we need to hunt yetis."

Zyair frowned. He pushed at the embers of the dead fire with his foot, then followed the path of the tracks. "From what I can see, they're staying close to the road. They must have run into civilization along the way. You really suggesting we leave defenseless civilians to take care of them on their own?"

Daycia wanted to smack him for being so smug. Of course she wouldn't let that happened. "If we see trouble on our way, then we will of course stop to help, but we will not be detouring to satisfy your insatiable need for fighting."

"As you wish," Zyair acquiesced, giving Daycia an exaggerated bow.

100101

Travelling through Caledon was like traveling in an artist's representation of the perfect landscape. Dirt paths blended into graveled roads wide enough for two carts to pass each other safely. Gently rolling hills dotted the landscape, peppered with delicate blooming flowers.

If it wasn't for the weight of thick leather armor with its metal reinforcements dragging her shoulders down, and the tension of those around her, Daycia could have believed she was going on a leisurely stroll through the countryside.

They passed several small villages with no incidents and Daycia started to hope that the yetis had retreated back into the hills where they belonged. Daycia started to believe she would reunite with Oleana, providing the support the Heirs needed. A panicked shriek cut through the air, dispelling all such hopes.

"Yetis?" Zyair asked.

Daycia nodded her head. What else could it be?

"Do we fight?"

Daycia looked back at the line of troops behind them. More than a hundred men and women were following. They had joined to fight, agreeing to leave their homes behind and throw in with the Heirs of Eternity, and a better future. They weren't crossing the realm to put down a few yetis. They were there to change the future.

"We split up. Ten come with us, Paley you lead the rest to Central City. We will catch up."

"I don't want to leave you," Paley objected, her eyes so stubborn.

"This is more important. They need to get to Central City. I need you to do this."

Paley nodded. Zyair picked his men. Daycia gave Paley one last look before following Zyair and his group toward the noise. Daycia didn't want to fight but one always seemed to find her.

Over the first hill Daycia drew up short, not able to believe what her eyes were seeing. She saw a sea of red, but not in the way she had expected. Twenty men and women were rounding up a pack of the yetis that had invaded the farming town nestled in the valley. Daycia never thought she would see the day when ten yetis could be herded together like docile sheep.

At the heart of the soldiers was a woman on horseback. Daycia smiled thinking it to be Oleana, then she saw the long dark hair spilling over the woman's breastplate. She looked to be the same height as Oleana, and same lean build, but it was not Oleana.

One of the yeti broke through the containment ring. Zyair charged forward, his built-up momentum nearly carrying him through the yeti. Instead, the beast got a face full of horseflesh. Daycia was quick on his heels. When the yeti found its feet, red streaming down its face, Daycia finished it off with a sharp blow to the head with her baton. The dull thud of metal against bone rattled Daycia down in her teeth. The yeti hit the ground like a felled tree.

"Nice job," the mystery woman said, pulling up beside them. Her horse snorted as if to say he wasn't as impressed.

"Looks like you have the situation under control," Daycia replied looking around. The rest of the yetis were sufficiently corralled. A few of the villagers were brave enough to venture forth from the wooden building they had taken shelter in.

The more she saw of the place, the more Daycia realized the little border town would look just as at home in Arismas. Caledon was supposed to be the land of glass and steel, yet most of the houses in front of her had thatched roofs and wooden siding. Seeing such familiar things let Daycia start to feel that the outside world wasn't as strange and unknowable as she had feared.

"This is the third group we've run into," the woman said, sliding down of her mount with the grace of dancer. She flicked her hair out of her face, exposing her startlingly sharp green eyes. "They're getting harder to control. Any help we can get is much appreciated."

"We are at your service my lady," Zyair said. Daycia cut him a stern look. The yeti problem couldn't distract them. Oleana needed them. "Where are my manners? Daycia of Solon, let me introduce you to Lady Lillian Starson, first lady of Caledon."

Daycia smiled. "We were actually on our way to see you and your husband. We brought some help."

Lillian looked past Daycia to the ten men lined up behind her. "Your communication said a contingent of troops. Thanks for the help, but ten men aren't going to solve our problems."

"The rest are headed for Central City. We didn't want them getting sidetracked," Daycia explained.

"Well you couldn't have come at a better time. We are stretched thin. I've been doing my best to keep things under control, but with so many of our troops gone it's hard to keep up."

Daycia looked around. "I don't understand, where is Nadir? Where's Oleana? And the other Heirs?"

"They're on the march to Evermore."

CHAPTER TWENTY-ONE: SPLIT

"I haven't been part of a squad in over thirty years," Oleana said, trying to scratch her head through her new helmet.

Lysander nodded, barely listening. His mind was on fire trying to sort through all his conflicting thoughts. The current crisis forced him into action without a moment to consider all that happened last week.

Now on the slow march to the border, with the wild zone, was the first time he got to turn his thoughts inwards since he'd been cured. Even then he could still feel the tendrils of the others' minds wrapped around his own, like some phantom limb. Lysander felt a faint melancholy when thinking about how big his world had been when joined to them, the power he tasted.

The march to Evermore brought its own type of stress. Everyone tried to stay on high alert but after two days of inactivity, even the most seasoned soldier found it hard to remain tense. Lysander's mind wandered, dreaming up future dangers and, mourning the life left behind.

He feared that the reset had changed him in some fundamental way. He waited for the new version of himself to seize control and banish him to some deep dark abyss where he became an observer of his own life. Oleana tried to assure him that it wasn't a shift in personality, just a reset of his body. Lysander didn't know if he could trust what she said. Their melding of personalities left its own shadows.

When he looked at his mother, he loved her as his mother, the same as always, but he also held some jealousy toward her and the life she'd managed to secure for herself. He knew those alien feelings were Oleana talking, but knowing in his head didn't make the emotion in his heart any less powerful. Separating his truth from the ghosts of the other Heirs clinging to his insides proved harder than Oleana once claimed it would be.

Lysander had to admit the change in his body was significant. He'd always felt awkward in his own body. No matter how hard he trained, how disciplined he became, his body didn't respond the way he wanted it to. Lysander couldn't put words to what the change was in himself, but he felt different, whole for the first time.

"Troops spotted eastward," came the call down the ranks.

Lysander panned right to confirm the sighting. The fire squad soldier had good eyes. Lysander caught the dim outline of movement downhill as heavy feet kicked up the dirt as they moved.

"Tighten ranks. Shields on the eastward," Lysander ordered. The command made it down the line and the members of his squad moved seamlessly into their new positions.

"Looks like Ivar's men," Oleana said peering out her brass binoculars. She swung her gaze along the horizon. "No sign of the yetis."

"How many are we looking at?" Lysander asked. He needed to know whether it was more feasible to fight it out and eliminate the threat, or try to outrun his foe.

"Ummm, crap. Incoming," Oleana responded.

Lysander looked up to see the mass of arrows hit the peak of their arch before heading back down toward them. The line of soldiers tightened around him, forcing him to rub shoulders with Oleana and others. The shielders lifted their namesakes high, blocking his view. Lysander flattened his body low over his mount and put his free hand over the back of his neck, hoping the dragon scale armor would protect him if anything got through.

Arrows beat against the line of shields like pebbles against a brick wall. Lysander imagined himself being soothed by the rhythmic clacking if the circumstances were less deadly. He heard several cries of pain down the line but there was no room to look, or to attend the wounded until the onslaught was over. Lysander grit his teeth hoping whoever was hit could last until the break came.

When the noise ebbed, the shields came down and the archers were ready to return fire. Ivar's troops were in full retreat. Lysander staid his men knowing the enemy was out of lethal range. Letting arrows fly would be nothing more than a waste of ammo. Lysander cursed the cowardice of his enemy.

"Report," Nadir ordered from the head of the line.

Lysander looked over his squad. One of his men suffered a small abrasion as an arrow slipped between the gap where the arm and chest piece met.

"Moon reporting one minor," Lysander yelled.

The other squad leaders sounded off, "Two minor. No injuries. Three minor." The attack seemed overall ineffective. Lysander questioned the purpose behind it.

"Repair on the move," Nadir ordered. The troops slid back into arrowhead configuration at a more cautious pace. Lysander pushed away his idle wondering and kept his eye on the horizon.

100101

The sun was waning, and with it Oleana's patience. Five blitz attacks and the entire camp was feeling the strain. At first Oleana couldn't see the reasoning behind the fight and run tactics. Now that her nerves were shot and her behind was chaffed from riding through the day without a break she saw the endgame, wear them down so they'd be easy to pick off when the real attack came.

When Nadir finally called for a rest, Oleana collapsed against the fallen tree that she and the other members of her squad had made their seat. Every inch of her was sore and tired. They hadn't eaten all day and she was starved, but didn't feel up to expending the energy required to reach her saddle and search for what little food was left in her pack.

The sun hung low in the sky throwing off bright orange and blue melting into a rich purple. The evening refused to die and all Oleana wanted was for night to fall so she could sleep. She didn't even mind using the rotting bark as her pillow. All she needed was some quiet so she could curl up and drift off.

"This isn't working," Leith said after plopping down in front of the fire. He pulled up his legs wrapping his arms around them and laid his head atop his knees.

"Agreed," Lysander said. He stood by his mount, tied to a nearby tree. He stripped his arm guards off and slung them over his horse. Red splotches dotted his olive skin. Oleana had areas she knew had the same chaffing but she chose not to examine them since there was nothing she could currently do for it.

The smell of bitter sweat and desperation was thick enough to overcome the odor of damp mildew and rot that permeated the bank of trees. Trees, grass, and rounded hills stretched out around them in an endless teasing game, promising shelter was just over the next hill but never delivering.

Oleana spent a lot of her life on the move, walking or riding from one place to another. Never before had she been so ready to find a comfortable place to just sit and stay. She didn't care where it was, would have even agreed to live out the rest of her days in Solon with its bitter cold winters, as long as she didn't have to keep running.

"We present too big and slow a target," Oleana said. "They attack and run before we have a chance to retaliate."

"What do you suggest we do about it?" Nadir asked coming up behind her.

Oleana craned her head back to look him in the face and she heard her neck crack. It felt good, next she needed someone to walk on her back and relax the muscles there. Nadir's face was taught and the big vein running through his forehead was throbbing. He took a long drag from his water canteen before looking down at Oleana. A drop of water splashed against her face which she quickly wiped away.

The weight of her head soon strained tired muscles so she had to right herself. "We split." Oleana said, more to herself than as an actual suggestion, but the volume control on her mouth wasn't working. The others stared at her as if she were a stranger that wandered in. "What other choice do we have? We continue this way and wait for them to wear us down to the point that the next attack does serious damage, and they'll come full force and wipe us out. Or, we change things up. Split into smaller groups. The change alone will slow them down. The next time they attack we can be just as quick with our own charge and make them think twice about coming after us."

"Coming after you," Nadir corrected. "After you and Lysander, Leith and Lorn. That's who they want. The rest of us are just getting in the way. We split up, what keeps them from barreling down on you with a massive force in the hopes that taking out one the Heirs is better than splitting up and trying to go after all of you?"

"Let them come after me, then the rest of you will be safe to reach Evermore," Oleana said. "I've been itching to fight since we started off, and moving in this giant convo is just stifling. They come after me and they'll learn that I'm not to be messed with. They'll regret getting in my way."

"And if they see Lorn as a more acceptable target, or Lysander, or Leith. What'll you do then?"

Oleana wanted something smart to reply to Nadir but she had nothing. Instead she looked at Lorn, Lysander, and Leith in turn. "If you have a better option now is the time to speak it."

Nadir sat next to her. He hung his head low, gazing into the fire as the tendrils of flame darted back and forth in the soft wind. "I honestly don't know what to do."

Oleana caught the look of surprise that crossed Lysander's face. Hearing those words from his father must have been hard but it was an important lesson for the future king to learn. "Being a good leader doesn't always mean having all the answers. It means recognizing when someone else has a good idea and having the courage to acknowledge it," Oleana said staring at Lysander.

"Do you ever shut it off?" Nadir said.

"What?"

"That part of you that is the guardian. The part that can turn everything into a lesson to be learned. Watching you train my son in front of me is disconcerting."

"I'm sorry, I didn't mean to overstep," Oleana said. She rubbed at her face. "I'm tired and it just comes out."

"Thought it just me," Leith said.

"No, she does it to everyone. Try living with it for most of your life," Lorn grumbled.

"Try literally being her boss and getting lectured," Nadir added. "Do you know how much of a pain it was to be her squad leader? My father tasked me with training her, and keeping an eye on her. This version may be a little mouthier than I remember Mira being, but the stubborn streak is just the same."

"You guys are amusing. I love the witty banter in the face of danger, but can we please get back on topic?" Oleana said.

"Can't we just sit here for two minutes and just enjoy the outdoors? Maybe eat something, and in the morning, we can make all the life and death decisions you want," Lorn said.

"Let's not worry ourselves with little things like reality. We can just sit here and joke while Ivar's men move in to kill us. Or maybe the yetis will come and slaughter us in our sleep, make it quick and painless. Wouldn't that be nice? Would you all be happy then?"

"To answer your question," Lorn said. "No, she never turns it off."

Oleana wanted to slap the smirk off her son. If he didn't understand how important things were by now, he never would and she'd failed him. "Why do I even bother with any of you?"

"I think we should split," Lysander spoke suddenly, drawing everyone's attention. "Oleana has a point. We're never going to be effective against them in our current state. The only way we have a chance is to split into smaller groups." Lysander stared down at his feet. He picked at the scales on his chest plate, but no one spoke to interrupt him so he continued. "Look, there's no good way for them to tell who went in what direction, so they'll be forced to come after all of us. There's no way around it. Besides once we hit the marsh land it's going to be impossible to keep this big a group together anyway."

"I don't want you out of my sight," Nadir insisted.

"Dad, no offense, but my life was dangerous before it was confirmed that I'm the Master of Earth and all that entails. You've had to cope with it this long, there's no reason to get jumpy now."

"You're my son and I will always worry about you. There's no stopping that. And having that title hanging over your head puts you in line for a level of danger that's hard to even comprehend."

Nadir shook his head. "You have no idea. If it were up to me I would make you wear three layers of dragon scale from head to toe, and I would lock you up in a brick tower with a platoon of elites around you. But it's not up to me, so all I can do is worry." He let out a ragged sigh that sounded like a piece of his soul had escaped.

Oleana heard the hesitation in Nadir's voice and she knew, before he did, that she'd won. "You can't let that worry keep him from becoming what he needs to be," Oleana said as an aside. She really couldn't help herself.

The hard look in Nadir's eyes said he was wrestling with a decision. "Because you are my son, I trust you. We will split and meet up at Evermore."

"This way it should only take us about a day and a half to get there," Oleana said.

"Well then there's no point in waiting to get started. We have a lot of things to get together before sunrise," Nadir said.

Oleana groaned. So much for getting sleep. She guessed she could sleep when she was dead.

CHAPTER TWENTY-TWO: MARSH

Oleana found herself looking out over a wide stretch of marsh too vast to see the end. She glanced up at the sky. It was well past the height of day. They had maybe three hours of good light left.

"Looks like it stretches forever," Mason, leader of moon squad said. He looked like he could be a relative of Tycho's. He was tall and broad, like a statue carved out of a mountain. His brown curls were sprinkled with gray, which only added to the brightness of his hazel eyes. Oleana judged his age as close to Nadir's, so she wondered how she could have missed a man like him her first time around. The white line of a scar that bisected his chin said he'd been at the ranger game for a long time. Oleana felt safer with his experience at her side.

"Yes, and time is not on our side," Oleana said. "Do we search for a camp site now and delay crossing until the morning, spending even more time exposed, or do we cross now and risk having nowhere safe to bed down once nightfall comes?"

"Sir," someone said behind them. Oleana turned to see the young woman they'd sent out to scout for them. Bad news was written all over the pinched look of her face. "Captain, Failsea troops are moving in from the west. A compliment of thirty plus."

"I guess that answers that," Oleana said. She looked over the fifteen men and women around her. Her presence and their desire to protect her might get them killed, and she hated that reality. She wanted to stand and fight, but not at the risk of their lives. "We have to traverse the marsh."

"They've been making raids from this area for years. They know it better than we do," Mason reminded her.

"Yes, but they're chasing. That makes it our game to play. Speed and agility trumps knowledge."

"I hope so," Mason said. He turned to his troops. "Form up into arrowhead, we march into the marsh."

Oleana braced herself against the trek she knew was coming. The smell of the bog alone was enough to discourage her from wading into it. The fact that her horse fought her every step forward didn't improve her opinion of the situation. She wasn't one for horseback riding, Oleana preferred moving under her own power whenever possible.

Oleana was forced into the center of the arrowhead configuration with Mason in front of her, a man on each side of her, and men behind her. They moved so tightly together she could feel the hot, muscled flesh of the next man's horse pressed against her legs. She was at the heart of a cage of moldy marsh, straining horseflesh, and unwashed human bodies. Oleana hoped she didn't smell as bad as the others. She had to represent as a living legend. It would be undignified to die reeking of filth and sweat. Oleana wanted on the outside for at least a chance at fresh air. She felt like she would suffocate.

It didn't take them long to reach a portion of the marsh that failed to support the heft of horse and rider. Manson stepped forward and sunk in so far the mud came up to the belly of his mount and he nearly lost his shoe in the thick sludge.

"Halt," he cried, forcing a pileup behind Oleana as horses and men grunted their disapproval.

With help, Mason managed to back out of his hole. "Jax, Joel, spread out, see if you can find secure footing," Mason ordered.

The men directly to Oleana's right and left peeled away searching for a solid path. The one on the right made it four steps before sinking. Left made it a dozen steps before he met the same fate. Tension ripped through the group like a stiff wind would blow through tissue paper.

"We're too heavy," Oleana said. "Finding a path that would support us could take forever. If we leave the horses we can make a better way of it," Oleana said to Mason. She kept her voice low. She didn't need anyone thinking she was trying to undermine his authority. Mason nodded without looking at her as if he were thinking the same thing.

Oleana caught him stroking the horse's neck and she understood his hesitation. The horses didn't complain about the closeness of the formation, didn't object to sinking. They were more than just random mounts and Mason didn't want to just abandon them to whatever fate awaited.

Oleana remembered the hollow feeling she got when she had to just up and leave her farm to follow Lorn. She'd tried so hard to resist getting attached to anything, but she'd raised her son amongst those animals, tending to that field. Attachment happened whether she wanted it to or not.

"There has to be a solid path somewhere, we just have to find it," Oleana said.

"No, no. Time is not on our side. We leave the horses and anything else that might weigh us down."

"We can at least leave them by the stream that leads into the marsh," Oleana said.

Mason looked back at her and nodded. His gray eyes were soft. He would never have suggested it himself. Oleana was happy to take the burden off him.

"Okay all, we leave the mounts and extra gear streamside and move forward on foot. Five minutes," Mason called to his people. The burst of movement startled Oleana, she'd expected some hesitation, maybe even complaining, but these were soldiers and they had no room in the ranks for that.

She was projecting Lorn onto them. The thought of him made her ache inside. She could hear him go on about how he just got the horse. How Nadir wouldn't be happy they just let go of his prized property. Ever since she found him on the street Oleana hadn't been away from him for longer than a day, and never under such trying circumstances.

Back at camp she wanted to chide Nadir for voicing his nervousness about letting his son go while inside she was screaming at herself for even suggesting the idea. She closed her eyes and pictured him smiling at her. That would have to be enough to sustain her for a while.

Oleana dismounted and lead her horse to the water where it lowered its massive head to the cool stream right away. She grabbed her familiar pack, leaving the extra sword and shield the rangers gave her. She wanted to leave behind the armor. It was the lightest she'd ever been in, but after days of hard riding it chafed something fierce. As soon as she reached for the first buckle, Mason cleared his throat.

"Just adjusting it," Oleana assured him.

"Make sure it stays that way. I wouldn't be able to go home if I let something happen to the guardian on my watch."

"Well, Nadir will have my hide if something happens to one of his treasured squad leaders on my watch. Just remember that when you get the idea to do something heroic for my sake. I hate having Nadir yell at me. That vein in his forehead gets all throbby. It's not an attractive look."

"I'll keep that in mind, guardian."

"Call me Oleana, please."

"Yes ma'am."

"You're impossible," Oleana shook her head.

"Yes ma'am."

"I take that back about you being cautious. Just go ahead and live dangerously."

Mason laughed. It was a deep barrel-chested noise that made Oleana smile. "You and Tycho are what?"

"Cousins. My mother and his father are siblings."

"Explains the different last names. You look so much like him. Sound like him too."

"Something we are reminded of all the time."

"I'm sorry. I didn't mean to…" Oleana started.

"No it's not a problem. I love my cousin. Very proud of the man he is, and the family he's built."

"Sir," Joel said coming up behind them, "we're ready to move."

Mason nodded. "Take point. Stay tight. Move swift." His people grunted their acknowledgements.

Once again Oleana found herself in middle of a ball of flesh but this time Mason was beside her. They marched along and after a while straining to hear if the enemy had caught up was fraying on Oleana's nerves. She needed more than just the endless march to keep her mind occupied. Normally Lorn took care of that with his obsessive chatter but he was somewhere else keeping another hapless individual entertained.

"So, Mason what about you. Do you have a family I need to return you to?"

He hesitated answering and Oleana feared she'd hit an old nerve. "Umm, wife, no kids. Both too married to the job to have kids."

"She's a ranger too? She isn't out here in this mess is she?" Oleana said looking around then realized she had no idea what his wife looked like, so looking for her was useless.

"Guarding the capitol. We were both supposed to retire this year. Looking forward to a time when we see each other for more than a week at a time between assignments. Yet the call of war came and we both jumped without a second thought. Not sure if either one of us know how to do anything else."

"I'm sorry," Oleana said. "Everywhere we go we end up disrupting other people's lives. I try so hard to slip by unnoticed, and all I manage to do is bumble in and make a mess of things."

"Like I said, we both jumped at the chance knowing the risk. You will make a real difference in this world and that is worth every risk. I think about Tycho's grandbaby coming. This world is heading further into chaos. Without the hope that the Heirs offer that child, it will grow up in a world more violent than I have ever seen. If it takes sacrifice on my part to ensure that doesn't happen, then I'm happy to do it."

"Me too," Joel said, sparing a glance behind him.

"Yeah whatever it takes," another guy said behind Oleana.

"Yeah for us too."

Oleana didn't know what to do when confronted with fourteen faces shining with earnest appreciation for her. "You shouldn't umm," Oleana stuttered, and nearly tripped and fell into the muck, not paying attention to the man in front of her. Only Mason's hand on her arm kept her upright. "Thanks. Always suspected talking was hazardous to my health."

"You started it," Mason said.

"Yeah well," Oleana started, but the sound of hoofbeats interrupted her. "Please tell me that's our horses who can't stand to be without us."

"Failsea forces are headed around the bend. They will hit the edge of the marsh soon," one of the female squad members said. Oleana hated that she didn't know everyone's name, but it wasn't like they had time for formal introductions.

"They'll be slowed by the marsh, just as we were. Still, it's time to pick up the pace moon squad. Show this marsh what you're made of."

Oleana had to suck in the humid, moldy air to get her aching muscles to move any faster. She regretted complaining about the horse ride. At least then only certain areas of her body took a beating. Now it was a head to toe pummeling that threatened to have her flat on her face.

The new pace forced them to take a few missteps but the sound of horses faded, as well as the sight of any Failsea warriors that had been on their tail. There was no more time for talking. It was all about putting one foot in front of the other and hoping the muck didn't drag it down.

When they came across a clearing after an hour of jogging Oleana nearly collapsed with relief. They might actually make it to Evermore without a fight. They had maybe another hour of useable light. They had to get out of the wetland and find a safe place to bed down. The night would be hard, but solid ground would make things a little easier.

"Joel, scout ahead. Everyone else easy march," Mason ordered. Sweat beaded across his forehead in thick globs. His graying hair was plastered to his forehead and mud and decaying green gunk clung to his clothing, yet his voice was as strong as when they started. Oleana wheezed and huffed, jealous that a man twice her age was able to out-stamina her. Life on the farm had made her soft.

"Incoming!" someone screamed.

Oleana had her weapons at the ready and her eyes scanned the horizon. She saw the men on horseback coming in from the east of the clearing. Their head start had been trumped by a shortcut. Oleana's first instinct was to retreat, but they would be quickly caught by the enemy and would have to fight on the run.

"We stay here, in the wet, force them to expend themselves," Mason said. "Circle up."

The others formed a circle around Oleana and no matter how hard she tried to make a space in the outer line, they maneuvered her back inside.

"I know how to fight," Oleana insisted.

"Back inside," Mason ordered.

"But I can help!" Oleana shot back.

"If they get through us," Mason said. "I made a promise to your son."

Oleana let herself be swallowed up not knowing what she could say to that. When the sound of metal crashed against metal, Oleana was jostled and bumped by the press of people around her. The fighting became a blur. She held her weapons at the ready for a fight she hoped would never make it through to her, because that would mean too many people were dead or dying for her.

When Oleana saw an opening, she charged for it despite the warning. She couldn't sit back while others fought. She dove under a padded elbow and came up in front of a chestnut mare and her sturdy front quarters. Oleana rolled to the left to keep from getting stomped on, to land against something hard.

She looked up to see Mason staring down at her. He knocked his opponent flat with a bone shaking blow with his forearm. Then he offered her a hand up. Oleana read the look of disappointment on his face clear as day, but he spared her a wordy reproof.

"I'll split them," Oleana offered.

Mason nodded. Oleana pushed her way through the line of Caledon soldiers and took off running with what strength was left in her legs. The adrenaline of battle and fear gave her a speed she hadn't thought possible so late in the game, but Oleana didn't question it, she just continued forward. Joel and Mason stayed by her side as the others limited the amount of Failsea troops that followed.

Oleana lead them out to a narrow strip of solid land, solid in comparison to the murky mess around it. Standing still in it caused Oleana to slowly sink, but it was sturdy and wide enough to let the three of them stand abreast. The first pursuers tried to follow them on horseback only to have their mounts complain, then sink. They were forced to come forward on foot.

"We do it in twos and rotate," Mason said.

Oleana had to dig deep into her past life to remember the maneuver. Pulling it off took more than a basic understanding of the steps. It also required muscle memory, a sense of proper timing, and trust in your partners to step in when needed. Oleana didn't have time to think about it.

The first Failsea trooper reached her. He was as tall as Mason but thin as a rail. He had a thick black beard that looked like it hadn't been combed in weeks, and the look of desperation in his eyes almost unseated the anger. Oleana dug her heels into the muck and blocked his sword's downswing, twisting it out and to the left.

With her other sai flat against her forearm she brought it up against his jaw. She heard his teeth crack. Felt his head jerk back. She kicked him hard in the middle. Before another could take his place she took two steps back. Mason filled the space she left. He and Joel faced the next two giving Oleana a second to breath and assess the situation around them.

Between the two groups Oleana saw five members of the enemy troop down. She didn't detect any serious injuries on her side, but she couldn't get a good look at the other group. They were still significantly outnumbered, but they had the superior position and that mattered in cases like this.

Oleana heard a sharp thud and a splash, and knew it was her turn to step forward. Joel stepped back and Oleana slid in forced to duck low under a vicious axe swing. She stumbled onto her knees and managed to get both sais up in defense in time to save her head. Mason pushed his opponent into hers, sending them both off the solid ground. With the loss of anything solid to grip onto they sunk into the muck trying to swing away, but only wasting energy on open air. Oleana rolled left to face the next two, while Mason finished them off.

They went through nearly a dozen men that way before Oleana's arms threatened to fall off. She knew her swings were getting wild, she had less energy and precision for blocking, yet the enemy kept coming. An axe came down at her face and she was a little slow reaching up to block. Joel shoved her, taking the blow to his side. Oleana landed on top of bodies left to be eaten by the mud.

The sense was knocked out of her, and the back of her head impacted something hard. She struggled to get up, having to paw at the stiff chest of the man under her, before her eyes refocused. Angrily, she lunged forward without thought.

Her sai met the shaft of an axe and she twisted with the momentum of her whole body, wrenching it from her enemy's grasp, but now her back was against him. She swung back with her elbow, connecting hard enough to make her hand tingle. She twisted around, using the side of her sai against his face and he went down, blood pouring from the gash on his cheek.

Oleana didn't have time to worry about him. She knew Joel had to be hurt. He was kneeling, clutching the side of his neck, eyes staring off into nothing. Oleana skidded to him, clamping her fingers around his. The blood oozed out around them, sliding down her arm in rivulets.

"What do I do, Joel you idiot, what do I do?" Oleana said, not liking the panic in her voice.

Joel opened his mouth but only a bloody moan spilled out. Oleana knew her hands weren't doing the job of closing the rip in his neck but she didn't want to risk taking them away and searching

for something else. Oleana thought about what she did for
Lysander, using her own energy to heal him and wondered if it
would work on Joel. She had to do something.

"Look out," he croaked.

Oleana felt the blade puncture her side before she could turn.
Anger burned through her more than the pain. She lashed out with
all she had. Claws and fist pummeled the faceless thing that dared
attack her. Her knuckles bloody and cracked, Oleana didn't stop
until she felt no resistance.

She turned back to Joel who was now slumped over in a pool
of his own blood. Oleana put her fingers in his wound and closed
her eyes listening for the bio signal that was distinct to him. It was
faint, barely an echo trapped under a jar, but she heard it. Then she
searched for the ones and zeros that made up that part of her that
was more than human. The part that made her an Heir. Before when
she used the trick to heal Leith she had a reserve of energy meant
for a lifetime to spare. This time she only had the tendrils sustaining
her now. She could give a little away. He just needed enough to tide
him over until the others could stitch him up.

The transfer was painful from the start and Oleana recoiled
from it at first. Instinct told her not to just give away something so
precious but Oleana pressed on. Her body screamed but her mind
felt free. She was part of Joel, part of Mason, part of the chaos and
it felt electrifying. Oleana was overwhelmed.

She forgot her purpose and moved to calm everything. She
pulled away from Joel and stood. She channeled the voice of the
Twelve and screamed, "Stop!" The world around her stopped. She
heard Joel's voice echo hers but it sounded wrong, hoarse, and
weak. Scatter, she ordered and she felt people move. She didn't
know how many, or on what side, but the progress made her happy.
She could let go.

Oleana came back to herself in a rush and it felt like her body
was too small to contain her. She felt like she was crammed into a
box two times too small. Her nerve endings were on fire. The cotton

of her underclothing felt like sandpaper against her skin, and even the gentle breeze that flowed in from the east felt like nails across her cheeks.

"Oleana," someone called. "Oleana can you hear me?"

Oleana looked to see Mason. He placed his hand on her shoulder and she jumped back. He froze as if afraid to startle her. "I'm sorry. I didn't mean to. Are you okay?" she asked. "Joel."

Oleana turned and knelt down. He was still breathing, no matter how shallow, and the wound at his neck was scabbed over. The bleeding stopped.

"By the Twelve, Oleana your side," Mason's eyes were impossibly wide as he pointed at her.

Oleana grabbed at the side where she'd been hit to find a short sword still lodged inside of her. She reached to pull it out when Mason's hands clasped over hers.

"Don't. You'll bleed out. They've retreated. We need to find shelter and get you both taken care of."

Oleana nodded. She released her hand and looked everywhere but at herself, fearing the sight of it would cause her to be reckless. What was left of their compliment staggered toward her, bruised, and battered. Oleana found her feet, afraid that they were coming to capture her. She wouldn't fight but she might be able to flee.

"You saved us," Paul said. Others behind him nodded. "Whatever it was that you did, thank you."

"Henry, Paul, help with Joel. Arissa you help Oleana. All those still able to fight take the lead. Priority is speed and shelter. Move," Mason ordered.

Oleana let Arissa take her arm. Together they walked toward the clearing and hopefully a nearby shelter. Oleana didn't think she had enough in her to walk for long.

CHAPTER TWENTY-THREE: ALONE

After they stumbled onto a system of caves carved out by some long gone raging river, the same one that died in the marshland, Oleana was patched up, as best as possible by the resident medic, Fallon. They had a little tiff about it since he wanted to treat her first, but Oleana insisted he tend to Joel. She tried to get some rest while she waited but there was no way for her to lay down with the hilt still sticking out of her.

Mason held onto her the whole time. His right eye was bruised and swollen, his lip split, his knuckles bloody, and he walked with a limp, but still he insisted on keeping her calm. For medical purposes Oleana was permitted to consume a flask of brandy, down to the last drop. It was like liquid happiness sliding down her throat.

The dark liquid calmed a screaming urge that she'd pushed to the back of her mind. She almost forgave him for the mind shattering agony that shot through her when he pulled the sword out. She begged for more liquid painkiller to no avail. Oleana didn't remember much after that.

She woke up on a hard surface. The only light she had to see by was the fire crackling nearby. The smell of blood still clung to the air, mixing with the sharp mineral bite of rock and earth. Her armor's padding had been balled up to act as her pillow, and her midsection was wrapped in so many bandages she was sure they'd exhausted their supply. Oleana wished they wouldn't have gone through so much. She didn't need to be coddled.

Two male voices whispered across the space. Oleana levered herself up on her elbows to get a look at who they were. Mason and Fallon were talking with their shoulders hunched and their eyes pointed away from each other, out the cave entrance. Oleana couldn't make out what they were saying but both men held themselves so tight Oleana thought they might snap.

Biting her lip to keep quiet, Oleana got up on her feet and using the rocky walls as support she climbed over several sleeping bodies to reach them.

"What she gave him helped but it just…." Fallon looked up and his face went blank but Oleana caught the edges of grief written in the deep creases of his crow's feet.

"You should be resting," Mason chided.

"Joel is dead," Oleana said more of a statement than a question.

Fallon looked away. "A few minutes ago. What you did helped, but there was too much damage, too much blood loss. He couldn't recover. I'm sorry."

Oleana slammed her fist against the wall. "Years I sacrificed off my life. Years I gave to him only to have it go for nothing. Why did he save me? What makes me worth saving? Maybe I was ready to go. Did he stop to think that I might be tired of the running, and fighting, and tearing people's lives apart as I pass by?" Oleana helplessly rambled on in her grief.

Mason clamped his large hand over her mouth, cutting off any further ranting. "I understand your pain, but I won't let you disrespect Joel like that. I've said it before, but I'll say it as many times as it takes for you to get it. What you represent is more important than you or me, or anybody else here. We'll die, to the very last man here, if it means saving you, so you can accomplish what the legends say you will. We'll die for the hope that lives in you.

I can't imagine how heavy a burden that must be, and I'm sorry you have to bare it, but you must, for the sake of humanity."

Oleana pushed Mason away as soon as his grip lightened. The movement sent her teetering and she slumped against the wall, falling on her behind. Tears welled up in her eyes, but she didn't need them. She needed her anger. It was the only thing strong enough to keep her insides from falling out.

Fallon reached for her. "Are you..."

"I'm fine," Oleana said, brushing his hand away. "I'll live." Pain burned its way up her back and into her head and she wanted to curl up into a ball and die, but Oleana wasn't going to share that with them. Instead, she sat as still as she could, taking shallow breaths, trying to still her pounding heart.

"We have to find somewhere to bury the body and hope that once things settle down someone will be able to retrieve him for a proper funeral, along with the others," Mason said.

"How many did you lose?" Oleana asked, making sure to keep her voice under control. She didn't wish to anger Mason further.

"Four including Joel." Mason looked her over. "Four more seriously injured."

Oleana guessed that included her. She couldn't disagree. The walk, of all of five steps, took all she had. She'd be sleeping at the mouth of the cave if no one carried her back to her makeshift bed. She hadn't done her hand any good by putting it against the rock wall. If her back didn't hurt so much she would have been really worried about the pain.

"And after you finish with that, what's the plan?" Oleana asked Mason. She needed to focus on the next step. Drown out what her body was screaming at her. Keep focused and moving forward.

"This cave is secure. I think we should send out for help and hold down here until it comes. I can't move the injured, and I can't leave them. It's the only option I've got."

"How long do we wait before admitting they might not be coming back?" Oleana asked unable to stop herself from thinking the worse.

"If the next night comes with no sign of rescue, then we move on to plan B."

Oleana heard a twig snap and she reached for her sais but they weren't there. She didn't even have the sheaths strapped to her thighs. Mason held his hand out to stay her. He whistled two quick tones. Three long returned.

"It's okay," Mason said.

A young man, looked close to Lysander's age, parted the bushes and stepped into the cave. Oleana recognized him from the squad. He was pulling up the rear of their march to the caves. His face was covered in mud and his armor showed signs of the battle he'd fought hard in.

"Bring me good news Henry," Mason ordered.

"Sorry sir. The two messengers got away clean, but on my way back I spotted yetis on the search. Don't think they noticed me, took a roundabout way back here, but I don't think we are going to stay hidden for a day."

Mason didn't say anything for a long moment and Oleana thought this would be the straw that broke his patience, his courage. Oleana was scared. She couldn't even defend herself if the yetis came. Feeling helpless was not for her.

"Take Jax and explore the cave. Paul, and I will shore up this entrance. We just need to survive the next day. Fallon, take who you need and move the wounded as far inside as you can, that includes you, Guardian."

Oleana frowned at the return of the formal address, but she didn't have the energy to argue. "Yeah, I can't move without help," she admitted.

Fallon put one arm behind her back and one under her legs. Oleana wrapped her hands around his neck. She let him lift her, and while the sensation still sent pain through her, she was grateful for his smooth delivery.

Following Henry's lead, they moved further in until only the light from Henry's torch lit their way. The further they moved back, the more the ceiling sloped at odd angles forcing them to stoop and bend. There came a fork in the cave leading two different directions. At first glance neither of them looked appealing. Dark and rough.

"Stay here for now while we search out these two," Henry said.

"Won't be going anywhere," Oleana said after Fallon lowered her to the floor.

"You sure you're okay," Fallon asked.

"As okay as I'm going to get."

"Okay I'm going to go round up the others."

Oleana waved him away. She didn't need him hovering over her. Fallon and Henry left in different directions leaving her with only a hastily started baby of a fire. The noises of the cave whispered doom in her ears. Her choices yelled at her from the shadows. Sit by and wait in fear. Be selfish and do what it takes to save yourself. Do something for someone else and send Mason into a tizzy.

The first question was, did she have the ability to do the second two? Oleana took three deep breaths, bit down on her lip and pushed herself into a standing position. Her legs felt like lead weights but she took her first step forward. Oleana carefully scooped up the discarded torch and relit it. Then she stumbled her way forward knowing if she stopped to think about what she was doing she would lose her nerve.

100101

Lorn stared up at the Crystal Tower, mouth open at the breathtaking beauty of the structure and the knowing that he was finally there. Four lifetimes of trying and he finally stood in front of the place he yearned for the most. He may not have been able to remember the other three lifetimes, fragments lingered in his mind from his mother's memories, but the weight of them pressed in on him. Reaching Evermore, seeing the tower, it gave him a sense of relief that was too old for his sixteen-year-old self. It was a feeling that cut back through time and generations, a culmination of a century's worth of effort.

After the constant strain of being on the run for days, Lorn felt near collapse. His heart thudded against his chest and his legs felt too weak to support a feather, much less the weight of his body. The hundred feet between him and the tower seemed like an impossible distance to cover.

The tower itself radiated an energy that called to Lorn. Looking at it directly hurt his eyes. The sharp angles of the crystal structure captured the light and spit out different colors, oranges, greens, and reds, to the point Lorn wasn't sure what color was true. Except for the arched doorway, Lorn saw no breaks in the surface for windows or a veranda.

Still, more striking than the building itself was what it represented, a chance to reunite with those he cared about. Leaving his mother, Lysander, and Leith, felt like a torture too hard to bare. Every second without them in sight, he couldn't help but think about where they may be or if they'd found safety.

His route to the tower took several steps back toward the border before it was clear enough to move forward. He knew a lecture about being stealthy and fast lay in his future, and for the first time Lorn looked forward to it. Three sleepless nights and all he needed was to hear his mother's voice, even the angry version, and he could finally get the rest he needed.

"Sir we need to move to cover," his second in command said. The man was young, close to Lysander's age. He even carried some of the same features, dark olive skin color, tall and lean with the Caledon accent that Lorn was starting to get used to. The young man taught Lorn a lot about survival over the last couple of days and Lorn was grateful, but he preferred his mother.

"Lead the way," Lorn said, nodding to the man.

Before they got to the door, they were greeted by a dozen Caledon soldiers who popped out of a dozen different hiding spots as they approached. "Identify yourself," the one closest to the door yelled.

"Come on," Lorn replied irritated by the hindrance. "You see who we are as clearly as I see you as part of desert squad, Leith's squad."

The guard at the door look unimpressed by Lorn's answer. After days on the run like a hunted animal, he was near hysterical at being stopped so close to his goal.

"Let me through or I will let myself in. You don't want to mess with me," Lorn said. He emphasizing his point with the tip of his sword aimed at the man's face.

His second stepped in between Lorn and the guard. "Lieutenant Stillwaters and crescent squad reporting to the tower as ordered. Passcode, dragon five nine ranta three."

The guard nodded and Lorn watched his companions disappear back into their dark holes. "Passcode accepted. The others inside will be glad to know you've finally arrived," he said moving aside. "And sir I'm sorry, but I'm just following orders."

Lorn waved him off without another thought. Stillwaters pushed the door open and Lorn was inside searching for any sign of his mother. He ran down the corridor not worried about what passed by in a blur but moving toward the voices he heard. The hall lead to an opening with a massive set of crystal stairs leading up far enough for Lorn to lose track.

He peered around them to see another room with one of its double doors open and people coming in and out. He nearly ran into Daycia as she was coming out.

"Lorn my boy, why in such a rush?"

"How did you get here before us?" He waved the question off before she could answer. "Never mind, I'm sure we can talk about it later. Where's my mother? Is she okay? Are the others okay?"

"Come inside and we can talk about all of that," Daycia said, laying her hand on his shoulder.

Her touch was light and warm, but Lorn was not comforted. She tried too hard to be gentle and it made him suspicious. "What's wrong? Is my mother okay? Just tell me."

"She's not here. Come inside and the others can explain it better than I."

"She's not here yet? Since we were forced to bed down for an entire day I was sure we'd be the last ones to filter in," Lorn said. He let himself be led by Daycia inside the grand room behind the stairs. He glanced up to see two dozen men and women either gathered around a large rectangular table centered in the room, or milling about in groups of two or three at the edges. "Maybe we should go back out, see if we can find her, bring her in where its safe."

"They can explain everything," Daycia said in a diplomatic tone.

Lorn spotted Leith and Lysander at the table looking over a map with a woman who was clearly something other than human. Her skin was a pale cream color with a shimmer to it as she moved. Her oval eyes were green on green with no black pupil and she was as tall as him with a similar slender build.

Leith was the first to spot him. Looking up from the map relief washed over his face at spotting Lorn. His shoulders relaxed noticeably then he lowered his eyes as if it was too hard for him to look at Lorn.

"Ah, Lorn you made it," Lysander said standing up.

Lorn embraced each of his brothers in turn. "Good to see you both alive and in one piece. They didn't make the trek here easy. The longer Mom stays out there the more danger she's in."

"Daycia didn't...?" Lysander asked.

"I figured it was best if it came from you," Daycia said.

"Maybe you sit first," Leith said offering Lorn a chair.

He let himself be maneuvered into a chair, hoping that if he stayed quiet long enough they would stop fidgeting and tell him what he wanted to know. He bit the inside of his cheek to keep his mouth shut.

Lysander knelt in front of him, the length of his sword, still strapped to his hip, scraping against the hard tile floor. "Moon squad returned after being cornered by Cornelius and the men of Failsea." Lorn would have jumped out of his seat if the movement wouldn't have knocked Lysander over. "They suffered severe injuries after the first attack but managed to take cover in some caves. Oleana knew her men couldn't take another assault so she…" again Lysander looked away as if he couldn't bear to look at Lorn, as if the knowledge he held was too horrible to let out.

Lorn shook his head. He knew his mother couldn't be dead. He would have felt that, he was sure of it.

"She went alone to save her men. No sign a her out there," Leith finished.

"She's not dead. We would have felt it."

Leith nodded. "Wit Cornelius just a matter of time."

Lorn did stand on that note, forcing Lysander back on his hands before falling on his behind. Lorn sidestepped the crowd that had gathered around him. "She may be out there hiding, waiting to be rescued. Did you think of that? You're all standing in here, relaxing, patting yourselves on the back for surviving while she could be out there injured, counting on us to find her. What a disappointment we all turned out to be."

"Calm down, my boy, getting yourself all worked up isn't going to help anyone," Daycia said. She grabbed his shoulder spinning him around to face her. Lorn tried to struggle free of her grip but the power in her long slender fingers was beyond normal. "Look at me."

Lorn looked up at Daycia. The earnest worry in her eyes froze him, brought him to the brink of tears. His anger was nothing compared to her soft voice and warm eyes.

"You say she may be out there, okay I trust your instincts, we can send some people out to be sure, but I can't let you go. So many have risked everything to get you here. I can't let you throw that all away. You have more important work to do here."

"There is much to be done here," the odd woman said, finally standing up. Lorn had forgotten about her in the chaos. Now with her closer he realized who she must be.

"You're the keeper of the tower." Lorn smacked his forehead for not thinking of it sooner. The tower was only a safe haven but it was the Keeper who held the power. She would test their fitness to be king. She would crown them if she deemed them worthy. The Keeper of the Crystal Tower was the oldest living being on the face of Euphoria and Lorn had spent much of his life dreaming about meeting her.

The woman nodded. "Kameke, and you are the Master of Skies. I too lament the absence of the Guardian. Her presence would have been much appreciated. I would have loved to finally meet her, but like the half-breed said we have much for you to do."

"Hey what's with the name calling?" Lorn said. He looked to Daycia, wondering why she didn't defend herself.

"That's what she is, is it not?" the Keeper asked looking thoroughly confused.

"Her name is Daycia," Lorn said.

"Forgive her Lorn, she has been isolated here for some time," Daycia said.

"That's no excuse," Lysander said.

"I am sorry if I caused offense where none was intended. It's important for you three to trust me as we move forward. The trials will be hard and they must be conducted with all haste."

"Sorry, what bout trials?" Leith asked.

"The trials of the three. Do you not know anything about the legend of the Heirs of Eternity?" Lorn chided.

"I don't bother myself with tales," Leith replied.

"Ironic." Lysander said.

"Did the guardian not prepare you for what was expected?" the Keeper asked.

"We were in a bit of a rush, other things came up," Lorn said.

"That's no excuse," the Keeper said.

"Don't worry, I'll explain everything he needs to know," Lorn said.

"The trials cannot be delayed."

"I know the legends. I can go first," Lysander offered.

"Is it agreed that the Master of Earth will volunteer for the first trial?"

"Are you sure?" Lorn looked to his brother. He'd had half his lifetime to prepare for the trials and they still made him nervous. The journey to the tower wasn't exactly easy. They needed time to recuperate but the circumstances around them wouldn't allow for that. It didn't feel right to Lorn to let anyone else go first.

"I've been here the longest. I know what's coming. I can do this. Don't worry."

"I agree," Lorn said.

"Me too," Leith seconded.

"Master of Earth, you will face the trial of Power."

CHAPTER TWENTY-FOUR: CAPTURED

Oleana stumbled through the brush, holding tight to the wound on her side. No matter how slowly she moved or how shallow her breaths, pain shot through her middle with every movement. She made it to a small clearing that she decided was as good a place as any to sit and wait to be killed.

From the gathered leaves and broken branches, it looked like some other animal had once called the spot home. The smell of animal musk and urine lingered in the air, mixing with the background aroma of wet leaves and moss. Whatever made its home there left it some time ago. Feeling so drained it was an effort to keep her eyes open, Oleana didn't care what found her first, animal or enemy.

She lowered herself to the ground, leaning up against a fallen tree trunk that was rotten down the middle. She tried not to think of the community of bugs that must have been calling it home. As long as they stayed inside and away from her, things would go smoothly.

Her still lit torch was clutched tightly in her free hand. It was the only thing she had left. No food or weapons, just an oversized lit match. Oleana pushed some leaves and sticks together, setting the torch in the middle of them to start up a fire. She knew it would draw attention.

That was what she wanted, needed. After finding a narrow exit out of the cave and being careful to hide the way back to it, Oleana had stomped her way through the forest, breaking every branch she had the strength to. Setting a couple small fires along the way. She needed everybody's attention to be on her and only her. Mason was going to be furious, but she wouldn't live long enough to be yelled at.

Oleana wondered if Cornelius would show up. She didn't want her last life to end the same way as her first. There were worse things than dying at the hands of the wannabe god. Sitting back and doing nothing while Lorn and the others got killed was at the top of her list. They were so close to Evermore, so close to becoming the kings the world needed. Oleana couldn't fail them now. If it took her life, then she would gladly give it to see that they succeeded.

Oleana heard a crunch and nearly jumped out of her skin. When she turned, and saw that it was a leaf blown by the wind she knew she had to find something to do to take her mind off what was coming. She lifted her shirt to check on her wound. The bandage was stained red, her injury reopened with all her exertions. She grabbed the pocket of her pants, thinking to rip it off and use it to trap the bleeding, but she felt a bulge there.

She remembered Kaithlen handing her a slice of cake as a reward to keep her going on the road. It was no bottle of whiskey, something she really could have used at that point, but it would do nicely. Oleana abandoned her wound care and sat back as comfortably as she could manage on the hard, cold earth, to eat her treat.

Oleana pulled back the paper wrapping, swiping every bit of precious chocolate off before turning to the cake itself. Taking the first bite, Oleana remembered the first time she had cake. It wasn't until her second lifetime. That first go around her training and searching for the others dominated her life to the point she had no room for those simple things a lot of people took for granted.

With her mind on more pleasant things, Oleana's eyes drifted close. She didn't know how much time passed when a noise startled her awake. Deep in the brush a branch snapped. Oleana strained to see, but the sun was low and her eyes refused to adjust. She heard a snort that suggested an animal tracked her trail.

"Come get me beasty," she said hating how high and weak her voice sounded bouncing amongst the trees. Oleana caught the outline of a large angular head and broad square shoulders level with her eyeline, so it must have been walking on all fours.

At first Oleana thought it might have been Tannin come back to haunt her. The damage Lysander caused him on the fields of Central City would have been fatal to most, but the multiform had a pedigree that could have given him a chance at survival.

Oleana stared into the impossibly blue eyes searching for the sharp intelligence that Tannin possessed. As the creature eased closer to the fire, Oleana spotted its elongated fangs glistening in the flickering light. Its coarse fur and curved claws all screamed yeti.

Relief flooded Oleana. She may have been resolved to die in her head, but her heart still wanted to live, and she knew a fight with Tannin meant certain death.

Good to know I left a trail clear enough for something as dumb and wild as you to follow." Oleana looked around, surprised to find one of them out by themselves. "Why don't you go ahead and call in your brethren? I might be bleeding, but it's going to take more than one yeti to take me down."

The beast eased closer to her, apparently oblivious to her words. It carefully skirted the fire, moving forward until its front legs brushed against Olean's feet. The smell of decaying earth clung to its fur. It's breathing came in heavy gusts out of two wide nostrils, brushing against Oleana's face.

The oddly calm behavior sent a chill deep into Oleana's spine. She fought against the yetis since the beginning and never had one acted so reserved, so curious. Oleana leaned forward mesmerized by the look in its eyes. With her free hand, she reached for a nearby branch, the only weapon available to her. It wouldn't even pierce through the yeti's thick fur but it would startle it, maybe get it to yell out and attract others.

Oleana gripped the branch, swinging across her body with as much strength as she could manage, pulling at the burning wounds along her middle. The edge of the branch caught the yeti across the cheek, stopping against its nose. Oleana felt something wet fall on her arm, she wasn't sure if it was blood or mud.

The yeti snatched the branch from her hand, taking some of Oleana's skin with it. The yeti leaned in closer to Oleana and grabbing her face in its meaty hands, it's sausage fingers covering half of her mouth. "Father wants you alive," it croaked in a rough, shaky voice, as if his vocal cords weren't often used, "otherwise I'd make you pay for that."

Oleana's mouth would have fallen open had it not been held by the yeti. "You talk," she mumbled. "How can …?" Oleana never finished her question. The yeti squeezed Oleana's neck until she saw oblivion.

<u>100101</u>

"Guardian."

Oleana opened her eyes, her head swimming. The light reached her eyes and she doubled over gagging on what little was in her stomach.

"Disgusting," someone complained next to her.

Oleana tried to wipe her mouth, but found her hands were bound behind her back. She remembered staring up at the talking yeti before the lights went out. She'd expected death, had already come to terms with it. What they had in store for her, she didn't know if she could handle. Oleana wiped her mouth on her shoulder as best she could before struggling into a sitting position.

"To think I actually worried that Seth did you irreparable damage."

Oleana squinted against the black spots in her vision to get a look at Cornelius standing several feet away from her. Being so close to him after so many years of being terrified of the mere thought of him, she didn't know whether to laugh or cry. Oleana's chest felt tight and tears pooled at the corner of her eyes. She opened them wide, taking in deep, steadying breaths. She refused to show him any more weakness.

"Since when do your rabid dogs talk?" Oleana said ignoring her fear and focusing on the thousand questions in her head. She looked around trying to find anything familiar to latch onto. "Where am I anyway? And why did that pathetic genetic experiment you call a son not kill me when he had the chance?"

"No, my dear, I've learned my lesson. Kill you, and I just have to work that much harder to find you again." Cornelius said. He leaned over her much as his son had done not long ago. His breath on her skin was frigid like icy mountain air, sending chills skipping up her arm. "I plan to eliminate the threat you Heirs pose once and for all, and you are going to help me."

"That knock on the head must have scrambled my brain, because I know I heard you wrong."

"For what I need your help with I don't require your consent. Just your body."

Oleana coiled up when Cornelius reached for her. The thought of him touching her was enough to make her stomach turn. Her heart pounded against her chest and rubbing her palms together she felt the sweat building there. His long fingers brushed the side of her cheek and cold seeped into her skin so deep her teeth ached.

"You're not going to damage that pretty body too bad? I was hoping to get some kind of compensation for having such a dangerous thing tucked away in my camp."

Oleana looked around Cornelius to see Ivar standing in the far corner, picking at his teeth. The hungry look in his eyes made Oleana feel exposed.

"You won't touch her, you hear me," Cornelius said, staring down Ivar. "Not until I get what I need out of her."

Oleana never thought she'd be grateful to Cornelius for anything, but for the briefest second she wanted to thank him for sparing her from Ivar. That was until he grabbed a fist full of her hair, pulling her head up at a painful angle. "I'll start with something small, but if that doesn't get my point across, say goodbye to a limb. I'll give you time to think about which one," Cornelius said before he sliced through her locks with his razor-sharp claws. The black tresses with their rainbow threads laced throughout fell limply in his hand.

What was left of her hair fell down in Oleana's face setting off a rage that she couldn't clamp down on. "What in the name of the Twelve did you do that for? Do you know how long it took to grow those? Eight years of hard work and you ruin it to make a point. I'm sick of this crap. Sick of being scared of you. Wish you would just kill me and get it over with." Oleana said raising up on her knees, spitting her words as her voice got louder. Her abdomen burned, reminding her of how injured she was.

"The girl is mad," Ivar said. He laughed, making Oleana all the more furious.

"Why don't you shut your fat mouth and leave me alone? Why are you even here? I thought you were all about getting your precious river. How is that going for you? How much help was your new partner here?"

Ivar's eyes narrowed and he put his hands down at his side balled into fists. "It will be taken care of in due time. You have no place to talk. You're under my guard. You should be nicer to me."

"You untie me and I'll show you how nice I can be." Oleana lunged at Ivar who stepped back bumping into the wall.

Cornelius laughed. "Looks like this version of the Guardian is far from tame." He pulled Oleana back by her shirt, placing her squarely on her behind against the cold stone wall, the rough edges scraping her back. "Behave or I take the limb now and savor the look on the others' face as I present it to them."

The thought of Lorn cut through Oleana's anger. She could image how scared he must be knowing that she'd surrendered herself. She hoped he would understand her decision, that she had no other choice. She taught him as best she could, and she had to trust that he was prepared enough to face being a king, and to face Cornelius without her.

"They aren't going to give you what you want. My boys aren't as dimwitted and desperate as Ivar."

"Stupid, cocksure..." Ivar spat.

"Hold your tongue Ivar. If you can't handle a few insults, leave," Cornelius ordered.

Ivar stared at Oleana, his jaw clenched so tight Oleana worried he might crack his teeth. "Your help better be worth all this," Ivar said before turning to leave. The wooden door smacked closed behind him.

Oleana laughed, amused by how easily Ivar was rattled. "Your partner is sensitive. Might crumble under real pressure. I'd keep my eye on that one if I were you."

"Just remember that while I'm dealing with your fellow Heirs, he'll have unrestricted access to you. Maybe it wasn't such a good idea to make him so mad."

Oleana put on her best scared face. Cornelius smirked. He gripped his prize tighter, her long locks clutched in his skeletal hand. Oleana watched him leave wishing it would be the last time she would ever see him, but knowing they would face off again too soon.

CHAPTER TWENTY-FIVE: POWER

While volunteering for the first trial seemed like the right thing to do when Lysander said it, facing the truth of it was another matter. The trial of power required him to do on a grand scale what he'd only recently learned how to do on the small. The last time he'd given over to his power so completely he'd had a seizure bad enough to knock him out for a few days. While he'd proved able to use the ability without consequence after Oleana's reset, it still scared him.

"Master of Earth do you understand what is required of you?" the Keeper asked, her voice was soft but her words cut through him.

The group had gathered at the top of the Crystal Tower on the observation deck. They were still surrounded by the otherworldly crystal but the shell was at its thinnest, to the point where if Lysander caught it at the right angle he lost track of the wall and looked directly out onto the street below.

Up so high, they could see for miles. Lysander never thought of himself as being afraid of heights, but looking out from the tower made him re-think things. He focused on the area of the horizon that mattered.

"You want me to clear out the overgrown mess that lies two hundred yards due north of us, and then replace it with a living wall of pyracantha from the seeds you had one of your people deposit. Why, pyracantha? I mean out of all the things to choose, why them? Is there something significant about them? Am I missing something?" Lysander couldn't stop talking. He felt like he was channeling Lorn again, whether out of nervousness or residual effects from their joining, he didn't know, but either way he wanted it to stop.

"The plant is not native to this area and has a low bio signal, making it harder to manipulate," the Keeper replied.

Lysander swallowed hard. "I shouldn't have asked."

"You have twenty minutes to complete the task or you will be deemed unfit to be crowned," the Keeper said. Before Lysander could agree, she wound her timepiece. Its loud ticking reverberated in his ears until it was all he could hear, other than the all too fast beating of his heart.

"Lysander, you can do this. Just remember to clear your mind," Lorn encouraged.

"It's the Guardian's job to mentor you through this process, but because she is absent is it agreed that Lorn will act as her replacement?" the Keeper asked.

Lysander turned back to look at Lorn. The kid knew more about the trials than anyone else around. The mini course he gave Leith as things were being prepared was as thorough as he could have hoped. "Yes, please," Lysander said, ready for any help he could get.

"I'm not... I didn't think," Lorn stuttered.

"We need help," Lysander said. Leith nodded. "You're what we've got, and that's more than good enough for me." Lysander felt his time ticking away, slipping through his fingers. His nerves felt like they were on fire.

Lorn rubbed at his eyes and Lysander wondered if they were asking too much of the boy. It was hard enough for him to be without Oleana, now they were asking him to replace her. For Lysander having his father close was a comfort too important for words, but he still longed for his mother, wondered if she was safe. Lysander was ready to rescind his plea, take the burden off Lorn.

"Yes, its agreed," Lorn said.

Lysander wouldn't have called the look on the boy's face happy, but he did look determined. The skin around his eyes was tight, and his lips were pressed into a thin line. The weight of multiple lifetimes showed through in the lines of his face. Lysander felt a moment of regret that Lorn had to grow up so fast, but that fate had been hanging over all of them from the start.

"Come on, let's do this. Make a plan, then work the plan," Lorn said. "First step?"

Lysander tore his eyes away from the timepiece and looked out to his target. The mushroom-shaped tops of the trees swayed in the gentle wind. His target area was marked by a row of dying trees at the end of the street that led to the tower.

Rust colored rot interwove its way through the dark brown of the trees' bark. Limbs were devoid of leaves, or had become sickly yellow things, that looked like they would crumble in on themselves with a stiff breeze. Reaching out to them, Lysander could feel the disease as an ache in his joints, a bitter taste on his tongue.

"Break down the plants there to enrich the soil so it will be ready for the new growth," Lysander said. He licked his parched lips. Nervousness crawled under his skin like a thousand angry ants.

"Don't forget about the seeds. Break them down and you'll have nothing to start fresh with," Lorn warned.

Those stupid seeds. How was he supposed to find them in all the background noise? Before the Keeper sent them out he had a brief moment to study them, get a feel for what their signal sounded like. It was a slow, gentle pulse. The tone was in the soprano range with a four count that repeated. The trees on the other hand were big baritone drums that pounded away in a fast six count.

Lysander searched for his seeds. He heard a dozen different signals, some he recognized and others were a mystery, but none of them were the ones he wanted. What he did get was a throbbing at his temples that threatened to blossom into a severe migraine. Frustrated, he let go of all the sounds bombarding his mind.

Lysander's frustration bubbled over. He slapped his hands against the nearest wall. "This is ridiculous. How am I supposed to isolate a handful of tiny seeds in the midst of all that chaos?"

"Listen, I'm not a hundred percent sure how your abilities work, but if they are anything like mine you can make even the smallest signal louder when you block everything else out," Lorn said. Lysander had to admit he preferred Lorn's gentle tone over the underlying tinge of irritation that Oleana always spoke with. "We are standing at the height of a giant amplifier. Use it." Lorn managed to sneak the irritated tone in at the end.

Lysander placed his hands against the flat of the wall. He could instantly feel the vibration of the crystal. It was less of a movement and more a buzz of energy low level enough to not generate much heat, but enough to make the hairs on the back of Lysander's hand tingle.

When Lysander first opened himself up, using the tower as an extension of himself, the feedback was too much. He fell to his knees, overwhelmed by the noise. He felt a hand on his back, turned to see Lorn kneeling beside him. His mouth moved, but all Lysander heard was a monotonous buzzing in his ears.

"Lysander, are you all right?" Lorn asked.

Lysander waved him away. He didn't have time for sympathy or setbacks. Once his feet were under him, Lysander placed his hands back on the wall and eased the floodgates of his mind open a little bit at a time. It took time to adjust to the press of input but Lorn's words were clear, block out everything he didn't need.

The ticking of the timepiece faded away. Then he pushed away the booming of the trees. Next, the pulsating rhythm of the different flowers and the steady drone of the earth beneath them. It left him with the higher registers of the different fruits. He discovered a line of mulberries on the other side of the road at the start of blooming. Lysander didn't let them distract him for long. He caught the trace of his pyracantha, delicate little songbirds that they were.

Locked on, he could feel them nestled in a bed of lilies. Focusing in on their unique tone, Lysander used the special properties of the tower to amplify the rhythm of the pyracantha so he could let the other signals back in. After the symphony was organized in his mind Lysander could clear out what he didn't need.

"Lysander," someone behind him yelled.

He stepped back for the wall, startled, losing all sense of the symphony he'd so carefully constructed. His head swam because of the sudden disconnect. He tried to take a step but his feet weren't where they were supposed to be and he stumbled. Lorn's support kept him from hitting the ground. Leith came up on his other side standing close enough to lend help if needed. Lysander was quick to wipe the blood tinged beads of sweat from his forehead before his brothers could see them.

"Did I run out of time?" Lysander asked staring at his feet. He couldn't bear to face failure in the eyes of his brothers. "I pushed it as hard as I could. I was almost there. Just another minute..."

"Look," Leith said, his voice surprisingly hard.

Lysander looked up to see several guards had entered the room. The Keeper was busy talking to them. With his ears still buzzing he couldn't make out what they were saying.

"What's going on?" he asked.

"Troubles coming," Leith said.

The Keeper turned from her men. "Troops have surrounded our city, yeti and human. Your people were forced to pull back to the tower."

Lysander stared out the window, expecting to see the cruel ice god smiling up at them. Lorn stiffened beside him. They exchanged a look of dismay. The haunted look in Leith's eyes told of his fear while he remained silent.

"Send everyone you can after them and cut them down," Lorn said. Lysander and Leith nodded their agreement. Cornelius had forced them to flee Caledon, separated them from Oleana. The ultra and his warriors needed to be eliminated.

"This city is neutral, always has been. I will not compromise that for you," the Keeper said. "We will only act in defense if they try to breech the tower."

"Do you think for a second Cornelius will honor the rules of this city? Lorn asked. "He didn't gather his troops along the border to have a chat."

Lysander's eyes were drawn back to the timer still running out. He thought about the pyracantha seeds ready to sprout. The people of Solon built the great wall to keep the yetis out. Evermore needed a temporary fix until things could be sorted out.

Lysander put his hands back on the Crystal Tower wall, searching for that connection with the tiny little seedlings. He was a solider, not very good at being aggressive for himself, but there was no way he would let others come to harm.

The decay had done its job. Lysander felt the cold spot of decay around the gently pulsing song of the pyracantha. Lysander could change their song from one of passive survival to one of explosive growth. He used the tower's focusing powers to send the instructions to the tiny seeds, like turning a flute solo into a grand orchestral symphony.

"What are you doing?" the Keeper asked, her dulcet toned voice barely registering on Lysander's conscious.

"I'm going to build you a wall," Lysander said, not breaking his concentration, "keep the enemy out, and your city safe."

"You sure bout that?" Leith asked.

Lysander brushed their concern off. The first bush sprouted, its song deep and throaty. The second and third were easier to get going because Lysander already knew the right sequence to spur them into over-growth. Seconds ticked by and then they blossomed, and Lysander's brain exploded with a million new songs springing into the air.

At first, he panicked. It was so much at once he didn't know how to control it and the seeds needed to go where he wanted, otherwise the wall would be chaotic and ineffective. Lorn's hand fell on his back and another hand on the wall next to his.

The wind picked up the seedlings and scattered them in an even layer around the city. Lysander wanted to thank Lorn, but forming the words were beyond him, his mind stretched to the limit. He was forced to keep three complex, overlapping songs straight at once. Preparing the soil for the seeds, sprouting new pyracantha bushes, and interweaving the thick bramble bushes with the existing trees creating an impenetrable living wall.

Lysander felt like his brain was going to overheat and liquefy, his body was going to shake apart. He vaguely registered the impact of his knees against the floor as the simple act of standing became too much work.

"They're surging forward," the Keeper said.

Lysander opened his eyes briefly but it took a few moments for him to be able to see anything but the notes of the song. He could see the first group of soldiers trying to make their way through the growing mound of living wall.

"You must stop this or you'll kill them," the Keeper insisted.

The sky darkened and rain drenched the ground in sheets of gray. The soil became pliable and hungry for more seeds. Then just as quickly Lorn cleared the clouds and the sun beamed down showering the starving new plants with needed nutrients.

"You stop and we all die," Lorn yelled, his nails digging into Lysander's back. "Keep going."

"Give 'em a break," Leith urged.

Lysander heard Lorn's voice, but saw Oleana's face just behind his eyes, Leith's worry faded. He remembered what it was like being inside her head, knowing exactly how proud she was of them and yet how scared she was that she couldn't protect them. One of those nameless soldiers could have been the one that took her away from them. Lysander couldn't let that go unpunished.

He let his anger and fear feed the pyracantha plants, pouring every ounce of energy he could spare into the building of the wall. He could make out the vague outline of the slaughter as thorns the size of hands pierced flesh. Lysander felt the violence as blood seeped into the soil strengthening the mutant plants.

Lysander built his wall on the bodies of his enemies and it scared him, but he couldn't stop himself. The wall grew five feet thick and six feet tall. Lysander felt less human and more like a carnivorous plant as his creation swelled, stripping the ground of the all the nutrients it could get.

"Stop this," the Keeper yelled.

Lysander felt Lorn's hand leave his back. The lack of support felt like the wind was knocked out of him. Lysander collapsed and only a shrill ringing was left in his ears. His head swam, unable to wrap around what he'd just done.

Leith kneeled beside him, mouthing something that Lysander couldn't make it out. His whole body felt like he'd been dunked in a boiling hot spring. His breathing came ragged and he could taste blood and dirt on his tongue. Lysander couldn't help but focus on the screams of the Keeper. She'd told him to stop and he'd ignored her. Lysander wondered what that meant for the test. Was his desire to avenge Oleana for nothing? Had he ruined their chances of being crowned?

Lysander swallowed hard and summoned his courage to ask, "Did I fail?" he croaked, his throat feeling as if he'd swallowed a pound of sandpaper.

Leith shrugged. "You okay?" he asked, helping Lysander to sit upright.

Lysander pushed Leith away and struggled to his feet. His vision blurred and he had to steady himself against the wall, but his question remained the same. "Did I fail?" he shouted not worried about the pile of bodies he'd left in his wake, or the tornado swirling around behind his eyes. None of that mattered half as much as passing the first test.

"You saved us all," Lorn said standing in front of Lysander. The boy grabbed Lysander's chin lifting his face so that their eyes met. "That's success in my book."

Lysander turned to the Keeper. While he appreciated Lorn's sentiment, that's not what mattered. He needed to know what she would say. "Did. I…." he couldn't bring himself to say the word again, though it kicked around in his chest. Failure. In so many ways that's what he'd always been, a failure.

His body often failed him. His fears and doubts overwhelmed him. He failed to be the son his father wanted, failed to be the perfect soldier his people expected. Now when it was most important, had he failed again?

"You showed a tremendous control of your abilities." The Keeper indicated the line of dark green thorn bushes stretching out around the city as far as he could see, and as tall as the tallest tree in sight, "Your wall is a thing of power and function. I would not have expected such a thing from one so young." She glanced at the timepiece, her face rigid, giving nothing away.

Lysander wanted to scream at her. Demand she hand down the verdict. He also wanted to run away and hide. If he never heard the words, then he could always pretend he'd done the right thing. "You completed the task and more, with time to spare. While you disobeyed my order, you did not violate the neutrality of the city as you built it in defense and not in attack. You, Master of Earth, have passed your first trial."

Lysander laughed. It started small, at the back of his mouth, then burst forth bouncing off the angular walls of the observation room. "It only took the slaughter of dozens of people to be able to call myself a success," he said in a whisper so low he could hope no one else heard him.

"Need to rest," Leith said, coming up beside him.

Lysander realized his legs were still shaking, and he was drenched in sweat. The pain in his head was only growing.

The Keeper nodded. "You may all go rest. I will direct the others to keep an eye on the wall."

Leith and Lorn helped Lysander down the spiraling staircase. He let them move him without resistance. His mind was torn between thoughts of Oleana and thoughts of the people he'd just killed. They were his enemy, but Lysander had never given over to the power surging within him before. He'd never been so excited by the violence of it all.

It took several heartbeats for Lysander to realize that they'd stopped moving. He looked up to see a couple of the farmers of Evermore had rushed in to meet them at the bottom of the stairs.

"What is it?" the Keeper pushed past him.

"Cornelius sends a message. He wants to talk."

"Now he wants to talk. He tells us where my mother is and then we can talk." Lorn sounded as if he was sure Oleana was alive, but Lysander didn't hold out the same hope.

"As I said, this place is neutral," the Keeper explained. "If he wishes to talk peacefully then we will allow him. And him only," she told the two farmers.

They nodded and ran off.

Cornelius. The name sent a chill down Lysander's spine. He didn't have the strength left to deal with the ultra face to face.

"This stupid. Man's a killer and you wanta talk it out," Leith said shaking his head.

"He could say the same of you," the Keeper said. She waved it off as if their complaints meant nothing to her. "Go get him food and water so you will be ready to talk with a clear head." She walked off before anyone could object.

"Cornelius," Lorn said, as if the name were a curse that had befell them. "This will not end well."

100101

Two guards with dragon scale armor on from head to toe, and twin axes in their hands, escorted Cornelius into the great room, yet the wannabe ice god stole all the attention. With ten-foot-high ceilings and an eighty-square foot room around them, Lorn still felt claustrophobic being in an enclosed place with the ultra. The smug smirk on Cornelius' face made the feeling worse. What did he have to be smug about surrounded as he was by the enemy? Yet he strode down toward the crowd as if he were in his own ice castle, held his shoulders back, and walked with the speed of a man confident in his surroundings.

"Cornelius, Ice Ultra, welcome back to the Crystal Tower."

Cornelius looked up at the ceiling and the creation mural painted there in exquisite detail. It started with the formation of the rings in which the Twelve reigned over Euphoria, moving on to the descent of the Crystal Tower, then the shadow figure spread of the ultras, and ending in the forming of the five realms. "Even after five centuries away this place still feels like home. And you, dear sister, you still look the same."

The Keeper failed to show any reaction to Cornelius' words. "You requested a chance to make your case before the Heirs. Do so now."

"I came to broker a truce. Your display with the wall was impressive, but it will only delay an invasion. You have the forces of Caledon pull back and let Ivar have his river. I pull my yetis back to Mount Elmire and you three return to the various realms that you came from," Cornelius stated flatly.

"Why would we do that?" Lysander asked.

The three Heirs stood in the center of the room. A dozen or more armed guards where spaced throughout all ready to attack Cornelius if he showed any intention of raising arms against them. Daycia, Nadir, and Tycho stood off to the side for support. Even with all that, Lorn felt so small and unprotected with the Ice Ultra so close.

Cornelius reached in the back pocket of his pants and pulled out an odd bundle wrapped in twine. The second Lorn saw the color, a deep black with purple and yellow threads coming loose from the rest, he knew what it was. The others didn't catch up until Cornelius undid the binding and let the severed locks hit the floor in a shower of hair and thread.

Tears fell against Lorn's cheeks and he exploded forward, rage burning through him hotter than the fire heating the giant room. Lysander's firm hand arrested his forward momentum. How Lysander anticipated his reaction, when Lorn himself didn't know it was coming, surprised him, but wouldn't stop him.

Lorn clawed at the hand that kept him in place. "What have you done!" he yelled. "I'll kill you, I swear to the Twelve, I'll kill you," Lorn felt the spittle land on his chin but he didn't care. His body was ready to shake apart and his chest felt like it weighed a ton. The air around him was as thick as mud, making it impossible to take in a full breath.

More hands grabbed him and pulled him back. Lorn fought against every inch, to Cornelius' amusement.

"I think there is something amiss with this generation. They've gone rabid. The Guardian acted similarly when I severed those from her head. Who knew such a simple thing as hair could cause such a fuss? Trust me young one, when I left her she was unharmed, though I don't trust Ivar to keep her that way. She insulted him rather profusely. The longer it takes you to agree to my terms, the greater risk your guardian is under."

Lorn stopped fighting. He closed his eyes, focusing on just breathing. In the darkness, he could see his mother's face, feel her calloused hand brush his cheek as she assured him they would see each other again soon. He didn't want to leave, didn't want her out of his sight. Everything in him told him it was a bad idea to split up. And here he was facing the ice god without her. How could she do this to him? He had to get her back, if only to tell her how wrong she had been to doubt his instincts.

"You set her free first."

"Lorn wait," Lysander warned.

Lorn waved him off. "You set her free first and we acquiesce to your demands."

"What makes you think I would trust you?" Cornelius asked.

"We're not the ones that started this fight. We're not the ones who kidnap and kill. We aren't the ones who...."

"Exactly, so no point in giving him what he wants," Leith said, interrupting. "We agree and we all dead anyway."

"We need to confer amongst ourselves," Lysander said, before Lorn could object. He grabbed Lorn's arm and spun him around, moving them both toward the door before Cornelius answered.

Out in the hallway, with the door closed behind them, Lorn sucked in air so hard he thought his ribs might crack. His mouth was dry and his throat tight. The moment Lysander released his iron grip, Lorn started pacing. He couldn't stand still. His mind and heart raced. His mouth couldn't form words fast enough to express all that he felt.

"You can't give in to him," Daycia said.

Lorn looked at his mother's mentor. At the woman who had instantly become his friend, someone he trusted. Her tone was flat but the terrified look on her face spoke more than she ever could.

"Are you telling us to just let her die?" Lorn raged. "Just let your student, the Guardian, one of the Heirs of Eternity die without lifting a finger to save her?" Lorn heard the words come out of his mouth but they were too horrible to contemplate. "I can't! We can't." Lorn looked each one of them in the eye, challenging them.

"What you suggest we do?" Leith said. He turned his favorite dagger over and over in his hand. Lorn wondered if the familiar movement actually brought him some comfort.

"Lorn, you know as well as I that none of us would make it back to our homes. Cornelius is not one to let his enemies regroup and try again," Lysander said. "We have to be rational about this."

"How?" He demanded. "How can we be rational? That's my mother he's talking about."

"It's the world that hangs in the balance," Lysander reminded him. "You know better than I how hard things have gotten in this world. People are withering under tyrants like Ivar and Emmaray. Even a land as prosperous as Caledon is suffering under the constant fighting between realms. The yetis have already cut a bloody swath through Arismas. Things will only get worse if we give even an inch to Cornelius. Your mother fought over and over again to get us here. She'd never forgive us if we gave it up for her."

Lorn wanted to scream. Frustration coursed through his body. He slammed his fist into the wall. Pain cut through him, giving him something to focus on. He was too young to lose the only parent he'd ever known, too young to have the weight of the world on his shoulders. "We tell him no, and she dies. We kill her. Can you live with that?" Lorn challenged them.

"No other choice," Leith said, but his eyes refused to meet Lorn's.

"It's better than the alternative," Lysander added, "but we'll follow your lead."

Lorn needed some place to run. Needed time to think, but there was no place for either. They were right about one thing, he had only one choice. Lorn wiped his face. Cornelius had seen enough of his tears. "Then let's go."

Lorn thought of nothing but his hatred for the thing that would call itself an ice god. All the pain and sorrow he felt now, he would be sure to visit it on Cornelius a thousand-fold in the future.

"Ah the rabid one, have you convinced your fellows to see reason?"

"We have made the only choice you left us with," Lorn said. He was proud of how steady his voice sounded.

"I knew you were a smart boy the moment I set eyes on you."

"We reject your terms and propose new ones. You leave this place knowing that we will do everything in our considerable power to hunt you down and destroy every last trace of your despicable presence on this planet. That we will live up to the legacy of the Heirs of Eternity and do what you could not and unite humanity under the cause of hating you."

"You'll regret the…" Cornelius started to yell.

"You'll flee from here, with your tail tucked between your legs, happy that we met on neutral ground, but know that your days are numbered." Lorn could feel the air in the room change. An electrical charge danced along his skin. He didn't have to look up to know that in his anger he was pulling together moisture in the room to form a freak storm cloud. "If I were you I would release the guardian and pray to the Twelve that is enough to stem our anger, because if nothing else in this world is certain this one thing is, her death will be the end of you." Thunder boomed making the ground shake and Lorn's ears complain. Lightning cut through the air blinding him for a moment until he saw the scorch mark inches from Cornelius feet. "Next time I won't miss."

Cornelius turned and left, leaving a trail of ice crystals on the floor behind him. Lorn watched as the Ice Ultra receded, kept staring even when the door blocked his view. The others said they could live with it, but Lorn didn't think he could. He said it was the end of Cornelius but Lorn knew it was the end of him too.

"Master of Earth, Master of Skies, you have both completed your trials of power."

Lorn blinked. The transition was too much for him to process. He laughed.

"How can that be?" Lysander said.

"Your wall is strong, and the clouds above us proves his power. All three of you pass the trial of Integrity, putting the world ahead of the guardian. That leaves only the Master of Animals to prove his power, then we move on to the final test. Intelligence."

CHAPTER TWENTY-SIX: THE TWELVE

Oleana said the code phrase as she had a dozen times before. Without having a clear view of the outside, she didn't know if the signal would be clear, but it was better to try and fail than never try at all. Oleana felt her mind pulled out over Euphoria. She tried to hold on to the feeling, tried to find a particular signal amongst all the chaos. She didn't know how far she was from Evermore, but her previous attempts to search came up empty.

Being stretched so thin hurt. Oleana's mind was forced to process too much incoming data and she had to fight against the intended path from her to the Twelve. Desperation overrode pain and Oleana clung to the open signal with all she had.

The snapback was brutal. Oleana heard the Twelve screaming at her like a million needles piercing every nerve ending. Oleana was sure her head would explode. She lost herself in the cacophony. She couldn't tell what thoughts were hers and what belonged to the collective.

"Guardian."

Oleana heard Four's voice and latched on to it, building her reality around it. Four was a star and Oleana was the proto-planet forming in its gravity well. Piece by piece Oleana pulled herself together. "G.u.a.r.d.i.a.n."

"Is Lorn safe? And the others. Tell me please."

"We are not here to be your…"

"Please just tell me." Oleana pleaded. She dug her nails into her palms. Her body felt taught as if she'd been stretched over a boulder and left to dry in the sun. "I didn't get to say goodbye. I need to know. Just this once don't stand on ceremony and do this one thing for me."

Silence filled the black space behind her closed eyes and Oleana thought that the connection had been severed. Oleana would bang on that door until her head cracked open if that's what it took to find out about her boy.

"The Master of Skies' bio signal is strong. It is at the heart of Evermore with the Master of Animals and the Master of Earth."

"Can I talk to him? I tried to connect with him on my own, but I just don't have the strength. Please."

"This is very unusual," One said joining the conversation.

"Cornelius has me. I don't know what his plans may be for me, but I know they won't be good. As you must know, I spent the last of my resurrection energy saving Leith. There is no coming back for me. I just want to say goodbye to my son. After all that I have done in your name, for the cause you forced upon me, do I not deserve this little thing?"

"The quality of the connection will not be up to the standard you have become accustomed to," One said. His voice was tight and Oleana swore she detected sorrow in his tone. "Prepare yourself."

Oleana nodded. Her words of thanks caught in her throat. She felt another voice join them, but it was grabbled. One said something, but it sounded like the shadow of a distant echo. She strained to make sense of it. If she could just make out a word. One word and the rest would fall into place.

"Lorn," Oleana screamed. "Lorn, can you hear me?"

"Hold on, we are adjusting," Four explained.

"Mom."

Oleana's heart fluttered. She wished she could see Lorn's face. The image her mind conjured looked incomplete, intangible, and to ethereal to hold. "Lorn, my boy. I'm so sorry. I'm so sorry I can't be there for you." Oleana felt the tears roll down her cheeks and she didn't care who saw them. If saying goodbye to her only child wasn't a good enough reason to cry, there never would be.

"No mom I'm sorry. Cornelius was here. He said he would free you if we surrendered. We had to...."

Even without seeing his face Oleana knew Lorn was torn. She could hear his pain in the high register of his voice and the deliberate way he spoke every word as if it hurt to let them out. Oleana didn't have to stretch her imagination far to guess what Cornelius put before them.

Oleana felt her last hope slip away from her. She knew Lorn and the others couldn't forsake the rest of the world on the off chance that Cornelius would actually keep his word and set her free. That didn't mean a part of her hadn't hoped they would find some way. In the back of her mind a piece of her still clung to the hope that she would make it out alive.

"Lorn, you did the right thing. You made an impossible decision and you choose well. Never think otherwise."

"But he'll...."

"Cornelius and I have done this dance before and while I had hoped it would turn out differently for me this time, I surrendered myself to save you and the others. Nothing matters to me more than that." Oleana swallowed hard against the jagged lump of dread in her throat. She wanted to hold her son one last time, but her words would have to be enough. "I'd die a thousand times for you, Lorn. Just promise me you'll earn your crown and finish the work we started together. You deserve that life. The sooner you rid this world of Cornelius and the other ultras like him, you can live the life of peace I always wanted for you."

"Mom, I'm sorry. I can't." Lorn's voice was so high and hoarse Oleana barely recognized it. "I can't do this without you."

Oleana kept herself hard and strong for her son. "You can and you will. Don't be like me, weighed down by my mistakes. Be better. Move swift. Be safe. I love you."

"Mom, I…" Lorn's voice cracked. He cleared his throat and tried again. "Love you too, Mom."

Oleana felt the connection drop and she was left alone. She refused to open her eyes. The room around her didn't have Lorn in it. With her eyes closed she could hold on to the image of him and then maybe things weren't as bad as them seemed.

She could see him smiling back at her. Hear him talking so fast his words ran together into one excited jumble. She could feel his silky curls as she ran her fingers through his hair.

"I would die for you a thousand times," she told his shadow. "I just hope this once is enough."

CHAPTER TWENTY-SEVEN: MAZE

Leith didn't like the sound of the test of Intelligence. It wasn't exactly his most prized quality. Leith knew he wasn't as stupid as most people judged him to be, but the other trials proved to be more than just simple tests. His teacher, Lorn, was practically comatose due to his grief. Leith had no idea how to console the boy. He didn't feel up to being cheerful himself.

He may not have known Oleana long but the impression she made on him was a good one, and getting over her loss would not be a simple matter. The Keeper, Kameke proved to be a cold-hearted taskmaster, not giving them a moment to process their grief before pushing them into the next, and final trial.

"Lorn," Leith said touching the boy's shoulder.

The boy shrugged it off and didn't bother to look up at him. "I'm fine. We can do this. The intelligence test is the most straightforward of the tests. The fourth and fifth floors of the tower are built into a maze. Navigate it in the time given and you pass. There are no tricks to the maze. Nothing I can teach you to help. Just run the maze. You don't need me for that." Lorn walked away leaving Leith to look into Kameke's cold eyes. They may have been a striking green but they held the same reptilian look that Cornelius had. What made her their ally and him their enemy?

"Are you prepared, Master of Animals?" she asked in that sickly sweet little girl voice that set him on edge.

"If I say no, do I get a pass?" he asked, only half joking.

"If you do not complete the final test you cannot be crowned king, and neither can the others."

"Thanks for the pep talk."

"I don't understand," she replied tilting her head to the side like a curious dog.

"I'm ready." Leith said irritated.

Kameke picked up the hourglass. "You have until the sands run out to reach the heart of the maze and ring the bell, then you will be shown the way down and the next Heir will have his chance." She flipped it over and Leith couldn't help but watch the first sands fall.

When he could tear his eyes away from the hourglass, Leith bolted up the steps into the dimly lit fourth floor. The idea of facing a maze didn't bother Leith. Every time he had to run from the city patrol he ran the gambit of the city, finding back alleys and shortcuts no one else knew about. Where the test of his intelligence would come in, he didn't know, and that worried him.

Lorn had to have known more, but he clearly wasn't in the mood for talking. Leith tried to cut the boy some slack. He did a hard thing telling Cornelius off the way he did. Leith didn't know if he would have had it in him if the roles were switched.

They did the right thing, Leith knew that, but he didn't know if the boy was strong enough to live with it. Even with her other flaws, Oleana never missed an opportunity to teach, to protect hers. Lorn stepped into the position, but was falling short when they needed him most. It wasn't the time for mourning, for being angry at the people that were there for him.

Leith was so wrapped up in his worrying he came to a dead stop inches away from the first wall of the maze. It was ten feet high, reaching all the way up to the ceiling and made of the same crystal that covered much of the rest of the building, except this version was completely opaque. He glanced behind him to see what he had missed on his way in.

The stairs weren't easily visible. He'd traveled some way without realizing it. He could barely make out the top of steps a dozen feet behind him. As he looked up at the wall in front of him, Leith noticed the markings on the wall. Three hash marks were etched into the green crystal. Ordinarily Leith wouldn't have thought twice about them, but if there were marks on this wall they had to be important.

Leith retraced his steps to find another way. Six steps back he found a branching corridor that curved off into the dimness. As soon as Leith breached the entrance a tingling crawled up his spine that made him stop. He didn't believe what his body was telling him. The guardian didn't keep wild animals locked up in her maze, did she? Leith reached out to whatever was making him uneasy.

First Leith caught the signal of a dozen different things bouncing around at him from odd angles. Leith shook his head and rubbed at his temples trying to undo the headache building there. Then all the signals flickered out of existence like some giant wave had extinguished their flames all at once.

"What game you playing?" He asked the maze.

When nothing but silence returned, Leith tried again to pinpoint what had set him on edge. Again, the multiple signals assaulted him out of nowhere. The thought of facing that many unknowns in the tiny confines of the narrow corridor made him want to head back down the stairs and demand of the Keeper a restart, an explanation, or something that would take the blame off him and on to the circumstances he found himself in.

In the monotony of the maze, Leith's mind returned to the image of the sand pouring down through the hourglass and the haunted look in Lorn's eyes. The boy faced his greatest challenge with boldness and courage. What could Leith say if he gave up on his trial at the first sign of trouble? He had to fake some courage if he couldn't find any in his heart.

His first steps into the corridor were shaky, but he was determined to keep going. The corridor took a sharp turn that made Leith think it must have followed the curve of the exterior of the tower. The further he moved into the hall the darkness thickened, and the stronger his sense of dread became. So intent was he on looking out for danger, he nearly missed the markings on the wall.

Four dash marks stood out on the wall. The more he looked at them the more they looked like claw marks. Were the marks just a numbering system for the corridors? If so, where were one and two? Leith just filed the marks in the back of his mind for future reference.

A fork in the road came up. Two choices. Leith tried to narrow down where the feeling of danger came from. It bounced around from everywhere and nowhere all at once, then flickered out with as much randomness as everything else.

Right. His dominant side, so he chose the right fork because he had no other criteria to go on. This corridor was marked eight. The big jump in numbers angered Leith but he pressed on. Time ticked away and he had others counting on him. Leith came across another side corridor, but he didn't know whether to keep going, or take the turn.

A deep throated howl came from deep within the side corridor and Leith backed away from it, holding his dagger up, ready for the attack. He stood there for a good three minutes but nothing happened. He felt foolish standing there staring into nothing.

He didn't understand. Using his powers had come so naturally to him before, but now when he needed them he couldn't detect an animal that couldn't have been more than a dozen feet in front of him. If Oleana were with him she would have said something clever that explained everything and fixed it all up.

Instead, all he had was the cold echo coming off the high, thick walls, and a vague sense in the back of his mind that Oleana was still alive even though he knew her time had to be limited. And worse yet he knew, because of their brief mind meld, that she had no life in reserve to call on when Cornelius ended her.

Her energy flowed through him, a sacrifice Leith would never have asked of her. No wonder Lorn couldn't even look at him. Because of Leith his mother would never come back to him. Leith couldn't waste that life on some stupid maze. He ran away from the noise and straight into a wall.

The placed was cursed, Leith thought. The last time he looked he had clear space, but now a solid wall stood where there was none seconds ago.

"Your mind playing tricks," he insisted.

Leith went back, passing the corridor with the howl and back toward the fork. Apparently right was not the way to go. Leith walked and walked. The corridor circled around in a way he didn't think it had before. He felt like he was going in a circle. Finally, he came upon an exit but his eyes caught the number on the wall. Twelve.

That couldn't be. All he did was turn around and go back the way he'd come. He made sure he didn't miss a side corridor. How could he have come back out on a mystery corridor? Where did twelve come from?

Leith searched for the other corridor that made up the fork, but it was nowhere to be seen. Instead, what he got was a splitting headache, as if some invisible drill was being tapped into his temples. Leith looked around terrified that a herd of ranta were going to descend on him with teeth and claws. Grabbing his head, Leith balled up, doing what he could to protect his face and neck.

Again, nothing came. Leith waited in agony, tasting the bitterness of his fear on his tongue. When Leith couldn't take the wait anymore, he stood. Around him were four chambers. Two, five, seven, and nine. The impossibility of it scared Leith as much as the possibility of attack.

"How am I 'posed to navigate a maze that changes shape when my eyes close?" Leith asked himself.

The pain in his head ebbed to a dull throbbing. It came from one distinct place. Corridor number two. Leith couldn't be sure of how much time had passed. Couldn't be sure of his own instincts. Couldn't even be sure of what his eyes were telling him. What he did know was that he'd run away from that signal before, only to run into more trouble. He may have been simple, but he wasn't stupid.

Leith chewed on his lower lip trying to summon up what courage he could muster. He ignored what his instincts told him and walked straight into danger, straight down corridor two. When he got more than a dozen steps into the corridor with no attack, Leith started to relax. For the first time since entering the maze he felt like he might actually be on the right track.

Corridor one came to a dead end with two choices in front of him. Corridor three veered off at a 45-degree angle to the right, and number four 45 degrees to the left. He'd tried four to no use, so he picked corridor three.

The sense of unease stayed with Leith. There was no real direction to it, as if he were in the middle of a nest of predators.

Leith left Solon with what little he could carry and three certainties; Oleana would be there to guide him through whatever happened, his power would only increase, the road ahead would be dangerous. Now all he was left with was the danger. How he let himself be convinced anything was certain, he didn't know.

Leith almost ran into the wall, his mind focused as it was on his internal conflict. He was presented with two choices again. He didn't know how he had looped back around to corridor four, but it was staring him in the face, along with its cousin corridor five.

Leith first thought that maybe it was time to try four again, follow the linear path he was on, but something at the back of his mind said that wasn't right. Some half-understood piece of knowledge, left over from the mind joining he'd experienced with the other Heirs of Eternity, told him there was another pattern he had to follow.

Leith followed five. Then seven, eleven, and finally he stood in front of thirteen. Thirteen was special. Thirteen had a door.

When Leith felt the familiar warning bell dancing across his skin, he thought nothing of it since his power had proved to be unreliable from the beginning of the trial. The door to thirteen opened into a shadowy room. Leith walked in before his eyes fully adjusted.

He got a face full of angry animal for his trouble. Back out in the light of the hallway, Leith got a look at his attacker. The animal looked like a cross between a muscular pig and a porcupine, with the only quills along its spine. Leith grabbed it around its neck, feeling an overwhelming sense of déjà vu.

The creature's jaw snapped close with a click as it tried to bite Leith's face off. Trying to keep it away from his face, Leith's hands slipped down to its shoulder and over an engraved symbol on its leathery skin.

As soon as Leith's thumb brushed it a warm yellow glow shimmered along the creature's skin and its attack was temporarily halted. Leith crawled out from the frozen creature noticing that it was the number thirteen that Leith had touched. A dozen other numbers were etched into the creature's skin.

The porcupig shook free of its fit. Leith was ready, delivering a boot to its face. He racked his brain for the secret behind the numbers that brought him this far. It was something Lysander had studied in his many years of schooling. Prime numbers. The sequence got him this far he just had to continue it.

Leith twisted out of the creature's reach trying to get a better look at the numbers. Playing a game of dodge, Leith kept on the move, staying out of the creature's reach and looking for his opportunity.

Quick reflexes helped Leith tap the seventeen, nineteen, and twenty-three. Twenty-nine was the highest number he saw, but Leith couldn't reach it on the underside of the creature at the apex of its ribcage.

After several failed attempts, Leith knew the only way to get it was to let the creature at him. Staring into the porcupig's beady black eyes Leith braced himself for the pain that was coming his way. The creature charged. Leith took the brunt of its weight without fighting it, landing hard against the crystal floor. Before gleaming white teeth could come down on his face, his fingers found twenty-nine.

The porcupig froze, leaving Leith to pant on the floor under it. At the center of the room a door opened up. When his breathing was under control and Leith was sure the porcupig was done, he pushed it over and stood, finding his way to the trap door.

At the bottom of a set of stairs stood the guardian, the halted hourglass in her hand. She looked up at him with a blank look on her face.

"Two seconds to spare," she said calmly. "You have passed the final test."

Leith wanted to jump and scream. Instead he just nodded. He wondered if he should explain to her that it wasn't his knowledge that had gotten him through. He'd borrowed the learning of another.

There were things more important than his honesty. He completed the trial. He would be king. Oleana's sacrifice would be worth something.

CHAPTER TWENTY-EIGHT: KINGS

A loud crash startled Oleana who'd been passing the hours alone thinking about the good times with her son. She opened her eyes in time to see Cornelius rip the doors of her cage off its hinges in his haste to get to her. The look in his impossibly pale blue eyes was pure madness. Oleana smiled at the sight of it because she knew it meant he'd tasted his defeat and it scared him.

A noise so loud and animalistic escaped his thin-lipped mouth it rattled Oleana's teeth. "You think you have won," Cornelius shouted, "but I'll crush those kinglings."

He reached for Oleana and she pushed back instinctively. Cornelius snatched her by the arm, claws ripping into her flesh, lifting her off the ground. Cornelius flung Oleana across the room, her back slamming into the hard rock wall before she slid to the floor.

"Without you they'll wither and die, and you'll once again have to die knowing you failed them."

Cornelius grabbed her around the neck and cold spread from his hand all over her skin. Oleana strained against the ropes keeping her hands tied behind her back. "Enjoy your sleep, Guardian because you'll awake to a world ruled by me."

Oleana struggled to breath. Her chest felt like a brick wall had fallen on it. The cold that invaded her body was so intense her fingers curled into a vice-like fist. She could feel her nails digging into her palms. Her eyes were frozen, starring up at the smug smile on the ice god's lips. Her jaw was stuck open in an impotent gasp as the ice overtook her.

100101

All the people in Evermore that weren't on patrol were gathered in the throne room for the coronation. Lorn pulled nervously at the blue vest he borrowed from Lysander. He cinched the golden threaded belt tighter along his waist to get the proper fit. He smoothed out his black pants and ran his hands through his curls.

"You look fine," Daycia said standing behind him. Her hand fell on his shoulder, stilling his jittery hands.

Lorn turned to give her a smile. "This isn't how I pictured this going," he said, swallowing hard against the lump of grief in his throat. He glanced over at his brothers standing on either side of him. They exchanged looks that said more than words could ever express.

They passed the trials and they should have all been very proud of that. Lorn was proud of it. But with every step he took forward he couldn't help but think about who should have been there with him.

He'd said his goodbyes to his mother. She told him to be better. He would try, for her, but he couldn't fill the big space she left. He wanted to be excited about finally being crowned, but in the back of his mind he held out this hope that he would be able to save her. Lorn wanted to run into the night searching for her.

The music started, the dulcet tones of the harp blending in with the deep vibrato of drums, giving Lorn the cue to start his march. Tycho and Nadir were in front of them, clad head to toe in polished red armor. Daycia and Zyair were behind them, decked out in their finest gear.

Moving to the steady tempo of the music, Lorn march down the center of the diamond-shaped room. Its ten-foot-high ceilings made it look open and wide, even with more than a hundred people crowded in it. Pastel purple silk drapes wrapped around wooden pillars marking off the boundaries of the room.

The center aisle was large enough for the three of them to walk abreast with room to spare. It ended at a raised stage with two steps in front of it. Three high back chairs carved out of crystal was spaced evenly on the stage. Each one marked for each king.

Lorn let his left-hand play over the raised mark on his arm, He remembered as a child sitting cross-legged on his bed gazing at his mother's face as she regaled him with tales of the Master of Skies. To hear her tell it he was and always would be a brave man, untethered from the bonds of the earth, a free spirit with great power tempered by a kind heart.

For the first time Lorn felt trapped by the ground beneath him. The sky and the world it looked down on was too wide, too dark, and too cruel a place. It took a mother away from a boy that already knew the pain of being orphaned. Lorn thought the second time around would be easier to handle. Instead he couldn't come to grips with a life that could be so savage.

Tears welled up at the corner of his eyes. Lorn felt the weight of all those looking at him. He sucked in a deep breath through his teeth and shut out the tumultuous thoughts racing through his mind. He had to focus on the moment at hand.

They stopped at the foot of the steps with the beautiful Kameke looking down on them with an attendant at her side. The music died and with it Lorn's heart slowed to a more natural rhythm. Nadir climbed the steps, followed by Daycia, and Jonathan of Darten.

Nadir presented himself to the Keeper. He bowed before speaking, his slicked back black hair catching the afternoon light coming in from the crystal walls. "I, Nadir Starson, representative of Caledon stand in observance of this coronation." Nadir removed the crest of Caledon pendant that was clipped to the right shoulder of his armor and passed it to the Keeper, Kameke.

She took it, looking over it carefully. Then nodded. "Nadir Starson you are accepted."

Jonathan went next, handing over the seal of his realm and the Keeper accepted. When it was Daycia's turn to step forward the Keeper looked wary. Maybe she didn't approve of Daycia representing one particular realm or maybe she just simply didn't approve of Daycia at all. Lorn couldn't guess, but Daycia handed over the crest of Arismas as she had been authorized to do. Lorn looked away, afraid that the tower keeper wouldn't accept it.

"Daycia you are accepted," Kameke said. Lorn could breathe again. The Keeper turned to look down at them. "Present yourselves."

Lorn, Leith, and Lysander climbed the stairs together. They spun around facing the crowd. Lorn tried in vain to take in all the different faces, to the point that they just became a wiggling blur in front of him. His stomach was in knots and he almost forgot what he was supposed to do.

Lysander, no stranger to facing large crowds, stepped forward first. He pushed up his sleeve and raised his arm. "I, Lysander Starson present myself as Master of Earth to be crowned as King of Euphoria. I have passed the trials. I have proved myself. Do you accept me?" The crowd erupted in generous applause. Many banged their weapons against their shields. A few yelled out Lysander's name in a chant of solidarity.

Kameke held up her hand and the noise died like someone sucked out all the air. Lysander turned to the representatives of three of the five realms. They each gave their acceptance.

Leith stepped forward next. He gave his bare arm to the air. "I, Leith Underwood, present myself as Master of Animals to be crowned as King of Euphoria. I -," Leith hesitated.

Lorn looked over at his brother. Leith looked back, there was something in his eyes, a secret he was holding onto. There was a moment of panic that shot between them. The moment passed and Leith turned back to the crowd.

"I have passed the trials. I have proven myself. Do you accept me?" Again, the crowd erupted. Again, the representatives gave their acceptance.

"I, Lorn Paysan present myself as Master of Skies. I have passed the trials. I have proven myself worthy. Do you accept me?"

Lorn didn't really pay attention until it was Daycia's turn. His gaze found hers. She smiled at him in a way that made him think, for just a second, that things would be okay. "Arismas accepts you," she said, and Lorn felt it like warm tea sliding down his parched throat, its soothing warmth spreading through his body.

Kameke stepped forward, facing the three Heirs of Eternity. "Lysander, you have been accepted," she placed a crown upon his head. "Lorn, you have been accepted." Lorn bent down so she could place the ring of onyx around his head. It rested lightly just above his ears, but Lorn found himself standing straighter because of it. "Leith, you are accepted," she finished, her voice holding a hint of excitement.

Turning to the crowd a hush fell over the room as thick as fog. Everyone took a collective breath. The weight of a legend being fulfilled descended on them. "Ladies and gentlemen, the esteemed of Euphoria," Kameke's voice filled the grand room, like a songbird starting the day. "I present to you... the Kings of Euphoria!"

The crowd erupted, shaking the very walls in their triumph. Some rushed forward, held back by the guards around the stage. Leith and Lysander came in closer, each wrapping an arm around Lorn as they stood together, newly minted kings.

Part of Lorn wanted to smile, to let relief and joy wash over him. They were kings, after such a long journey, after lifetimes of trying, they finally made it. They were kings, yes, and now the real work would begin.

Sneak Peak: *Kings of Euphoria*
Tentative Release Date: December 15, 2017

Gaeth.

Cornelius never liked stepping foot on the hot and humid island. He hated even more the way the people treated him, like some outsider encroaching on their territory. Speaking with Emmaray was important enough to endure it. The second he stepped off the borrowed Failsea ship, Cornelius felt the heat hit him in waves. He secured his frozen face mask over his mouth to prevent breathing in too much of the hot air. The feel of it against his exposed fleshed gave him a sharp reminder of the flames Daycia had threw in his face not long enough ago. He caressed the scared side of his face, feeling the gentle ridges there where his burns had healed just a little off, marring the once clean lines of his face.

"This way," his guide urged, pulling Cornelius back to the present.

The man was one of the Elevated, a special class of elite soldier on Gaeth. He wore the black and crimson red of their order. He was a tall man, for a human. Coming up to Cornelius's shoulder. The sides of his head were shaved and the swath of hair at the top was dyed a startlingly deep red. Four golden rings punctured his right ear, which marked him as a lieutenant in the order.

The fact that Emmaray sent such a high-ranking escort gave Cornelius some hope that things would work well between them. It boded well that she gave him enough thought to send one of her best to make sure he made it to their meeting.

Cornelius didn't need an escort. He could have found Emmaray in the middle of a dessert with his eyes closed. He'd known her longer than her new sycophants could even image. There was a connection between them that brought them together when they were in need, and just as much repelled them when things between them weren't going well.

He had every intention of playing on those feelings to get her to do what he needed of her. Those Heirs hurt their son. There was no answer that would get him to leave other than her complete cooperation.

Cornelius nodded to the man and followed him along the rock path into the jungle. The thick leaves slapped against his arms as they climbed in elevation, leaving the flat, wide open beach far behind. After several minutes of walking through the barley contained wilderness Cornelius was almost convinced there was no civilization to be found on the island.

Then the tree line broke, a clearing spread out before him, and the first signs of humanity became visible. Cornelius was surprised by how far Gaeth had come in his absence. A hundred years and Emmaray had done her best to replicate the delicate structures only seen in Evermore. The towering volcanic rock buildings started at the heart of the city and spiraled out in regular intervals with what looked like single family homes taking up the gaps in between. It gave the place an odd sense of balance and organization yet blended into the wild seamlessly, as if there was no beginning of one and end of another but a hybridization of the two.

Far in the background lay the string of volcanoes that made Gaeth in the first place. The last time Cornelius left the island, the highest mountain, Mt. Kilana was sputtering and spitting smoke out of her top, agitated by Emmaray's fury. The ground beneath his feet shook as he stalked down the hillside and back to his boat, leaving his son Tannin behind. Yet Tannin, when strong enough to make his own choice despite his mother's wishes, choose to come be with his father.

When he first reached out to Emmaray, warning her that he had bad news about their son, Cornelius was sure she would greet him with a fireball, blaming him for any ill that befell their child. She'd already lost her first child to the pull of the humans. Now he had to tell her that he'd failed to protect their son. It would not be easy, but now she must see the need to join the fight and defeat the

Heirs once and for all. Otherwise people like him, and Emmaray, and Tannin would all be exterminated. The Heirs of Eternity would make sure of that.

They snaked their way through the city, plenty of brown faces, bronzed by the relentless sun, starring at him as he passed. Cornelius wondered how many of them would be coming back with him to fight a war that they knew nothing about. They would do whatever Emmaray ordered them to.

At the center of the city Emmaray's castle sat at the center of a spiral. Its was a dark sister to the Crystal Tower in Evermore. A shorter, less imposing version. One with more curvy, natural lines. Much like Emmaray herself compared to the Keeper of the Tower, Kameke.

The guide pulled open the dark wood door with its intricate leaf and flower carved design. Cornelius was surprised to find the building was mostly one large room with a loft area and catwalk along the perimeter.

Emmaray sat on her throne, draped in shear turquoise green dress that fell over her knees. Her red curls cascaded over her shoulders and brushed the top of her thighs. As many villagers as he spotted outside were sitting around her. Many had baskets in theirs hands or various offerings ready to give up to her.

Two women stood in front of the throne. They were older women, gray hair gathered in neat ponytails atop their heads. One was thin, so frail looking at her Cornelius didn't know how the weight of her hair didn't break her in half. The other had some meat to her but her skin looked dried out from too many years in the sun, her caramel skin covered in dark blotches that made her look like an overused pin cushion.

Cornelius couldn't hear what they said, but whatever it was had everyone's attention, and the thin elderly woman in tears. Emmaray smiled at them as if they were wayward children she needed to correct. Of course, Emmaray always had that look in her eyes. She thought everyone was a child compared to her. In her defense one long look into her shimmering violet eyes ad many people were reduced to childish behavior.

Emmaray didn't give Cornelius a second glance as he overtook his guide and moved closer to within feet of the throne. Cornelius wanted to cut through the crowd and get on with his business but he knew trying to rush Emmaray would only result in her shutting him down. So he took as close a position to her as he dared and watched her work. She was the goddess of this island, worshiped by its inhabitants for generations. She was the only ultra on the planet that had such a large and devoted following and she kept it that way by not interfering in the plans of others. Cornelius knew he had an uphill battle to fight with her, but he also knew how to dig in and wait for the right moment to strike.

The older women continued with their tale of woe. "… the last piece of our family that we had. My sister and I have nothing left. No other means to support ourselves. Without your mercy," the thin woman's voice broke. Her frail body shuddered as her sister hugged her tight, "we will die on the streets. We wish not burden you with our problems. We know of your great mercy toward your servants."

"We are asking for that mercy now," the other sister continued. "We both lost our husbands to your service. We just ask that you please take care of us in the last days of our lives."

Cornelius could only imagine what the husbands of these two women died doing. There were plenty of jobs in the service of Emmaray that were more dangerous than she would ever admit to. Now they were asking for help. Cornelius knew Emmaray wasn't as merciful and kind as these two women claimed she was. If they truly believed the words they said, desperation wouldn't have been dripping from ever word out of their shaking lips.

Emmaray glanced over at him, as if she sensed what he was thinking. Maybe the Fire Goddess could tell by Cornelius body language that he doubted her. She offered him a smug smile then returned her attention to the women in front of her. Emmaray rose from her throne with a flutter of brightly-colored fabric, stepped down to the floor level, and placed her hands on the thinner woman's shoulders.

"My dear faithful women, of course your loyal course will be rewarded," looking out into the crowd, Emmaray gave them the full power of her soft, concerned public mask. "You should have come to me sooner. I would never have let you suffer so long. If you had only reached out for my help at the onset of your problems I could have spared you such indignities." Emmaray turned to the guard on her left, another of the Elevated. Two rings in his ear, a scimitar in his hand, and broader in build than the one that led Cornelius in. His hook nose distorted the otherwise baby look of his face. "Jotham here will escort you to the Temple of Plenty and the sisters there will provide you what you need." Emmaray looked out to the crowd, making sure all were aware of her generosity. "Let no one say Emmaray is uncaring. That she lets down those who serve her with a complete heart. I give much, it is up to you to come to me with your burdens."

The gathered beat their hands on the ground in the ceremonial sign of their jubilation. The women smiled, crying all the harder now that their burden was lifted. Jotham stepped forward and lead the women away.

"My people I'm sorry for the interruption but another matter calls my attention. I will open up my doors again tomorrow and keep them open until sunset to assuage any inconvenience that this may cause you. Peace be with you, and I will see you again." Emmaray blew kisses to the crowd then sat back on her throne dismissing the gathered with a wave of her hands.

No one so much as groaned as they got up to leave. By the looks on their faces plenty of them were upset but they most likely feared making any noise about it. Cornelius appreciated the iron hold Emmaray had over her people. A hold she managed to keep for centuries. Despite her isolationist attitude she would prove to be the best ally he could have.

Ivar did his part. His eagerness and raw resources made up for his lack of intelligence and his short-sightedness. But it was now time for Cornelius to find an equal partner. One that brought in as much as Cornelius did, and Emmaray was that one.

When it was just the two of them, the guards at her side fading into the background, Cornelius finally dared to move up on the steps that lead to Emmaray's throne. "That was an impressive display. You always had a way with your people that I admired."

The beginnings of a smile tugged at the edges of Emmaray full lips but she tightened up, sitting straighter in her high-backed seat, chest out, back arched, arms gripping the padded arm rests. "Get to your business Cornelius. Having you here doesn't sit well with me. The sooner you state your case, the sooner I can be rid of you."

Cornelius bit back the ball of rage that collected in the back of his throat. He wasn't used to being talked to that way. It stirred up the blinding anger that sat in the back of his mind, always straining to get free. But the task at hand was more important than his pride. He thought of Tannin locked away. Thought of how sweet the victory over the Heirs would be with Emmaray at his side.

"I apologize for disturbing you so Emmaray. I come to explain to you what has happened to our son and beg for your help to right the wrong."

Emmaray stiffened. Her eyes narrowed, but she said nothing.

Cornelius powered forward. "The news must have reached even you by now but the Heirs of Eternity resurfaced recently. They showed up in my backyard and I was forced to confront them before I was completely ready. Tannin went after them and that Guardian of theirs injured him gravely."

Emmaray stood, her dress billowing around her as she closed the distance between them in the blink of an eye. Her cheeks blistering red from the anger burning inside of her. She grabbed the collar of his shirt. "Where's my son? What has happened to him? Why didn't you explain this in your letter?"

Cornelius stood his ground, not willing to give her anger and inch. "I saved Tannin. Froze him to give his body time to heal itself."

"If he'd stayed with me none of this would have happened. He would have been safe. Why did I let him go anywhere near you. I knew you would bring him nothing but pain."

"I don't think you had much choice," Cornelius stated flatly. Emmaray reared back as if she were going to slap him but Cornelius pulled away from her. "I only meant he is as stubborn and strong willed as you. That fight would have been never ending."

"So you have told me of Tannin. Now can you be off?"

"No," Cornelius closed the gap between them and snatch Emmaray wrist before she could turn away from him. "While the incident with Tannin is unforgivable it is only a symptom of the larger problem. The Heirs have been crowned. They wage war against our kind. They will not stop at the sea and continue to leave you to your paradise. It is time to pull your head out of the sand and stand and fight with me. They must be destroyed, otherwise they will destroy us."

Emmaray looked down at Cornelius' hand on hers. He dropped her like a hot stone. Still she stared down lost in thought. "I can't leave my people. I have promises to keep. What can I do for you."

Cornelius sighed. He was hoping for more but at least she didn't shut him out or try to run him away as she had before.

"You don't have to leave your island to be of help. You have trained soldiers and resources beyond mine. Join in this fight and lend me men to fight with. I will bring you the heads of those who dared to hurt our son."

Emmaray looked him in the eyes and smiled. It was a mischievous look that brightened her face. "You know that I reward my loyal ones. All you had to do was ask and I will grant all that I can to demonstrate my power in your behalf."

If you liked what you read, please consider writing an honest review on:

Amazon.com

TM

Goodreads.com

TM

Acknowledgements

In no particular order
Thank you so much to my design crew Debra C. Cyndi B. Ernesto M.

Thank you to all those who took the time out to read over rough versions. Rose W. Katie M.

A big shout out to the work crew, without y'alls discipline and encouragement I would not have made it through. Malissha J. Tierra S. Char H.

To the family members who keep me grounded. Ruth J. LaToya P. Jeremy P. Pat P. Joyce I. Christina P. and Terrence P.

To my twin who is sick of hearing me talk about writing Shante J. And to my friend who forces me out into the world so I can write about it better Kate D.

If I missed anybody I am so very sorry, but I know that writing a book takes a team and I have the best around me. I am more grateful to you all than I can ever express.

Love you all.

 Franc Ingram is a Sci-Fi writer who loves to write about damaged heroines/heroes and extraordinary technology. Personally, Franc is an animal lover, having a Lab mix named Mya. Franc loves planes, green tech, a fine white wine, good food, and books of all genres. Lives and works in Northeast Ohio.

Find Author online at:

Urwhatureadblog.wordpress.com

www.facebook.com/steampunkwriterxx

Goodreads: Franc Ingram

60869335R00155

MAY - - 2017
3545472

Made in the USA
Lexington, KY
21 February 2017